The Culture of War

Literature of the Siege of Paris 1870–1871

Studies in Modern and Contemporary France   6

Studies in Modern and Contemporary France

Series Editors

Professor Gill Allwood, Nottingham Trent University
Professor Denis M. Provencher, University of Arizona
Professor Martin O'Shaughnessy, Nottingham Trent University

The Studies in Modern and Contemporary France book series is a new collaboration between the Association for the Study of Modern and Contemporary France (ASMCF) and Liverpool University Press (LUP). Submissions are encouraged focusing on French politics, history, society, media and culture. The series will serve as an important focus for all those whose engagement with France is not restricted to the more classically literary, and can be seen as a long-form companion to the Association's journal, *Modern and Contemporary France,* and to *Contemporary French Civilization*, published by Liverpool University Press.

The Culture of War

Literature of the Siege of Paris 1870–1871

COLIN FOSS

Liverpool University Press

First published 2020 by
Liverpool University Press
4 Cambridge Street
Liverpool
L69 7ZU

This paperback edition published 2023

British Library Cataloguing-in-Publication data
A British Library CIP record is available

ISBN 978-1-78962-192-1 (hardback)
ISBN 978-1-83764-413-1 (paperback)

Typeset by Carnegie Book Production, Lancaster

Contents

Acknowledgments   vii

Introduction   1

Part I: On Stage

1   The Boulevards Lose their Theaters   25

2   Hugomania   51

Part II: Off Presses

3   The *Feuilleton* at War   71

4   The Dubious Battle of Reichshoffen   97

Part III: At Home

5   Letters to No One   119

6   Historians of the Present   139

Part IV: In Print

7   De-Modernizing Publishing   165

8   To Make the Past Public   189

Coda: The Siege and State Violence   207

Bibliography   217

Index   231

Acknowledgments

We are lucky in nineteenth-century French studies to be able to rely on a community of engaging, prolific, and friendly people. This book, from initial conceptualization to final proofs, has been made possible because of the people I am privileged to call colleagues. I want to thank Edmund Birch, Heidi Brevik-Zender, Scott Carpenter, Andrew Counter, Robert Doran, Elizabeth Emery, Jennifer Forrest, Andrea Goulet, Anne Linton, Anne O'Neil-Henry, Raisa Rexer, Kirstin Ringelberg, and Claire White—among many others—for welcoming me into the profession and for their inspiring work.

I am grateful, too, for the help that I have received from historians of France, whose guidance makes interdisciplinary work like this possible. John Merriman, Rachel Chrastil, Quentin Deluermoz, Dominique Kalifa, and Miranda Sachs have exposed me to the bright and welcoming world of historians. Like many others, I have benefitted from the work of archivists at the Archives nationales, the Bibliothèque historique de la Ville de Paris, and the Bibliothèque nationale de France.

This book is an expansion of my dissertation completed with the support of the members of the French Department of Yale University. They generously continued to help as the dissertation transformed into a book. Morgane Cadieu, Thomas Connolly, Alice Kaplan, and Chris Semk have a knack for asking the right question at just the time you need to hear it. Howard Bloch and Chris Miller encouraged me to see the shape of the book when it was not clear to me. Annie de Saussure, Liz Hebbard, Jessica Kasje, Robyn Pront, and Richard

Riddick have offered valuable advice and invaluable commiseration. Maurice Samuels deserves much more than I can say about him here. His relentless encouragement is rivaled only by his thoughtful and keen critique, both of which have shown me—and many others—the way through challenging research questions.

As this book took shape, a number of people offered the kind of incisive insights that come from deep wisdom: Jann Matlock, Susan McCready, and Rachel Mesch are among them. Nicholas White and his brilliant approach to 1870–1871 can be found behind every page of this book. The staff at Liverpool University Press have created a publishing process both rigorous and creative, in particular thanks to the efforts and expertise of Chloe Johnson. I want also to thank my reviewers, who gave the gift of an honest and thorough reading.

My students and colleagues at Austin College have created the type of atmosphere in which research and teaching work together, making both better in the process. Within Classical and Modern Languages, I want to thank Lourdes Bueno, Bob Cape, Ruth Cape, Truett Cates, Patrick Duffey, Julie Hempel, Wolfgang Lueckel, Mary Yetta McKelva, Elena Olivé, Marty Wells, and Wendy Wilson. The kind of interdisciplinary work at the heart of the liberal arts finds its best voice in my colleagues: Tom Blake, Erin Copple-Smith, Alex Garganigo, Max Grober, Felix Harcourt, Mindy Landeck, Lisha Storey, Randi Tanglen, and Elizabeth Terry are some who put me on the right path. I don't know what I would have done without Stacey Battis, who only speaks truth.

I am constantly trying to find ways to thank my family, my parents Susan and Roger, and Cynthia Rush, without whose support I would not even be in the position of writing acknowledgments to a book. I especially want to thank my grandmother, Gabby, whose life is as inspiring as her words, and to whom this book is dedicated.

Introduction

Like many lower-level government employees, the clerk in charge of France's national bibliography kept his job even after the Second Empire fell. On September 4, 1870, the Prussian army captured Napoléon III, but the imprisonment of France's head of state seemed to have little effect on the clerk's daily task of logging the title, author, and printer of every book and periodical published in France. When the Prussians eventually encircled Paris on September 19, his job changed slightly, but only slightly. There were no more books coming from the provinces as the Prussians had cut off all routes into and out of the capital. Nonetheless, he diligently continued to record all the books published in besieged Paris for the next four months.[1]

We can learn a lot about this clerk from his record keeping. He was not very thorough, often forgetting to mention a book's printer, its author, or how many pages each copy contained. His negligence is rather inexcusable, as it was likely that he had access to these books as he recorded their important information. His job was to maintain the *dépôt légal*, which, despite a hiatus (1790–1793) during the Revolution, is the result of a law requiring French printers to send a copy to a central, government-run library since 1537. While there are some discrepancies, the *dépôt légal* is more or less an accurate reflection of all the printed, non-periodical books published in Paris during the Siege,[2]

---

1   The result of his efforts can be found at the Archives nationales, F18 III 128.
2   Another source is Firmin Maillard, *Les Publications de la rue pendant le siège et la Commune: satires, canards, complaintes, chansons, placards et pamphlets* (Paris:

meaning that our clerk—despite being lax—still took his role seriously even as the city around him suffered through one of the most dramatic moments in Parisian history.

What is surprising about this clerk, charged with one of the most important administrative jobs in literary history, is his ignorance of all things literary. He seemed unaware, for example, that a curious book called *Les Châtiments* was written by one of France's most famous living authors, Victor Hugo. On two separate occasions, he records the publication of this book with the indication "s.a.": *sans auteur*, or *without author*. Almost no one in Paris was unaware of Hugo's massive bestseller during the Siege, making this clerk's omission rather impressive. Distracted from his toiling, his thoughts may have wandered to the city that was falling apart around him.

The Siege of Paris, lasting from September 19, 1870 to January 28, 1871, was the final stand-off in the Franco-Prussian War. When the Prussians began their military blockade, they did not expect that Paris was content to resist. For four long months, Parisians watched mournfully as their supplies of food and fuel dwindled and as Prussian artillery shells fell sporadically on the city. Through cold, famine, and shelling, thousands of Parisians lost their lives during the Siege, which eventually ended when the provisional French government surrendered. The story of the Siege is one of resistance in the face of the inevitable, of Parisian pride of place, and of drastic changes to everyday life. This book is about the tragedy that befell Paris, as documented in the thousands of diaries, newspapers, books, poems, pamphlets, and plays produced during the blockade. It is about how culture unexpectedly flourished as the fog of war fell upon the city of lights.

But this book is also about institutions and the people who represented them, such as our clerk who witnessed history unfolding in the form of titles, authors, and print runs. For the clerk and the catalogue he left behind, the Siege was not a moment of rupture or a pivotal turning point in French history. Instead, his work reveals that institutions impose continuity onto chaos. The banality of the majority of these books' titles—*Nouvelles et romans choisis, Le Maître d'école, Marianne Aubry, La Vie de Madame Elisabeth*—does little to

---

Aubry, 1874). Maillard, a journalist, historian, and bibliophile, also wrote a less complete *Histoire des journaux publiés pendant le siège et la Commune* (Paris: Dentu, 1871), which I discuss in Part II.

signal that the city was under siege, threatened by enemy occupation, struggling through a regime change, and fighting off famine. On the other hand, there were hints of the extreme situation outside of this clerk's office, like the constant republication of *Les Châtiments* or the increase in political pamphlets published by unknown or anonymous presses with energetic titles like *L'Heure suprême* and *Le Cri de guerre*, but in the unhurried and clear writing of the clerk, there is no alarm, no astonishment, and no reason to think that Paris's publishers had changed the way they operated during the Siege.

While publishing, reading, and attending the theater could be and was interpreted as heroic, as an example of Parisians stubbornly remaining Parisian through the continued production and enjoyment of culture, it also meant in a more practical sense that cultural industries performed surprisingly well when most other sectors of the economy came to a grinding halt. Our government clerk logged roughly eight hundred and sixty new non-periodical books during the Siege. He likewise noted that the number of newspapers in publication nearly doubled during the same four-month period. Some authors who later found international fame, such as Théodore de Banville, enjoyed their first literary successes behind the lines of military investment. After an early hiatus, Parisian theaters performed sold-out shows. The massive industries behind the production of literature chugged forward, printers printing, actors acting, authors writing, and clerks recording.

The industries of culture had their own politics, independent of the politics of the authors and the texts they published or performed. Pockets of Parisians may have been clamoring for the return of Napoléon III and his Empire, the reinstatement of the Republic, the return of monarchy, or the establishment of a revolutionary regime, but the capitalist logic of industry proved sluggish and opaque. Institutions that had prospered under the Second Empire were wary of change, unwilling to embrace either a return to political normalcy or a revolution. These newspapers, theaters, publishing houses, and the people who represented them were concerned with the future of the French state, but only insofar as that future state benefitted the well-being of each cultural institution, so dependent on the status quo: the continual publishing of books, the functioning of the presses, the financial stability that only political stability could offer. However, some institutions and individuals wanted to rock the boat, disrupting national politics in the process.

After the provisional government lifted many regulations curbing the freedom of the presses and of booksellers, there was an explosion of new literature in the city, driven by writers and printers finally able to publish without fear of censorship or without the burden of costly start-up permits. The one hundred and sixty new newspapers that appeared during the four-month Siege threatened the market share of the dozens of larger-distribution papers that had been in operation for decades. Small printing presses began churning out new books and pamphlets written by the besieged, for the besieged. Turning away from established authors like George Sand, Jules Michelet, and Ponson du Terrail, these new printers instead published engaged texts like political manifestos, first-hand accounts of fighting on the ramparts of the city, and political poetry written by soldiers. The exception to this rule, Victor Hugo's anti-Napoleonic book of poetry *Les Châtiments*, became the bestseller of the Siege. His official printer, Claye, ran out of coal to run his presses. Smaller, upstart printers were happy to print their own editions without Hugo's approval, often leading to confusion such as that of our government clerk. Newspapers, urged to document this unique moment in French history, began printing stories written by ordinary Parisians, sometimes without citing their names, as if this literature emerged from the city itself. Author advocacy groups actively tried to suppress what they saw as literary misdemeanors, threatening to bring legal complaints against underground printers and upstart newspapers. Popular boulevard theaters experimented with new types of spectacle that explicitly mocked the fallen regime and performed plays and recited poetry written by soldiers or by unknown authors, while official state theaters like the Comédie-Française, clinging to their prestigious repertoire, struggled to articulate their relevancy. Outside of the walls, the war was between France and Prussia; inside, it was between traditional literary industries and the cottage industries born of the freedoms of the Siege.

This book takes as its premise that no literature is produced in a void, and that in order to become a part of culture, there must be some organization or industry that is willing and able to make it public, even in the form of self-publishing. Changes arose in publishing practices only as manifestations of internal conflict between competing conceptions of literature as an economic or political reality, or as a result of material or practical concerns such as the lack of coal. In other words, new forms of culture arose only because new institutional configurations or constraints made them possible. The major struggle of the Siege was not between competing definitions of the future of the French nation, but between the different institutional systems that could provide and disseminate such definitions. Behind every text that appeared during the Siege there is the story of its production, its promotion, and the industry that made it possible to become a text in the first place.

This is not to say that the content of literature—what was actually published—did not change. On the contrary, there was a boom in new types and new iterations of old genres of media during the four months Parisians were left to their own devices. Beyond new periodicals, theaters began experimenting with new spectacles that verged on community morale-building, integrating classical French theater with topical lectures on how to resist the enemy. Hundreds of ordinary citizens took up their pens to write Siege diaries, articulating a form of history writing in opposition to professional historical methodology. Self-styled soldier-poets composed rhymes around bivouacs and on the defensive ramparts of the city. The Siege changed the face of literature, but it was only through a popular opposition to traditional forms of publication that this new literature arose.

The literature produced during the Siege has long been absent from scholarship on this period. In a study of daily life under siege, historian Victor Debuchy declines to engage with Siege literature on the grounds that it is not worthy of our attention.[3] Stéphane Audoin-Rouzeau's foundational 1989 work on the Franco-Prussian War comes closer to recognizing the literary output of the Siege, but falls short of studying anything but a few published diaries, noting conservatively that for theaters, "a few shows often of a patriotic tone were nonetheless given until the end of the Siege, thanks to the softening of legislation."[4] The two other major historical works on the war, by Michael Howard and Geoffrey Wawro, completely ignore literature.[5]

Even some writers in 1870 believed that literature ended during the

---

3   Debuchy, "La vie intellectuelle," in *La Vie à Paris pendant le siège* (L'Harmattan, 1999).
4   Audoin-Rouzeau, *1870: la France dans la guerre* (Armand Colin, 1989).
5   Howard, *The Franco-Prussian War: The German Invasion of France* (Macmillan, 1961); Wawro, *The Franco-Prussian War: The German Conquest of France in 1870–1871* (Cambridge UP, 1990).

Siege. Émile Zola thought that these times of national tragedy were inhospitable to authors, claiming that "this terrible war has made my pen drop from my hands."[6] It was only in February 1871, one month after the Siege, that Edmond de Goncourt felt "something like the appetite for literature,"[7] even if he kept a notoriously loquacious diary during the period of military investment. Despite these high-profile accounts, there was a veritable explosion of popular culture within the walls of the city. Faced with the sheer number of poems published, the printer and editor Damase Jouaust concluded that "the sound of cannons could not extinguish the voice of our writers."[8] What happened to this literature? Why was it so divisive and yet now so forgotten?

The particular economic, political, and material conditions of the Siege did not bode well for the production or consumption of literature. The blockade sapped the primary resources of literary industries. With limited coal for printing presses, limited paper for newspapers, and without access to the larger market of provincial readers, literary production faced serious obstacles to financial viability. With most Parisian industries also shut down due to lack of markets, consumers, and materials, many Parisians found themselves out of a job, and therefore potentially unable to afford a theater ticket, a book, a newspaper, let alone wood to heat their homes.

Despite these odds, Parisians found unlikely solutions to the problems that limited resources posed. As a result, literary production burst into new growth markets, reaching out to new groups of readers. Literature has for so long eluded scholars of this period precisely because it was not authors with recognizable names like Zola that wrote within the walls of the besieged city. However, this was seen as a novelty during the blockade, as a community spirit brought people together in ways that even the public culture of the Second Empire had not. The anonymity of writers constituted their appeal, and in some cases their motivation to write in the first place. Anonymous diarists, poets, pamphleteers, and journalists fell under the spell of an *esprit de corps*, despite or perhaps

---

6 Quoted by Paul Alexis, *Émile Zola: notes d'un ami* (Paris: Charpentier, 1882), p. 173.

7 Goncourt, *Journal des Goncourt: mémoires de la vie littéraire*, Vol. 4 (Paris: Charpentier, 1892), p. 219 (February 24, 1871).

8 Jouaust, "La littérature pendant le siège." *Lettre-journal de Paris: Gazette des absents*, January 14, 1871.

due to a divisive political atmosphere. This literature imperative gave Parisians the tools and the materials to not only survive this moment of national mourning, but also to tell the story of their survival to others who were not present, those outside of Paris whom they designated "les absents." The corollary to the fact that Parisians were isolated from the world was that the world was unaware of what was happening within Paris during the Siege. The literature produced during this moment constitutes a collective history of the Siege of Paris written by those who lived through it.

This cultural record eluded us for so long because much of it was ephemeral and often difficult to justify as a subject of study on aesthetic grounds. However, the study of minor or popular manifestations of literary culture sheds light on larger social, political, and economic practices. Before, during, and after the Siege, literature appeared in the pages of newspapers, books, diaries, and on the stages of theaters high and low. The majority of these texts were overtly political, deploying hardly subtle rhetoric in an attempt to come to terms with the fall of Napoléon III and the subsequent proclamation of the new French Republic. Propaganda, often, is simply dismissed as such. However, this propaganda hardly ever came from the government; it emerged in response to market forces and, more pressingly, to the perceived need for morale-boosting literature. This was populist propaganda, spilled from the pens of ordinary citizens.

Writing in Dark Times: The *Année Terrible*

From our current perspective the Siege was not an isolated event. Its entanglement with another historical moment in 1871, the Commune of Paris, suggests another reason why the literature of 1870–1871 has been forgotten. While I focus specifically on the literature produced during the Siege, this event was just one of two related moments that Hugo summarized as the *année terrible* or the "terrible year."[9] After Napoléon III declared war against Prussia on July 19, 1870, the Prussians quickly seized control, rolling into France and capturing the emperor on September 4 at the battle of Sedan. A new

---

9   As he titled his book of poetry, *L'Année terrible*, published in 1872.

French Republic was declared, but enemy troops reached the capital undeterred on September 14, when the blockade of the city began. Just before the armistice on January 29, 1871, Germany officially unified its various states in a ceremony held in the Hall of Mirrors in the palace of Versailles. However, as France began to cement its provisional government into permanency, a Parisian revolt led to the establishment of the Paris Commune, a revolutionary government unsatisfied with the regressive and undemocratic political composition of the government. The French army, under orders from the Versailles government, rolled through Paris in May of 1871, indiscriminately executing and imprisoning Parisians for the crime of having stayed in the insurgent capital. Paris was thus twice besieged, once by Prussia and again by France. Tens of thousands of Parisians lost their lives during the so-called Bloody Week or *semaine sanglante* and in the ensuing decades as French authorities continued to chase down the perpetrators, real and imagined, of the revolutionary Commune.

When Zola spoke of the war making him drop his pen, he anticipated twentieth-century trauma theory, which suggests that traumatic events resist representation. Given the ensemble of events that occurred in 1870–1871, contemporaries might have agreed with theorists like Elaine Scarry, who argues that, in the context of psychoanalysis, the *année terrible* might have fallen victim to the essential disjuncture between experience and language. Shoshana Felman and Dori Laub have dubbed the desire and subsequent inability to express trauma as the "crisis of witnessing," especially as the phenomenon relates to Holocaust victims and survivors.[10] In the 1870s, it was difficult to speak of the Commune as a singular event due in part to governmental suppression of the memory via censorship, but a trend in publishing also suggests that the two events were packaged together as a way of eliding the trauma of the Commune. Titles like *Les Femmes de France pendant les deux sièges*,[11] *Les Deux sièges de Paris: album pittoresque*,[12]

10   Felman and Laub, *Testimony: Crises of Witnessing in Literature* (Routledge, 1992).
11   Henri de Trailles, *Les Femmes de France pendant les deux sièges de Paris* (Paris: Polo, 1872).
12   *Les Deux sièges de Paris, album pittoresque* (Paris: aux bureaux du journal *L'Eclipse*, 1871).

Paris pendant les deux sièges,[13] and *La Comédie-Française pendant les deux sièges*[14] collapse the specificity of each "siege" into a seemingly coherent whole, eliding both the trauma of Bloody Week and the French government's culpability in laying this second siege. This trend is far from over, as evidenced for example in the 2016 publication of a book entitled *Les Deux sièges de Paris: 1870–1871*.[15] Historiography of the events of 1870–1871 still tends to blur the "two sieges" together. This historiographic practice furthers political arguments that wish to ignore the role of state violence against its own citizens in both the Siege and the Commune. To do so, it anachronistically spreads the trauma of the Commune over the entirety of the so-called terrible year. This book attempts to cut through ambiguity in a way that allows the Siege, and by extension the Commune, to be allowed to speak for itself rather than to share the same memorial space.

Taking a cue from the ample literary, historical, personal, anecdotal, and visual publications related to 1870–1871 that appeared in the 1870s and '80s, historians and scholars still often read the Siege in the light of the Commune. This perspective has certainly been very fruitful for our understanding of the longer moment of September 1870 to May 1871, but it privileges the Commune over the Siege, during which of course the future was uncertain and revolution not yet tangible. For some, the Commune must be understood as a direct result of the Siege, as Parisians, disillusioned with the armistice, the lack of social reform resulting from the proclamation of the Republic on September 4, and the decidedly bourgeois composition of the new government, attempted to enact the changes they felt they had been promised.[16] Others, such as John Merriman, have taken care to show how the events of the Commune reflect long-term and larger societal and class-based attitudes towards the poor and working-class citizens held by the bourgeois elite who opposed and eventually suppressed them through both bodily and discursive violence.[17] By focusing on

---

13   Louis Veuillot, *Paris pendant les deux sièges* (Paris: Vivès, 1876).
14   Édouard Thierry, *La Comédie française pendant les deux sièges (1870–1871). Journal de l'administration générale* (Paris: Tresse et Stock, 1887).
15   André Bourachot and Henri Ortholan, *Les Deux sièges de Paris* (Bernard Giovanangeli, 2016).
16   See in particular: Robert Tombs, *The War against Paris 1871* (Cambridge UP, 1981), and *The Paris Commune, 1871* (Longman, 1999).
17   See Merriman, *Massacre: The Life and Death of the Paris Commune* (Basic, 2014).

individual narratives of the Commune, Merriman shows a comprehensive range of voices of those who lived and suffered through it, a perspective that I have applied to the Siege. Within history, current trends are deeply indebted to the work of Jacques Rougerie,[18] who was one of the first to rehabilitate the *année terrible*. In literary studies, most of the focus on the Commune has come from Rimbaud studies and spatial theory.[19] Despite these different approaches, the above-cited studies lend credence to the assertion that "[the Commune] is not dead,"[20] but that it is obscuring the Siege for better or worse.

In order to explain and analyze the Commune, it is necessary to understand the Franco-Prussian War and the Siege. Many of those who became prominent players in the Commune first expressed their ideas during the Siege. A group of self-proclaimed *communards* stormed the *hôtel de ville* on October 31, 1870, which led to the creation of two newspapers called *La Commune de Paris*, at least three political clubs devoted to the movement, and innumerable references to that ur-Commune of the Revolution of 1789. Studies of the Commune are quick and right to point out these precursor moments.

Taking the opposite approach, I read the Siege in its own time, as the people who were writing and reading understood it in the winter of 1870–1871. While I hope that this perspective will help to understand the mentalities and political forces that determined reactions to and apologia of the Commune, this is not my primary frame of reference. Once unburdened of the need to explain the events of 1871, the Siege becomes a much more interesting moment in French history, capable of explaining how cultural institutions co-opted the revolutionary nineteenth century to ensure their own viability. Applying to the Siege a similar type of thick description

18   See his *Procès des Communards* (Juillard, 1964), *Paris libre 1871* (Seuil, 1971), *Paris insurgé* (Gallimard, 2006).
19   Murphy, *Rimbaud et la Commune, 1871–1872* (Classiques Garnier, 2009); Ross, *The Emergence of Social Space: Rimbaud and the Paris Commune* (University of Minnesota Press, 1988) and *Communal Luxury: The Political Imaginary of the Paris Commune* (Verso, 2015).
20   The title of a popular song written in 1886 ("Elle n'est pas morte!") by Eugène Pottier and of a scholarly study of the reception of the history of the Commune by Éric Fournier, *La Commune n'est pas morte: les usages politiques du passé, de 1871 à nos jours* (Libertalia, 2013).

that Merriman uses for the Commune might help disentangle the events of 1870–1871, a period Quentin Deluermoz has called "a chaotic collision of temporalities."[21]

Among scholarship on the Siege as an incident isolated from the Commune, Hollis Clayson's *Paris in Despair: Art and Everyday Life under Siege (1870–1871)* has set the standard, not least because it is the first book-length investigation of cultural and artistic practices during the Siege. A study of the visual arts, *Paris in Despair* also theorizes the psychosocial circumstances of the isolated city, of which culture is a reflection and a product. From this perspective, Clayson conceptualizes boredom as the primary psychosocial experience of the besieged over whom "immobility rather than violence prevailed."[22] If commentators in the 1870s and '80s shifted the trauma of the Commune onto the memory of the Siege, Clayson encourages us not to take the bait. With Parisian industries shut down, and skirmishes conducted sporadically, inefficiently, and at long distances far beyond the walls of the city, it is difficult to speak of the Siege as a traumatic event for all who experienced it. Clayson theorizes how this "interlude of boredom, restlessness, claustrophobia and anxiety"[23] informed the lived experience of the Siege, showing that immobility brought about drastic changes in everyday life and explaining the nervous linguistic and literary activity that Rebecca Spang has called "a near epidemic of writing and speaking."[24]

Yet even if the primary experience of the besieged was one of boredom, wealthy Parisians nonetheless knew that others were suffering. Boredom fell unevenly on Paris. It is not a contradiction to claim that some Parisians found the Siege boring and others lost their lives to it. In 1873, the playwright Léon Beauvallet summed up the problem by evoking the terrifying prospect of death aside the equally mortifying reality of boredom: "The men were dying while bored ... the women were dying of boredom." His solution really only addressed

---

21 Deluermoz, "Le Crépuscule des Révolutions: 1848–1871." *Histoire de la France contemporaine*, vol. 3 (Seuil, 2012), p. 307.
22 Clayson, *Paris in Despair: Art and Everyday Life under Siege (1870–1871)* (University of Chicago Press, 2002), p. 5.
23 Clayson, *Paris in Despair*, p. 55.
24 Spang, "'And They Ate the Zoo': Relating Gastronomic Exoticism in the Siege of Paris," *Modern Language Notes*, vol. 107, no. 4 (September 1992), p. 754.

the latter problem, by suggesting "The theater, by Jove!" as a way to "distract everyone."[25] Beauvallet acknowledges that death formed a part of the period, but his tone and his wordplay pass over these deaths in favor of a different history of the Siege, one in which cultural institutions could simultaneously alleviate boredom and give voice to tragedy. Mortifying boredom was amplified and given a public venue by institutions that profited from the twin motors of idleness and a sense of civic obligation. It benefitted theaters and newspaper directors, for example, that Parisians thought of themselves as bored in a way that made them sympathetic to those suffering from more mortal afflictions. Theaters such as the Comédie-Française and the Odéon offered what Beauvallet called distractions, but they also functioned as field hospitals where nurses and actors cared for the wounded. Newspapers established subscription services to raise funds towards the founding of cannons. Diarists openly acknowledged that they wrote from a place of boredom, but the city they described was upended by suffering, by famine, and by sickness. The writers that eventually published their diaries often insisted on anonymity in order to avoid appearing to profit from tragedy.

Very few besieged Parisians suffered in any acute way, but most suffered in a chronic way that one might qualify as boring as long as one also acknowledges that it was a form of suffering. The texts in this study arose from the stillness and silence of living through the Siege, but they take suffering as their subject and tragedy as their tone. While the Prussians bombarded the city only in January, those falling shells nonetheless killed dozens of people, including children.[26] As wood and fuel dwindled, Parisians began cutting down the trees lining the boulevards and burning furniture to keep warm. Many of the poor who lived on the streets succumbed to the coldest winter in recent memory. The Prussians had completely cut off supply routes into the city, forcing Parisians to ration their food in improvised municipal shops. Bakers added sawdust and rice to their bread. Many Parisians died of malnourishment and starvation. Stéphanie Sauget estimates that

---

25   "Les hommes mouraient en s'ennuyant ... les femmes s'ennuyaient à mourir." Léon Beauvallet, preface to Franz Beauvallet, *Le Forgeron de Châteaudun* (Paris: Tresse, 1871), p. 3.
26   Simonin, "Le Canon Krupp et le bombardement de Paris, par un officier de secteur." *Revue des deux mondes*, 2ᵉ période, vol. 91 (1871), pp. 467–468.

Parisians funeral services in December 1870 buried 120 to 140 percent more than during "ordinary" periods.[27] The literature produced during the Siege spoke directly to this collective tragedy, even if many of the writers avoided personal tragedy due to their status and wealth. Rachel Chrastil has shown that, during the Siege of Strasbourg, when the Prussians were *en route* to Paris, those who suffered the most from the war tended to "shift 'victimhood' onto others" and saw themselves "as actors trying to make the best of a difficult situation."[28] This new way of approaching the writing of trauma informs my perspective; Parisians wrote about the tragedy of others, or of the collective tragedy of the nation. According to the literature of the Siege, France was the ultimate victim.

The Shape of Literature

The sudden complete freedom of the press and of publishers opened the floodgates to all sorts of literature. I use the term "literature" to designate any cultural product whose meaning is primarily conveyed through language. The breadth of this definition is intentional, as it does not distinguish between so-called high and low literary culture, scholarly bias towards the former having obscured the popular culture of the Siege. More emmeshed in the economic and political constraints surrounding its creation and dissemination, popular culture reveals how such invisible structures determine the production and dissemination of all forms of literary culture, including print media such as newspapers and pamphlets, as well as more ephemeral products such as theatric spectacles.

By reading texts within the context of their production—the material and ideological forces that acted upon the institutions and figures who participated in that production—this book shows how the literary industry defines the shape and tenor of national debate. As Gisèle Sapiro shows for the *années noires* (1940–1944), writers become engaged in politics in part due to their institutional affiliations, and the "logics"[29]

27   Sauget, "Enterrer les morts pendant le double siège de Paris (1870–1871)." *Revue Historique*, vol. 317, no. 3 (July 2015), p. 566.
28   Chrastil, *The Siege of Strasbourg* (Harvard UP, 2014), p. 13.
29   Sapiro, *La Guerre des écrivains* (Fayard, 1999), p. 9.

that determined the conditions of the literary profession through those affiliations. Adopting this sociological methodology, I show that the literature of the Siege did not happen *ex nihilo*; material conditions, institutional politics, organizational rivalries, and interpersonal conflict largely determined the types of literature being produced and who was doing the producing. Within each part of this book, I remain conscious of the major actors, organizations, genres, and material specificities that organized each site of literary production (that is, adopting Sapiro's definition of institutional "logics"), and show how these logics influence our reading of the texts that were produced, performed, published, or commissioned. However, none of these sites was completely isolated from any other, forming in their aggregate a map of literary production.

I have chosen to structure this book according to sites of production—theaters, newspapers, personal writing, and publishing houses—because it indicates how the altered geography of the city created new centers of culture. These sites correspond to physical spaces (theaters, newspaper offices, homes, publishers' offices) and also to the different actors and institutions involved in production and consumption. For example, theaters existed as the ensemble of actors, directors, authors who contributed to productions as well as the public that attended performances. Newspapers had offices, but were consumed primarily in the streets, and contained many different types of literature (news, essays, fiction). Some diaries were written for later publication, but others were deeply personal writing with no readership intended other than the author or the author's family and friends. Finally, book and pamphlet publishing involved a complicated system of influence and control between authors, editors, and printers. By using sites of production as the primary classification of different literatures, I intend to describe not just what types of literature emerged, but also how they emerged through social and industrial processes, and the changes the Siege brought to both the what and how of literature. The story of Siege literature can only be told through analysis of networks of authors, editors, publishers, and readers: the history of literary institutions. Since most of the texts during this period were published almost as soon as they were written, ignoring the conditions of their production would make them nearly incomprehensible.

A lot of the literature of the Siege was about politics. This is due to the relaxing of censorship, the lack of appropriate civil servants to police literary production, and due to the fact that France's emperor, Napoléon III, had just been captured, leaving an unelected republican government in his stead. This meant that literature became a place of public debate over the future of the French state, and is why culture was never understood purely as a form of escapism. Literature revealed itself as an ideal medium for disseminating political opinions, of which there were many. On the first day of the new Republic, the government abolished all censorship of the press, meaning that newspapers profited from a rare moment in pre-twentieth-century French history: complete freedom to print whatever political opinions editors saw fit. The political spectrum was thus laid bare in print with the advent of dozens of new dailies that formed "a fervently patriotic and fervently revolutionary press."[30] The Republic was fragile, so the stakes were high for adherents of every political regime. Radical republicans, often called "red" republicans, began to clamor for a Paris Commune as early as October 31, 1870, when a group stormed the *hôtel de ville*. This group was perhaps best represented by Auguste Blanqui, who raged against what he saw as the conservative composition of the government in the pages of his militant newspaper, *La Patrie en danger*. On the other side, there were royalists like Louis Veuillot with his newspaper *L'Univers*, who hoped for the return of a French monarchy. However, most of the literature that I study here falls somewhere onto a spectrum of moderate republicanism, ranging from the revolutionary Henri Rochefort, who held a ministerial position in the new regime, to Adolphe Thiers, the chief executive of the provisional government, erstwhile monarchist, and eventual first president of the Third Republic.

What makes literature such an appropriate vehicle for the dissemination of politics during the Siege? As Paris was effectively isolated from the rest of France and the world, the literature produced *intramuros* served as a way of reaching readers who were absent. Writing for *les absents*, Parisians encoded their political and historical arguments into literary representation. For example, personal diaries allowed for readers to experience the Siege on a day-to-day basis just as their authors had. In this way, the literature of the Siege anticipated later

30 Pierre Guiral, "La Presse de 1848 à 1871." *Histoire générale de la presse française*, Vol. 2, edited by Claude Bellanger, Jacques Godechot, Pierre Guiral, and Fernand Terrou (Presses universitaires de France, 1969), p. 366.

pedagogical works like *Le Tour de France par deux enfants* with its implied readership of citizens who may bring with them different regional identities. Theatric productions functioned as reminders of community, of the bodily presence of compatriots, at the same time performing the fall of Napoléon III and bolstering physical and mental resistance against the Prussians. As one lecturer put it, literature acted as a "moral nourishment"[31] at a time when more bodily nourishment was hard to come by.

Political debate filled each site of literary production. Alongside reporting on daily happenings, newspapers also highlighted the importance of literature in times of war as journalists and authors theorized how the complete freedom of the press, only briefly established during the Siege and then formally in 1881, constituted the basis of a democratic society. Publishing houses and editors rushed to publish new texts that spoke directly to the present moment—*pièces de circonstances*—often written by amateurs and attesting to the desire to represent ordinary voices in public discourse; literary industries democratized, pre-empting political debates about the replacement of imperial and monarchic authoritarianism. As the Siege coincided with the highest literacy rates France had ever seen, consuming literature became the best and only outlet for the education of citizens, at the same time offering them the possibility of engaging directly with the building of a republican state through their own writing, as the diary impulse attests. Each site of literary production revealed itself to be uniquely situated to reflect on and adapt to the changes happening in everyday life.

Throughout the nineteenth century, newspapers had always been a vehicle for the dissemination of drastically different genres of text, from the news to the *roman feuilleton* or serialized novel, leading Marie-Ève Thérenty to claim that the nineteenth-century newspaper was composed of "literature."[32] During the Siege, the structure of newspapers did not change, but the types of stories they told coalesced into one literature with many voices, all speaking about the Siege. Any articles that appeared below the fold nearly always had a

31   Ernest Legouvé, "De l'alimentation morale pendant le siège." *Conférences parisiennes* (Paris: Hetzel, 1872).
32   Thérenty, *La Littérature au quotidien. Poétiques journalistiques au XIXe siècle* (Seuil, 2007), p. 12.

direct link to current events: an essay on the previous sieges of Paris throughout history, a fictional account of the Napoleonic Wars during which France invaded Germany, poetry written by ordinary Parisians. The types of new periodicals also demonstrate how the Siege made newspapers more political: serious left-leaning newspapers appeared as well as more satirical ones like *La Cave*, which jokingly offered delivery to basements in case of bombardment. Newspapers also had to abandon their reliance on the news, since the blockade had interrupted any flow of information from the outside world. As a result, they became even more self-referential, even less interested in the "new" since, paradoxically, everything was new given Parisians' heightened sense of living through a historic moment.

Alongside the feeling of witnessing history there was the utter monotony of the actual experience of the besieged. This paradox—time is standing still and yet moving too quickly—found its expression in personal diaries. Most sectors of the economy had shut down, except those related to cultural production, leaving some Parisians feeling lethargic and literary at the same time. Even if these diaries—mostly written by well-off Parisians who did not suffer in any acute way—preserve a record of the Siege as "a time of tedium,"[33] they also document how the besieged integrated national issues into their personal lives. Boredom may have initially encouraged Parisians to put pen to paper, but what they wrote expresses a desire to bear witness to the history passing before them. The confrontation of the personal and the political transformed the diary into a form of history writing in the present tense and in the first person, a corpus of so many textual attempts to integrate the self into events that seemed beyond individual understanding. The diary is a perfect genre for such a communication of experience. As it is written daily, the author cannot know the end of the story, and therefore cannot alter or curate observations and conclusions in order to support a historical narrative. The results are decontextualized observations about the world around the diarist, and about the diarist's often contradictory interpretations. Reading them is a way of experiencing the confusion of the Siege, the anxiety it produced about the future, and the impressionistic way that the besieged experienced it. Nowhere more than in these diaries do we

33   Spang, "And they Ate the Zoo," p. 761.

find that the Siege existed outside of time, as a sort of parenthesis to history rather than as a pivotal moment. Literature thrives in times of national tragedy because of its generic flexibility and its fuzzy relationship with fact. Surely one person's experience of the Siege does not constitute collective reality, but the way people collectively express their experience—the genre they choose to write about it—tells us about how living through such moments changes one's relationship to historical time.

Theaters also changed how they produced and what they produced. Theater directors, in particular Édouard Thierry of the Comédie-Française, began to look outside the normal repertoire for performances, relying on shows that combined poetry recitations, isolated scenes of plays, song, and speeches. The fall of the regime gave theaters a chance to rebrand themselves, turning away from the leisure politics of the Second Empire and towards spaces resembling political clubs. In this way, some theaters during the Siege gestured towards revolutionary theater, hosting what Susan Maslan calls an "alternative space for developing the practices of participation, scrutiny, interpretation, and judgment"[34] during the French Revolution. On the other hand, more established institutions took a middle road between politics and tradition, fashioned into civic spaces oriented towards apolitical patriotism. Theaters themselves took on new social functions as impromptu hospitals to house and care for the wounded, the female actors of these theaters often performing the role of nurses. These changes represent theater's role not just as a space for the dissemination of literature, but also as spaces of community engagement and morale building, presenting a "certain defiance in the face of the enemy, a refusal to give up the pleasures of society"[35] as Susan McCready writes of theater during the First World War. The types of populist, democratic representation one saw on both the stage and in the audiences of Siege theater may have suggested a type of revolutionary fervor, but most theaters as institutions were only engaged in the patriotism of wartime, the defense of the *patrie en danger.*

The structures of publishing houses also changed to reflect Parisians'

---

34   Maslan, *Revolutionary Acts: Theater, Democracy, and the French Revolution* (Johns Hopkins UP, 2005), p. 3.
35   McCready, *Staging France between the World Wars: Performance, Politics, and the Transformation of the Theatrical Canon* (Lexington Books, 2016), p. 20.

interest in literature about the Siege produced during the Siege. This required a de-modernization of publishing practices, which the success of the publishing industry had made bureaucratic and administrative. The rupture of publishing practices during the Siege upholds Jean-Yves Mollier's argument of the profit-driven pivot of the publishing industry in the early years of the Third Republic[36]—the *de facto* deregulation of the war made profit even more of a motivating factor, anticipating later debates. Christine Haynes has argued that the rise of the *éditeur* (often translated as *publisher*) from the 1830s onward cemented that social and economic role independent of the bookseller and the printer, leading to a politicization of the role as industry lobbyist.[37] The Siege either formally or informally saw these legal and social networks crumble albeit temporarily. While major publishers continued to respect contractual relationships with authors who may have left the city, new printers emerged to satisfy Parisians' thirst for literature of the moment without the need of a publisher intermediary. Notably, many non-periodicals were printed without the intermediary of an editor. This direct relationship between printer (during the Siege, this meant anyone with access to a press) and author was a departure from normal publishing practices of the late nineteenth century, when the editor had acquired the role of gatekeeper in the publishing industry.

Studying this literature allows us to map the literary economy that the nineteenth century had created, and how the Siege upended that institutional modernity. Rather than describing only the peaks of literary production, this book also describes its valleys and the composition of its bedrock, the ground from which literature sprouted. In this sense, I read the city under siege as a textual landscape, frozen in time. Many Parisian authors noted that time seemed to stand still during the four months of blockade. Reading the texts produced during one moment in time allows for a broader understanding of the mechanics of textual production. While paying some attention to chronology within the Siege itself, this book primarily treats the literature of the Siege as a

---

36 Mollier, *L'Argent et les lettres. Histoire du capitalisme d'édition* (Fayard, 1988). For other early examples of the cultural turn in book history, see Robert Darnton and Roche, editors, *Revolution in Print: The Press in France 1775–1800* (University of California Press, 1989).
37 Haynes, *Lost Illusions: The Politics of Publishing in Nineteenth-Century France* (Harvard UP, 2010).

coherent whole, sacrificing causality for thick description of what, how, and why certain types of texts sprang from this moment.

★   ★   ★

Each of the four sites of literary production I identify—theaters, newspapers, diaries, and publishing houses—contained a number of institutions that were competing for market share or for discursive supremacy. For theaters, I focus primarily on the Comédie-Française and the Théâtre de la Porte Saint-Martin precisely because their institutional missions were so opposed and clashed in ways that illuminate those missions. The Comédie-Française, as a guardian of French *patrimoine*, was less likely to engage with republican propaganda than the Porte Saint-Martin, eager to anchor itself as the theater of a bright republican future. Each newspaper and publishing house I discuss could be considered an individual institution with its specific policies, culture, history, and personnel, but the Siege brought in new players who were opposed to these older institutions in ideology, structure, or intended audience. Diarists, as amateur authors of historiographical texts, existed on the periphery of the institution of professional historians at the Sorbonne, invariably leading them to write in opposition to that institution. I will discuss the specific limitations and opportunities the Siege offered to each of these institutions and the new types of literature that resulted from these changes.

In Part I, "On Stage," I look at Parisian theaters under siege. This is the story of Victor Hugo's return to Paris from exile and how his book of poetry *Les Châtiments*, available for the first time in France, became a sensation on the stages of Parisian theaters. In a bid to legitimize the new republican regime, the city organized a free reading of these poems at the most unlikely venue, the Opéra de Paris. Three thousand Parisians from all corners of the city were invited to invade that Second Empire monument to the pleasures of the rich. Hugo's skirmishes with the director of the Comédie-Française reveal how the most storied and iconic French theater struggled to shake off its aristocratic reputation and retain control of its image. Theaters' imbrication into Parisian public space made them particularly vulnerable to changes in Parisians' way of life, but also ideal spaces to remind the besieged of their bodily presence in a community.

Newspapers are the focus of Part II, "Off Presses." With censorship abolished, one hundred and thirty new periodicals went to press, many presenting themselves as overtly republican. However, I show that this revolutionary freedom of the press made possible by the Siege was not a freedom for all. Shrinking paper supplies and rising prices threatened the very foundation of the public sphere by favoring older, conservative newspapers with greater access to raw materials, over their new republican rivals, demonstrating that unregulated markets reproduced the policies of censorship in all but name. In the competition for readership, many newspapers turned to repeating false information in order to raise morale. One such story, about the likely fictional bravery of French troops at the battle of Reichshoffen, became so popular that it lived on as a foundational myth of the Third Republic. The French general in that battle, Patrice de Mac-Mahon, claimed that it was the success of this myth that won him the presidency of the Republic in 1873.

Part III, "At Home," studies the breadth of personal writing that emerged during military investment. I highlight the writings of Caroline Chaumorot, a woman whose honeymoon was interrupted by the war. Through close readings of her diary as well as of others drawn from Parisian archives, I argue that these chronicles of the Siege—national epics on a personal scale—represented a new form of grassroots historiography set against the grand narratives of the Romantic historians and the scientism of the rising *école méthodique*. However, nearly all professional historians denigrated the genre of the diary, seen as either too feminine (and therefore not serious enough) or too popular to stand in for narrative accounts of the historical moment. "At Home" engages with the historiography of the present, how people understood their own history as they were living it, and how this form of historical consciousness changed during the Siege.

Part IV, "In Print," discusses publishers of non-periodical books and the publishing industry in general. I discuss how these institutions were assisted by government-sponsored publication efforts to expose the Second Empire's secrets while reshaping a new industry around the idea of spreading information and knowledge to the public. Publishers saw their goal as the making public of information, through traditional publishing, municipal libraries, or simply through cataloguing and curatorial efforts. This part presents, among other texts, the Siege-time revival of the eighteenth-century literary genre of the *libelle*, arguing that these erotico-historical tracts that detailed the sex lives of Napoléon III's family, along with the unedited publication of his most private papers, participated in a revolutionary tradition stretching back to the symbolic and literal toppling of the *ancien régime*. On the other hand, more bureaucratic efforts like those of clerk of the *dépôt légal*, who recorded all publications made in the capital, those of the Société des gens de lettres, whose advocacy relied on promoting the status quo, and those of the myriad government employees engaged in the publishing industry, ensured that this industry would continue uninterrupted despite the tumultuous events of the Siege.

The literature of the Siege attests to the emotional and ideological contradictions of this moment in French history. Literature is capable of expressing such contradictions without fear, and especially since many industries were more concerned with financial self-preservation than ideological consistency. In such moments of abrupt economic and political upheaval, traditional histories often fall short of expressing the anguish and frustration felt by those who lived through them. As their literary production makes clear, average Parisians were inconsistent in their convictions, unsure of their future, and while they expressed unwavering faith in the resilience of their fellow citizens, they were nonetheless prone to bouts of the most fatalistic pessimism. Taking these stories at their word, studying them within their historical context, without historical teleology or anachronistic conclusions, this study gives voice to the collective and individual experiences of a people caught in that nebulous space between past and future. In her study of such moments of rupture in history, Hannah Arendt has articulated the mingled feelings of opportunity and despair that plague writers caught in the gap, when "the actors and witnesses, the living themselves, become aware of an interval in time which is altogether determined by things that are no longer and by things that are not yet. In history, these intervals have shown more than once that they may contain the moment of truth."[38] This book elicits that truth through an exploration of the prolific literary output of just such a historical moment.

---

38 Arendt, *Between Past and Future* (Viking Press, 1961), p. 9.

Part I

On Stage

Chapter 1

The Boulevards Lose their Theaters

For many, boulevard life and the theaters that dotted the long, wide avenues of Paris represented the politics of the Second Empire. An example of how closely Napoléon III and his regime were associated with Parisian theaters can be found in Jules Claretie's 1907 novel *Le Mariage d'Agnès*. The novel takes place during the Siege and centers on the love between two young actors, one of whom who has just been accepted among the troupe at the prestigious Comédie-Française. During a walk through the besieged city, the lovers linger in front of the theater, growing pessimistic about its future and of our protagonist's once brilliant prospects:

> They were grouped in front of the posters announcing, in their wooden frames, this lugubrious phrase, these letters of mourning that had become the slogan of the country: "On Hiatus." One small, forgotten poster retained the title of the last performance, Monday September 5, by the regular actors of the Emperor, "Le Lion amoureux" [...]
>
> "Ponsard is in vogue. But they closed on two hundred and seventy francs in receipts! See you later, theater!"
>
> And the [...] young group stared at this forgotten poster, asking themselves sadly, now that the curtain had closed on the play, when it would be raised again and what individual tragedies would be played in this great, empty theater.[1]

Claretie understood the importance that theaters played during the Siege as markers of history. The inscription "comédiens ordinaires de

1 Claretie, *Le Mariage d'Agnès* (Paris: Fasquelle, 1907), p. 82.

l'empereur" ("regular actors of the emperor") was no longer relevant after Napoléon's fall, an anachronistic designation that emphasized France's uncertain political future—and the intertwined fate of the city's theaters. The meager revenue from a performance of a popular playwright attests to how difficult it was to imagine literary performances in a moment of national crisis. The deceptively frivolous "See you later, theater!" hides an anxious fear that the very idea of theater as defined by the Second Empire may not survive the war. This scene in Claretie's novel emphasizes the uncertainty of the moment: what was Paris without its theaters? What kind of city would it become after the Siege?

The doors of the Comédie-Française did not stay closed as the military investment continued. Those meager receipts on an otherwise popular performance also became a thing of the past; theaters during the Siege found ways of performing to full houses, integrating themselves into the circumstances of the blockade. This transition from vestigial limbs of the Second Empire to morale-raising (and profit-making) theaters of war came at the cost of a difficult reorganization of the institutional missions and social presence of Parisians theaters. Caught between a sense of civic duty and an awkward incongruity in times of war, theaters had to shake off their reputations as places of entertainment while ensuring some kind of income for their actors and administrators. To make matters worse, theaters faced new competition. The Siege itself was spectacle enough for many Parisians, obsessed with the transformation of everyday life in the city. Why, for example, watch Sarah Bernhardt or Marie Favart perform the roles of tragic heroines when millions of Parisians were experiencing their own immediate tragedies? To survive the Siege, theatric institutions had to align their social contribution and their aesthetic mission.

The sentiment of national mourning brought about by the Siege did not allow for what many deemed frivolous distraction. Hollis Clayson defines the boulevard as "the principal locus of the transformation and consequent diminution of the material and symbolic dimensions of Parisian public life during the war,"[2] a diminution caused by the claustrophobic conditions of blockade, but also by the closing of the

---

2   Clayson, *Paris in Despair: Art and Everyday Life under Siege (1870–1871)* (University of Chicago Press, 2002), p. 56.

theaters, restaurants, and other public establishments. Claretie's *Le Mariage d'Agnès* can attest to this, but one may not need look further than the forcible closing of public establishments at 10:30 p.m.—a curfew in all but name that killed boulevard life and the theaters on it.

As the boulevard shrunk as a locus of daily life, other parts of Paris expanded, new spectacles emerging during the short theatrical hiatus. As the war seemed to offer an alternative to the spectacle of boulevard life, Parisians began to disassociate theaters from the Second Empire. When the police initially closed theaters at the beginning of the Siege, it was ostensibly because the public did not want to go. However, these so-called spectacle-averse besieged found new things to see, flocking to the ramparts to spy on Prussians, strolling around encampments to see military maneuvers, and observing the long lines of Parisians eager for a ration of the dwindling supplies of food. Parisians turned the Siege itself into a spectacle.

The war became spectacular and theaters, conversely, militarized. New performances re-enacted parts of the war and that made Parisians feel like they were participating in the effort of resistance to the enemy by coming to see a show. Under the guise of raising morale, Parisian theaters managed to alleviate the boredom of the upper classes, ensure revenue streams, and unmoor themselves from the fraught political association with the Second Empire. Far from offering a distraction, theater during the Siege was engaged in representing the present. Parisians did not go to the theater to see their favorite actors perform their favorite plays; they went to participate in the fall of the Second Empire, to find courage in the company of fellow citizens, and to witness the transformation of theatrical space into political venue.

However, theaters were not inspired by patriotism or republican fervor in their Siege-time transformation into sites of community. Instead, directors like Édouard Thierry of the Comédie-Française were motivated by institutional inertia, trying to keep the lights on by selling tickets and making themselves indispensable during a moment of national crisis. As a result, continuity imposed itself on change, the Siege revealing itself as a hiatus rather than a rupture. The same Second Empire logic spread under siege as theaters, actors, and playwrights competed for relevance in a changing city. The inertia of the theater industry resisted revolutionary rhetoric. Susan Maslan has written that theaters during the French Revolution had the newfound mission of the "formation of the nation and its citizens."[3] During the Siege, the majority of cultural institutions promoted spectacle that only *performed* revolutionary culture, and that were less invested in revolutionary politics. Instead, Siege-time theater more clearly resembles the phenomena of spectacle in times of war, as a "certain defiance in the face of the enemy, a refusal to give up the pleasures of society,"[4] as Susan McCready writes of theater during the First World War. Militarized spectacle offered new definitions of patriotism and citizenship without espousing one political regime over another.

The Spectacular Siege

The announcement of the Republic on September 4, 1870 coincided with defeat at the battle of Sedan, which meant that alongside feelings of patriotism and republican fervor there was a distinct atmosphere of mourning in the capital. French defeats in the fall of 1870 were far more common than even small victories, and as a result the population did not want to be entertained by the theaters that were still open or those that were about to begin their active season. Admission sales plummeted in the days following the defeat at Sedan. By September 9, the provisional police prefect Émile de Kératry announced the temporary closing of all theaters. His official decree sums up the feelings of many depressed Parisians:

> Considering that the country is in mourning and that the opening of theaters stands in contradiction with the general attitude of the Parisian population [...] As of September 10, theaters will be closed.[5]

Nearly every newspaper published Kératry's decree, and many commentators approved of the edict, even theater critics like Timothée Trimm of *Le Petit Journal* and future director of the Comédie-Française Jules

---

3 Maslan, *Revolutionary Acts: Theater, Democracy, and the French Revolution* (Baltimore, MD: Johns Hopkins UP), 2005, p. 30.
4 McCready, *Staging France between the World Wars: Performance, Politics, and the Transformation of the Theatrical Canon* (Lexington Books, 2016), p. 20.
5 Most newspapers published Kératry's decree: see, for example, *Le Petit Moniteur* of September 11, 1870.

Claretie. The fate of theaters nonetheless seemed grim. The actor Frédéric Febvre called this "the somber period that nearly caused the disintegration of the Comédie-Française."[6] The newspaper *L'Entr'acte*, which normally detailed performances in major theaters in the city, ceased production on September 11, the day Kératry closed the theaters, telling readers that the newspaper would begin again "the day—very soon, we hold the patriotic conviction—that theaters reopen in Paris."[7] Despite the population's initial refusal to frequent the theaters they had so loved just a few weeks earlier, popular sentiment and official law very soon reversed completely. The *Entr'acte* was right: it was patriotism that soon led Parisians back to their old haunts, or at least the desire to appear patriotic. By the end of November, some theaters had become used to sold-out shows.[8] Instead of being an amoral distraction, theaters came to represent patriotic duty and resistance to the enemy.

The early twentieth-century doctor Lucien Nass claimed exultantly that theaters "wanted to [...] remind Parisians that they should always ensure the artistic reputation of their city anyway."[9] This sort of self-congratulatory revisionism ignores the fact that theaters underwent a civic transformation that, according to Clayson, "deeply disturbed"[10] theater critics such as Francisque Sarcey, invested in artistic reputation even during wartime. During their dormant period, theaters underwent a radical restructuring of repertoires and pricing, and most importantly, articulated the pressing need to alleviate the atmosphere of boredom and idleness in the besieged capital. Parisian audiences had to believe that going to the theater was a civic duty, and to this end, theaters staged performances that spoke directly to the present moment. Poems, plays, and speeches[11]

---

6   Febvre, *Journal d'un comédien*, Vol. 1, 1850–1870 (Paris: Ollendorf, 1896), pp. 236–237.
7   *L'Entr'acte*, September 11, 1870.
8   Given the rarity of archives for many of the boulevard theaters, it is difficult to give exact data on the number of spectacles or tickets sold at any given theater, let alone for the entirety of Parisian theaters. When making broad claims like this one, I am relying on secondary information such as newspaper reviews.
9   Nass, *Le Siège de Paris et la Commune* (Paris: Plon, 1914), p. 72.
10   Clayson, *Paris in Despair*, p. 84.
11   Nineteenth-century spectacles often combined different generic elements in a single show, but these multimedia performances were *de rigueur* during the Siege. In a three-hour block, spectators could have seen an act of *Phèdre*,

were quickly written, based on brief news articles, rumors of events outside the capital, or even about daily life in Paris itself. When the theaters finally opened, they donated the proceeds from many of their performances to patriotic causes like the founding of cannons and care for the wounded. Wealthy Parisians came to the theater because they were bored, but also to feel like they were contributing something to the defense of the city that they knew must be suffering, somewhere. They could give to charitable causes and go the theater at the same time. They had their cake and ate it, too.

Theaters had become so central to everyday life during the Second Empire that their sudden disappearance seemed to sap the city of its soul. Entire industries relied on them: from the directors and actors who depended on their financial success, the well-heeled public who filled their seats, to the newspaper critics who ranted and raved to make a name for themselves. If the fall of the Second Empire meant the closing of theaters, was it even possible to imagine their existence under a republic? Could Paris still be Paris?

Paris, the city of boulevards, *flâneurs* (strollers), and nighttime debauchery, reverted to a diurnal city. Many Parisians echoed the sentiments recorded by one anonymous diarist:

> The theaters, concert halls are closed, the boulevards are deserted at the moments when they used to be the most animated, meaning from 8 to 11 at night [...] Paris, so vibrant so gay around 9 at night, is now monotonous [...] The state of siege has changed Paris into the countryside.[12]

Everything that seemed to make Paris what it was had disappeared under the strict conditions of siege. The desertion of the boulevards, the extinction of gaslights, and the closing of theaters suddenly deprived Paris of its vital energy. Napoléon III's urban renovation projects had transformed Paris into a cosmopolitan capital,[13] but none of that seemed

a collection of patriotic poems, a rousing rendition of the "Marseillaise," and a speech condemning the rationing of bread.

12   Bibliothèque historique de la ville de Paris (BHVP), Ms 1073, entry of October 23, 1870.

13   There has been much written about the Second Empire's urban renovation projects, often called "Haussmannization" after one of the prime urban architects, the Prefect of the Seine region, Baron Georges Eugène Haussmann. See, among others, David Harvey's *Paris: Capital of Modernity* (Routledge, 2003), David

to matter during the Siege. Even if the wide boulevards remained, the *flâneur*, its primary inhabitant and consumer, had disappeared.[14]

Siege-time correspondence shows people still attempting to live in Paris in the same way they had before, constantly colliding with the limits of the blockaded city. Observers walked the very same streets, but now the city, without actually changing in any structural way, was a different place to inhabit. The poet Théophile Gautier wrote in the *Journal officiel*:

> It seems that Paris is an enormous city capable of tiring the most tireless stroller. Well, ever since our inability to go outside, the immense walls of the city trouble and restrict the hips of the Parisian population as would a belt that is tied too tightly.[15]

Almost in reaction to the enclosing Prussian lines, the limits of the city seemed to shrink, leading to what Clayson calls the "claustrophobia" of the besieged city, "a spatial affliction" that "produced the kind of unease that normally occurs after remaining too long in constricted indoor space."[16] No one knew what life (or strolling) was like outside of the walls, as the rest of France sank into what Nicholas White has shown to be a muddy imaginary, a geography "unstable, shifting in battle sometimes on a daily basis, as its status await[ed] determination by the definitive outcome of the war."[17] No longer could one even participate in the collective consciousness of the crowd since there were no crowds in which to lose oneself. The writer and *flâneur* Edmond de

---

Jordan's *Transforming Paris* (Simon & Schuster, 1995), and John Merriman's *The Margins of City Life* (Oxford UP, 1991). For a broader look at how radically the city had changed in the nineteenth century, see Colin Jones's *Paris: Biography of a City* (Penguin, 2004).

14   For more on the rise of boulevard life and the *flâneur* during the second half of the nineteenth century, see Christopher Prendergast, *Paris and the Nineteenth Century* (Blackwell, 1992); and Vanessa Schwartz, *Spectacular Realities: Early Mass Culture in Fin-de-Siècle Paris* (University of California Press, 1998).

15   Gautier, "Voyages dans Paris," *Journal officiel*, October 5, 1870. Gautier's column "Voyages dans Paris" was later published in part as *Tableaux de siège: Paris 1870–1871* (Paris: Charpentier, 1871) a title that completely ignores the essentially experiential nature of his articles.

16   Clayson, *Paris in Despair*, p. 56.

17   White, "Zola and the Physical Geography of War," *Dix-Neuf*, vol. 21, nos. 2–3 (2017), p. 157.

Goncourt walked the streets like a ghost, his *Journal*[18] becoming more and more terse as the Siege wore on. If the Second Empire allowed visitors to "write" the city as Goncourt had done, when the lights went out in the capital it became "illegible and unknowable."[19] Theaters once stood for the complicated intersection of leisure, boredom, and urbanity—in a word, Second Empire modernity. Now that those institutions were closed, modernity seemed like a thing of the past.

In the meantime, Paris under siege became a sort of theater, a "metamorphosis bestowing new structures and positive functions" on the city, as Clayson argues.[20] New urban spaces associated with the war, such as the ramparts, offered a spectacle that did not feel like a distraction because they served a purpose. Hastily improvised in the early weeks of September, these defensive structures had the double benefit of being both entirely new in the urban environment and directly related to the war. Our anonymous Parisian who earlier bemoaned the deserted boulevards remarked in his diary about the curiosity the ramparts inspired:

> The very different aspect of these formerly charming places doesn't seem at all sad, since despite the devastation the whole area is full of animation and the curious crowds abound, armed with lorgnettes to try and see the Prussians.[21]

He uses the word *animation* to describe the atmosphere on these defensive outposts, the same term he used in the previous citation to describe the streets of the city during the Second Empire. The site of animation, the boulevards, simply shifted to the ramparts. Note also that these onlookers brought their lorgnettes—an essentially theatrical accessory—to spy on the Prussians as if the Grande Duchesse de Gérolstein might be on the field of battle. The interest in catching a glimpse of these new structures and the panoramas they offered increased to the point that crowds of curious onlookers made military

---

18   Edmond de Goncourt continued writing the *Journal* after the death of his brother and co-author, Jules de Goncourt, on June 20, 1870, complicating his relationship to besieged Paris.
19   Mairi Liston, "'Le Spectacle de la rue': Edmond de Goncourt and the Siege of Paris," *Nineteenth-Century French Studies*, vol. 32 (2003–2004), p. 65.
20   Clayson, *Paris in Despair*, p. 58.
21   BHVP Ms 1073, entry of October 3, 1870.

operations impossible, leading to an official edict forbidding citizens from loitering around them.

Where newspapers used to run theater criticism, they now ran articles documenting the changes to the city under siege. Since their jobs depended on it, theater critics also saw besieged Paris as a spectacle to be reviewed. These articles reveal that, much like for the crowds of *flâneurs*, newspaper critics also sought spectacle elsewhere. At the end of the Second Empire, Théophile Gautier maintained a consistent theater column in the *Journal officiel* but was obliged to stop once the theaters closed their doors. He continued to write for this paper, now under the control of the Republic, but his column switched to the changing atmosphere of Paris under the title "Voyages dans Paris." While the new direction of his articles may seem arbitrary, he remained consistent in tone and terminology. Gautier never really stopped writing about Parisian spectacles, even when describing a train ride he took around the city:[22]

> At intervals, the sudden darkness of a tunnel made necessary by an overhead road or by changes in the level of land snuffed out the view, like in a theater when one lowers the lights to simulate night, then the perspective opened again with blinding light.[23]

Gautier kept the essentially theatrical elements of his column even if he was the spectator of a different performance. The succession of days and nights under blockade resembled the theatrical effects used to suggest the same on stage, time voided of experience and compressed into lightness and darkness. The geography of the city, interestingly, does not stand in for set décor; the overpasses are instead part of the machinery of the stage, as if the city were responsible for Gautier's warped sense of time and not the Prussian blockade. If this is a play about the Siege that he is describing, there are no protagonists, no enemy to be fought. Viewed from his train wagon, Paris has become an empty theater where time accelerates for no one but himself. His isolation within a seemingly abandoned city might have been a way of evoking the isolation of

---

22 Gautier was obsessed with trains during the Siege. His fascination was due in large part to the effective impossibility of normal train travel imposed by the blockade. In the *Journal officiel* of October 26, he wrote: "Nothing makes you think of locomotion like knowing you cannot escape a certain circle."
23 Gautier, "Voyages dans Paris," *Journal officiel*, November 2, 1870.

Paris itself. Gautier may have also been trying to find an outlet for his boredom. As he wrote in the *Journal officiel* on September 5: "The work of human genius never stops, despite the terrible grandeur of events." Even if Paris offered no more plays, he found the spectacle of the Siege itself to be a suitable alternative for his intellectual activity.

The impulse towards spectacle that brought so many Parisians out into the streets and onto the ramparts was not shared by all. Many of those on the ramparts were there on military business, since the majority of male inhabitants had been incorporated into the National Guard, or the *garde mobile*. One such impromptu soldier was Théodore de Banville, who became, along with others like Catulle Mendès, Albert Delpit, and Victor Hugo, a major poet of the Siege. Banville's prolific poetry, mostly published in the newspaper *Le National*, was later collected and published under the title *Idylles prussiennes*. Banville wrote notably about the sites of the Siege but did not share many of his contemporaries' thrill at the spectacle of war, as we can see in his poem "La Soirée" ("Evening"), which describes the masculine pleasures of military duty to one's country as a substitute to the effeminate vices of the Second Empire:

> When returning from the ramparts
> Where, full of warm faith
> He watched at his post,
> The father slips off his pea coat
>
> And there he rests until tomorrow!
> He forgets you, bitter breeze that blows
> On the rampart, and with a hand
> So happy, dons his slippers. [...]
>
> So the happy father
> Doesn't miss the theaters,
> Where adventurous jewels
> Bedecked false Cleopatras,
>
> Nor the cafés, uglier still,
> Where unpolished, pale Phrynes
> Blazed under their golden locks,
> Like scarlet beasts.[24]

24   Banville, "La Soirée," *Le National*, October 17, 1870.

Banville's poem contrasts the terrible but very real scenes of the Siege with the escapist theater of the Second Empire. His references to Cleopatra and Phryne (the latter a famous courtesan of ancient Greece) imply that Paris, the hedonistic modern Babylon, was no more—note the shift to the past tense. By making a father the subject of his idyll, Banville even suggests that the end of the theaters allowed for the rediscovery of familial pleasures: the hearth, slippers, the satisfaction of a day spent in civic service. The gendering of theater as feminine, through the use of two feminine theatric figures, contrasts with the manly pleasures of a war well-fought. Banville encouraged his readers to view the Siege as a moment of rebirth, where the physical and moral tribulations of war forged a new France. In order to do so, he suggested, Paris had to rid itself of its theaters and embrace a more masculine culture.

Many staunchly republican newspapers like *La Patrie en danger* and *Le Combat* welcomed the shuttering of theaters as a sign that the government and the population of Paris in general had its mind set on defeating the Prussians rather than returning to the debauchery of the Second Empire. Another "red"[25] republican paper, *Le Réveil*, upon hearing rumors of debate around the topic, issued a prophecy on October 24:

> We know that the measures taken to close the theaters will be upheld. When the Prussians encircle Paris in a ring of iron, when a part of the population suffers in misery and hunger, the reopening of theaters would be a scandal.

Certainly, many of these bellicose republicans saw theaters as an extension of Napoléon III's politics of bourgeois appeasement, but they also violently adhered to the waging of all-out war—*la guerre à outrance*—which left little room for entertainment. Even once theaters were allowed to reopen, *Le Combat* refused to report on what was being shown, instead running a column detailing the goings-on and ideas

---

25   The term "red" (*rouge*) was used during the second half of the nineteenth century to designate the radical left. The color was often associated with revolutionary causes and was notably proposed as the official color of the republican flag during the working-class revolution of 1848. During the Siege, bourgeois critics used the adjective pejoratively to designate the movement that led to the Commune of Paris just a few months later.

generated by various republican political clubs, which were perhaps after all just another space for political performance. For these critics, theaters represented the ironic, flippant, and, worst of all, apolitical culture promoted by Napoléon III. Theaters would have to rebrand themselves during this time of national strife. Luckily, the Parisian population seemed ready to accept a new type of theater for the circumstances of the Siege.

The Transformation of the Comédie-Française

Because of their affiliation with the boulevard culture of the Second Empire, Parisian theaters risked being left behind after its fall. While the city insisted that their doors remain closed, they found new ways of participating in the national war effort, perhaps cynically as a way to remain relevant amid the shifting political climate. By converting their spaces into *ambulances*, or makeshift hospitals, these institutions could carry the flag of the Croix-Rouge, not only potentially sparing them from bombardment but also contributing to the defense of the nation. In doing so, however, theaters had to accept charitable aid from nuns, display religious iconography for the sick and dying, and allow priests to perform rituals within their halls. The invasion of religion into theaters posed a problem for certain critics, especially those *vieilles barbes* of the Revolution of 1848, who looked back fondly to the anticlericalism of the first French Revolution in 1789. How could the new French Republic maintain a strict separation of church and state when these *ambulances* were organized in what were after all sites of French cultural heritage?

In the early months of the Siege, theaters had many competing, often contradictory forces pulling them in different directions. On the one hand, administrators such as Édouard Thierry of the Comédie-Française worried about paying actors, stagehands, workers, and themselves. With the theaters closed, an entire industry of workers would not get paid. On the other hand, the public scrutinized theaters due to their association with the political culture of the Second Empire. Thierry offered a solution: theaters could participate in the populist spirit of the Siege, offering up their spaces for representative assemblies. Shaking off their reputation as temples of pleasure, they could instead become temples of patriotic propaganda aimed at the population at large, rather than a small subset of upper-class strollers of the boulevards. Many theaters looked favorably on this suggestion, staging readings of Hugo or other incendiary poets, allowing ample time for spontaneous outbursts of "La Marseillaise," or giving lectures on the importance of patriotism in times of national struggle. However, the specific case of the Comédie-Française, one of the oldest theatric institutions in France and an official state theater, shows that the reorientation of theaters towards national interests often came at the cost of exposing these institutions to the vagaries of politics. While Thierry believed that converting the Theater[26] into an *ambulance* displayed his willingness to participate in the growing patriotism of the city, his gamble to rebrand his institution had mixed results.

The Comédie-Française was not the only theater that opened its doors, but most followed its lead by offering rhetorical spectacles that implicitly or explicitly argued for theaters' relevance in times of national tragedy as a space of public unification. The specific conditions of the Siege made this difficult. Since so many people had fled Paris, theaters were working with skeleton crews. Theaters offered performances irregularly and often without their usual complement of troupe actors, décor, and costumes. Many theaters never opened due to these circumstances.[27] The reasons theaters stayed closed indefinitely varied widely, ranging from practical concerns like the absence of actors or directors to moral qualms about performing during a moment of national crisis. Perhaps paradoxically, those that opened did so because they believed theaters were necessary in a time of national crisis. The imperatives that forced debate around the relevance of theater in times of war were not only those of boredom and resistance, but also the need for new plays that specifically represented Parisians' present moment.

The impulse to represent the moment was what tied all literary activity during the Siege together, but theater's place in this nation-building

---

26 Another name for the Comédie-Française was the Théâtre-Français, which I will call either the Comédie-Française or the Theater.
27 A short list of the major theaters that were regularly open includes la Comédie-Française, le Théâtre de la Porte Saint-Martin, l'Opéra de Paris, la Gaîté, l'Ambigu-Comique, les Bouffes-Parisiennes, le Théâtre du Château d'Eau, les Délaissements, l'Athénée, le Théâtre de Cluny, and les Menus plaisirs. A list of theaters closed during the Siege includes l'Opéra comique, le Théâtre lyrique, le Théâtre du Châtelet, le Gymnase, les Variétés, and le Théâtre du Palais-Royal.

process was particular in that it maintained a meta-discourse on the importance of timely fiction. Many theatrical performances in the nineteenth century included media other than just plays, and this was especially true during the Siege. For example, a performance at the Bouffes-Parisiennes of January 4, 1871 included four poems from Hugo's recently published *Les Châtiments*, two acts of *Le Cid* where the titular character was dressed as a national guardsman, and a poem written just one month before by Eugène Manuel. Musical interludes were very common, as was interspersing discourses by public intellectual figures between acts of a classic or contemporary play. This meant that theatrical spectacle had the largest variety of modes of representation available to it, and furthermore was able to comment on its own cultural and political significance through readings and lectures. Much like newspapers, theaters became a site of many different types of literature.

The scholar, poet, and dramatic author Ernest Legouvé gave one such lecture that caused a sensation. On October 25, 1870, he took to the stage on the opening night of the Comédie-Française to give a lecture called "De l'alimentation morale pendant le siège,"[28] a slight wordplay obvious to Parisians in search of more physical types of *alimentation* (nourishment) once the blockade began. The night was an important one as it was the first performance authorized by the police prefect since the closing of theaters. While the city had cautiously sanctioned the opening of theaters for such events as this lecture, the terms of what would be acceptable were still unclear. Would the government allow future performances? Would dramatic censorship, banished after the fall of Napoléon III, return under republican rule? Legouvé's lecture was a test, and as such garnered a lot of attention.

Legouvé tackled the topic of theater in times of war directly in his lecture, as a sort of apologia of spectacle as a way to boost morale. His speech reads as explicit instructions for how theaters—and cultural institutions in general—should present themselves to the public in a moment when it seemed that culture had no place. However, Legouvé did not explicitly address other actors, publishers, theater directors, or writers: he spoke to the population of Paris at large. This means that he had to speak the language of patriotism without espousing any particular

---

28   Published in Legouvé, *Conférences parisiennes* (Paris: Hetzel, 1872).

political beliefs. He had to chart a future for the nation without actually placing any legible signposts. His speech was therefore not a specific set of recommendations for how to weather the storm of war, but an empty rhetorical vessel in which a Parisian of any political persuasion might project their own beliefs. Debate, tension, disagreement, and dispute—the types of drama one might expect to find on the stage of a theater—gave way to reflection, community, commonalities, and solidarity. His selection of topics, as one might imagine, also tried to form consensus rather than inject new ideas into popular discourse. In a quarter hour, he discussed subjects ranging from the absence of loved ones and the duty to defend the country, to what kind of republic they should build. He presented a litany of topics identical to those endlessly discussed in newspapers and ostensibly in Parisian homes.

Legouvé brought the space of the theater into the discursive geography of the city under siege. The beginning of the speech situates the theater within social space:

> Given the terrible circumstances in which we find ourselves, without a doubt nothing is more useful than thinking of nourishing our bodies; but it is just as important to nourish our souls [...] Terrors throw [the soul] into panic, dejection overwhelms it, separation rips in it half ... This, too, is a wound! A wound that is inflicted in all parts of the city. Not a single house exists that is not an *ambulance* that cares for this type of victim.
>
> It's because of these wounds that I want to be with you today and before you to seek reasons for courage, the causes of confidence, the means for comfort that we have left; I want to glean all the grains, all the sprigs of hope, and to turn these into a sheaf to nourish the sickly.[29]

The first thing the audience would have picked up on is the metaphorical use of the term *ambulance*, as a real *ambulance* was in the very building they were occupying. Audiences—and the general public—were fascinated by the transformation of theaters into hastily assembled hospitals and often visited theaters to get a glimpse of the metamorphosis. The theatrical *ambulance* even became a part of the spectacle

29 Legouvé, *Conférences parisiennes*, pp. 211–212.

when later, during a performance of *Tartuffe*, the cries of a wounded soldier echoed throughout the room: "in the middle of all of this," wrote the director of the Theater, "the representation continues, and the groaning that rose from the stretchers was heard echoing through the terrified hall."[30]

Legouvé understood that theaters could be something more than just *ambulances*, however. In this excerpt, he begins to describe what is particular about performance with his situational phrase "with you [...] and before you." Spectacle presents an immediacy that no other cultural medium can, he argues. It can even be a sort of conversation, as the audience, the room, and the sounds of the sick nearby can change the meaning of the performance itself. During the Siege, spectacle addressed itself to a collective for whom the very act of coming together was meaningful when the community was threatened and its future uncertain. His speech appealed to audience participation.

By turning theaters into a space of potential meta-discourse on the situation, Legouvé argued that they served a specific purpose during this terrible moment. In fact, he was performing his argument by delivering it aloud in a theater. Legouvé implicitly claimed that his speech itself was one of these moral nourishments that Paris so desperately needed:

> In ordinary life, in the course of habitual occupations and pleasures, the "know-thyself" of Socrates has little place. We only rarely listen to our consciences; we are for ourselves but an acquaintance that we see from time to time; we do not speak deeply with ourselves. But the forced idleness of the Siege, the long shifts on the ramparts, serious reflections, born from the gravity of events, prompt us necessarily to take our moral inventory.[31]

Turning the arguments against theater on their head, Legouvé instead claims that the unprecedented nature of the Siege requires theater as a moment of reprieve, an introspective reorientation of the conscious. In a tautological gesture, he claimed that the fact that his audience sat

30   Édouard Thierry, *La Comédie-Française pendant les deux sièges (1870–1871)* (Paris: Tresse et Stock, 1887), p. 256.
31   Legouvé, *Conférences parisiennes*, p. 235.

before him was the proof that Parisians had something to gain from going to the theater. He knew that many of them had come merely due to the "forced idleness" of the Siege, hoping at best for some sort of "moral inventory" and at worst just for some distraction. But the theater offered a respite from daily life in which monumental events can be seen in their fullness. They could, he says, be distracted and engaged at the same time.

Legouvé's speech defended the nation less than it defended the Comédie-Française itself. He delved into the mental state of the city under siege, proposing the theater as a place of refuge and of self-reflection without proposing any particular policy or strategy for the future. The theater allowed for the city to know itself, which might lead to a satisfying moral inventory but leaves aside practical questions of how to resist the Prussians or elect a new government. It was implicitly political insofar as it entertained the notion that the city had the luxury of reflection when the government had little authority and the enemy was outside the gates. In a critique of Legouvé's lecture, the newspaper *Le Combat* wondered what "the faces of the spectators would have looked like if, in the middle of his academic eloquence, an artillery shell had interrupted the cadence of his speech."[32] This morbid fantasy implicates the Comédie-Française in a more general attitude of many wealthy Parisians, for whom the Siege could have been a moment of Socratic reflection rather than a struggle for the future of the nation and ultimately for one's life. While Edmond de Goncourt slurped down the last oyster in the city, while theater-goers applauded the idea that the Siege might be a moral event rather than a political and military mess, hundreds of Parisians were dying of cold, famine, and direct confrontation with the Prussian army.

Édouard Thierry intended this emphasis on the theater itself to be an argument for its relevance in times of war. He knew that any overt politics—which were also being hotly debated in other discursive spaces like newspapers and in homes—would have doomed his theater as a partisan institution. Thierry's attitude towards political regimes was one of wariness. While some of his contemporaries accused him of crypto-Bonapartism, it is more likely that he simply considered his theater to be apolitical: "French," rather than "republican" or

32 *Le Combat*, October 27, 1870.

"imperial." Speaking specifically about the Opéra de Paris, scholar Deborah Cohen remarks on the challenge of Parisian theaters to remain both disengaged from the present and still put on performances in times when the present seemed all-encompassing:

> One of the distinguishing elements that define institutions is their relationship to time. In this regard, we could say that the Opéra sees itself as an entity impervious to the vagaries of history and politics, guided only by its internal logic: the history of the musical institution and the history of politics are incompatible.[33]

The Comédie-Française, like the Opéra, had certain aesthetic and immaterial responsibilities to uphold. The municipal edict closing the theaters certainly resolved Thierry's impossible situation of running a timeless institution in a revolutionary moment. When the edict was lifted, however, Thierry felt he had an obligation to Parisians, who needed stimulation, and to his actors, who needed to be paid.

While many theaters were dealing with the same material constraints and the same abstract quandaries as the Comédie-Française, none had as storied a past as this institution. None certainly had as central a role in the state or in theatrical tradition. The Maison de Molière was not an upstart boulevard theater and so it did not need to follow the same trends, able to exist independently from the vagaries of aesthetic attitudes and serious economic concerns. In a sense, no other theater could compete with the Comédie-Française as it enjoyed a legal, exclusive right to its repertoire, which was without a doubt the most prestigious in France. It was not just the only place one could see current and classic plays, it was the very symbol of the French dramatic tradition. The critic Frédéric Loliée summed up Thierry's institutional mindset as maintaining "the equal balance between tradition, which it needed to uphold, and the demands of modern mindsets, which it needed to follow and understand in order to preserve the continuity of theatric creation."[34] However, "modern mindsets" had changed so quickly since the onset of the Siege.

---

33   Cohen, "Une institution musicale entre repli et implication politique: le quotidien de L'Opéra de Paris pendant la guerre de 1870 et sous la Commune," *Le Mouvement Social*, vol. 208 (2004), p. 8.
34   Loliée, *La Comédie-Française: histoire de la Maison de Molière de 1658 à 1907* (Paris: Lucien Laveur, 1907), p. 304, cited in Sébastien Le Jean, "La

Thierry, like his Theater, was being pulled simultaneously towards the past and towards the future.

After the theaters reopened, one of the first major questions of "modern mentalities" was that of stage costumes. Many male actors, like most men in Paris, had joined the National Guard either through a sense of duty or a desire for a stable salary while the theaters were closed. When they reopened, the actors remained enlisted, wondering if they should perform in their military uniforms. Even Victor Hugo was swept up in military fervor, buying a *képi*—the distinctive headgear of the National Guard—on October 7, almost as a sort of souvenir.[35] As uniforms became the costumes of the Siege, it is unsurprising that they also became the costumes of Parisian theaters. The actor Henri-Polydore Maubant recited a monologue from *Le Cid* in his National Guard uniform.[36] Édouard Brindeau often recited the "Marseillaise" in similar dress.[37] In his memoirs, the actor Frédéric Febvre recalls that, given the style of growing one's beard when serving in the military, "in the middle of all those military costumes, the public had difficulty recognizing the troupe."[38] Théophile Gautier, writing his daily column in the *Journal officiel*, published a review of a performance of the *Andromaque* at the Comédie-Française in which he addressed the unusual costume decisions:

> Since the sets and costumes had been placed in storage for safety, in a basement or in a room secured against bombing, they would perform the play in tail-coats and street clothes in front of simple stage design. This idea is charming. Tragedy, such as the masters of the seventeenth century understood it, does not concern itself with "local color." It did not know the expression or the concept. Even if Racine was a grand Hellenist, he certainly did not imagine, when representing *Andromaque* or *Iphigénie*, looking

Comédie-Française et ses administrateurs (1849–1871)," in *Les Spectacles sous le Second Empire*, edited by Jean-Claude Yon (Armand Colin, 2010).

35   "Acheté un képi" is the full entry in Hugo's diary for October 7, published as *Choses vues* (Gallimard, 2002).

36   Gustave Labarthe, *Le Théâtre pendant les jours du siège et la Commune* (Fischbacher, 1910), p. 95.

37   Frédéric Febvre, *Journal d'un comédien*, Vol. 1, 1850–1870 (Paris: Ollendorf, 1896), p. 237.

38   Febvre, *Journal d'un comédien*, p. 238.

at a Greek vase or consulting an ancient medallion in order to arrive at a more accurate *mise en scène*.[39]

Gautier lauded the actors of the Comédie-Française for performing "en toilette de ville" (in their everyday clothes) because he thought Racine would never have intended his characters to be dressed in Greek clothes as the topic of the play might suggest. However, the decision to perform without costumes was out of Thierry's hands. The danger of bombardment forced him to put the Theater's décor and costumes in storage, obliging the actors to perform in street clothes. While most spectators would have thought it was inherently circumstantial—a sign of the times—to see Andromache in contemporary dress, Gautier saw it as timeless.

While the audience seemed to revel in the unlikely costumes, Thierry did not. In his diary, he made no remarks on the unlikely aesthetic of *Andromaque* but seemed to regret the decision: in all subsequent performances, the actors of the Comédie-Française performed in costume or they did not perform at all. The director of the Théâtre de la Porte Saint-Martin frequently asked Thierry for costumes, who always refused. Thierry saw his refusal in terms of competition, as he writes in his diary: "The Comédie-Française refuses to lend them the costumes for *Cinna*. Always foolish to lend when one never borrows."[40] Denying his colleagues the type of community togetherness his actors promoted on stage, Thierry aimed to set his theater apart from others. For him, the novelty of the Siege was not in seeing uniforms on stage, but instead in seeing theater costumes during the Siege as a sign of continuity with theatric history: the actress Marie Favart, who played the titular role of Andromache, visited some wounded soldiers after her performance, still dressed in character: "she went to the *ambulance* to show off her costume to the poor Milon [a wounded soldier], who asked her to do so."[41] Thierry wanted to keep his Theater above the fracas of war and politics, but his gamble was dangerous. By distancing the Comédie-Française from other theaters and by prohibiting his actors

---

39   Gautier, *Voyages dans Paris*, in the *Journal officiel* of November 13, 1870. Gautier's articles were later compiled in *Tableaux du siège* (Paris: Charpentier 1871).
40   Thierry, *La Comédie-Française pendant les deux sièges*, p. 130.
41   Thierry, *La Comédie-Française pendant les deux sièges*, p. 135.

from performing in military uniforms, he ran the risk of seeming to ignore the tragedy that had befallen Paris.

Thierry's willingness to open the Theater to the wounded and their caretakers could be seen as engagement with the conditions of siege. However, he made this decision as a form of public relations, as its aftermath shows. With the Comédie-Française's transformation into an *ambulance* also came the presence of nuns, who worked alongside actresses to tend to the considerable number of wounded French national guardsmen along with a small number of Prussians. The presence of nuns in a theater, albeit conspicuous, was not cause for alarm; it was how the Theater accommodated them that became another thorn in Thierry's side. During the Theater's transformation into an *ambulance*, someone slipped a sheet over a famous statue, *Voltaire assis*, completed by the sculptor Jean-Antoine Houdon in 1779, which had been displayed in the Theater since 1781. The presence of this statue in the halls of the Comédie-Française speaks to Voltaire's enduring status as a symbol of French literary heritage. However, Voltaire, an anticlerical writer revered by republicans during the Revolution of 1789, became a political lightning rod during the Siege. The news of this scandalous veiling reached the editors of *Le Combat*—a staunchly anticlerical and antimonarchist newspaper:

> While the French Republic allows mass to be celebrated in the streets, one of its civil servants, Monsieur E. Thierry, director of the Comédie-Française, has covered the statue of Voltaire under the pretext that the sight of this philosopher is out of place in an *ambulance*.
>
> All we have left to do is parade the relics of Saint Genevieve in the streets of Paris, with the provisional government at the head of the procession!
>
> If Paris wants to remain the great Republic of rationalism, it is time to instill seriously in it the rationalism of the Republic.[42]

Calling Thierry a "fonctionnaire" (civil servant), the editor of *Combat* implied that he had an obligation to serve the interests of the nation. A nation, the editor reminded readers, should respect the strict separation of church and state in keeping with the traditions of the

---

42 *Le Combat* of September 21, 1870.

rationalist Enlightenment that gave France its First Republic. Voltaire had come to represent secular Enlightenment virtues. According to *Le Combat*, veiling his statue amounted to an attack on those values.

Often held up as a republican hero for his views on civil rights, his insistence on the separation of church and state, and his anticlericalism, Voltaire had been denounced by conservative leaders for the same reasons. Thierry was named director of the Comédie-Française in 1859 and had done well at its helm, successfully identifying the growing bourgeois population of Paris as a lucrative demographic, lowering ticket prices and including plays by bourgeois authors such as François Ponsard and Émile Augier.[43] His relationship to the Second Empire was one of benign indifference. Thierry didn't rock the boat, and Napoléon III mostly left him to manage his establishment. However, the article in *Le Combat* was about to put his entire project in jeopardy: veiling Voltaire was tantamount to attacking the new Republic.

It is unclear whether Thierry actually had any ideological reason for covering Voltaire in the Comédie-Française, just as it was unclear why he preferred his actors in costumes rather than in military uniforms or street clothes. His diary seems to suggest that covering *Voltaire assis* was an innocent mistake. Since the Theater's transformation into an *ambulance*, the charitable nuns who now worked there would have been scandalized, said Thierry, by the statue of Voltaire. However, all good intentions aside, the "affaire Voltaire" was already making headlines and dividing the city. As Thierry wrote in his journal on September 25:

> Gustave Coquelin came to see me tonight at 9:30, carrying a letter written by L. Guillard, whom Monsieur H. Brisson, accompanied by two other magistrates, had aggressively demanded to remove, without delay, the veiled structure covering the statue of Voltaire.[44]

Reading through Thierry's shorthand, we can see that he was uncomfortable with his business becoming public and the internal affairs of the Theater coming under the scrutiny of officials like the deputy mayor of Paris, Henri Brisson. In Thierry's understanding, the Comédie-Française should not entangle itself in politics by allowing

---

43   On Thierry's tenure as administrator, see Le Jean, "La Comédie-Française et ses administrateurs (1849–1871)."

44   Thierry, *La Comédie-Française pendant les deux sièges*, p. 86.

the government to dictate how it dealt with its own artistic holdings, the statue included. Thierry argued that the statue of Voltaire was as much a part of France's history as the history of the Comédie-Française. The political aspects of the debate over Houdon's *Voltaire assis* exasperated him: "People refuse to notice that, even if the state of Voltaire is covered, next to it can be found a beautiful bust of Voltaire, another masterpiece by Houdon, that is not covered."[45] Clearly, he saw himself at the center of a larger debate, in which the facts of his veiling or not veiling mattered little. Instead, republicans and religious conservatives were staging a war with his Theater at its center.

The "affaire Voltaire" soon spiraled out of control. Louis Veuillot, the Catholic editor-in-chief of the newspaper *L'Univers*, took up his pen to admire Thierry's actions and to condemn his so-called partisan critics: "We must conclude that all these 'red' journalists, idolaters of Voltaire, have never read a word of the author's works, whom they would condemn as an aristocrat to be guillotined as quickly as possible."[46] The allusion to the guillotine cast the "red" republicans as inheritors of the Terror, the scourge of violence and beheadings that followed the Revolution of 1789. According to Veuillot, since the Comédie-Française had become an *ambulance*, the statue of Voltaire ("truthfully, very repugnant" in Veuillot's words) was an affront to the religion of the nuns who had been called in to assist in providing succor. They had to work "in a place where the devil is honored in his most immoral form." Veuillot casts Thierry's critics as worshippers of false idols, idols—he continues—that they do not even fully understand: he claims that, despite their adulation of the figure of Voltaire, they are not even familiar with his writings. By endorsing Thierry's decision to veil Voltaire, Veuillot inadvertently enlisted him in a war against the Republic and the revolutionary tradition it had inherited. Suddenly, Thierry and the Comédie-Française were thrust into the middle of a public debate about the signs of belonging to the new Republic. Veuillot almost succeeded in making Thierry look like an aristocrat, an enemy of the people he had been working to court.

Parisian *ambulances* also posed a problem for the anticlerical members of the new government. The stakes were unusually high, since these

45   Thierry, *La Comédie-Française pendant les deux sièges*, p. 89.
46   *L'Univers* of September 27, 1870. All citations in this paragraph are from this article.

theaters were not only important sites of cultural patrimony (and thus represented the nation) they also played made important contributions to the war effort as makeshift hospitals. This unstable mix of civic service, religious accommodation, and popular celebrity made theaters even more visible.

Before she became an international celebrity, Sarah Bernhardt was a nurse in the besieged Théâtre de l'Odéon. Bernhardt may not have been trained in medicine, but she knew that she could advocate for those who suffered from the circumstances of the Siege. When she heard that the Prussians were closing in on the city, she decided to stay rather than flee, "feeling useful."[47] She ended up founding one of the first *ambulances* in the city at the Odéon. From the windows of her theater she often observed an unfortunately common spectacle of the Siege: women waiting in line for rations at the municipal butcher shops. She describes the scene in her memoirs, published in 1907:

> I saw them from the windows of the theater. I saw them huddled together, blue from the cold, stomping their feet to keep them from freezing, for this winter was the cruelest that we suffered through in twenty years. Often, I was brought one of these silent heroines, who had fainted from exhaustion or been taken suddenly by congestion due to the cold.[48]

The actor is now the spectator, the besieged streets the stage. The performance of poverty prompted Bernhardt to advocate for her *ambulance* and the women who fell ill and those who tended to them.

In this role as actor-cum-civil servant, Bernhardt also tried to rebrand her institution, and herself, as useful. As rations were dwindling even in the early days of the Siege, Bernhardt called on the mayor of the sixth *arrondissement*, Anne-Charles Hérisson, for help.

> Indeed, the mayor, Monsieur Hérisson, had arrived accompanied by a high-placed civil servant to take a tour of my *ambulance*. This illustrious personage implored me to remove the pretty white Virgin Marys placed on the fireplaces and pedestals, and to take down the crucifix hanging in each room that housed the wounded. Upon my refusal, a little insolent and very final, to

47   Bernhardt, *Ma double vie* (Paris: Charpentier et Fasquelle, 1907), p. 209.
48   Bernhardt, *Ma double vie*, p. 219.

act according to the wishes of my visitors, the famous republican turned his back to me and gave the order that City Hall would refuse me everything.[49]

Bernhardt noted that the refusal of the *hôtel de ville* to grant her request for rations was solely based on the religious paraphernalia that her visitors may have found comforting, linking this aversion to religion to the mayor's republican values. Perhaps the mayor was right to worry about the rebellious act of displaying this iconography: Bernhardt had been a close friend to both Napoléon III and the Empress Eugénie, a relationship she was happy to highlight in her memoires. Nevertheless, Bernhardt used her popularity and remnant political influence to pressure the mayor into reversing his order, eventually succeeding. The Odéon kept both its crucifixes and its rations. The republican battle for the separation of church and state was already being waged in the most improbable place: the halls of Parisian theaters.

While Bernhardt made her independence from the government known, Thierry abstained from making any overt political statements both during the "affaire Voltaire" and in his diary. This reticence was the hallmark of his attitude towards politics, which his actions during the Siege make clear. On September 5, not twenty-four hours after the declaration of the Republic at the *hôtel de ville*, Thierry took down the official imperial insignia that was on display in the theater. Instead of destroying these imperial trappings, however, he merely put them in on-site storage, from which he recovered the republican tricolor banners and flags that had been fabricated for the Theater after the proclamation of the Second Republic in 1848. The basement of the Theater had everything he needed to quickly adapt to any regime change. In Thierry's cautious worldview, Napoléon III could still return, in which case he would simply dust off the imperial seal. In order to weather any political storm that came their way, the directors of the Comédie-Française had to be prepared for any and all revolutions. For Thierry, the present was an ever-changing mess of politics that existed outside of the hallowed stage of the Maison de Molière. Seeing Andromache in street clothes was for Thierry merely the first instance of the present's

49   Bernhardt, *Ma double vie*, pp. 227–228.

encroachment on the timeless tradition of French theater of which the Comédie-Française was the anointed custodian.

However, staying neutral became more and more difficult, as the scandal of the Voltaire statue made evident. At a time of republican fervor and patriotic scrutiny, the refusal of the Comédie-Française to participate in nation building was immensely suspicious. Despite his attempts to resist the atmosphere of revolution, Thierry eventually had to make concessions. As the "affaire Voltaire" seemed to lose its public appeal, another challenge presented itself. With the return of Victor Hugo to Paris, after eighteen years of exile, Thierry had to find a way to welcome the popular hero, the obstinate exile, the poet of the people, the adamant republican, without seeming to enter into politics.

Chapter 2

Hugomania

In late November 1870, Victor Hugo was surprised to find the Parisian police prefect Ernest Cresson at his doorstep. At the instigation of the Société des gens de lettres, the city of Paris had decided to stage a free and open-to-the-public reading of Hugo's book of poetry, *Les Châtiments* (*Castigations*), an invective the poet had written in exile targeting Napoléon III and the Second Empire. The only venue that could possibly accommodate the expected crowds was the Opéra de Paris, the crown jewel of the Second Empire entertainment industry.[1] And they did indeed expect a crowd. Official estimates, Cresson told Hugo, indicated that nearly eighty thousand people would descend on the venue to claim the woefully inadequate one thousand eight hundred seats.[2] The besieged capital held nearly as many inhabitants as it does now—two million—meaning that around 4 percent of the population wanted to hear Hugo's work according to Cresson's estimate. Even given Hugo's immense popularity in 1870, the moment he returned to France after eighteen years of exile, this would be an incredible turnout. Cresson hoped the poet could help decide how best to handle the crowds.

Cresson and Hugo settled on a course of action. The night before the reading, they authorized each *arrondissement* of Paris to hand out

---

1 Construction of the Palais Garnier Opéra began in 1862, but the venue was only officially inaugurated on January 5, 1876. Many events—including the Siege, the Commune, and the budget problems posed by the postwar period—delayed the process. The Opéra on the rue Le Peletier, where the Hugo reading took place, was destroyed in a fire in 1873.
2 They ended up distributing three thousand tickets, effectively leaving nearly a thousand spectators standing in the aisles and crowding the boxes.

a share of the total possible tickets on a first come, first served basis. Each *arrondissement* would receive a number of tickets proportional to its population, meaning that every Parisian had an equal chance of obtaining a ticket to what was quickly becoming the biggest performance of the Siege. What began as a measure to reduce chaos at the ticket windows ended up a democratic allotment of seats. Parisians both high and low could attend as representatives of their districts: from the aristocratic Faubourg Saint-Germain all the way to popular Belleville. All to hear Hugo's poetry recited on stage.

Why was this spectacle so popular? Why would the city open up the Opéra to stage the incendiary poetry of a former exile? Why was it so important that a representative assembly of the city attend? Every French revolution had its *assemblée constituante*, a representative body of legislators charged with composing a new constitution: both the transformation of the Estates General in 1789 and the creation of the constitution of 1848 had established such a tradition, both moments like that during the Siege when France was declared a republic. However, the fall of Napoléon III and the proclamation of the Third French Republic happened when France was at war with Prussia, Paris isolated, and a national representative body near-impossible. Instead, the recitation of *Les Châtiments* had to do the social and cultural work of declaring a new regime.

According to those who were invested in the financial well-being of such spaces, theaters allowed Parisians to separate themselves from reality and yet still feel like they were engaged in political acts. For as much as theaters intended for their spaces to act as political assemblies, these performances did not achieve the unity they proposed. Guy Debord's claim that "spectacle presents itself simultaneously as all of society, as part of society, and as instrument of *unification*,"[3] explains why the new leaders of the Republic wished to instrumentalize spectacle as a performance of revolutionary politics: to avoid another revolution. In opening the Opéra to the masses, the City managed to turn the subject matter of *Les Châtiments*—the castigation of Napoléon III— into a re-enactment of his fall from grace. By attending such an anti-imperial performance, Parisians could feel as if a revolution had already occurred.

3   Debord, *Society of the Spectacle* (Black and Red, 1983), p. 2.

Victor Hugo had been in exile since Napoléon III seized power in 1851. Famously dubbing the emperor "Napoléon le petit," Hugo remained outside of France despite an amnesty offered him in 1859. His writings from exile were mostly banned in France, including *Les Châtiments*. However, upon Napoléon III's capture in Sedan and the subsequent declaration of the third French Republic on September 4, 1870, Hugo re-entered Paris to near-universal acclaim, finding that his exile had only increased his fame. *Les Châtiments* was published legally for the first time on French presses almost immediately, in September of 1870, and quickly became the bestseller of the Siege. Parisian readers of *Les Châtiments* who had been critical of the Second Empire were given the opportunity to feel that they had been exiles in their own country, waiting for their hero Hugo to return. Hugo had become a powerful reference for anyone wishing to make sense of the national tragedy. The comforting myth Hugo represented was that the Siege was not Paris's fault, that blame fell squarely on the shoulders of the disgraced Emperor.

The idea of a public reading of *Les Châtiments* was born of political necessity. Many different political factions were vying for legitimacy, and besides the outright Bonapartists, monarchists, and *communards*, there were also those who welcomed the Republic but were not necessarily convinced that it would last. From the monarchists came the claim that France had been under illegitimate rule since the Revolution of 1789. From the left came the suspicion that undercover Bonapartists still lurked in powerful positions, plotting his return. Still others complained that there was nothing at all republican in France's new regime. Looking at the composition of the government itself, one found republicans like Henri Rochefort alongside people like the newly proclaimed president Louis-Jules Trochu, who had once published monarchist propaganda but had also held a high position in Napoléon III's Ministry of War. Scholars have long noted the odd make-up of the new Republic as a "bourgeois state [...] unburdened with social promises to be fulfilled,"[4] whose leaders felt "only a minimal attachment to its institutions or its principles."[5] However, for better or worse, France was officially a republic, and the government

---

4 Sanford Elwitt, *The Making of the Third Republic: Class and Politics in France, 1868–1884* (Louisiana State UP, 1975), p. x.
5 Philip Nord, *The Republican Moment: Struggles for Democracy in Nineteenth-Century France* (Harvard UP, 1995), p. 3.

had to convince the people of its legitimacy in the absence of popular insurrection.[6]

Hugo's presence made it feel as if France had turned a corner in the course of its history. It is almost impossible to overstate the excitement that his return caused. The journalist Odilon Delimal described it in evangelical terms: "May his arrival wake still sleeping consciences, urge on weakened resolves and souls laid low by this reign, shame of the nineteenth century, that began in assassination and theft, and ended in cowardice and treason."[7] These sentiments were echoed in many daily papers, among the Parisian literary elite, and by the Société des gens de lettres, the literary advocacy group whose remaining members offered Hugo the interim presidency of their organization. His arrival signaled the end of Napoléon III and more broadly the end of an era. For theaters, it was a chance to declare themselves by the people and for the people: their directors positioned them as places where, in the words of Delimal, consciences came to awaken.

What Victor Hugo managed to do was rally support around himself, and by extension, around the idea of regime change in France. If the public was sometimes unenthusiastic in their support of the Republic, they were more than happy to have their prodigal son return, the poet who had prophesized the end of "Napoléon le petit" and the end of the regime that has brought them war. But while he certainly encouraged it, Hugo had little control over the frenzy surrounding his return. His indifference to his own political legacy left open the interpretative space for Hugo to represent multiple political beliefs, to be co-opted into any institutional bid for legitimacy. Hugo's popularity brought many different parties out of the woodwork. Theaters seized the opportunity to align themselves with him, as an endorsement from Hugo provided immunity from politics at a time when the future of theaters was uncertain. He was beloved by everyone, most of all by the

---

6 Following a *communard* takeover of the *hôtel de ville* on October 31, 1870, the *gouvernement provisoire* offered a referendum to the people of Paris to invest the government with more authority. This referendum, which took place on November 3, resulted in a stunning victory for the current establishment: 557,996 "oui" against 61,638 "non." However, some critics, like Auguste Blanqui, protested that much of the Parisian population voted for stability because of the war, not because they approved of what he saw as a conservative government.

7 Delimal, "Les Châtiments," *Le Combat*, October 24, 1870.

influential bourgeoisie, indignant at Napoléon III since the war became disastrous. Meanwhile, a committee charged with taking inventory of the Louvre palace found that Empress Eugénie had a complete set of Hugo's works in her library—all dedicated to her by the author.[8] Hugo's reputation as a republican survived the discovery. It seemed that Hugo could survive anything.

Les Châtiments sold at least twenty thousand copies during the Siege.[9] Parisians took a certain pleasure in reading Hugo's poetry, especially since the very things he prophesized—the fall of Napoléon—had already happened. This allowed its readers to pretend they had always known Napoléon III would fall. The discourse around Hugo and the ways in which his poetry was implicitly cited made it seem like it was the poet himself who had deposed the despot. In an article in the newspaper *le Petit Moniteur* of November 16, for example, the journalist Victor Cochinat wrote:

> never would we have dared think that, during the very lifetime of he [Napoléon III] against whom was directed the scourge of this terrifying Nemesis, we would find, in the middle of Paris, in the middle of a theater, before a greedy public carried away by enthusiasm, a reading of this book of iron and gold, where are inscribed with an irony more bitter than that of Dante all the crimes of those whom the author has branded forever with his relentless pen.[10]

While it is true that both Dante and Hugo wrote invective against their respective homelands in exile, the symmetry ends there. Dante was exiled on pain of death, whereas Napoléon III offered amnesty to the brooding Hugo. In his praise, Cochinat also compares Hugo to Nemesis, the Greek goddess of revenge, since he punished the hubris not only of Napoléon III, but of Paris itself: Cochinat insists on his surprise at hearing Hugo in the middle of Paris, and in a theater no less, one of the most privileged spaces of the Second Empire. His enthusiasm borders on exaggeration, indicative of the atmosphere of praise and hope that Hugo's return inspired.

---

8 For more on Eugénie's personal library at the Tuileries, see Chapter 9.
9 This meant that one in one hundred Parisians—men, women, and children— had a copy of *Les Châtiments* by the end of the Siege.
10 Cochinat, "Les Châtiments," *Le Petit Moniteur*, November 16, 1870.

Cochinat shares the lyrical prose of other commentators of Hugo's return. The similar tone of these accounts is a form of flattery: they are writing pastiches of Hugo's style in *Les Châtiments* and about his poetic mission. Here is a passage from one of the most performed poems during the Siege, entitled "Stella," originally written in 1853 while in exile:

> O Nations! I am burning Poetry,
> I shone upon Moses and I shone upon Dante.
> Ocean, that lion, burns for me.
> I come. Rise up, courage, virtue, faith!
> Thinkers, wits! Climb the towers, sentinels!
> Eyes, open! Light up your gaze!
> Earth, shake your furrows; life, wake your rustle;
> You who sleep, stand up;—for what follows me,
> For what sends me first ahead,
> Is the angel Liberty, is the giant of Light!

Hugo's poem is written from the perspective of poetry incarnate, who promises to open eyes, awaken consciences, shed light on the injustices of the world. In their zeal for his return, these journalists interpreted the poetic "I" as Hugo himself. They turned Hugo into a prophet upon whom shone the same light that shone upon Dante. Who was the intended readership of this poem? Its introductory apostrophe, "O Nations," pluralized, implies a community defined not by geographic territory but by a shared desire to protect itself against tyranny. The "sentinels" the poet speaks of are the people of Paris, who were now happy to find themselves enlisted in the ranks of Hugo's war against their fallen Emperor.

Given the poetry's success in bookstores, theaters decided to stage readings in the early days of the Siege in a bid to influence the "general attitude" of the population, in the language of the police prefect. In keeping with his desire to remain relevant, Édouard Thierry was the first to propose a reading of *Les Châtiments*, whose benefits would have gone to charity had the reading taken place. On October 23, a month before Cresson approached Hugo about the spectacle at the Opéra, the director of the Comédie-Française visited the poet at his residence to ask permission to perform "Stella," the poem cited above, at the Theater. To Thierry's surprise, Hugo acquiesced, even offering to waive his right to collect royalties. However, there was a catch:

the Comédie-Française must perform all of *Les Châtiments*, not just "Stella," or Hugo would not give his permission. Thierry, suspecting that reading all of *Les Châtiments* would be too ostentatious a political act, demurred. A playwright and actor associated with the Theater, Ernest Legouvé, suggested that they could dedicate a whole day to the enterprise, having different actors and actresses read different poems. In his diary, Thierry seemed hesitant: "Victor Hugo offers everything or nothing. No "Stella" by itself. All of *Les Châtiments* and right away. To reopen the Comédie-Française with *Les Châtiments* would be a real stunt."[11]

Again, Thierry struggled between politics and what he considered the essentially eternal aspect of French cultural institutions. He had been concerned that Paris might have condemned the Theater as an "aristocratic institution"[12] during the "affaire Voltaire." Reading Hugo could have dispelled that fear but reading *all* of *Les Châtiments* veered too far in the opposite direction. Thierry feared it would represent a declaration of revolution. Many of the Theater's actors believed that he would buckle under the pressure of public acclaim for Hugo and accept the poet's demands. Perhaps the most famous male actor of the day, Edmond Got, wrote to the Société des gens de lettres to protest the potential reading, even going as far as promising to boycott the performance if it were to take place: "I admire *Les Châtiments* as much as anyone [...] but even if I was one of the rare members of the opposition in the past, please permit me today to stand apart from the too numerous blowhards of the future."[13] In this appeal for moderation, Got insisted even more than Thierry that artists should abstain from making decisions based on politics and more importantly should ignore the vagaries of public opinion. During the Second Empire, he had kept his distance from the regime; under a republic he wanted to do the same. Got wanted to be an eternal dissident without espousing revolution. The stakes for Got were not the same as for Thierry,

---

11   Thierry, *La Comédie-Française pendant les deux sièges* (Paris: Tresse et Stock, 1887), p. 120. The French ends with "ce serait un grand coup," which could be understood as a "stunt" or as a "shock." I choose to interpret the term "coup" pejoratively here, considering that Thierry did not wish to perform the entire book.
12   Thierry, *La Comédie-Française*, p. 109.
13   Letter related in: Alfred Carel, *Histoire anecdotique des contemporains* (Paris: A. Chevalier-Marescq, 1885), p. 168.

however. The latter had to keep in mind the future of the Comédie-Française. In his role as its director, he acted as an extension of the institution itself.

Others urged Thierry to reconsider his refusal to read the incendiary, populist *Les Châtiments* on the Theater's stage. The next day, Jules Simon, the Ministre de l'Instruction publique, pressured Thierry to agree to Hugo's terms. That same day, three representatives of the Société des gens de lettres showed up at the Theater—"on behalf of Victor Hugo"[14]—to ask Thierry to relent. Thierry dug in deeper. When the Theater opened on October 25, Ernest Legouvé took the stage to give a speech on the need for theater in times of national tragedy. Snubbing Hugo and his *Châtiments* roused the ire of some of the more hard-line republican higher-ups. Hugo had been Bonaparte's Nemesis, now he was playing the same role with Thierry.

Correctly identifying Thierry's delicate situation, Hugo's "all or nothing" offer was a test of the Comédie-Française, an institution he saw as intimately tied to whatever regime was currently in place. In the 1830s, Hugo had two of his plays performed in the Theater, *Le roi s'amuse* and *Angelo*, both of which were poorly received by politicians of the July Monarchy. The Theater, fearing reprisals, ceased all performances of both plays. Hugo brought its administrator to court for failing to honor their contract, but the courts decided in favor of the Theater. Hugo meant for the trial to determine much more than financial responsibility. In effect, his loss in court proved that the July Monarchy still practiced a form of *de facto* censorship despite its formal abolition.[15] Hugo staged his face-off with Thierry in 1870 as another attempt to expose the Theater's allegiances, just as the trials of 1830 uncovered the hidden networks of collaboration still operational between literary institutions and the government.

Once again, Thierry was in a difficult position. On the one hand, he had to protect his authority over the direction of his theater. Letting Hugo dictate performances would have been an abdication of the Theater's autonomy. On the other, he had to prove to both Hugo and all of Paris that the Comédie-Française was a theater for the people, not the current regime. And, once again, his commitment to keeping

14   Thierry, *La Comédie-Française*, p. 120.
15   See Odile Krackovitch, *Hugo censuré: la liberté du théâtre au XIXe siècle* (Calmann-Lévy, 1985).

the Comédie-Française out of politics prevailed. In the aftermath of the *Les Châtiments* stalemate, he ultimately convinced Parisians that the Theater was neither Bonapartist nor revolutionary, and yet nonetheless an important site of French literary heritage. To do this, Thierry staged his own stunt.

The Comédie-Française held the exclusive performance rights to many plays that were already French classics. Besides being the "Maison de Molière," the Comédie-Française was also the House of Hugo, having staged among others his play *Hernani* in 1830, a performance that led to one of the most ferocious aesthetic battles of nineteenth-century theater and established Hugo at the head of a new literary genre now known as Romantic drama. This meant that the Comédie-Française held the exclusive rights to the performance of Hugo's now-infamous play. When, on November 15, 1870, the director of the Théâtre de la Porte Saint-Martin asked Thierry for permission to stage *Hernani*, Thierry obstinately refused. "M. Thierry is a strange obstacle," wrote Hugo in his diary on hearing of the refusal.[16] However, the gauntlet had been thrown; Hugo had to concede given that he had no legal authority to help the Porte Saint-Martin obtain rights to his own performances. There was no denying that the Comédie-Française had a politically complicated past, but it had nonetheless been the theater on whose stage *Hernani* had changed the literary landscape of France. Thierry was implicitly arguing that the Comédie-Française was just as French as the stubborn Hugo. His stratagem won out and on November 24, Hugo allowed the Theater to read some—and just some—of his poetry during a literary matinée. As a final conciliatory gesture, Thierry offered Hugo a private box from which to watch the spectacle that would only feature three of his most popular poems. Hugo declined to attend.

By the time Thierry and Hugo arrived at this détente, the Comédie-Française had already lost the race to be the first theater to recite *Les Châtiments*. While Thierry was snubbing Hugo, other theater directors stepped in to woo the public with readings. The Théâtre de la Porte Saint-Martin performed the first public reading of the entirety of the book of poems on November 8, raising 7,000 francs for the founding of a cannon, which they christened "le Victor Hugo." This success

16   Victor Hugo, *Choses vues: Nouvelle série* (Paris: Calmann Lévy, 1900), p. 292. Entry of November 16, 1870.

inspired Hugo to stage yet another reading, again at the Saint-Martin, this time raking in 8,000 francs.[17] The Société des gens de lettres, eager to participate in Hugomania, spoke to a series of members of the government, including Jules Simon and the police prefect Ernest Cresson, to organize a free reading at the Opéra.

The government's enthusiasm for Hugo and *Les Châtiments* is difficult to explain using official documents. However, an examination of other receptions of Hugo's return, the publication history of his poetry, and Hugo's own interpretation of his success make it easy to see what Hugo represented in political terms. Hugo wrote in his diary: "The government cannot refuse me anything."[18] He noted that by late November his work was being performed all over Paris without his permission, leading him to proclaim magisterially in his published diary: "je suis une chose publique!" ("I am a public phenomenon!").[19] The play on words is telling: *une chose publique* (literally, "a public thing") being a possible translation of the Latin *res publica*—also rendered as "republic." Hugo, and most likely the government as well, saw the promotion and reading of his poetry as directly linked to the project of populist state building. Hugo even went so far as to claim that he himself had become public property, a mythical unifier invested with authority through his populist appeal. Around two hundred years before the Siege, King Louis XIV was said to have proclaimed "l'État, c'est moi!" ("I am the State!"). Hugo responded that he was the Republic.

The spectacle at the Opéra was important because it was intended to bring together a representative assembly of the city. Perhaps its organizers, especially the police prefect, were happy that the performance was less representative than they had initially thought. Paris was, as it is still, a very diverse and socioeconomically compartmentalized metropolis. The nineteenth-century urban renewal projects, undertaken in large part by the prefect of the Seine, Baron

---

17   These profits were unthinkable during the early days of the Siege, pre-Hugo. In early September, empty houses meant meager returns—two to five hundred francs if the Saint-Martin was lucky. On November 6, a particularly successful performance at the Comédie-Française only netted 3,023 francs. Theaters were most certainly aware of the profitability of reading Hugo.

18   Hugo, *Choses vues*, p. 294. Entry of November 24, 1870.

19   Hugo, *Choses vues*, p. 296. Entry of November 27, 1870.

Eugène Haussmann, had the effect of pushing many of the urban poor communities scattered about the center of the city to the peripheries, areas that inspired "bourgeois fears of ordinary people."[20] The northeastern corner of the city in particular welcomed these displaced families into a community composed of the lower working class, the working poor, and the flat-out poor, in impromptu and unhygienic housing situations. The buildings were not connected to the sewer and water systems that Haussmann had been improving in the center of town. The very attempts to create a unified, modern Paris had brought about these squalid periphery communities. The Opéra, seated at the center of new Paris, was as much a monument to modernity as it was a physical manifestation of the polarizing policies of the city. A resident of popular Belleville would not have felt at home in the long, clean boulevards around the Opéra. Which might explain why Belleville did not show up even when the Opéra opened its doors.

The stakes of the performance were high. Victor Cochinat's disbelief in seeing Hugo at the Opéra ("in the middle of Paris, in the middle of a theater") stemmed from the improbable location of the reading. The Opéra was not built for the periphery communities, discouraged by the difficulty of travel along the muddy streets of the outskirts and the prohibitive ticket prices. Reading Hugo, the man of the people, the defender of the downtrodden, the popular hero of Paris, at the Opéra was a veritable revolution in itself, according to some commentators. The organizers wanted to signal to Parisians that no neighborhood and no citizen was unwelcome in the process of nation building. Hugo, the *res publica*, was enlisted in the project of a revolutionary republic that would redefine urban space and literature as inclusive rather than exclusive, unified rather than segregated. Hugo's take-over of the Opéra implied a radical reorientation of the social geography of Paris, an acknowledgment that space is always political. Kristin Ross has argued that the revolutionary Commune had operated such a radical geographical shift on the city where previous labor-based distinctions broke down. The reading during the Siege gestures towards the "wrenching of everyday objects from their habitual context to be used

---

20   John Merriman, *The Margins of City Life: Explorations on the French Urban Frontier, 1815–1851* (Oxford UP, 1991), p. 3.

in radically different ways,"[21] without ever managing to achieve such a reinvention of the Opéra or the boulevards it represented. It is not even clear that the reading was intended to operate such a spatial revolution. The institutional conservatism of the Siege allowed optics to stand in for revolution. Even critics of the reading did not question the claim that something as simple as a populist invitation to the Opéra might prove something about the legitimacy of the new Republic.

The reading of *Les Châtiments* took place on Monday November 28, 1870. Reviews indicated a packed house, endless applause, and numerous spontaneous bursts of overlapping renditions of the "Marseillaise," a rowdy performance where the audience was as much a part of the show as was Hugo's poetry. Many newspapers took the opportunity to reflect on the nature of spectacle during revolutionary moments. The *Electeur libre*, normally so hostile to anything it deemed frivolous, wrote what amounted to a defense of theater in times of tumult, inaugurating Parisian theaters into a narrative of populist revolutionary ideology: "As we see, the *montagnards* of 1870 can come without fear to applaud the verse of Corneille, of Molière, and of Hugo. Their ancestors will not begrudge them this."[22] Such appeals do not argue that the theater can be revolutionary, but that going might also not be a betrayal of political beliefs.

Even critics of the performance bought into the myth of Siege-time theater as populist assembly. The cynicism of administrators like Thierry and the opportunism of the new provisional government in seizing upon Hugo as a national hero did not go unnoticed. Reviews were mixed, but all accounts of the spectacle hinged on the public that attended, meaning that these reviews linked the legitimacy of the spectacle to who showed up. The democratic allotment of seats should have meant a broad public, from wealthy *boulevardiers* to

21   Ross, *The Emergence of Social Space: Rimbaud and the Paris Commune* (University of Minnesota Press, 1988), p. 36.
22   *L'Electeur libre*, November 17, 1870. The *montagnards* of 1793 were members of the staunch republican party that included Danton, Marat, and Robespierre—names synonymous with the Comité de salut public and the Terror but also with sensitivities to the public opinion of Paris. They opposed the *girondins*, who advocated for a unified front against threats external to revolutionary France. The implication in 1870 is that one could be worried about France's internal unity and still be seen at the Opéra—as long as one was applauding authors such as Corneille, Molière, and Hugo.

le peuple, the working-class and proletarian citizens on the margins of the city. "*Le peuple* are the true public," suggested *Le Rappel* on November 30, 1870, "and at the Opéra, it was the people." On the same day, *Le Constitutionnel* called the performance "splendid." *Le Petit Journal* insisted on "a magnificent crown" that had been thrown on stage, seeing in such an act "a token destined to perpetuate the memory of the day." Théodore de Banville, writing a long article in *Le National* also on November 30, questioned the success of the event despite these signs of populist patriotism: "Among the few thousand spectators in the room, only one old man with a long white beard was wearing overalls." Banville points out that the reading, which was intended to be a sort of representative assembly, did not actually do the political work it had intended, with only one obviously "proletariat" attendee, identified by his overalls.

The organizers, Banville argues in this review, misunderstood *le peuple* of Paris in a structural way. But he criticizes the spectacle only as an unsuccessful revolutionary performance, never going so far as to critique the idea of politics as performance. Even though the city had offered tickets on a first come, first served basis, the entire concept of waiting in line to receive a ticket went against the spirit of open-doors assembly, claims Banville:

> The people, eternally oppressed and beaten down by thousands of so-called rules that are in fact perfectly useless, are wary of anything that looks like regulations, like a cat fears cold water! For them, a free performance would still mean, perhaps always mean, one where the doors are open wide and they are told, "Go wherever you like!" but the people will never feel at home in the midst of so many ushers and bayonets as there were yesterday at the Opéra.

Banville's review only makes sense within the context of this performance during a moment of revolution, ignoring the fact that Paris was not traversing a revolutionary moment. At best, we might call his critique optimistic that the performance could have inspired Parisians towards political engagement. While the provisional government did not explicitly say why this performance needed to take place, it was nonetheless Jules Simon who commandeered the Opéra for this spectacle. Banville even seems to approve of the original intent of using Hugo for revolutionary performance, claiming that it was not the actual crowd of "a half-literate public," but "the people" who had "this naïve faith whose virtue makes them capable of embracing the highest ideas and renders them equal to the poet himself." According to Banville, the performance had not failed, they had just invited the wrong people. Hugo, who by all accounts did not attend the reading, tersely gave his own review in his notebooks: "Huge crowd."[23] Interestingly, only one newspaper questioned the intentions of the organizers, and only in passing. "Certainly, the poetry of *Les Châtiments* is a considerable work that has sealed the reputation of the great poet," concedes *Le Figaro* on November 29, 1870, "but is this really the moment for reciprocal hatred, and do we not owe the Prussians and the future all of our attention and all of our thoughts?" After all, the war was still raging outside of the city walls.

This performance ultimately helped theaters more than it unified the Parisian population. Theater directors and critics enlisted Hugo, Corneille, and Molière in a battle that was ultimately less concerned with the future of the nation and more with the future of theaters as economic and cultural institutions. In fact, Hugo's poetry was, in 1870, essentially backward looking. *Les Châtiments* was more anti-Bonaparte than it was pro anything, but this was precisely what made it susceptible to inclusion in a fuzzy republicanism. These readings criticized Napoléon III but offered little in terms of political alternatives. In *Les Châtiments*, one thing was certain—Bonaparte and his band would be punished—but beyond that, the future was indistinct. Even Hugo's conception of Bonaparte's ultimate fall constantly referred to Bonaparte's past rather than France's future, for example in his poem *L'Expiation*:

> [...] The emperor,
> Discouraged, cried out in horror into the shadows,
> Lowering his eyes, raising his terrified hands.
> Marble Victories sculpted still at the door,
> White ghosts standing beyond the dark sepulcher,
> Making signals with their fingers and leaning on the walls,

---

23   Hugo, *Choses vues*, p. 296. Entry of November 28, 1870. Interestingly, he uses the same term to describe the crowds of *communards* outside of the *hôtel de ville* when it was seized on October 31. Hugo writes, however, that he "refuses to associate with" those who led the uprising (p. 288).

Listened to the titan crying in the darkness.
And he who screamed: "Demon of deathly visions,
You who follow me everywhere, who I never see,
Who are you?" "I am your crime," said the voice.
The tomb then filled with a strange light
Similar to the clarity of God when he takes vengeance,
The same as the words that Balthazar saw shine,
Two words written in the shadows lighting up Caesar,
Bonaparte, trembling like a motherless child,
Raised his head and read: EIGHTEEN BRUMAIRE!

In this poem, Napoléon III is haunted by his own past, assaulted with visions of his own trespasses, hounded by a voice that announces itself as the manifestation of his crime, the coup d'état of 1851 when he seized power. Hugo wrote this poem eighteen years before Napoléon III was captured in Sedan, so it was in a prophetic mode that he imagined the Emperor's fall. And yet, the words that condemn Napoléon III come from the distant past: *dix-huit brumaire* being the day on the revolutionary calendar that his uncle, Napoléon I, carried out his coup d'état in 1799.[24] Hugo shows us a Bonaparte haunted by the success of his uncle, constantly reminded of his own insignificance. Hugo telescopes time, jumping over an entire century of revolutions to focus on two moments—one noble (1799) and one disgraceful (1852) in his telling. He encourages his readers (and spectators) to lament the distance that separates the two Bonapartes. In doing so, he props up Napoléon I as a French hero, whose exploits deserve a proper afterlife. If others look to 1848, 1830, or 1793, Hugo suggested that 1799 also continued to haunt French politics.

In indirectly praising Napoléon I, Hugo articulated yet another conception of French history and French republicanism. He gave a conscience to French history, a sort of divine fatalism that rewards and punishes. Despite its brimstone visions, *Les Châtiments* reveals itself ultimately as an optimistic account of France's past and future: errors will be repeated, but sins will be forgiven. He never blamed the French people for the actions of their despot. This divine forgiveness

---

24 This also echoes Marx's condemnation of Napoléon III's coup as it is presented in his *The Eighteenth Brumaire of Louis Bonaparte* (New York: International Publishing Co., 1898).

(or "expiation") to which Hugo pointed in his poetry was only possible once Bonaparte had fallen, his crimes revealed and his reign denounced by the public. Through this interpretation, the public reading at the Opéra amounted to a collective atonement that purged France of its sins. The republicans of 1870, in promoting Hugo's poetry on such a representative, egalitarian stage, cast themselves as the descendants of the ur-revolutionaries of 1789, the *montagnards* of 1793, and of Napoléon I on the eighteenth of Brumaire. But for the larger Parisian population, staging Hugo at the Opéra amounted to a public denunciation of their former ruler.

Hugo's success would not have been possible without the transformations the Siege had brought to Parisian theaters. They needed him as much as he needed them. In their bid to legitimize spectacle during a tragic war, theater directors, actors, and journalists redefined the public role of theaters to contribute directly to national causes. In the halls of the Odéon, the Comédie-Française, and neighboring theaters, the wounded found solace in the care of nuns and in the company of actors. Proceeds from special performances turned iron into cannons, helped feed the needy, and kept an entire industry of theater staff from going hungry. Many spectators went to the theater for distraction, but what they found there was very different: they were roused by countless renditions of the "Marseillaise," reminded of the treasures of French culture, urged, even, to consider the Franco-Prussian War as a fight between neighbors with a shared culture and history. Most importantly, Parisians theaters taught spectators that their resistance against the enemy mattered, not just for their own lives, but for the future of France. These public assemblies consecrated the Siege as another foundational moment in French history, performing the revolution that, in the minds of many Parisians, should have occurred on September 4.

Without inciting a revolution, the reading of Hugo's poetry at the Paris Opéra represents one moment in a long history of popular theater as political event. The intention behind the democratic allotment of seats, as suggested by the police prefect and supported by Jules Simon, indicates a desire for this spectacle to legitimize a political regime through populist overtures, or perhaps more optimistically, to transform the theater into what Susan Maslan has called an "alternative space for developing the practices of participation, scrutiny, interpretation, and judgment."[25] This alternative space, Maslan argues, solidified and then dissolved during the Revolution of 1789. Others contend that the political possibilities of popular theater did not disappear, but simply changed focus. In her study of popular theater and political activism from 1870 to 1940, Jessica Wardhaugh notes that "as early as the mid-1870s, politicians began to redefine and reorganize the role of the arts" within the Third Republic's Ministère de l'instruction publique, des beaux-arts, et des cultes as a part of this government's "desire to use culture—especially festivals and theatre—to create active citizens."[26] What these two understandings of populist theater have in common is their focus on education and the types of political skills that theater can be used to teach. They both are interested in the citizen-spectator's engagement in a political regime seeking stability.

The theater of the Siege only participated partly in revolutionary culture, and even then with some serious differences to the type of theater Maslan and Wardhaugh describe. Maslan states that the playwrights of the Revolution "expressed the belief that artistic creation was deeply bound up with the history-making events in which they found themselves and in which they participated" to which Hugo in 1870 would have strongly agreed.[27] But Hugo as a "res publica" was not the only political actor within Paris during the Siege, and the populist (at least in theory) reading of *Les Châtiments* was not the only spectacle that engaged with revolutionary traditions. Like the Comédie-Française, the majority of cultural institutions promoted spectacle that simply performed revolutionary culture, and that were less invested in national unity than in the longevity of theater as an economic and institutional reality within Paris, a city that by 1870 had been through a dizzying century of revolutions and counter-revolutions. Thierry may have finally negotiated a performance of *Les Châtiments*, but the imperial insignia of the Comédie-Française still sat in storage just in case the Emperor returned.

25 Maslan, *Revolutionary Acts: Theater, Democracy, and the French Revolution* (Johns Hopkins UP, 2005), p. 3.
26 Wardhaugh, *Popular Theatre and Political Utopia in France, 1870–1940* (Palgrave, 2017), p. 30.
27 Maslan, *Revolutionary Acts*, p. 11.

Part II

Off Presses

Chapter 3

The *Feuilleton* at War

During the Siege, Paris suffered from a debilitating shortage of paper. This paper crisis provoked debates about the freedom of the press and the duty of publishers to disseminate information to citizens, and thus became a crisis that threatened the very foundation of the Republic. At the beginning of blockade, *Le Moniteur de la papeterie française* presented the crisis in no uncertain terms: "Paris, which possesses bread in abundance, this commodity of primary importance to the body, is already starting to run short on paper, this commodity of primary importance to the mind."[1] The war had disrupted regional logistical networks, robbed Paris of able-bodied workers, and broke down materials markets, all leading Parisian printers to rely on their own paper stockpiles throughout the entire period of military investment. After London, Paris was the largest consumer of paper products in Europe, but only had enough paper *intramuros* to supply short-term demand. *Le Moniteur* wondered: "Is besieged Paris able to meet demand in the long term given its stockpiles?"[2]

And yet, the Siege saw a dramatic rise in the number of publications. Demand for paper increased during the blockade, due to both the advent of new publications and the obsessive reading habits of besieged Parisians. The city itself seemed covered in paper. Political broadsides, lithography offprints, and single-sheet images bearing caricatures and crude jokes inundated streets, "plastered on kiosks and on the newsstands"[3] and

1   *Le Moniteur de la papeterie française*, November 1, 1870.
2   *Le Moniteur de la papeterie française*, November 1, 1870.
3   Jean Berleux, *La Caricature politique en France pendant la guerre, le siège de Paris, et la Commune* (Paris: Labitte, 1890), p. xii.

"over the *képis* that everyone wears, suspended on a string between trees."[4] Such images, however, only constituted one part of the rain of paper that fell upon Paris, and their diffusion usually understood as a manifestation of the *blague parisienne*,[5] a tendency to reduce every serious event into a punchline which, in its caricatural manifestation, one nineteenth-century historian called the "moral depravity of the street during this troubled time."[6] In contrast, newspapers benefitted from a serious and patriotic reputation, propped up as pillars of democratic debate, but also deemed sources of falsehoods and blatant exaggerations. Their contradictory reputations certainly did not impact their popularity, however. They, too, multiplied in the streets and in homes. An anonymous diarist remarked that "never have newspapers been as read as in this moment," noting that the ubiquitous hawkers made 2 francs 5 centimes per hundred copies sold[7]—a respectable haul at a time when most industries were on hiatus. By one estimate, seventy-six new daily periodicals were created,[8] all in need of paper. However, the archival records of the *dépôt légal* attest to at least one hundred and thirty new periodicals.[9] This estimate includes projects that only printed one edition and others that continued well into the Third Republic. The growth of the periodicals market was unprecedented. The official clerk for the *dépôt légal* ran out of space in the register, resorting to writing in the margins. The paper industry could not satisfy demand for the very material upon which new publications were catalogued.

Le Moniteur de la papeterie française warned that "the abundance of newspapers, the enormous circulation of many among them, increases

---

4   Edmond de Goncourt, *Journal des Goncourt: mémoires de la vie littéraire*, Vol. 4 (Paris: Charpentier, 1892), pp. 45–46.

5   There were of course serious images that were circulated within besieged Paris, including lithographic and photographic copies of Puvis de Chavannes's *Le Pigeon* and *Le Ballon*, which sold around fifty thousand copies within a few days, according to Bertrand Tillier in *La Commune de Paris. Révolution sans images?* (Champ Vallon, 2004, p. 238). Tillier holds up such allegorical images as "icônes" of the Siege. The circulation of images drew on different paper stockpiles, which, as far as I can tell, never sank to the point of sounding alarm.

6   Berleux, *La Caricature politique*, p. xii.

7   BHVP 1073, October 24, 1870, p. 36.

8   Firmin Maillard, *Histoire des journaux publiés pendant le siège et sous la Commune* (Paris: Dentu, 1871).

9   AN F18(IV)/158–161.

the consumption of paper every day."[10] Given the scarcity of and yet pressing need for news, readership of both new and old periodicals tripled. Before the Siege, readers often only consulted one or two publications and received these mostly through subscription. However, given the frenetic pace of both political and military events, "[t]he passerby that used to buy one newspaper on the way home in the evening now takes off with an assortment of three of four."[11] Edmond de Goncourt noted the nightly "assault of newsstands and the triple line of newspaper readers around every lamppost,"[12] feeding their despair with the "fibs, lies, and untruths of journalism."[13] Auguste Nefftzer, the editor of the influential daily *Le Temps*, saw newspapers as complicit in this paper frenzy: "All newspapers lie a little," he confessed, "even my own, in order to raise morale."[14] It didn't hurt sales either.

Newspapers depended so essentially on paper, their institutional identities so wrapped up in their specific material reality, that the conditions of the Siege altered not only their format, but also their scope, content, and ideology. Fewer pages meant that space was at a premium. Every story, every *chronique*, every *feuilleton* had to state clearly its relevance to the present moment to earn precious page space. The demand for news translated into the disappearance of certain cultural *feuilletons*, including serialized novels, that editors and readers deemed escapist and frivolous, and the emergence of new *feuilletons*, usually historical fiction or historical essays, that better articulated the role of literature in moments of national struggle. The shortages of the Siege, as well as Parisians' heightened awareness of the extraordinary moment they were experiencing, made newspapers more homogeneous in the types of texts they published. The myriad texts contained within the paper—editorial, *feuilleton*, and *fait divers*—all became muddled, sharing content and mixing media. Dominique Kalifa has argued that the *fait divers* did not disappear during the Franco-Prussian War, but it "adapted," marking the beginning of the "fait-diversification" of the news in the last third of the nineteenth century. This process "reduces

---

10   *Le Moniteur de la papeterie française*, October 1, 1870.
11   These estimates on consumption and demand are reported in *Le Moniteur de la papeterie*, November 1, 1870.
12   Goncourt, *Journal des Goncourt*, p. 19.
13   Goncourt, *Journal des Goncourt*, p. 153.
14   BHVP Ms 1113, reported by Barthélemy Hauréau, August 27, 1870.

all information to the realm of the *fait divers*,"[15] a short and generically ambiguous newspaper category that mixed news, anecdote, and tall tales that found extraordinariness in the ordinary events of daily life: an outlet for the cultural imaginary of a society. However much the poetics of newspapers as a genre may have motivated "fait-diversification," the material conditions of the Siege collapsed newspapers, distilling their contents, their genres, and their politics. What Marie-Ève Thérenty has called the "literature"[16] of nineteenth-century newspapers coalesced into one collective chronicle of the Siege.

The newspaper became a chronicle in that it was written *sur le vif*, in the heat of the moment, without an obligation to follow-up or to conclude. Unlike novels, newspaper literatures—the *fait divers* and the *feuilleton* this chapter focuses on—do not create a generic expectation of conclusion. More like a chronicle, the *feuilleton* in particular always points towards the next page, promising readers that they will find more without ever promising a narrative with a beginning, middle, and end. The never-ending parade of urgent news, repetitive updates, and never-substantiated rumors reflected and exacerbated the fatalist epistemological limits of the besieged.

The nineteenth-century newspaper had always been a hybrid object, both literary text, political commentary, producer and curator of culture, and historical artifact of the present. These literatures presented a self-referential system of different types of texts in whose codependence alone a coherent narrative might be found. This development began with the *feuilleton*, or the space of nineteenth-century newspapers dedicated to literary texts, cultural criticism, serialized novels, and non-political gossip. The *feuilleton* helped "to create a new type of newspaper based more on transmitting information and providing entertainment than on shaping or discussing political opinions."[17] Scholars credit the editor Émile de

---

15   Kalifa, "Faits divers en guerre (1870–1914)," *Romantisme*, vol. 97 (1997), p. 90.

16   Thérenty, *La Littérature au quotidien. Poétiques journalistiques au XIXe siècle* (Seuil, 2007), p. 12.

17   Maria Adamowicz-Hariasz, "From Opinion to Information: The *Roman-Feuilleton* and the Transformation of the Nineteenth-Century French Press," in *Making the News: Modernity and the Mass Press in Nineteenth-Century France*, edited by Dean de la Motte and Jeannene M. Przyblyski (UMASS Press, 1999), p. 160.

Girardin with revolutionizing the relationship between literature and the press in the late 1830s by encouraging the *feuilleton* and by monetizing newspaper space through advertisements: the media model that made newspapers an "ideological but also socioeconomic universe."[18] The *feuilleton* introduced a new poetics to the textual landscape of newspapers, offered a venue for new modes of reading and writing, and made literature a contemporary, ongoing activity like the reporting of the news. Novels now appeared in installments, right next to advertisements and political diatribes, transforming the newspaper into a patchwork of different literatures.

The *feuilleton* also made newspapers profitable as a mass-market industry. It comes as no surprise then that the *feuilleton*, as cultural space and economic good, underwent changes as the unusual economic and social conditions of the Siege made fiction seem possible and tightened budgets. What Kalifa noted as the "fait-diversification" of the newspaper during the Franco-Prussian War, the besieged experienced as a monolithic "feuilletonality." Each newspaper *rubrique* (section)—news, chronicles, opinion pieces, etc.—seemed to end in a cliffhanger for the dual reason that the Siege was an ongoing—some might have said interminable—event, and that cliffhangers kept the reading public coming back. Like the Siege itself, you cannot flip to the last page of a *feuilleton* to learn the ending.

Parisians witnessed an unprecedented expansion of the types of newspapers in circulation alongside an extreme reduction in the types of literature published within them. Marc Martin points out how "uncommon" it was for a war to be the impetus for a complete "demolition" of governmental regulation,[19] but this was no common wartime scenario: not only was France waging war against its neighbor, the end of the Second Empire meant that "a fervently patriotic and fervently revolutionary press"[20] smothered the capital in news. The entry of new, politically charged publications electrified the political

18   Alain Vaillant and Marie-Ève Thérenty, *L'An 1 de l'ère médiatique: étude littéraire et historique du journal* La Presse*, d'Emile de Girardin* (Nouveau Monde Éditions, 2001), p. 7.
19   Martin, *Médias et journalistes de la république* (Odile Jacob, 1997), p. 49–50.
20   Pierre Guiral, "La Presse de 1848 à 1871," in *Histoire générale de la presse française*, Vol. 2, edited by Claude Bellanger, Jacques Godechot, Pierre Guiral, and Fernand Terrou (Presses universitaires de France, 1969), p. 366.

discourse of even those dailies that most identified as apolitical, but as Pierre Guiral points out, most new arrivals in the Parisian press "did not separate the country to defend, the Republic to construct, and the socialism to expand,"[21] leading to a collapsing of content and a confusion of mission: a pile of rhetoric which entranced readers but threatened to exhaust material resources. Once paper had become a limited resource, Parisians debated what would be the best use of this medium. The answer was unequivocal: Parisians longed for texts that obsessed, like them, over the novelty of the city under siege. The paper crisis brought on by the conditions of the blockade had the effect not of introducing diversity into newspapers, but of intensifying their similarity in terms of format, pricing, and content.

Paper Shortage: The Nation in Crisis

> The regular production of paper is one of the necessary elements of the intellectual life of a civilized people.
>
> *Le Moniteur de la papeterie française*, October 1, 1870

Behind the veneer of patriotism and national duty plastered on the front pages of Siege newspapers, the political beliefs of editors were often more an expression of economic realities than of revolutionary crusades. Print content revealed more pressing concerns about how to remain profitable during the tumultuous months of blockade. Squeezed by rising costs and fixed resources, publishers resorted to increasingly drastic means to hold onto their readership, usually through entering into debates around the future of the French nation and the orientation of all sections of the newspaper towards such debates. The more dire a newspaper's financial situation became, the more willingly its editors resorted to inflammatory rhetoric, outrageous claims, and complete falsehoods.

The two major economic upheavals of the Siege were closely related. One of the first actions of France's new government was to abolish the censorship laws and eliminate the one-time tax (*caution*) on new periodicals. For the first time in eighteen years, anyone could

---

21   Guiral, *Histoire générale de la presse française*, p. 367.

publish a newspaper devoted to anything they wanted—even politics. This complete deregulation opened the floodgates to all sorts of new publications, inundating the market with competition. On the other hand, the Prussian troops began cutting off supply lines to Paris, leading to rising costs for manufacturers who then passed those costs onto publishers. With a reduced market share per publication and rising costs all round, the ground beneath Paris's massive newspaper industry began to erode. While the two economic forces of deregulation and rising costs were both products of the war, they established a new reality for publishers that lived on beyond the period, renewed again in 1881, when France reaffirmed its commitment to complete freedom of the press.

The major dailies that had been in publication for years—*Le Petit Moniteur, Le Siècle, La Presse, Le Constitutionnel,* etc.—had little to fear at the start of the blockade. These institutions benefitted from a large enough distribution network and relied on such a large amount of paper for their daily business that they naturally had their own stockpiles lasting them, in some cases, until the end of the Siege. For precarious or new periodicals, such as *Le Combat, La Patrie en danger, Le Moniteur des arts,* or *Le Conseiller des dames,* things were different. The price of large-format paper swelled to such a level that these smaller-scale papers had four options: they could raise prices; they could opt to publish one sheet rather than the industry standard of two; they could reduce their paper size to that of the *petite presse,* which by 1870 had already established itself as an alternative[22] to the *grande presse;* or, as a last resort, struggling publications could scrape the low-end paper suppliers for a crude material made from the coarsest pulp called *papier bulle.* Editors-in-chief used this as a last resort and only temporarily, always returning to more respectable paper after a few days. The quality of paper indicated the type of the text printed on it. *Le Moniteur de la papeterie* reported, most likely referring to Louis Veuillot's conservative Catholic newspaper *L'Univers,* that some editors "have resigned themselves to color paper, and we have seen the curious

---

22   Jean-Didier Wagneur states that these "petits journaux" had a smaller, folio format that nineteenth-century readers would have recognized as a separate category of press "without ambiguity" ("Les Chiffonniers de la petite presse. Hottes et crochets médiatiques." *Revue d'histoire littéraire de la France,* vol. 118, no. 3, 2018, p. 551).

sight of conservative writers [*écrivains-ultra*] printing their incendiary prose on water-green or rose-tea paper, as if it were the most banal writing for young ladies."[23]

By and large, editors preferred to reduce their format rather than increasing their prices or printing on colored paper. Ernest Picard, the political director of *L'Électeur libre*, felt that he needed to explain his newspaper's decision to reduce its format, letting his readers into the intricacies of industry struggles:

> Despite all our efforts, we could not procure the ordinarily formatted paper of the ELECTEUR LIBRE in a sufficient quantity. We must therefore resign ourselves to following the example of many of our fellow papers, and temporarily reduce our format. But the administration of the ELECTEUR LIBRE is taking measures to end this state of affairs as soon as possible: soon our paper will assume its normal dimensions.[24]

Format became a point of pride for papers, editors feeling the need to insist to readers that they were working to solve the problem—a problem that, Picard nonetheless insists here, is shared by many. An article the following day informs readers that the Compagnie de l'Est, one of the major railway companies, was warning that "the shipments of paper cannot pass through Paris except via the Marais factory, situated near Coulommiers, and via the paper mills in certain areas of the Vosges."[25] The following day, an article indicated that the Compagnie de l'Est has lost access to Paris following targeted Prussian sabotage with explosives.

Why did papers reduce format rather than raise prices? One reason is that the divisions of currency restricted the practical pricing structures for newspapers in the second half of the nineteenth century. Editors were at the mercy of the different denominations of their readers' pocket change. In 1870, the small-format editions of the *petite presse* cost 1 *sou* (5 centimes, or 1/20 of a franc). Large-format newspapers sold at 10 or 15 centimes (2 or 3 *sous*). The next highest practical price per issue was 20 centimes, which would have been prohibitively expensive. To give some

---

23   *Le Moniteur de la papeterie française*, November 1, 1870.
24   Picard, *L'Électeur libre*, September 15, 1870.
25   *L'Électeur libre*, September 16, 1870.

perspective, national guardsmen were paid 1 franc 25 centimes per day,[26] a dinner and show at a *café-concert* cost 7 francs, and a head of cabbage sold for 70 centimes during the Siege.[27] This rigidity in pricing practices meant that it was easier to reduce format than to increase prices.

Most text-based papers oriented their texts towards the population of readers in Paris. The illustrated press looked outward. Michèle Martin has shown how the illustrated news in London depicted the Franco-Prussian War in ways that "shap[ed] British social imaginary."[28] Parisians involved with Parisian illustrated presses pounced on this, sending images via balloon and often reduced in size via microscopic photography in order to be included in foreign periodicals, means that were developed "for political and military purposes."[29] While non-illustrated news was also sent via balloon to influence foreign perceptions of the Siege or to encourage diplomatic or foreign intervention, these outward-looking publication strategies did indeed carry more political and military motivations than did the press under examination in this book, which acted according to economic concerns and internal politics. One such non-illustrated paper, *Le Journal-Poste*, was published in the form of a post card, with patriotic news on the front, announcing events like *actes officiels* that were very flattering to the Government of National Defense. Within Paris, such announcements carried a heavy gloss depending on the politics of the paper that printed them. The economic constraints exacerbated such internal divisions. Carving out a space for a new publication in the newly open market often required smearing competitors. Fights between editors were ferocious, and often took place on the front pages of the newspapers they headed.

Other than producing very real economic constraints, the paper shortage brought out hidden ideological differences among editors as a result of competition. Publishers worked on tight profit margins and

26   As most industries were shut down by the investment, the National Guard's salary of 1.25 francs per day is the best estimation of income for a large portion of Paris's lower classes during the Siege.

27   These prices are provided by an anonymous diarist in BHVP 1073.

28   Martin, "Conflictual Imaginaries: Victorian Illustrated Periodicals and the Franco-Prussian War (1870–71)." *Victorian Periodicals Review*, vol. 36, no. 1, 2003, p. 42.

29   Michèle Martin and Christopher Bodnar. "The Illustrated Press under Siege: Technological Imagination in the Paris Siege, 1870–1871." *Urban History*, vol. 36, no. 1, 2009, p. 74.

so many new dailies had increased competition to such an extent that even a slight price increase or slightly reduced readership could have bankrupted newcomers. When the Government of National Defense abolished political restrictions on newspapers, Auguste Blanqui took full advantage, but his difficulties in getting his newspaper off the ground expose the politized economics of publishing. Blanqui had appeared and reappeared often during the revolutionary nineteenth century: a *carbonaro*[30] at the fiery age of nineteen, he participated in countless movements against successive French governments, including the revolutions of 1830 and 1848, and often found himself in prison for his approach to political upheaval. Openly hostile to Napoléon III, he was nonetheless pardoned by the emperor in 1869, only to then attempt two insurrections in 1870. In September 1870, he founded *La Patrie en danger*, a leftist newspaper that announced its mission of dedicated resistance to the enemy both within and without:

> The undersigned, setting aside any particular opinions, offer the provisional government their most energetic and absolute support, without any reserve or conditions, only that the government maintain the Republic, and will be buried alongside us under the ruins of Paris rather than negotiate the dishonor and dismemberment of France.[31]

Of course, "the enemy" is a slippery identification. As long as Blanqui believed that the government was still republican, he would support it, but he seems to imply that the government itself could become the enemy. After declaring that the editors' support was unconditional, he then gave two conditions, one of which was that Paris should be destroyed rather than sign an armistice. The government quickly violated Blanqui's conditions. On September 21, he wrote that the "gouvernement de la capitulation nationale" ("the government of national surrender")[32] paid its Bonapartist collaborators handsomely

---

30 Named after the secret revolutionary cells of coal workers in Italy, the "Carbonari" movement quickly spread to Restoration France in opposition to King Louis XVIII. The movement lost focus after the Revolution of 1830, but their name has always been associated with liberal revolution in France.

31 *La Patrie en danger*, September 7, 1870.

32 A play on the government's official title, "le gouvernement de la défense nationale."

while the people starved. As a result, his newspaper garnered enemies on the right and even many on the moderate left.

Le National was also a relative newcomer, since its first issue was only published in 1869. The Second Empire, however, had close ties with its director Ildefonse Rousset, who defined the newspaper's mission in anti-revolutionary terms:

> Dedicated to democratic ideals, we wish to wage honest and loyal war against revolutionary tendencies, from whatever area they arise. We respect all religious beliefs, we believe that the priest should not cross the threshold of the temple, and we energetically reject any clerical involvement in political matters.[33]

Read at the end of the Second Empire, the message is clear: *Le National* was moderate, but espoused republicanism insofar as its editors advocated for a separation of church and state, a revolutionary commonplace since 1789. Read during the Siege, Blanqui interpreted this selective adoption of revolutionary values as a clear indicator of a conservative allegiance to Napoléon III.

When *Le National* derided *La Patrie en danger* for reducing their format to two pages from four, Blanqui saw shots fired across his bow. There were rumors that *Le National* had been receiving money from the Second Empire government since its very beginning in 1869, suggesting that Rousset had plenty of money to spare during the privations of the Siege. Blanqui went on the attack:

> But, dear little *National*, while you were making money selling for five centimes what cost you ten or twelve, and with this money you stockpiled paper, the editors of *La Patrie en danger* were in prison or exiled […] During this time, you cornered the paper market, and when the Republic gave us back our voice by abolishing the *caution* and tax stamps, we found only rare stockpiles of paper that we had to buy at a premium.
>
> And this is why, malicious *National*, we only publish two pages.[34]

Blanqui's criticism rightly points to the most glaring of the inadequacies of the free market. Despite the end of censorship, despite the abolition

---

33　Rousset, *Le National*, January 19, 1869.
34　Blanqui, *La Patrie en danger*, October 4, 1870.

of fees, older newspapers still had the financial advantage. *Le National* had directly benefitted from governmental support under a system that discouraged dissent; in the new, supposedly egalitarian system, its editors were still indirectly profiting from their collusion with the former government via their stockpile of paper.

Blanqui's criticism, while perhaps valid in theory, got the facts wrong. Before the Siege, *Le National* sold for 15 centimes, not five as he claimed. When the government stopped requiring a publication fee in early September 1870, *Le National* responded by dropping its price to 5 centimes. However, not two days after Blanqui called the paper out for its enduring privilege, *Le National* raised its price back to 15 centimes with an apology to its readers: "In turn, *Le National* must, regretfully, given the scarcity of advertisers and paper, which translates to an increase in costs."[35] *Le National* obviously did not cite Blanqui's claims when announcing its price rise, as doing so would have been an admission of defeat. Blanqui essentially put *Le National* in a double bind in linking prices to legitimacy. His argument was that high prices represented political independence and, conversely, low prices meant that a newspaper had benefitted from collusion with the Second Empire. Increasing the price of *Le National* right after this criticism looked like an acceptance of his premise that higher prices indicated some sort of authenticity, a political independence that conferred respectability. However, *Le National*—like every other paper that benefitted pre-Siege—nonetheless faced very real financial constraints: the lack of advertisers and the rising cost of paper. Keeping prices low would have meant paradoxically taking a financial hit and gaining a reputation for being a Second Empire holdover. The price of a newspaper meant more than pocket change.

In the end, many papers took a route different than that of *Le National* by sidestepping the dilemma of pricing altogether and cutting costs in other ways. These decisions also reflect something other than simple internal finances. As paper rarified, the costs of paper production landed squarely on the primary consumers of paper—the editors of newspapers—irrespective of their politics. Louis Veuillot wrote in his "ultra" Catholic *L'Univers*: "Certainly, the paper material for newspapers is becoming scarce in Paris, and one cannot procure it

35 Rousset, *Le National*, October 6, 1870.

without undergoing a rise in prices."[36] The crisis also put the squeeze on Charles Delescluze's left-wing *Le Réveil*, which apologized for the drastic measures taken to reduce paper consumption by reducing format:

> We alert our readers in Paris and elsewhere that despite our efforts and the sacrifices we have imposed on ourselves, the impossibility of procuring paper in a sufficient quantity, beyond even its exceptional price, requires us to publish *Le Réveil* in reduced format.[37]

The entire political spectrum felt the effects of shrinking supply. Like Blanqui's *La Patrie en danger*, many decided to reduce format or total number of pages. Félix Pyat's *Le Combat*, Charles-Eugène Gibiat's *Le Constitutionnel*, Ernest Picard's *L'Électeur libre*, papers old and new, all opted to reduce format rather than raise their prices. Many, including *La Patrie en danger*, eventually ceased production rather than push costs beyond 10 or 15 centimes. As seen in the exchange between Blanqui and Rousset, the price of a newspaper represented political authenticity; it said something about the identity of the editorial staff and about the identity of its supposed readership. Changing prices represented a betrayal of those identities. Blanqui adopted this mantra to the point of allowing his newspaper to fold rather than reduce his format or raise his price.

The Collapse of Content

Debates over pricing and format revealed that the economic conditions of the Siege were fought in political terms. The newspaper, as a physical product in an economic market, had to adapt to gain or retain dominance. Reduction, however, became a necessity in sizing and in content. The battle over market supremacy also affected the content of newspapers, which began to exploit Parisians' obsession with their situation under siege: "notre situation" as it was often called on the front pages, imposing urgency, geographical and temporal precision, and social homogeneity on besieged readers. The newspaper had always

36 *L'Univers*, September 13, 1870.
37 *Le Réveil*, September 15, 1870.

been the text of everyday life, but never had it engaged so blatantly and so uniformly in the propaganda of daily life, aligning all of its constituent parts towards convincing readers of something they already knew: they were living in unprecedented times.

Or perhaps we should say that they were witnessing unprecedented times. By the end of the 1860s, the internal poetics of French newspapers developed such that they "could no longer describe [...] they had to witness."[38] Thérenty notes that this form of eyewitness reporting required that news correspondents become "the observing consciousness of the century,"[39] and that war reporting was "created by the need to give precise information quickly on different conflicts."[40] Martin has written that the poetics of witnessing also spread to the illustrated press, that "the first-hand experience of the artist and of what they were seeing" became a guarantee of authenticity.[41]

This eyewitness imperative spread to all parts of non-illustrated newspapers. Even articles that were ostensibly not about the war or the Siege were written in the first person or from a perspective that approximated or delivered first-hand information. They may actually have been written by the same person, as many staff writers had fled the capital before the investment. Given Thérenty's claim that this had been a while in the making, it is not surprising that the Siege only amplified this poetics. It is more surprising that even the fictional elements of the newspaper also came to be based on first-person accounts.

The literary *feuilleton* did not disappear during the Siege, it spread to promote the propagandization of the Siege. As purely literary, fictional *feuilletons* rarified, the poetics of the text published in serial installments contaminated other sections of the paper. In *Le Petit Moniteur*, for example, the serial publication that began on August 12, 1870 of Fortuné de Boisgobey's novel *Les Gredins* slowly trickled off in late September. One of Boisgobey's earliest works, *Les Gredins* looks at the more criminal, hidden classes of society in the same vein as in works of Émile Gaboriau, the originator of the French detective novel. Indeed, Boisgobey went on to become a key player in the creation of

---

38   Thérenty, *Littérature au quotidien*, p. 22.
39   Thérenty, *Littérature au quotidien*, p. 37.
40   Thérenty, *Littérature au quotidien*, p. 297.
41   Martin and Bodnar, "The Illustrated Press under Siege," p. 82.

an imaginary underworld of Parisian society[42] and one of the many precursors to modern-day crime fiction. During the Siege, these stories of the seedy underbelly of Paris no longer held any interest. Octave Féré's *Le Dernier criminel*, also in this genre, appeared in less and less frequent installments in the *Figaro*. In its place appeared another type of crime fiction: Henri D'Audigier's *Marianne de Hohenzollern: ou, le secret du roi Guillaume*, a lascivious romp through the sex lives of the Prussian noble family.[43] *Le Temps* also began to stagger publication of Paulin Capmal's *Lorenzo Cellini*, a picaresque novel set in fifteenth-century Italy. In its place came a series of articles by Francisque Sarcey under the title "Courrier de Paris," where he recounts life as a national guardsman on the ramparts. In most instances, newspapers suspended *feuilletons* that had begun before the Siege in favor of ones that were being written *sur le vif*: in the moment, on the ramparts, or happening right outside the city gates. The poetics of the *feuilleton* best responded to the serialization of daily life.

The most noteworthy example of this new political *feuilleton* was Émile Gaboriau's *La Route de Berlin*. Its serial publication in *Le Petit Journal* began on July 24, 1870, only five days after France declared war against Prussia.[44] The novel stands out for two major reasons. First, it is one of Gaboriau's rare novels that does not take as its cast of characters the police or the criminal population of Paris. Gaboriau's crime novels are well known, such as *Monsieur Lecoq* (1868), the story of a cunning detective who solves the mystery behind a series of nasty murders in Paris. However, in *La Route de Berlin* there is no mystery to be solved, no motives to be revealed, and no criminal or investigative mastermind. All the novel's secrets have already been discovered, as it is a historical novel: the action of *La Route de Berlin* takes place in 1792, during the French Revolutionary Wars. The title is doubly significant, as when it was first published in the summer of 1870, France was still

---

42   See Dominique Kalifa, *Les Bas-fonds: histoire d'un imaginaire* (Seuil, 2013).

43   This book resembles many others that were published during the Siege, bringing back the eighteenth-century genre of the *libelle*, which I discuss in the chapter on publishing houses.

44   We have every reason to believe that Gaboriau was writing *La Route de Berlin* as it was being published. As I mention earlier, most *feuilletons* were written in this way during the Siege, so as to remain relevant. Gaboriau was present in Paris, and this novel had not appeared anywhere to my knowledge before its publication in *Le Petit Journal* on July 24.

optimistic about its chances against Prussia, still marching along that road to Berlin.

The story of *La Route de Berlin* has one foot in the present of 1870 and one in the past of the Revolutionary Wars. In the novel, a veteran recounts his participation in the Revolutionary Wars to his grandchildren in order that they take revenge against the Germans on his generation's behalf, completing France's long march towards liberty. This brings up the second remarkable aspect of the novel, which is its surprising willingness to espouse republican rhetoric as early as July 1870, months before the fall of Napoléon III at Sedan. It becomes obvious in the novel that these double marches towards Berlin represent France's century-long transformation into a durable Republic. Even if it declares a decidedly eighteenth-century republicanism based on the Revolution of 1789, the novel nonetheless invites its readers to draw comparisons between the French Revolutionary Wars—which resulted in the First Republic—and the Franco-Prussian War, resulting in the Third. In this way, the novel does not merely inspire patriotism, it argues for a conception of the Republic that is assailed on all fronts, foreign and domestic, and one that must be defended continuously and violently: *une patrie en danger*.

La Route de Berlin can be read as a historical telescoping of the Franco-Prussian War, a way to talk about the present by talking about the past. When the Prussians invaded France in 1793, the narrator explains their motives in a way that rang true after the declaration of the Republic in 1870:

> So, why would they come? Why! Because they know our border defenses are lacking, because they believe that the difficult birth of our freedom places us at their mercy ... because Prussia is a predatory nation and it expects to gain something from us; a fortress, a city, a province maybe ...[45]

During the French Revolutionary Wars, Prussia did not end up taking any French provinces. On the contrary, France extended its borders west of the Rhine. The narrator's last allusion can only then be interpreted in the context of the Franco-Prussian War, when these territories—Alsace and Lorraine—again found themselves stuck

---

45   *La Route de Berlin*, in *Le Petit Journal* of July 28, 1870.

between competing nations. If we are to assume that the narrator's fears were legitimate at the onset of the Revolutionary Wars in 1792, they inspired just as much fear in the hearts of the French of 1870. While other *feuilletons* were suspended, this novel continued to be published thanks to the double meaning of its passages, linking France's Republics new and old. Europe had once attacked France for its revolutionary ideas, and the Franco-Prussian War merely continued that long struggle.

While *La Route de Berlin* was published in its entirety before the proclamation of the Republic on September 4, it nonetheless anticipated this event in provocative ways. During the French Revolutionary Wars, when this book's action takes place, France's internal disputes left it open to attacks from European monarchical powers fearing the spread of revolution. However, in 1870, Prussia was not invading France in order to put an end to the new Republic. It had declared war against the Second Empire, not a new or revolutionary government. On the other hand, it is hard not to read this line as imbued with meaning for the present of 1870, since the narrative framework of *La Route de Berlin* informs the present with a story from the past. Gaboriau seems to imply that France's fight for revolutionary freedom justified the 1792 conflict, but this motivation was lacking in 1870. Why was France still fighting? What ideals, if any, were behind France's resistance against the enemy? For what noble notion were so many French giving their lives, if the Republic was not fundamentally threatened? The *feuilletonization* of the newspaper allowed these questions to go unanswered, as if the next installment might offer some clarification.

Gaboriau's *feuilleton* also acted as a running critique of the other parts of the newspaper, themselves also caught up in the serialization of the present. Despite *Le Petit Journal*'s publication of *La Route de Berlin*, its editors were less subtle than Gaboriau in their war mongering. On August 9, 1870, *Le Petit Journal* struck a patriotic chord with its readers: "EN AVANT" ("FORWARD MARCH") spread across the front page, a militaristic slogan that echoed Gaboriau's ambitious title, urging the French towards the German capital city. In a long article, editor Thomas Grimm wrote that "from today onward, the entire country is on its feet!" The language is reminiscent of the infamous *levée en masse* ordered by the Convention government in 1793, a complete conscription of all eligible Frenchmen to fight foreign invaders. However, no such *levée en masse* occurred in 1870. Readers of

1870 would also have been reading these patriotic outbursts in context with the more nuanced tone of the novel. Gaboriau's installment of August 9 also included a description of France suiting up for war, this time in 1792:

> I must tell you, because it's the truth, that France was feverish and worried. There was not a single patriot who, walking in front of the *hôtel de ville* that didn't feel a pang in the heart at the sight of the permanently hanging banner where was written: the country is in danger.[46]

Gaboriau presents patriotism cautiously, with less gusto and more nuance than Grimm. The latter informed readers that "the entire country is on its feet," but further down the page Gaboriau seems to criticize Grimm, suggesting that such patriotism is often "feverish and worried." Just a few days later, in the edition of August 19, Gaboriau's narrator described the feelings of antipathy of many of his compatriots of 1792: "Some of us had not experienced the raising of ideals, the power of a nation that fights for its independence and its freedom." In other words, some of them were too young to know why they were fighting. Could not the same be said for anyone in 1870, scant few of whom had lived through the Revolution of 1848 and likely none the Revolution of 1789? Gaboriau pleaded for caution, for thought, and for a reason to fight if fighting must occur, all the while his newspaper published propaganda designed to rile its readers. A growing disconnect between the cautionary tale of the *feuilleton* and the political propaganda of the newspaper would have made readers question their commitment to the war effort.

The dialogue between editorial and *feuilleton* sharpened when *Le Petit Journal* began publishing unsubstantiated and deceptive rumors as if they were fact. On September 5, in the completely disorienting atmosphere of news relating to France's terrible defeat at Sedan and of the capture of the emperor, *Le Petit Journal* nonetheless was emblazoned with the erroneous announcement of the "VICTOIRE DE SEDAN."[47]

---

46   *La Route de Berlin*, in *Le Petit Journal*, August 9, 1870. Recall that Blanqui's newspaper was named *La Patrie en danger*, yet another echo of late eighteenth-century republican fervor.

47   *Le Petit Journal* was the only newspaper to get this one wrong. Given the intense competition for readership, I imagine the editors were just taking a bet

Le Petit Journal never issued an apology for or a retraction of its claim of a French victory in Sedan. It did, however, nod to Gaboriau's conception of a war for self-determination when it reported the revolution of September 4: "We have just witnessed a pacific revolution. Paris, rendered inconsolable last evening by the news of the Sedan disaster, has taken control of itself and prepares to fight energetically against the enemy."[48] Paris taking possession of its own destiny recalls *La Route de Berlin*'s narrator's claims of the necessity of self-determination in war, but in the context of 1870, is it really the Republic that is under threat? *Le Petit Journal* was now arguing that the real war had begun, that the war that would decide the future of the new Republic, but it is only through the intertextuality inherent in the newspaper that this sort of reading is possible. The editorial staff's vague references to self-determination only become comprehensible when read in light of Gaboriau's historical novel about the century-long march to reclaim the original French Republic. Readers of the newspaper had to read everything within it—the myriad constituent parts of its "literature"—in order to gain a clear understanding of what interpretations were being presented. Newspapers themselves, given editorial practices such as including different genres like the *feuilleton*, saw their rhetoric transformed from blatantly and perhaps uncritically patriotic to nuanced and persuasive, arguing for things like the necessity of war when the Republic fell under siege and the need to look to the past to understand the current conflict and national identity.

The *feuilletons* of the Siege affected, or at least attempted to affect, their readers in social ways. Judith Lyon-Caen has shown that the emergence of novels in the pages of newspapers in the 1830s and 1840s inaugurated a period of social engagement in literature. As literature became imbricated in newspapers it also stitched itself into the everyday lives of its readers, establishing collective and personal identities and bringing readers closer to authors.[49] Lyon-Caen notes, however, that these social functions of literature broke down after the 1848

---

that at best could keep them on top of the kiosk piles, and at worst humiliate them until readers forgot a few days later. They got lucky, as the news of the proclamation of the Republic quickly overshadowed their embarrassing blunder.
48 *Le Petit Journal*, September 6, 1870.
49 Lyon-Caen, *La Lecture et la vie: les usages du roman au temps de Balzac* (Tallandier, 2006).

Revolution. The Siege brought back this intimate relationship between newspaper, reader, and author, but this time it was through political literature. The collective identity that newspaper *feuilletons* imagined during the Siege was a national identity. No longer under the threat of censorship, newspapers did not completely revert to publishing politics *tout court*: their ideological positions, their conceptions of the new French state appeared also in fiction.

There was another category of newspaper text that further complicated readers' task of interpreting the everyday: the *fait divers*. These short, pithy anecdotes about everyday occurrences in Paris tended to cover criminal activities, seemingly random acts of violence, and the inexplicable mysteries of daily life. While they had their heyday in the latter decades of the nineteenth century, their origins can be found in the newspapers of the Second Empire and the Siege. The *fait divers* created a space for the spectacle of daily life, and this was no truer than during the Siege, when daily life itself changed so drastically. The Siege created the conditions that allowed for the *fait divers* to take on its role as dramatization of daily life under the Third Republic: at no previous moment in the nineteenth century had Paris been so disconnected from the world, so detached from its routines and industry, and so obsessed with the changes that were happening within it. The present *was* a spectacle in a literal sense and not a metaphorical one, as a thing to be read and dramatized, because the Siege was so unprecedented. The *fait divers* makes sense of "the chaos that breaks routine, finds within it expected surprises, and narrates the collective extraordinary."[50] The Siege flipped the *fait divers* on its head, chronicling when routine interrupts chaos, finding unexpected boredom, narrating the collective tedium.

All newspapers created new *rubriques* dedicated to the changing experience of living in the besieged city. These new columns presented information that would later be called *faits divers*, short takes on the quotidian spectacle of living in a city as complex as Paris. These Siege columns had names like "Paris au jour le jour" (*Le Figaro*), "Le Siège" (*Le Temps*), "Physionomie de Paris" (*Le National*)[51] in marked contrast

50   Anne-Claude Ambroise-Rendu, "Le Fait divers," in *La Civilisation du journal*, edited by Kalifa et al. (Nouveau Monde Éditions, 2011), p. 979.
51   This *rubrique* announced its mission directly and early: "Paris n'est plus Paris. Une ville nouvelle a remplacé l'ancienne." *Le National* of September 13, 1870.

to the previous, universal category of "Chronique" that had emitted the same type of news just a few months previously. These new *rubriques* concerned themselves with keeping readers up to date—as did the Second Empire *chroniques*—but insisted more heavily on the constantly changing nature of the city under Siege, and how constant change became expected. Editors needed to find new categories to explain the myriad changes to Paris's culture. These early *faits divers* did not need to invent or to sensationalize; the public already knew that they were living through an extraordinary moment in history. If, during the later Third Republic, the *fait divers* "implied that the everyday might be transformed into the shocking and sensational,"[52] there was no implication necessary during the Siege: the everyday was already shocking and sensational.

The early *fait divers* of the Siege were inverted forms of their later inheritors. Instead of showing the extraordinary in the ordinary, they highlighted ordinary events within an extraordinary historical moment. One example of this early *fait divers* can be found in the September 18, 1870 edition of *Le Petit Moniteur*, which describes the banal death of a solider:

> Assassination of a soldier—Thursday, at three in the afternoon, two soldiers [...] were drinking near Batignolles in a cabaret on the Avenue de Clichy. Next to them were two individuals in overalls, with suspicious demeanors, two of these prowlers on the outskirts of the city that live on marauding and misdeeds.[53]

When the soldiers finished their drinks and paid, one accidentally took out a 50 franc bill from his pocket. The criminals noticed, followed them outside, and slit their throats for the money. For readers during the Siege, this story typified how commonplace both tragedy and comedy had become. The "soldiers" were most likely national guardsmen, given their location near the ramparts of Paris, and also given the fact that they were drinking. As reported in *Le National* on September 21, bars caught serving visibly intoxicated soldiers were subject to forced closure by government decree: drinking among the enlisted had become a public nuisance. On the other hand, the violence

---

52   Vanessa Schwartz, *Spectacular Realities: Early Mass Culture in Fin-de-Siècle Paris* (University of California Press, 1999), p. 36.
53   *Le Petit Moniteur*, September 18, 1870.

of this anecdote is almost ironic. By their very vocation, soldiers confronted the possibility of death every day, albeit from different antagonists than highway robbers. This story articulates how Parisians' lives had changed, how the Siege had normalized some exceptions and exoticized what had previously been normal. This story was not interesting because it presented an exceptional crime—it even seems to imply that these types of "misdeeds" are common—but instead because this type of crime had become exceptional given the circumstances of the Siege. Soldiers were meant to die, but not at the hands of common criminals.

What made anecdotes like these especially interesting is that they were published alongside rhetorical editorials and literary *feuilletons*, influencing the ways readers encountered and interpreted them. The *fait divers* I present above came just as its newspaper, *Le Petit Moniteur*, was publishing a serialized novel, one of the few that continued even after the Siege began. The novel, *Les Gredins* by Fortuné de Boisgobey, participated in the growing genre of detective fiction, like those of Gaboriau I mentioned earlier in the chapter. The *fait divers* shares much with this genre of fiction with both insisting on the criminality of the metropolis and the unknown threats that lurk around every corner. Both, as I alluded to earlier, contributed to a growing cultural imaginary constituting the unseen lower spheres of society, perhaps best illustrated by Eugène Sue's *Mystères de Paris*, which is also noteworthy for being one of the first *romans feuilletons*. The *roman feuilleton* drew its source material from the *fait divers*—the lurid stories of murder, betrayal, and subterfuge providing the grist for the mill of fiction. This relationship was reciprocal, however, the *fait divers* "improv[ing] on the formula" of *romans feuilletons* by "creating sensation out of the quotidian."[54]

The *feuilleton* and the *fait divers* collided in their implications for the fate of Paris. During the Second Empire, a story about cutthroats lurking in the city might have had bourgeois readers clutching their pearls. A story about Parisian criminals killing the defenders of the city—defenders who were expectedly drunk—had implications for the outcome of the Siege. The *feuilleton* allowed readers to draw conclusions in the generic equivalent of an ellipsis: their lack of conclusion, lesson, or moral to be drawn influenced the *fait divers*, which took on a similar

54 Schwartz, *Spectacular Realities*, p. 34.

interminability. As a result, both *fait divers* and *feuilleton*, reflecting the uncertain future of the city, appealed to and created paranoia.

The literatures of the newspaper manipulated information in ways that influenced how readers behaved. The newspapers of the Siege created public attitudes at the same time that they reported on actions taken as a result of those attitudes, creating a feedback loop. For example, all newspapers, especially the more left-leaning ones, published frequent accounts of Prussian spies apprehended by the authorities: "Spies proliferate like the most unpleasant insects. In vain are they arrested or squashed by the hundreds, there are always more," wrote *Le Combat*.[55] Another newspaper, in a genre reminiscent of the *fait divers*, reported on a suspicious person arrested while writing in a notebook at the observation area at the top of the Arc de Triomphe: "'I am not a Prussian! I am English!' screamed 'the spy' as he was apprehended. But in vain: he and his notebooks were brought to the police chief."[56] The generic ellipsis at the end of this story is significant: was he an Englishman or a Prussian? If the former, the story's moral criticized the paranoia and surveillance in the city. If the latter, readers could be forgiven if they feared any foreigner might be a spy. *Le Petit Moniteur* issued a blanket warning to its readers (and perhaps to real spies as well) when it asserted that "It is a duty that we remind all citizens, and especially those in positions of authority, that danger exists within our gates almost as much as outside of them."[57] The alarm seems feigned. In the case of the Englishman, the newspaper hastened to dub him "the spy"; in the case of the blanket warning, this smacks more of fear mongering than of real, authentic concern. Léon Bloy wrote many years after the Siege that the author Barbey d'Aurévilly found himself manacled when another "good citizen" mistook his sober dandyism for a military Prussian aesthetic.[58]

When the city gates closed, scrutiny turned inward. The messiness of receiving news from the outside[59] meant that newspapers either had to speculate on outside dangers or invent ones from within.

---

55 *Le Combat*, September 21, 1870.
56 *Le National*, September 3, 1870.
57 *Le Petit Moniteur*, September 19, 1870.
58 Bloy, *Sueur de sang* (Paris: Georges Grès, 1914), p. 65.
59 The difficulty of reporting on news from outside the walls is the subject of Chapter 4.

Personal diaries attest to the difficulty in getting a straight story. One anonymous writer, faced with the difficult task of determining the origin and reason for a night of cannon fire heard from his apartment, explained the confusion: "At nine at night began terrifying cannon fire in the south of Paris ... there are two different ways to explain this. Either the Prussians attacked our forward positions unprovoked or they were just responding to an attack they believed us to have initiated."[60] Not only can the observer not find an explanation, one of them even relies on the confusion of the Prussians about a French attack. How to provide the news with imperfect information on all fronts? To resolve the problem, many newspapers took a grain of truth and imagined the plant it could grow into. Auguste Nefftzer, the founder and editor of *Le Temps*, confessed: "Every newspaper lies a little, even mine."[61]

One of the more cynical reasons for this indifference to the truth can be found in the intense battles for relevancy among a suddenly crowded market of newspapers. If just one of these newspapers increased its market share by publishing rumors, the others would quickly follow suit or risk being left behind. While I think this might explain editors' reasons for *publishing* half-truths, it does not go far enough in describing the experience of reading these rumors. As the above citation from our anonymous diarist shows, readers were often well aware of the competing information circulating around Paris and accordingly believed nothing or contented themselves with ambivalence. On the other hand, newspapers had a real impact on readers' behavior when it came to rumors of spies lurking among the population to the point that innocent foreigners and authors such as Barbey d'Aurévilly were taken into custody. In the next chapter, I focus on this second effect: the ability of newspaper articles to change people's perception of the truth, to distort their feelings and define their sense of civic duty. People thought it was the patriotic thing to do—a "duty" of each "citizen" as *Le Petit Moniteur* put it—to denounce their neighbors as spies. This pointing of the finger, to designate the dangerous other, was what defined them as French.

The exaggeration of the *fait divers*, the intertextuality of the *roman feuilleton*, and the atmosphere of fear generated by rumors all contributed to the heightened awareness of everyday life during the

60   BHVP Ms 1073, entry of October 18, 1870.
61   BHVP Ms 1113, Letter of Barthélemy Hauréau, August 27, 1870.

Siege. They also signaled to Parisians that the defense of the *patrie en danger* can be constructed from the stuff of everyday life: their experience of and relationship to daily texts like the newspaper, which itself acted as a chronicle of their experience. Citizenship was defined by this space between experience and text, between reading and writing. Newspapers, as cultural object, participated in the everyday lives of their readers, while at the same time, as text, newspapers documented, commented, and organized the experiences of those readers. So far in the analysis, this has acted as a symbiotic loop, the reader able to critically analyze the texts that supposedly represented their experiences. When our anonymous diarist encountered two competing news stories, for example, he knew to treat them both with caution rather than buy into the truth claims of one. A hypothetical reader of the false announcement of the "victory" at Sedan would have known to read that optimism with a critical eye, given the gloss provided by Gaboriau's historical *feuilleton*. This was experience writing itself through negotiation between individual (the reader) and institution (the media).

Chapter 4

The Dubious Battle of Reichshoffen

Rumors of spies and deceptive news about victories shaped the ways Parisians processed the War. While readers claimed that they should not trust everything they read in the papers, they tried to cobble together stories of the outside world with diverse fragments of truth and fiction. As Paris's isolation made it impossible to receive accurate information, the literatures of the newspaper were forced into close collaboration. One such story began to take shape after August 6, 1870, when the French lost a battle at Reichshoffen, a small *commune* thirty miles north of Strasbourg. Over the course of the Siege, this story jumped across different newspaper media and across the line between fiction and fact such that it became a national myth. The story of the defeat at Reichshoffen became such an important narrative of French patriotism because it emerged from newspapers, a medium that, in publishing war correspondence and news quickly,[1] sacrificed precision for authenticity. In publishing anonymous witness accounts of the event, newspapers functioned as war literature because they found a way to link the "experiential dimension"[2] of war with its social function "as an expression of collective values."[3] Where better than the newspaper, the text of everyday life, to find such values expressed? Newspapers' forcible

---

1 As discussed in Chapter 3, Marie-Ève Thérenty has identified the apogee of eyewitness war reporting during the Franco-Prussian War; see Marie-Ève Thérenty, *La Littérature au quotidien. Poétiques journalistiques au XIXe siècle* (Seuil, 2007), p. 297.
2 Catharine Savage Brosman, "The Functions of War Literature," *South Central Review*, vol. 9, no. 1, Spring, 1992, p. 85.
3 Brosman, "The Functions of War Literature," p. 91.

entry into national myth-making through literature reveals what Edmund Birch has called the "corrupt and manipulative practices"[4] that newspapers employed to convince readers that a certain topic was *d'actualité,* or topical and worthy of collective interest. By promoting the defeat at Reichshoffen as timely, important, and newsworthy, and by using the literary practices of war literature, newspapers ultimately convinced the nation that France's defeat had been heroic. It is easy to see how this narrative would have been appealing to Parisians under siege and for French citizens more broadly decades after the Siege was over. The story of Reichshoffen became a sort of narrative monument to the war. Since the French government did not rally public historical consciousness in the 1870s and 1880s around a "unified vision of the conflict," argues Karine Varley, "there could be no truly national commemoration of the Franco-Prussian War." Varley looks then to local commemorations of the war, whose "politically, geographically, and temporally fragmented nature"[5] can also be seen in the multimedia trajectory of the myth of Reichshoffen.

The story of Reichshoffen is one of improbable luck. An under-equipped and underprepared French force of around thirty-two thousand faced the third Prussian army, numbering about a hundred and thirty thousand. The French quickly realized their strategic disadvantage and miraculously escaped without surrendering. It was only on August 12 that more details emerged to explain this event: a corps of heavily armored cavalry called *cuirassiers* had stalled the Prussian troops long enough to allow the rest of the army to retreat:

> These men of iron know that they ride to their deaths. It was the first time they did so. No such cavalry had appeared on the battlefield since Waterloo, but these riders remembered what their fathers had done, and immediately renewed the legendary charges of the sunken lanes of Honain [*sic*].
>
> Despite the artillery, despite the gunfire, despite the pell-mell of tumbling men and horses, the *cuirassiers* arrive at the front lines of the Prussian regiments, breaking them, smashing them,

---

4   Birch, *Fictions of the Press in Nineteenth-Century France* (Palgrave Macmillan, 2018), p. 164.
5   Varley, *Under the Shadow of Defeat: The War of 1870–1871 in French Memory* (Palgrave Macmillan, 2005), p. 15.

pushing forward; the vanguard, shaken in the thick of things, retreats.[6]

The story—written by journalist and author Amédée Achard—presents many aspects of wartime reporting in the late nineteenth century: a sense of the majestic, the tragic, and the legendary. What makes it particular to the Franco-Prussian War is its willingness to look backward for legitimacy.[7] These *cuirassiers* could not just be self-sacrificing heroes, they also had to be the sons of those *cuirassiers* of Waterloo, who themselves died in a tragic battle. Both groups also died in service to a Bonaparte: Napoléon I at Waterloo and Napoléon III at Reichshoffen.

However, this gesture to the past brings with it many unintended consequences. First, Achard notes that Reichshoffen was the first time the French *cuirassiers* had seen battle in this war. And, indeed, the *cuirassier* had become more and more outdated throughout the nineteenth century. The Franco-Prussian War took place at long distance, usually with the advantage going to the Prussians and their advanced Krupp cannons. The French breech-loading Chassepot rifle shot very accurately at long distances, especially compared to the Prussian Dreyse rifle that was more reliable but less precise. This meant that for two distinct reasons, each army had an advantage at long distances. The *cuirassier* had been designed for Renaissance fighting, before the advent of movable artillery and devastatingly precise and powerful rifles that were now the standard issue in both armies. Even during the Napoleonic Wars, the *cuirassier* had a clear strategic purpose. But in 1870 they were cumbersome and ineffective, a historical footnote to military progress.

On the other hand, the memory of the *cuirassier* still radiated glory. All chroniclers of the Napoleonic Wars reserved a special place for these units, including Victor Hugo in his 1862 novel *Les Misérables*. Hugo's mention of the *cuirassiers* of Waterloo contributed to their mythical status, lending the specific vocabulary that came to be associated with them and their charge:

6   Amédée Achard, *Le Moniteur*, August 12, 1870.
7   The article is also typical of the Siege in its factual errors. The "sunken lane" of the battle of Waterloo was in the Belgian town of Ohain, not "Honain" as reported.

[T]he *cuirassiers* had just noticed between them and the English a ditch, a pit. It was the sunken lane of Ohain.

The moment was horrendous. The precipice was there, unexpected, gaping, vertical under the hooves of the horses, as deep as two measuring rods; the second row pushed the first into it, and the third pushed the second; the horses reared up, threw themselves backwards, fell on their backsides, slid their four legs in the air, folding and tossing their riders, no means of retreat, the entire column was but a projectile, the force amassed to crush the English had crushed the French, the unavoidable ravine could only be filled, riders and horses rolling pell-mell, grinding each other, become one flesh in this abyss, and, when the pit was full of living men, the others walked on top of them to pass.[8]

Achard's article quotes heavily from Hugo's description. The direct reference to the "sunken lane" aside, the *cuirassiers* in both accounts "poussent," "rompent," and "écrasent," the battle is a "pêle-mêle." On a sentence level, Achard reproduced Hugo's quick succession of verbs to render the force of the scene. Achard rewrote the myth established by Hugo but also mimicked his prose, weaving Waterloo and Reichshoffen into the same story. Through his textual borrowing, he was able to displace the tragedy of the chasm onto the tragedy of the entire battle of Reichshoffen, which, like Waterloo, ended in defeat. If in the past, when the *cuirassiers* took part in critical military tactics, they fell victim to poor intelligence and poor strategy, the *cuirassiers* of 1870, these anachronistic leftovers from an earlier age, transformed into cunning heroes bashing the Prussian lines to pieces, allowing the French infantry to escape. History repeated itself, but with some fictional improvements.

Achard's article proved to be particularly evocative for Parisians in need of information and morale. As more stories flooded in from those French who escaped the battle, the pictures became clearer, or at least certain facts echoed across newspapers. *Le Soir* related the following about the French general Patrice de Mac-Mahon, who was Marshal of France and had been dubbed the Duke of Magenta:

Mac-Mahon had already lost the battle.

"We must charge, continually charge, my children," said the Duke of Magenta.

---

8   Hugo, *Les Misérables* (Pléiade, 1951), p. 343.

The colonel of the regiment [...] approached the Marshal and said to him: "Marshal, in the state to which we've been reduced, to charge would be certain death, you must know that."

Mac-Mahon shrugged his shoulders a bit and murmured these words: "It's not important, colonel. But first let us embrace each other."

The regiment surged forth and made three successive charges.[9]

Already, the myth of the "*cuirassiers* de Reichshoffen" was taking shape. The dialogue here—highly stylized, highly reverential to Patrice Mac-Mahon, a future president of the Third Republic—borrowed from Achard's account, especially the knowledge of certain death on the part of the *cuirassiers* and their general. Added here, we see the humanity of Mac-Mahon and the inner turmoil of a commander sending his "children" to their deaths.[10] The myth had grown from an authoritative but distant account of the battle to an intimate scene tying together the heroism of these *cuirassiers*, surging forth not only from the retreating French ranks but also from history itself, charging from the past to help France defeat yet another foreign foe. The story was rich with cultural resonance, but it needed another push before it was engraved in the history of the Siege as well. These newspaper accounts were contradictory, ephemeral, somewhat crude narratives that nonetheless groped towards lyricism. In the next incarnation of the myth of the *cuirassiers*, it would leap from the front pages into poetry.

The poet-chronicler of the *cuirassiers*, Émile Bergerat, was not very well known at the onset of the Siege. In 1865, when he was only twenty years old, he wrote a one-act play called *Une Amie* that was performed at the Comédie-Française. However, given the complete obscurity of the author his play was billed as anonymous. Bergerat spent the next five years writing small plays, frequenting other Parnassian-inspired

---

9   *Le Soir*, August 14, 1870.
10   A decorated military commander since the Crimean War, Patrice de Mac-Mahon (also written "Mac Mahon" and less often "MacMahon") went on to head the Versaillais troops that brutally suppressed the Commune and its citizens, and eventually to become President of the Republic. Compare this trajectory to the commander Achille Bazaine, whom the public largely blamed for French military incompetence, especially during the battle of Metz, which garnered him the nickname "the traitor of Metz." Mac-Mahon's success resulted perhaps directly from these accounts of the battle of Reichshoffen.

poets and journalists, writing articles for various newspapers, and meeting Estelle Gautier, daughter of Théophile Gautier and Bergerat's future wife. When the war broke out, Bergerat had his perhaps second biggest theatrical break: a three-act play, *Père et mari* that was selling well at the Théâtre de Cluny. However, his career-making moment—and the subsequent poetry that would make him famous—came when he heard the story of the *cuirassiers* of Reichshoffen. The origin of his poem, he later claims in his memoirs, was in the news, even if he tried to hide this banality through the intervention of poetic inspiration:

> The news of our armies was being proclaimed in the streets. The news was not good. On July 30, Frossard had succumbed at Sarrebruck. August 4, it was Douay's turn, buried at Wissembourg in his defeat. Finally, August 6, Reichshoffen and the heroic charge.
>
> The story of this ride, a German ballad, set a fire under me even more than did my hero. Mac-Mahon played a role true to the admiration that he inspired within me. I came back to my home, shut myself in, and with verve and in one sitting, composed the ode, famous for so long now, to which I owe my modest reputation. It was called *Les Cuirassiers de Reichshoffen*. It was recited at the Comédie-Française by Coquelin and it carried away the room.[11]

The news that he hears begins with an indirect enunciator, the newspaper criers in the streets of Paris, whom Bergerat does not mention by name, instead constructing the sentence passively. This way, it seems as if the news emerged from the street itself. As the paragraph continues, it becomes even less obvious who is giving the information and who is receiving it. How does the "news" become "story," and then "German ballad"? When he calls the story a ballad, he must have been thinking of how he would transform the news into poetry. While in his diary he is quick to move on from its origins in

---

11   Bergerat, *Souvenirs d'un enfant de Paris*, Vol. I (Paris: Charpentier, 1911), p. 178. Bergerat continues: "It has been said and it could be said that the Ode to the Cuirassiers de Reichoffen brought Mac-Mahon to the Elysee Palace and predestined his presidency, but this overestimates the power of the lyre, and thank God, I don't need to blame myself for May 16." The May 16 he mentions is not related to the bloody repression of the Commune by Mac-Mahon, but his ultimate political defeat in 1877.

the news, his poem tells a different story, one that is fully based on these conflicting and kaleidoscopic news articles, making it obvious that Bergerat read the news slowly and widely in order to write his poem. The traces of the ballad's origins in newspapers can still be uncovered through textual evidence.

Reading Bergerat's poem, it becomes apparent that his inspiration for *Les Cuirassiers de Reichshoffen* did not come from a lyrical muse, but instead from the muses of the street, the newspaper criers and the articles themselves. He drew heavily on the numerous published accounts of the charge of the *cuirassiers*, especially the short dialogue published in *Le Soir*. These textual sources are most apparent in these stanzas of his ode:

> Mac-Mahon called his *cuirassiers* to him …
> Teach me words that will not perish!
> I need … I need an immortal language!
>
> [...] his gaze darkened.
> "Ah, I understand," he said, "there's nothing left but to do it.
> How many are there?" "They are countless": "This means death?"
> "Yes!" "I will go, Marshal," he said with effort.
> "Will you shake my hand? for I am a father."
>
> The man of Magenta did not shake hands,
> But opening his arms, and taking within them
> The man he sent to his death, not without envy,
> He embraced him before the army and before God,
> And, immortalizing him with this sublime goodbye,
> He made his death more beautiful than life.[12]

The similarities with newspaper texts are numerous. First, we see Patrice de Mac-Mahon as at once a tough and tender commander, cognizant of the dangers of his order and yet respectful of those who follow them. The masculine embrace common to both Bergerat and the anonymous author in *Le Soir* depicts this respect in human, homosocial terms. On the other hand, Bergerat does not wish to draw on the past to inspire the present. Here, there is no gesture towards the Hugolian sunken lane, but a claim to the timelessness of the charge of

---

12 Émile Bergerat, *Les Cuirassiers de Reichshoffen* (Paris: Lemerre, 1870), vv. 55–72.

1870. Mac-Mahon "immortalizes" the captain with his embrace, their dialogue spoken in "an immortal language," overdetermined attempts to elevate the news into a historical reference in its own right. Read in the light of the competing narratives of Reichshoffen circulating at the time of the poem's composition, its early lines ("I need an immortal language") could be read as an imagined plea for just such an elevation. In order for this event and those who participated in it to enter into history in their own right, they needed to shed the ephemeral language of newspapers in favor of the immortal language of poetry. They needed Bergerat.

This is the stuff of national epic, inspired by the past but updated to reflect what we can later recognize as Third Republic nationalism. Bergerat's poem recognizes the tragic futility of the charge, insofar as the battle was already lost before Mac-Mahon gave his order. The colonel is a father, a solemn affirmation of the sacrifice of the French forces during the war in service of their commander, their fellow citizens, and their country. But what kind of country is this? There is no mention in Bergerat's poem of Napoléon III or of his empire. Mac-Mahon sometimes bears the title "the Duke of Magenta" which Napoléon III bestowed upon him during the Second Italian War of Independence, but this name merely appears as a testament to Mac-Mahon's military glory and not as a reference to his Napoleonic ties. Instead, Bergerat takes a populist stance, describing France through the French who sacrificed during the war:

> Those among the line charged … Ah! I cry and I pray
> And I fall on my knees, o people, before you,
> You who march, martyrs of a sublime faith,
> At your heels carrying the Country.[13]

These general terms ("Country," "people") and the familiarity with which the poet treats them ("devant *toi*" in the French) indicate that the ode is written for them, the people of France, rather than in service of any particular government. He questions neither the motives for war nor the war itself, instead centering on figures like the people incarnate or Mac-Mahon himself ("ô peuple" v. 22; "ô Mac-Mahon" v. 98) for his apostrophizing, elevating French glory at the expense of political

---

13   Bergerat, *Les Cuirassiers de Reichshoffen*, vv. 21–24.

posturing. Furthermore, the history of France is whitewashed, as if France had always been simply France, rather than a series of Empires, Republics, and Monarchies. Even if Bergerat does not directly mention the anachronism of sending *cuirassiers* into battle, he alludes to their mythic status in the French imaginary:

> And the enemy said, "Do they dare?
> What fabulous combat do they propose?
> Nightly riders, do they make war in their dreams?
> They do! Here they are! [...]"[14]

In the eyes of the enemy, the *cuirassiers* seem to surge forth from a dream, their combat is "fabulous" ("fabuleux"), the stuff of fables, and yet they are real and face the enemy. If, for Achard, the *cuirassiers* emerged from the pages of history, for Bergerat this history has fully transformed into national myth, the dream of France. The *cuirassiers* charge forth almost magically from the fog of France's collective memory. Bergerat plays with this dreamlike quality of the *cuirassiers* by describing them metaphorically, again from the perspective of the enemy defending against their charge:

> The squadron entered into the mass of steel
> As into the bed of a stream of driven snow!
> Tighten your lines! Cross your irons!
> Unleash the guns ... They're slipping through![15]

Designated via synecdoche ("the mass of steel"), the *cuirassiers* confront the more mundane vocabulary of the Prussians ("cross your irons!"; "unleash the guns") in a move that places the French side of the combat in a legendary rhetorical structure that is one and the same with national myth building.

Bergerat tried to hide his debt to newspaper poetics in his poem, notably by eliminating historical references to Waterloo, a complicated historical touchstone after Napoléon III had fallen and France was declared a Republic. On the other hand, Bergerat could not have written such a successful poem if the Napoleonic source material had not already been known to his readers via newspapers. There were dozens if not hundreds of similar defeats suffered by the French

---

14 Bergerat, *Les Cuirassiers de Reichshoffen*, vv. 82–85.
15 Bergerat, *Les Cuirassiers de Reichshoffen*, vv. 86–89.

army, but none that featured the Napoleonic *cuirassiers*, their novelty on the battlefield inspiring these historical references. The main difference between Bergerat's poem and Achard's article is that in the meantime, between these two publications, the Second Empire had fallen. Napoleonic references were no longer as welcome in France's new Republic when Bergerat composed his ode. However, readers of Bergerat's poem—which was published in many newspapers during the Siege, closing the loop of intertextuality—would have had to cross-reference it with other articles about the battle in order to explain the relevance of these troops in modern warfare. Just as with Gaboriau's *La Route de Berlin*, presented in the previous chapter, the newspaper offered both the myth and a critique of the myth, encouraging readers to be wary of any version of events.

On October 25, 1870, the Comédie-Française again decided to perform one of Bergerat's pieces. This time, the famous actor Benoît-Constant Coquelin recited *Les Cuirassiers de Reichshoffen* and this time Bergerat's name finally appeared on the program. Théophile Gautier, writing in *Le Journal officiel*, praised his future son-in-law's modernity: "There is movement, courage, and a certain epic grandeur in this piece, where the challenge of dressing modern details in lyricism has been successfully overcome." Presenting *Les Cuirassiers de Reichshoffen* as an example of how the Siege has forced an unlikely marriage between current events and poetic rhetoric, Gautier continues: "Events present the most unexpected antitheses with a force that defies all rhetoric. Not so here, where nothing seems more natural."[16] Gautier tried to resolve the precarious situation of literature in times of war by framing the debate in terms of contingency versus lyricism. He found that the Siege was successful in creating good literature *despite* taking the present moment as its subject, at least in certain cases, including that of *Les Cuirassiers*. In short, he argued that newspaper articles could be elevated into epic poetry. He made this claim within the pages of a newspaper—the official newspaper of the government at that—bringing the story of Reichshoffen again back to its source.

Literary legitimacy changed during the Siege. Achard cites Hugo in order to place the *cuirassiers* into a longer French history, but Bergerat cites articles like Achard's in order to elevate the event of 1870 into its

16   Gautier, "Voyages dans Paris," *Le Journal officiel*, November 13, 1870.

own frame of reference. The poet frees the *cuirassiers* of Reichshoffen from their sticky entanglement with the past and allows them to live on without their citational baggage. Hence the necessity to describe his inspiration as having perhaps come from the street criers, but having taken shape within his own poetic imaginary, even if in reality he quotes heavily from textual sources. Since his published diary, cited above, *begins* with a lengthy ode to Hugo, we must imagine that Bergerat had read the portion of *Les Misérables* that glorifies the *cuirassiers* of Waterloo, even if this knowledge is only indirectly reflected in *Les Cuirassiers de Reichshoffen*. He specifically chose not to cite Hugo in his ode.

The work of national myth-making relied on the ability to incorporate these myths across media. A complex poetry congealed from a series of contradictory newspaper articles, but Bergerat's ode did not mark the end of the myth. On the contrary, the poem's success permeated every aspect of literary production during the Siege, beginning with its recitation on the stage of the Comédie-Française and its subsequent publication by the publisher Lemerre in 1870. Authors began looking to *Les Curiassiers de Reichshoffen* to bulk up their stories with the stuff of legend. The myth not only had staying power, but also a kind of inherent value: since the first-hand accounts had been published in nearly every newspaper, Bergerat had penned a very successful poem, and Lemerre had published it immediately after its performance at the most hallowed of French theaters, most of Paris would have been familiar with the gist of the myth of the *cuirassiers*.

A playwright, Franz Beauvallet, was another author to capitalize on the growing myth of the *cuirassiers*. He wrote a play entitled *Le Forgeron de Châteaudun* (*The Blacksmith of Châteaudun*) which was—like many other performances during the Siege—a *pièce de circonstance*, or a play that took the present moment as its subject. Critics used the term somewhat pejoratively, with the implication that plays like Beauvallet's would not be read after that present moment had faded because they represented the other side of Gautier's binary: works of art that failed to lyricize the present moment. In 1910, noted theater critic Gustave Labarthe wrote that for many of these *pièces de circonstance*, "just the titles of these plays alone are enough to show how little interest there is in knowing them."[17] His aesthetic judgment aside, some of these

17   Labarthe, *Le Théâtre pendant les jours du siège et de la Commune* (Paris: Fischbacher, 1910), p. 53.

plays speak eloquently to the ways in which the news was more than just news: it told Parisians how to conceive of their nation as one being constructed in the present.[18]

Beauvallet's play loosely took Corneille's *Horace* as its inspiration but placed the action of that tragedy in the town of Châteaudun during the Franco-Prussian War. The once-happy marriage of a German man and a French woman suddenly ripped apart by the war constitutes the essential tension of the plot. The double nature of the play as both inspired by history and engaged in the present is shown in the sources that inspired Beauvallet: a contemporary anecdote, and the structure and themes of Corneille's *Horace*. The subject matter came from yet another news item, this one about the battle of Châteaudun, in which a Prussian firing squad executed a blacksmith for his heroic defense of the city. The subject therefore was purely circumstantial, but Beauvallet gave the story a tragic plot pulled from *Horace*. The playwright Léon Beauvallet, in his preface to his son's play, asserted this as an intentional dramatic source. He anachronistically claims that *Horace* seems to have been written for the express purpose of furnishing its plot to the battle of Châteaudun.[19]

In taking a classic French play about war and giving it a new spin, Beauvallet showed how the present conflict compared to traditional French conceptions of patriotism, honor, family, and war. In particular, Beauvallet took *Horace*'s essential dichotomy between family and country and rejected it, opting for a more contemporary interpretation rooted in the unifying and universal nature of French nationalism and citizenship. This play is therefore a prime example of how Parisians inscribed their current situation—via viral newspaper articles—into a longer narrative, interpreting the subjects of the Franco-Prussian War as simply new iterations in an eternal French history.

Aside from Beauvallet's co-opting of Corneille, he props up his play with a modern myth: Bergerat's *Cuirassiers de Reichshoffen*. In the third act of the play, while the war rages outside of Châteaudun, a character enters the scene almost fortuitously: Pantruche, a citizen of Châteaudun who has returned home from battle, wounded and dying, transformed

---

18　For more on this play, see Colin Foss, "Engaged Theater during the Siege of Paris 1870–1871: Corneille Rewritten." *French Forum*, vol. 43, no. 3, 2018, pp. 375–389.

19　Beauvallet, *Le Forgeron de Châteaudun* (Paris: Tresse, 1871), p. 6.

from boy into man: "I am Pantruche, boss … do you not recognize me? The Pantruche who left not too long ago …"[20] The battle he returns from? None other than Reichshoffen. Pantruche had participated in the famous charge of the *cuirassiers*. The scene is almost lyrical in an otherwise prosaic play. During his long monologue, Pantruche often lapses into rhyming couplets. There are literary moments like this that recall not only Bergerat but the poetics of the many newspaper articles describing the event. Some of the same themes reappear, such as the recognition of certain death by both generals and soldiers: "Our officers tell us, 'Poor children, death is necessary!' 'Well good!' we respond, 'let us die.'"[21] This echoes the scene related in *Le Soir* where Mac-Mahon calls the *cuirassiers* "my children," and Bergerat's dialogue where death is certain but necessary ("'This means death?' / 'Yes!' 'I go, Marshal,' he said with effort"). During a pause in Pantruche's monologue, a bystander remarks with passion: "Oh! It must be good to die like that!"[22] recalling Bergerat's "He gave him a death more beautiful than life" with its message of nobility in a patriotic death.[23] Even the way in which Beauvallet relates the description of battle is reminiscent of earlier newspaper texts, the theatrical hypotyposis standing in for the first-person accounts published in the days following the bloody events of Reichshoffen. Both categories of text rely on a personal narrative to impress upon the reader/spectator the emotion and the sentiment of a larger historical event.[24] In this way, the authors not only describe the event but force readers/spectators to live it, framing their experience in nationalistic terms. A glorious death in battle, fraternity among generals and soldiers, resignation in the face of mortality, and the fictive first-person account of battle: themes certainly not unique to the event in Reichshoffen. Indeed, they have most likely always accompanied wartime writing in France, but their presence in accounts and fiction-alizations of the same event indicates intertextual borrowing.

20   Beauvallet, *Le Forgeron de Châteaudun*, p. 79.
21   Beauvallet, *Le Forgeron de Châteaudun*, p. 82.
22   Beauvallet, *Le Forgeron de Châteaudun*, p. 83.
23   As another intertexual reference, see *Horace*, which I offer in the original French: "Pour un cœur glorieux ce trépas a des charmes / la gloire qui le suit ne souffre pas de larmes." Corneille, *Horace*, Act 2, Scene 1. Or, the other Horace's famous verse, "Dulce et decorum est pro patria mori."
24   I will explore the tension between historical chronicle and personal anecdote more in Chapter 6.

Much like Bergerat, Beauvallet goes beyond simple citation of the news. The presentation of the event also mirrors the experience of reading the newspapers in search of a clear story that remains ever elusive. Pantruche's narrative is fractured—the character is dying, after all—and presents information in fragments, in disassociated verbs and subjects and a series of textual ellipses:

> What a battle! ... us others ... the *cuirassiers* ... we were in the battle ... immobile on our horses ... statues ... the others continued to fight ... we saw enemy battalions cut down like wheat ... But for as many helmets that fell, even more took their place ...[25]

The pell-mell of battle is reproduced in semantics and syntax. Who are the "others"? At first, it's the *cuirassiers*, but later it becomes the rest of the French army. The sentences lurch forward through the use of metaphorical appositives, redefining the subjects of increasingly fragmentary sentences. The *cuirassiers* are "statues," the enemy is "wheat" but then simply "helmets" through metonymical transmutation. The emphasis here, as in Bergerat's poem, is on lived experience and first-hand accounting rather than the historian's objectivity. It is the chaos of battle that the reader experiences through textual strategies. This again recalls the nature of news reporting during the blockade: many contradictory stories emerged, all circling around the same event, but never offering a complete picture. Beauvallet textually recreates the rocky epistemological landscape of Siege newspapers via Pantruche's monologue.

Readers of the time also felt that Beauvallet's play came more from the newspaper than from Corneille's tragedy, but not in a good way. Despite the play's success at the Ambigu-Comique, mostly due to the author's previous Siege hit, *Les Paysans Lorrains*, critics panned *Le Forgeron*. Jules Claretie, future administrator of the Comédie-Française and *académicien*, wrote in his diary about his experience watching the national epic:

> As a distraction, I went yesterday to the theater, the Ambigu. Again I saw there the daily preoccupation: the war. They were performing a drama full of clumsy intentions, *Le Forgeron de*

---

25   Beauvallet, *Le Forgeron de Châteaudun*, p. 82.

Châteaudun, a patriotic news item. It was not a play [...] Strange
way to understand national morale![26]

Claretie, a theater critic for newspapers such as *Le Temps*, *Le Soir*, and
La Presse, has an obvious bias in his critique of Beauvallet's play: it
was not really a play. Claretie insinuates that *Le Forgeron* was simply
pulled from the newspapers, designating it "une actualité politique"
("a patriotic news item")[27] rather than, say, a tragedy. Of course,
it is hard to disagree with him. On the other hand, this generic
ambiguity constitutes the entire interest of the play: it is certainly
based on newspapers and on patriotic poetry, but its very willingness
to participate in the dramatization of the news incorporated it into the
growing bibliography of national myth-making. Beauvallet laid his
stone on the path to a new narrative of French history based in news
media, one that held at least until the First World War.

What began as a simple rumor in the newspaper about a band of
cuirassiers who boldly ran headfirst into seemingly infinite Prussian
infantry changed over time as new voices entered the media sphere into
something larger, an echo of an earlier event in France's history: the
sunken lane of Waterloo. Once this slight shift of reference from *news*
to *history* entrenched itself, it paved the way for a poet like Bergerat to
immortalize the deeds of the *cuirassiers* and the words of Mac-Mahon
in an epic ode. The success of this poem, based on the accumulated
narrative elements that came before it, allowed for myriad interpretations including the all-too-journalistic *Forgeron de Châteaudun*.

How the News Became History

The myth of the *cuirassiers* of Reichshoffen lived on well beyond the
Siege. Bergerat claimed in his memoires that the popularity of his
poem perhaps propelled Mac-Mahon to become president of the Third
Republic in 1873.[28] Even if this claim was exaggerated—Bergerat

---

26   Claretie, *Paris assiégé: tableaux et souvenirs* (Armand Colin, 1992), p. 168.
27   A different translation could be "a political news item," but I have opted
for "patriotic" given the tone of the play and the common use of "politique"
during the Siege to designate patriotism rather than politics in such cultural
reporting.
28   Bergerat, *Souvenirs d'un enfant de Paris*, p. 178.

was hardly a kingmaker—one cannot deny the lasting influence of the myth Bergerat helped create. The charge of the *cuirassiers* was a foundational event in the narrative that made defeat seem like a morally advantageous outcome. Wolfgang Schivelbusch has written about the French attitude after the Franco-Prussian War,[29] claiming that in such a situation, France had to "invent an alternate, more comforting reality" to cope with the humiliation of defeat. One such invention was the myth of the *cuirassiers*. It is interesting that, among all the accounts of this battle, none employed the language of defeat. The language of loss, of death, of humanity—yes—but it never seems fully obvious that the battle was a decisive German victory. For the French, their resistance against the enemy made the case for a more nuanced interpretation of the outcome of the war. For Parisians specifically, the last, deadly resistance of the *cuirassiers* must have mirrored their own, very different resistance during the cold, quiet nights of the Siege.

In the decades following the Siege, the *cuirassiers* lived on in other ways, now fully independent of their original poetic and experiential ties to newspaper reporting. In keeping with Bergerat's revisionist history, the story no longer cited Napoléon or Waterloo. In November 1881, the *cuirassiers* saw perhaps their most spectacular representation since the Siege: a gigantic panorama of the charge, installed in the *rotonde parisienne* at 251 rue Saint-Honoré in Paris. The panorama as a technology essentially recreated the experience of "being" at an event in a similar way to Pantruche's vivid monologue. The spectator was led onto a raised circular landing, around which circled a mural depicting the event that stretched from below the spectator's feet all the way to the ceiling. Confronted with this all-encompassing vision, the spectator's body disappears, the canvas becoming reality.[30]

Aside from its experiential implications, this historical panorama issued imperatives for citizenship in the Republic. It presented an argument about national identity in the wake of defeat. Even if that defeat was already a decade old, it was still alive in the memory of

29   Schivelbusch, *The Culture of Defeat* (Granta, 2003).
30   For more on the panorama as representative mode, see: Ralph Hyde, *Panoramania: The Art and Entertainment of "All-Embracing" View* (Trefoil Publications, 1988); Maurice Samuels, *The Spectacular Past* (Cornell UP, 2004); Vanessa Schwartz, *Spectacular Realities: Early Mass Culture in Fin-de-Siècle Paris* (University of California Press, 1999).

the panorama's viewership. The panorama depicted the events of Reichshoffen, a city which no longer belonged to France after the annexation of Alsace at the end of the war; the very locale painted on the walls had ceased to exist as French. Every inch of this panorama reminded the spectator of the historical events that led to the present situation of France. The effect was to shape national identity, to produce a feeling of nostalgia for when Alsace could still have fought for its freedom, and to reopen the wound of the war, seconding Maurice Samuels's claim that "Through the consumption of popular and visually realistic forms of history, bourgeois spectators were able to envision the process of historical change that had created their new subject positions."[31] Napoleonic spectacles were not just a phenomenon of the revolutionary and imperial periods. They continued well into the nineteenth century, when their value was more nostalgic than historical. With the Reichshoffen panorama, we see that Napoléon I continued to haunt popular spectacle even when the nation and its history had moved on. The *cuirassiers*, those outdated soldiers fighting in a modern war, only make sense when understood in a Napoleonic field of reference. The viewers of this panorama were still encouraged to understand France's history in Napoleonic terms. The specters of the Reichshoffen story, its raison d'être, were the now nearly century old *cuirassiers* of Waterloo. Through the intertextuality of newspapers, which stripped away history in favor of a bold, new, and original republicanism, Reichshoffen became a Waterloo for the Third Republic.

I have refrained from making any factual claims about the charge of the *cuirassiers* for two main reasons. First, military documents seem to corroborate many of the claims regarding the event.[32] Second, and more importantly, it was the presentation and reception of the event through often-contradictory sources that most influenced the concept of republican citizenship. Even if most accounts—including fictional ones like that of Bergerat—got the details right, no one person had the authority to make truth claims about an event that quickly took on national significance. Analysis of newspaper articles and commentary

---

31   Samuels, *The Spectacular Past*, p. 270.
32   My primary investigative source has been Eugène de Monzie, *La Journée de Reichshoffen* (Paris: Palmé, 1876), which contains many official military documents.

shows that subjective, experience-based testimonials, even if contradictory, were the only means by which such an event was ever
imagined.

Newspaper journalists wrote competing, often fictive narratives of
events fully aware of the effect they had on shaping national identity
and of inspiring equally deceptive representations in other media. One
must start from the premise that newspapers did not aim for objectivity
in order to read the texts they brought together, whether during the
Siege or in the nineteenth century in general. Take, for instance, this
article written in 1893, about the former *cuirassier* Captain Peltier, who
visited the Reichshoffen panorama and found it a complete fabrication:

> "Ah, *sacrebleu*, my children, no. It did not happen like that! In
> Reichshoffen, you see, if only we had been able to reach the
> Prussians, we would have won the battle … But, gosh darn it!
> Those bandits were hidden in the bushes and, when we galloped
> over to them, they shot at us from two hundred meters away,
> like we were rabbits!
>
> "I was there, get it, and I'm telling you that we weren't able
> to touch a single Prussian. If we had reached them, my children,
> they would have been screwed!"
>
> And the captain shook his fist and the enemy then walked
> away, shrugging his shoulders.[33]

The article ends here, without any gloss to help its readers interpret the
captain's outburst. Was he right? Did the *cuirassiers* never actually reach
the Prussians? Even if the captain spoke the truth, he had nonetheless
fallen into the delusion of believing that a few regiments of *cuirassiers*
could have taken on hundreds of thousands of German troops. Or, on
the other hand, is this simply the fantasy of a vengeful veteran? If he
was wrong—if his memory was failing him—that would logically call
into question any witness account, even those published in 1870 in the
newspapers which eventually furnished the narrative sustained by the
panorama. In either situation, the reader is faced with an impossible
decision between two necessarily inaccurate sources.

The article posed a sort of riddle to its readers: Which version
of history should we believe when all of them fall short? The most

---

33   Paul Rovelle, "Le Capitaine," *La Presse*, January 5, 1893.

startling uncertainty of all is the one right before readers' eyes: how do we know if Captain Peltier even existed, or if this article was a pure fabrication? To my knowledge, no "Peltier" participated in the battle of Reichshoffen, meaning that the newspaper of 1893 may have been making the whole story up. If newspaper articles originally provided the source for the deceptive story told by the panorama, how can we even trust those original articles?

The mystery of Captain Peltier encapsulates the tricky business of national myth-making. From the earliest articles about the battle that appeared in Parisians newspapers, the *cuirassiers* had been intertextual figures, emerging from history via the front pages of 1870. Their mythic status relied on the blurring of lines between fact and fiction. However, as the 1893 article shows, this blurring disrupts the poetics of eyewitness reporting, calling into question the authenticity of the very first-hand accounts that formed the foundation of the national myth. We find that it is not the *cuirassiers'* coherence that makes them suitable fodder for history, but rather their resistance to unambiguous interpretation. To answer the riddle of national myth, to find its origins, we must read the newspaper as we would read any complicated literary text: as a story that works sometimes despite itself.

Part III

At Home

Chapter 5

Letters to No One

Between September 1870 and July 1871, Caroline Chaumorot wrote nearly one hundred and fifty letters to her friend Blanche. She did not send a single one. The Siege and the Commune disrupted their correspondence, which had been flowing uninterrupted since 1864, when Blanche left Paris for Nice to accompany her father, who was under doctor's orders to relocate to warmer climates. During the blockade, knowing that the Prussians seized all mail, Caroline continued to write but kept the letters stashed away until the postal network was operational again. In July 1871, that time had come; France was finally at peace. She bundled together the letters written during the Siege to send to her dear friend. Having written these letters behind the lines of military investment, with no way to send them or to receive any correspondence in return, Caroline realized that they constituted more of a diary—*un journal*—in which she chronicled not only her own life but the history of the Siege itself. Considering that she had written a sort of literary work, she decided to baptize her epistolary historiography with a preface:

> This was written for a close friend, another me. If it falls into the hands of a stranger, I would ask that stranger not to read it: they would not find a poetic story, serious and held together in a pure and elegant style. This is the outpouring of a heart urged on by patriotism (perhaps a blind patriotism) and troubled by the anguish of a dead silence on the part of family and friends. This was written to pass the long hours of the nights of siege when Paris, encircled by the iron walls of victorious Germany, fought to raise up its honor dragged through the mud at Sedan,

> and astonished the world by the military activity of its citizens
> so accustomed to pleasure and idleness.[1]

Caroline wrote this preface for strangers in 1871, but she also wrote this for us, readers of the twenty-first century, to ask us not to satisfy our curiosity and to leave these letters alone. However, her appeal whets our appetite even as it discourages us. She first entreats us to abstain from reading her letters, apologizing for their lack of elegance, but then reveals that they contain an emotional and possibly fascinating account of a troubled heart in troubled times. She tells us that we would be wasting our time in reading these letters, written during an extraordinary moment in French history when Parisians left behind their idle pleasures in order to resist an enemy that would inevitably stand victorious over the nascent French Republic. The letters, she promises, tell the story of a young woman who, while perhaps feeling betrayed by France's poor display of military heroism, found on the other hand a triumphant nobility in the resistance of ordinary Parisians faced with isolation from friends and family. Paradoxically, it is not despite but *because* of her preface that Caroline Chaumorot ultimately convinces us that this is perhaps the most honest, the most adventurous, and the truest history of the Siege that we might find.

The Siege turned Paris into a city of diarists. Urged on by an autobiographical impulse, Parisians who had never before written publicly took up their pens to document the changes to their city and to themselves. In this chapter, I argue that the historical and psychological circumstances of the Siege—at once a moment of idleness and of overdetermined historical importance—created a new form of personal writing that radiated outward from the self. Within each of these diaries, the author probes new readerships, expanding the scope of writing to encompass new, plural identities writing to larger audiences. The "I" becomes "we," as each author reimagines their historical, geographical, and gender identity in a city where time seemed to be suspended, daily life no longer meaningfully generative of knowledge of the world and the self. Similar to correspondence during World War I, Siege letters were "simultaneously dialogical and

---

1   Chaumorot, Bibliothèque historique de la Ville de Paris (BHVP), Ms 1074, fol. 91.

intimate" and "transcended the gender divide imposed by the war,"[2] even if such a gender divide fell differently on civilians under Siege. These diaries were intimate not because they, as Chaumorot falsely claims, expressed individual emotions normally reserved for domestic situations: they were intimate because they swallowed collective tragedy into a plural "I," allowing them to "shift 'victimhood' onto others," positioning their authors "as actors trying to make the best of a difficult situation."[3] This chapter addresses how the Siege collapsed all forms of personal writing (letters, memos, autobiography, etc.) into Siege diaries, defined as private documents written for public consumption. Siege diaries will be studied as a particular genre with particular conventions, all the result of war. The next chapter views these diaries in the aggregate, placing them within institutional historiographic traditions.

Siege diaries represent Parisians' attempts to impose order on time and space, to make their lives livable at a moment when the normal means of measuring one's identity had been thrown out of proportion. Hollis Clayson has described the experience of the besieged as primarily that of "an interlude of boredom, restlessness, claustrophobia, and anxiety," and argues that such discomfort "was both spatial and temporal."[4] Personal writing offered itself as a way of alleviating this boredom, of registering or inducing change in one's experience of an immobile city. In narrative form, written daily without knowledge of how the Siege would end, this testimony was the creation of the present, or, to use Michel de Certeau's language, an invention of everyday life. The grave circumstances allowed ordinary Parisians to benefit from "a carefree freedom by which each person attempts to best survive the social order and the violence of things."[5] And what was more violent than the constant and ultimately boring threat of famine and bombardment, what was more liberating than intimate writing? The Siege made every diarist aware of and complicit with the slow

2   Martha Hanna, "A Republic of Letters: The Epistolary Tradition in France during World War I," *The American Historical Review*, vol. 108, no. 5, 2003, p. 1342.
3   Rachel Chrastil, *The Siege of Strasbourg* (Harvard UP, 2014), p. 13.
4   Clayson, *Paris in Despair: Art and Everyday Life under Siege (1870–1871)* (University of Chicago Press, 2002), p. 55.
5   De Certeau, *L'invention du quotidien*, Vol. 1: *arts de faire* (Gallimard, 1990), p. 5.

march of time. They were writers of their time and outside of it, in the sense that they all believed they were ordinary people living through an extraordinary moment in history.

Dialogue in Isolation

Like most Siege diarists, Caroline Chaumorot uses complicated literary techniques to hide her authorship and ambiguously determine her reader. Chaumorot says that her letters were intended for "another me" ("une autre moi-même"), a way of designating her friend Blanche by referencing herself. The reader is the author, in a way. When she speaks to us, the unknown readers who might find her letters, she does not say "you." She speaks to us in the third person, saying that "they will not find …" ("il n'y trouverait pas …"). The most surprising part of this letter is what is not there. Chaumorot meticulously avoids using the pronoun "I" ("je"), hiding behind passive sentences like "This was written …" ("Ceci a été écrit …") and setting up the diary itself as a subject, as in "This is the outpouring …" ("C'est l'épanchement …"). This assortment of letters complicates the idea that correspondence is a dialogic communication between writer and reader, leading to the conclusion that they have to be a form of diary, an outward-looking diary that Katherine Roseau has called "a diary without the 'I'."[6]

Siege diaries were constantly in search of a recipient due to the geographical shrinking of the city. Since the Prussian blockade made postal correspondence impossible, many Parisians' letters never left their desks, like Chaumorot's letters to Blanche. So, how then is Siege correspondence any different than diaries? I argue that letters and diaries of the Siege coalesced into a new genre born from the isolation of blockade: the Siege diary. The "vous" and "tu" of these diarists—French ways of describing the recipient or author's interlocutor—became broader to encompass readerships that letters never imagined under ordinary circumstances, just as their "je" came to represent multitudes. However, the pluralization of singular pronouns—in other words, the individual's ability to speak for a

6   Roseau, "A Diary without the 'I': Embodiment and Self-Construction in Felix Hartlaub's Extrospective World War Paris Writings," *Textual Practice*, published online October 26, 2018. doi: 10.1080/0950236X.2018.1533574.

collective—does not preclude Siege diaries from epistolary literature, which Janet Altman has defined as "utterances that suppose a speaker or writer (*I*) and a hearer or reader (*you*),"[7] even if those two interlocutors became more abstract due to the blockade. Personal writing during the Siege always presupposed a bodily "I" and a bodily "you," which is what differentiates it from other literatures. Diaries maintain such a distinction between a writer in one physical and mental space and a reader in a separate physical and mental space, even if the intended reader is an alter ego of the author, another "moi-même" as Chaumorot termed it. Sam Ferguson has written that the literary aspects of diaries give the lie to the "persistent, comforting myth, of a self-identical, self-knowing subject writing spontaneously and expressing a unified 'self.'"[8] Siege diaries search for readership in the same way that they search for a new "I" to express the entanglement of the personal and the collective historical experience.

Writing to others requires infrastructure and freedom of movement; access that the Siege disrupted or denied. In laying out how letters are a unique form of writing, Janet Altman underlines their appeal to space, both physical and metaphorical: "To write a letter is to map one's coordinates—temporal, spatial, emotional, intellectual—in order to tell someone else where one is located at a particular time and how far one has traveled since the last writing."[9] The letter writer has not traveled, has not changed since the beginning of investment. The feeling that time (and space) was standing still was expressed so pithily by Barthélemy Hauréau, the newly named director of the Imprimerie nationale, when he stated in his letters that "nothing is more monotonous than a diary under siege."[10] There could be no exchange of information, the dialogic function of receiving or giving updates also rendered impossible.

The writers of correspondence during the Siege openly questioned why they wrote. Such was the situation of Hauréau, who wrote to his wife on October 4, 1870 that he had not been receiving her letters and feared that his own never made it to her either:

---

7   Altman, *Epistolarity* (Ohio State UP, 1982), p. 117.
8   Ferguson, *Diaries Real and Fictional in Twentieth-Century French Writing* (Oxford UP, 2018), p. 4.
9   Altman, *Epistolarity*, p. 119.
10   Hauréau, BHVP 1113, Letter 43, October 20, 1870.

> My letters must be coming to you mostly irregularly. That's because the balloon postal service is not yet regularized. Let's not complain. If the wind blew from the west to the east it would not even be possible to write you.[11]

Even if Paris turned to messenger pigeons and to newer technologies, such as hot-air balloons carrying thin-sheet letters[12] and microfilm to reduce weight, it was still difficult to maintain regular correspondence. The inaccuracy of balloon navigation not only meant that many of those that left Paris and the letters they carried never made it to their destination, but also that it was impossible to land a balloon in the city to receive return mail. Hauréau continued to send his letters by balloon,[13] unsure of their arrival, but others—pessimistic about their delivery or less inclined to have them lost—stopped sending them altogether.

Once it became obvious that letters would never reach their addressees, correspondence should have lost its dialogic function, but curiously this function simply switched addressees. Chaumorot constantly questioned why she continued to write letters to no one and found increasingly personal reasons as an answer: she was writing to herself. Recall that in her introductory letter, she claimed that in her diary the reader would find, "the outpouring of a heart urged on by patriotism (perhaps a blind patriotism) and troubled by the anguish of a dead silence on the part of family and friends."[14] Her description of her letters—which is in itself an act of self-writing—focuses on the emotional response ("heart") to a collective tragedy, implying that she continued to write as a way of understanding herself in her historical period. The telling adverb "perhaps" (in "urged on by [a ...] perhaps blind patriotism") points to a narrative of self-discovery and lost illusions, a hesitancy in proclaiming her opinions and how events have changed her.

11   Hauréau, Letter no. 40, BHVP Ms 1113.
12   This quality of paper, often called "Bible paper" in the anglophone world, the French of 1870 called "papier pelure d'oignon" (onion-skin paper). I explore the range of paper used in Siege-time Paris in Chapter 3.
13   Hauréau's letters were written on the lightweight paper that the post required for balloon service, but the real proof that he actually sent them are their broken wax seals. However, we cannot be sure whether they arrived at their destination in a reasonable amount of time, since the seals may have been broken after the war was over and the letters were finally found.
14   Chaumorot, BHVP, Ms 1074, fol. 91.

It is the problem of finding oneself in a troubled political geography, an uncertain person in uncertain times. Chaumorot struggles to define the genre of her own writing when she slides into these moments of "outpouring," like when she realized on January 13, 1871 that it was the eight-month anniversary of the day her husband gave her an engagement ring:

> Why do I lose myself here at this thought? Is this book not about politics? Is it not a diary of the Siege? Of course, but it is also the conversation of friends, and sometimes the wailing of my heart is so powerful that it is engraved in these pages. My dear friend, forgive this weakness, knowing that what I desire is my life-long dream.[15]

This is a political diary, one that traces the changes to Paris, but also the changes in her heart. It is not without irony that she remarks her dreams have come true during the trying times of the Siege. Her diary—"the diary of the Siege"—tells both of these stories, the history of Paris and the novel of her own life. Her intended readership is her "dear friend," designating Blanche but also Chaumorot's double: the besieged *parisienne* and the newlywed.

Barthélémy Hauréau, even if his letters were sent perilously by balloon, imagined his writing as personal and political in a similar way—he also calls his letters "a diary of the Siege,"[16] suggesting that he thought they would never arrive. Like Chaumorot, he wrote his letters to no one: not for a single person but potentially for all readers. Despite his attempts to describe the changes to Paris and to its citizens, he nonetheless slipped frequently into a self-contemplative mode, as if these letters were for him and him alone. On an eventual French victory, he writes that he is "not confident by nature, but [has] great hope," as if the mere fact of documenting his optimism might inspire him to towards confidence. He explains his presence in Paris in terms of patriotic duty ("For me, the horror of the Siege is being separated from you. This separation was necessary. My duty was to leave you behind"),[17] but this explanation seems to be a rationalization for himself more than for his family, who he thought would not

15   Chaumorot, BHVP, Ms 1074, fol. 114.
16   Hauréau, BHVP Ms 1113, fol. 45.
17   Hauréau, BHVP Ms 1113, fols. 50, 61.

receive the letter. Hauréau also finds himself professionally swept up in the new government when he is named director of the Imprimerie nationale[18] on September 5, 1870. His letters merged directly with his chronicle of Paris since he was participating in the new government he intended to observe. He wrote to his family that very day using the stationery of his new job merely to say that he liked his new office, at once offering an almost childish joy in the visible signs of his new authority and cognizant of the documentary and historical nature of his correspondence. For both Chaumorot and Hauréau, writing letters to no one offered a way to measure their lives, the changes that came over them during the months they spent isolated in the capital. The "you" of their letters became less and less specific as the days dragged on, eventually coming to represent a generalized reader—a transition that pulls their texts into the genre of history writing rather than personal writing.

The generalized "you" indicates that Siege diarists wrote with the goal of being published and reaching a broader public. The novelist and journalist Jules Claretie, for example, began to write daily entries in a diary as early as September 4, 1870, pages he later assembled into a book published in February 1871. In the preface to this book, he initiates the reader into the delicate process that goes into the decision to publish:

> I hesitated a moment before publishing the diary that follows. Maybe it is very personal, and if ever the "I" is contemptable, it is when it appears in the middle of such serious events as the Siege of Paris. But the witness who testifies in a trial, does he not after all have the right and perhaps the duty to make known his intimate thoughts and his feelings? His deposition only as good as his sincerity? We excuse him of speaking of himself if he helps us judge others.[19]

18   The new republican government was quick to take over France's official printing bureau, formerly the Imprimerie impériale. Hauréau's letter of September 5 bears the official insignia of the Republic, meaning they wasted no time in not only naming a new director, but also printing new stationery. This recalls Édouard Thierry's ability to swap imperial for republican insignia at the Comédie-Française in Chapters 1 and 2.

19   Claretie, *Paris assiégé: tableaux et souvenirs* (Paris: Lemerre, 1871), p. 10.

The decision to publish a manuscript seems, for the reader, to be binary: things are either published or not. For the reader, moreover, the decision is always affirmative. The very fact that a reader can hold this book in his or her hands means that Claretie decided in favor of it being made public. However, his preface indicates that this decision was not only taken hesitantly but that Claretie wanted his readers to be aware of the range of possible publication outcomes, which of course included publishing something with a caveat like this one. In laying out his reasons for publishing, and exposing just how precarious those reasons were, Claretie also implicitly referenced those innumerable Siege diaries that never went to press and now languish in municipal, national, and private archives.

The most important characteristic that brings together these Siege diaries is their precocious belief that the Siege was a noteworthy historical event and that the most appropriate way to chronicle it was through an unmediated personal diary. Take, for example, the diary of a man working for the municipal headquarters.[20] These letters are anonymous to the point of being impersonal. The only indications of the author's identity are his employment in the telegraph office of the *mairie* of the seventh *arrondissement* and his residence near the Boulevard du Montparnasse, but he only seems to offer these details in order to explain why the author had access to certain information, such as sites of enemy bombardment and census numbers. His diary begins on September 18, when he believed the Siege had officially begun: "Today is the day, strictly speaking, that the Siege begins. The Prussians are already blockading Paris on many fronts and the rail lines are suspended. Having not yet seen any preparations for siege, I am going to visit the exterior fortifications."[21] Synchronizing the beginning of his diary with the beginning of the Siege indicates that our man in the *mairie* thought the event was not only worth his observation, but that his observations also merited posterity.

Despite this anonymous diarist's attempts to couch his observations in the calm language of documentation, his experience under siege changed the scope and tone of his text as he was writing it, indicating that his diary was also a personal history. Whenever he tells an anecdote, he is sure to indicate that it is something the newspapers have

20   BHVP Ms 1073.
21   BVHP Ms 1073, fol. 1.

not yet mentioned and thus an authentic detail that he alone has the privilege to relate. These observations are always preceded by formulae like the following: "one fact that will not be reported."[22] The *reason* for the diary hides behind such formulae, revealing the curatorial mission he undertakes. He wanted to contribute to the documentation around the Siege that might serve later historians to reconstruct the event, a positivist conception of history described in the next chapter.

However, things changed for him: On November 25, he attended the meager and brief funeral of one of his colleagues from the *mairie*. This was the first moment that hints at any sort of emotion in our narrator, what Chaumorot called her "outpouring." It is not clear if he had anyone close to him, since he never mentioned family or friends, and the effect this funeral had on his spirits can only be read between the lines. After this point, his grammar became more and more lax, his sentences longer and riddled with the noncommittal semicolon to distinguish thoughts. On Christmas day, he wrote:

> Prussians, you are the reason that the most beautiful and happiest day of Paris is spent in an immense and needy sadness, made worse by the cold. All the houses seem destined for sleep, with the exception of a few lights here and there that seem to want to prolong the holiday, but they make no noises. The joyous conversations and the singing are replaced by rare and almost silent muttering.[23]

His address to the Prussians outside (a new "you" in his diary writing) merely masked another growing discomfort, more personal and perhaps tragic. Our observer remarked on the silence of what should have been a celebratory day, looking through windows into the lives of others ordinarily so joyful. But his own window, we must imagine, was also lit. When he described the lights that "seem to want to prolong the holiday," he was speaking also of his own light that illuminated the pages of his diary. The "rare and almost silent muttering" reflected not only the somber times, but also his own mutterings in his diary. He never reported his conversations with others, his own joys, leading the reader to believe that he either lived the quiet life of a bachelor civil servant or that those with whom he could have spoken had left

22   BHVP, Ms 1073, fol. 15.
23   BHVP, Ms 1073, fol. 108.

the city. The author, while clearly intending to write a chronicle of the city during the Siege, inevitably mused on his own isolation, his collective "we" slipping back to an individual "I." Like Chaumorot, he discovered that observing the changes in Paris was tantamount to observing the changes in oneself. Between diary entries, these writers may have contemplated the truth of Baudelaire's verses in "Le Cygne": "Old Paris is no more (the form of a city/changes more quickly, alas! than the heart of a mortal)."

The Political is Personal

Siege diaries show how this military conflict affected men and women differently, creating new categories of gendered action and thoughts. As a domestic, intimate genre, the diary negotiates and often ignores the boundary between private and public, allowing women—who were barred from military service—to articulate their engagement with the war effort. Writing about the British nineteenth century, Rebecca Steinlitz has pointed out that equating "women, diaries, and the intimate domestic [...] elides the engagement of nineteenth-century men's diaries with the intimate and the domestic."[24] For the Siege, too, the intimate and the domestic were not strictly feminine realms since, as Clayson points out, even men who were actively engaged in military service "commuted to war, splitting their time between their posts and home."[25] Thrusting national matters so visibly into domestic space, the conditions of the Siege thus made the home political. Juliette Adam[26] even went so far as to equate the history of the Siege with the history of its private life, writing in the preface to her published diary: "I am right to believe that my painting [*tableau*], as a genre painting, the painting of an interior, is the exact, truthful

24 Steinlitz, *Time, Space, and Gender in the Nineteenth-Century British Diary* (Palgrave, Macmillan, 2011), p. 99.
25 Clayson, *Paris in Despair*, p. 91.
26 Already well-known during the Siege thanks to her 1858 political essay *Idées antiproudhoniennes sur l'amour, la femme, et le mariage*, Juliette Lambert wrote widely on topics of national interest including feminism, women's rights, and republicanism. She published under many names including her married name, Adam, and "Lamber." Her diary credits the author "Juliette Lamber (Mme Edmond Adam)."

painting of Paris under siege."[27] Her diary, like all those written during the Siege, shows how the domestic had become another site of war, far from being simply where women could show their engagement, it was integrated into gendered practices that cut through the divide between private and public. "It is in the family that the country finds its ultimate counsel,"[28] wrote Adam.

If the diary as a medium of domestic expression reveals the home as less private, less feminine that one might imagine, the diary as a genre nonetheless affirms its status as a privileged genre for women. Readers of these diaries—even those written by men—should retain Adrienne Rich's claim that the diary is a "profoundly female, and feminist, genre"[29] since most professional publishing practices privileged men and masculine experiences of war. As primarily an unpublished genre, or at least one for which there was a realistic possibility of not being published, the diary escapes the publishing world's attempts to universalize the masculine.

Caroline Chaumorot's diary suggests a self-reckoning of the diarist's feminine "I" amid changing circumstances. Chaumorot was born in Paris on February 9, 1848, just two weeks before the Revolution of 1848 rocked the capital. The deplorable conditions of the working class to whom this Revolution gave voice, however, were completely unknown to Chaumorot, her family, and the bourgeois milieu they frequented during the Second Empire. Her father, Paul Amable Casimir Chaumorot, worked as an auctioneer (*commisaire-priseur*), sometimes in the Hôtel Druot, and dealt in all sorts of estate sales including jewelry and clothing. *Le Temps* reported that in May 1862, Paul gained a certain amount of notoriety in the sale of 750 pairs of men's and women's shoes that had been languishing in the auction house's storage for years. He also had a love of literature, which, combined with his flair for sales, led him to start another business: a rare book dealership he operated from the family's apartment at 40 rue de l'Echiquier. In short, Chaumorot's

27   Adam (Lamber), *Le Siège de Paris: journal d'une Parisienne* (Paris: Lévy, 1873), p. vi.
28   Adam, *Le Siège de Paris*, p. 9.
29   Rich, *On Lies, Secrets, and Silence: Selected Prose, 1966–1978* (W.W. Norton, 1979), p. 217, cited in Cynthia Huff, "'That Profoundly Feminine, and Feminist, Genre': The Diary as Feminist Practice," *Women's Studies Quarterly*, vol. 17, nos. 3–4 (fall–winter 1989), pp. 6–14.

life may have been ordinary, but only because political circumstances afforded her the luxury of believing it to be.

Caroline and her family represented the bourgeois ideal born of the Second Empire. She grew up surrounded by books and immersed in the culture of the *grands boulevards*, the playing ground of fashionable and idle Parisians. When she was not in Paris, she stayed at the Chaumorot estate in Passy, an aristocratic *faubourg* that, when annexed to the city of Paris in 1860, retained its affluent air. If Haussmann pushed poorer residents out to the ill-equipped settlements of the northeastern *arrondissements* in his quest to modernize the city center, he smiled upon the neighborhoods Caroline and her family called home. Caroline received a good education, judging from her family's position, her literacy, and her activities. She gave writing and reading lessons to a younger cousin whose spelling she often lamented in her letters. She studied painting under Nicolas-Eugène Trouvé, a genre painter whose house in Passy served as a *beaux-arts* school for young women. Two of her paintings hung at the eighty-eighth annual Paris Salon of May 1868: both pastels, both of flowers. When she received news of her acceptance, she wrote to Blanche: "Yes, little friend, your Caroline allowed herself to chase glory! But this glory is more a happiness for her mother and a testament of gratitude to her excellent teacher than a subject of vanity for herself."[30] Here we get a sense of Caroline's literary flair as she passes into the third person in order to displace the pride she feels in her work. Later in the same letter, she admits to calling her paintings "my dear children," a premonition of what awaits her two years later, when she will have actual children to care for. Her willingness to expose her work to the world, to chase glory as she puts it, suggests further that her coy opening letter—an excerpt of which I discussed at the start of this chapter—hides a desire to be read and to be public, to expose her ordinariness to the world as an example.

In contrast to her pictorial exhibitions, Caroline Chaumorot never published anything. The sheer mass of her letters to her friend Blanche indicates that she was familiar with writing correspondence, but the Siege forced her to start writing differently, experimenting with different genres. As she writes at the beginning of the Siege:

---

30 BHVP, Ms 1074, fol. 52.

> I have never written a diary, but I feel that there are circumstances that one enjoys reliving, and today while my dear husband writes at my side, in our little warm bedroom, I'm here to say a few words to you that will prove later that I do not forget you. From time to time I will make note here of a few reflections, a few circumstances.[31]

She had never written a *journal* (diary) before, but the circumstances she was living through seemed to warrant a change in vocation: the Siege made her a writer. Her language to describe this change suggests that she had to come to terms with what being a writer of history entailed. Common sense would dictate that a traumatic experience like the Siege should not be something that gives pleasure ("that one enjoys ..."), but for a writer, the representation of her experience could be pleasurable even if the experience was not. Maybe she felt the "carefree freedom" that de Certeau described as indicative of the invention of the everyday. Given the extraordinary nature of her everyday life, however, the Siege was not something that she could "relive," so she decided to capture the immediacy of the present in writing. With her newfound vocation, she came to see the event itself in a new light: not as something to live through, but something that could be relived by readers, even if one of those readers was herself in the future. Caroline saw the history of the Siege as intimately bound up in her own history, but in the act of writing, she sat outside of the flow of events.

For all the privacy she felt writing at home, she also theorized her public self as emerging from the private. Before the Siege began, many Parisians tackled the difficult question of escaping Paris or remaining during what could have been—and was—a long period of military investment. Chaumorot frames her deliberations in ways that make clear her status as a woman: "My husband was asked what he was going to do with his wife. The question bothered him, he handed it over to us. I declared that unless there is a law expelling women, I will stay at my post, that is to say, next to him."[32] Chaumorot does not scoff at the idea that her husband was asked first what he would do with her. She even seems to approve of this marital hierarchy in stating that her

---

31   BHVP, Ms 1074, fol. 93.
32   BHVP, Ms 1074, fol. 88v (August 31, 1870).

place is beside him, her obligations flowing from her status as wife. On the other hand, she rejects the idea that women could be expelled from the city, adopting for herself a feminized "post" equal to those of men. These gendered forms of duty show how Chaumorot's diary allowed her to develop new ideas of citizenship that could potentially run counter to both law and public opinion. Elevating what she defines as her domestic and feminine duties to those of her husband, Chaumorot suggests that the Siege had politized the personal.

Chaumorot's use of the word "circumstances" ("circonstances") to describe her civic duties is not unique to her. The problem of naming the Siege, of designating the collection of daily events, political reversals, as well as the emotions and states of mind that these events engendered, reveals the novelty of this moment in French history and the necessity of new ways of writing about that moment. Nearly all diarists used the term "circumstances" to describe the Siege to the point that it became a new word, at least in connotation, during the four-month blockade. It functioned as a catch-all, vague and yet semantically powerful, capable of collapsing different realities into one. Caroline and others swapped "present circumstances" ("circonstances actuelles") with other formulations like "our position" ("notre position") or "the situation we find ourselves in" ("la situation où nous trouvons"). While some terms point to the geographic specificity of the historical moment, others appeal to the collective lived experience of all those involved. Even for those like Chaumorot, whose life lay outside of politics due to her gender, "circumstances" most often referred to the political realities of the moment and to one's experience of those realities. "Circumstances" brought the political into the everyday. When our man in the *mairie* voted in the referendum of November 3 following the storming of the *hôtel de ville*,[33] he used "circumstances" in just such a way that imbricates the personal and the public:

---

33   On October 31, after 160,000 soldiers surrendered to the Prussians in Metz, Parisians rallied around leaders of revolutionary groups like Auguste Blanqui, Félix Pyat, and Charles Delescluze and stormed the main city hall of Paris (the *hôtel de ville*), calling for the removal of provisional president Louis-Jules Trochu and the establishment of a Commune of Paris. National Guard members loyal to Trochu quickly regained control of the building, putting an end to the organization of a new government. A referendum asked whether the population of Paris supported the "Government of National Defense." The government was upheld with votes of 557,996 to 61,638.

> I'm doing everything in my power to exercise my rights as a citizen in order to give my vote to the present government, which, given the circumstances we find ourselves in, is the only permissible one, the only one capable of getting us out of the situation and, I would add, it is also the most honorable one, the only one for which moderate and level-headed citizens should vote and in which my political thoughts and esteem are invested.[34]

Many believed that changing the government in the middle of the Siege would have spelled military disaster for the country, and this author was no different. However, he nuanced his claim by stating that the "present government" ("gouvernement actuel"), meaning the republican Government of National Defense, was the only valid, capable, and *honorable* choice available. Instead of making a claim couched in the rhetoric of defense of the country ("patrie"), the author made a broad political claim that the Republic was the only just government to lead them out of crisis. This passage is not merely theoretical; the author was an active participant in creating that honorable republican government through his vote. He suggests that the "circumstances" also created an obligation for him and his fellow citizens to take an active part in defining political reality. If his diary began as a way of documenting the "present circumstances," he pronounced imperatives along the way to ensure the proper functioning of the nation. He wrote a roadmap to democracy couched within a diary. The language he used was more akin to a political speech than a diary.

Others, too, articulated their own definitions of the Siege in order to highlight their personal participation in the event. Before Barthélemy Hauréau was named director of the Imprimerie nationale, rumors circulated that he would be named minister of the interior. He responds in his letters: "Not agreeing with them on the type of politics needed in these grave circumstances, I do not want to be any kind of minister."[35] The criticism here echoes a conservative refrain which holds that during such a tragedy as the Siege—what Hauréau calls "these grave circumstances"—jockeying for power is unseemly and unpatriotic. For

---

34   BHVP, 1073, fol. 50.
35   BHVP, Ms 1113, fol. 58. He changed his tune when he accepted, with obvious enthusiasm, the job of director of the Imprimerie nationale.

Hauréau, Chaumorot, and our man in the *mairie*, "the circumstances" refer to the complicated interplay between the Siege and personal politics. Writing in such a situation requires reconciling the two.

For no diarist was the Siege more personal, and therefore more political, than for Caroline Chaumorot, even if she did not hold a position in government. In May 1870, two months before the infamous Ems dispatch incited France to mobilize for war, she married a train engineer named Émile Dubois. She was twenty-two years old when the couple began their lives together and when war simultaneously interrupted it. In her letters to Blanche, we read about a happy couple arranging for their new life in Émile's apartment conveniently located near the Montparnasse train station:[36]

> We're still very busy. Tuesday, we picked out the curtains for the bedroom and the dining room: the former are gray rep with a band of blue velvet as trim, the latter are light with a dark, woody trim. Wednesday, we picked the wallpaper for the apartment, then we ordered a rosewood commode with white marble. The rest is M. Dubois's: bed, mirrored armoire, vanity, night table, then a buffet, a table, and oak chairs (old).

Chaumorot's joyful description of nesting contains within it a celebration of bourgeois material aspirations typical of the Second Empire: the sumptuous curtains recalling both royal velvet and warm rusticity, the tropical rosewood commode, and the chairs, vaguely yet intriguingly "old," all a testament to the idealization of the past and the ostentation of the present. Her husband's job as a highly trained train engineer—a relatively new career option—equally designates them as a modern couple, comfortably ensconced in the widening middle classes that were in some ways a product of Napoléon III's internal politics. Chaumorot and her husband were people of their time.

It is no surprise then that Chaumorot's ways of belonging to her time deeply inform her reaction to the war and the Siege, all the way down to her way of understanding politics. The fall of Napoléon III did not just represent the end of the only political regime she ever knew, it also coincided with her passage into married and adult life. In the same way, she wrote to chronicle the events of the Siege as they related to her changing personal and political identities. As she writes,

36   The anonymous author of BHVP Ms 1073 lived in this same neighborhood.

her obsession with current events increases, her citations of newspapers abound. If, at the beginning of her diary, she implies that she is writing because there are some circumstances "that one enjoys reliving," it is without hesitation that she later calls what she is writing a "book" about "politics." On January 28, 1871, when she learns of the government's surrender, she revolts:

> The Government of National Defense does not deserve its name, and when they tell us today that famine requires us to make sacrifices, it is our duty to respond: "Why did you wait until famine? Why did you allow the enemy to install such formidable artillery? [...] Now that you have allowed [Prussia] to execute its plan, you tell us that we are powerless ... It is you that allowed yourself to be reduced to powerlessness! ... All Europe should know this! Paris does not stand in solidarity with the ineptitude of its leaders, and the protests that emerge from everywhere can attest to this."[37]

Chaumorot's cozy "I" from the Second Empire has completely dissolved into a fiery "we" of the people of Paris. This almost reads as a speech in favor of the Commune of Paris, especially given Chaumorot's dialogic distinction between "we" (Parisians) and "you" (the Government of National Defense). Her complaints echo those of the *communards*, accusing the government of ignoring the will of the people it claims to govern. However, Chaumorot nonetheless reveals her class, forgetting that the famine being used as a pretext for surrender was not imaginary.

By the end of her diary, her "circumstances" are very different and, appropriately, so changes the meaning she gives to that word. Like Claretie, who imagined his writerly role as one of witnessing, Chaumorot states that, in the wake of the Siege, Parisians needed to "judge the actions of everyone in the great circumstances that have transpired in the past six months."[38] Her use of *circonstances* in French is just as awkward as in English translation, which draws attention to the word. To read this appropriately, to understand Chaumorot's meaning here, we must use the definition that diarists had been giving to this word since the beginning of the Siege. The circumstances of the Siege were not the politics, the bombardment, or the famine that

37   Chaumorot, BHVP, Ms 1074, fol. 124.
38   Chaumorot, BHVP, Ms 1074, fol. 126.

most certainly were extraordinary occurrences. Instead, Parisians'
found themselves in circumstance with one another, in constant
and cyclical dialogue with themselves and with those who were
absent from Paris. The Siege made dialogue near impossible, as the
Prussians excluded any possibility of speaking to the outside world. In
response, Parisians found others to address, as personal diaries adopted
an absent readership and as personal correspondence turned inward.
For as much as we, the readers of today, might wish to see Caroline
Chaumorot's preface to her letters as an appeal to us, she was also
writing to herself. Her letters had become an archive of her changing
self over the period of investment. When she writes that individuals
should be judged according to circumstance, she may also have been
putting herself on trial.

Chapter 6

Historians of the Present

Hundreds of Parisians picked up their pens to document the changes in Paris, to record their experiences, and to undertake a daily history of the event for others. These texts implicitly or explicitly asserted the historical importance of the Siege, implying that the story of this event must be written from the ground up, in ink spilt by citizens rather than by professional historians who perhaps had some sort of political bias or who had not experienced the event themselves. Each of these Siege diarists believed themself to be neutral, with neither axe to grind nor ideology to promote. By the very act of refusing to write a collective history, each of these texts claimed the authority to write an authentic history of the Siege and made their author an amateur historian. As a result, all of these diaries, memoirs, *souvenirs*, and private correspondence addressed themselves to the average citizen of France who would also be wary of the official version of events, that "poetic story, serious and held together in a pure and elegant style" as Caroline Chaumorot put it,[1] in favor of something more personal, more experiential, and, therefore, they implicitly argue, more true. These writers rejected the claims of professional historians: in 1870, this meant the old school Romantics, too *poetic*, and the emerging positivists, too *serious* and *held together*.

Diary writing constituted a new form of historiography during the Siege. The writers I will study here—from obscure citizens to well-known authors—believed that the nature of the tragedy befallen France was national, but that the only acceptable representation of

1 Chaumorot, Bibliothèque historique de la Ville de Paris (BHVP), Ms 1074, fol. 91. See Chapter 5 for an introduction to Chaumorot.

that tragedy was personal. In writing their diaries, they established a new vision of history that placed the tools and the responsibility to understand and write the past in the hands of individual citizens. Furthermore, they believed that the history of France happened among people in the streets and in their homes rather than in the halls of palaces. This form of grassroots historiography participated in a separate practice from the standard nineteenth-century tradition of history texts written by professionals—most of whom were journalists (male), authors (male), or politicians (male), or some combination of the three. The daily diary proved to be a perfectly appropriate alternative that was less interested in facts than the experience of everyday life during a specific historical period. According to Bonnie Smith, this type of amateur history writing has been gendered as feminine since it eschewed the "copious rules and procedures" set forth by professional historians of the nineteenth century, who viewed amateurs' writing as "a kind of impurity that the professional eliminated—a thicket of falsehoods he cleared away in order to find an authentic past and objective truth."[2]

The most specific rule these amateur historians broke was writing about the present as history. These narratives could not know how the event would end, or even if they were living through one event or many. Their observations, attitudes, and conclusions necessarily did not deploy a narrative explanation of the events that were unfolding. In his study of Zola's *La Débâcle*, Nicholas White suggests the expression "fog of war" to theorize "the sheer incomprehensibility of the battlefield, and its resistance to the rationalizing taxonomies of representation so often associated with nineteenth-century mimetic literature and art."[3] A different fog descended on Paris, rendering indistinguishable the personal and the collective and thwarting attempts to rationalize the experience of time. The resulting dynamism expressed itself in contradictory accounts, long parenthetical asides, and a mission to show how events look from the inside when the end is unknown, rather than as a series of conclusions about what went wrong. Siege diarists were not writing to make sense of their present as a link between past and

---

2   Smith, *The Gender of History* (Harvard UP, 2000), p. 7.
3   White, "The Fog of War: Impressionism and Zola Revisited," in *Lucidity: Essays in Honour of Alison Finch*, edited by Ian James and Emma Wilson (Legenda, 2016), p. 87.

future, but simply to participate in that present, and to encourage their readers to also feel as if they had been there, too. Juliette Adam wrote that her diary, "written daily, for [her] faraway daughter [...] at least has the merit of being sincere."[4]

When ordinary citizens put pen to paper during the Siege, they did not imagine themselves to be historians specifically because they intended to write a sincere history—a distinction they articulate explicitly. Many diaries owe their entire existence to the Siege, with the first entry corresponding to the first day of bombardment, the day the city gates closed, or the day the Republic was declared. The authors of these texts wrote with the impulse that what they were living through represented an historic moment for Paris and for France. This impulse often pushed them beyond their stated goals of documenting Paris, leading them past the city streets and into the emotional corridors of their own, personal tragedies. These texts explore uncharted territory, urging their authors to walk the streets in search of food, water, fuel, or simply to observe the spectacle of Paris. Beyond inspiring these individual perambulations that made *flâneurs* of them all, these diaries also pushed their writers to question the authority of professional historians who were sure to publish their own books in the aftermath. In fact, many of these diaries can be read as attempts to tell what their authors would qualify as the *real* story, the "more authentic and natural one,"[5] including the personal element that scholarly historiography often avoided. By writing their own stories, these diarists imagined a new form of historiography that placed anonymous individuals at the heart of history.

By the time the Franco-Prussian War broke out, the Romantic school had long dominated history writing in France, exemplified by the narrative-style histories of authors such as Prosper de Barante, Henri Martin, François Guizot, and Jules Michelet. These liberal historians began their nationalistic, stylistic, and historiographical revolution in the wake of the Napoleonic Wars and during the July Monarchy. Michelet in particular imagined "the people" ("le peuple") as the heroes of the nation, even consecrating a book to their history, *Le Peuple*, in 1846. In this book's dedication, he announces another foundational aspect of Romantic historiography, the voice of the

4   Adam, *Le Siège de Paris: journal d'une Parisienne* (Paris: Lévy, 1873), p. v.
5   Smith, *The Gender of History*, p. 7.

historian: "This book is more than a book: it is myself."[6] Born from the Revolution, this type of populist historiography had an appeal that still held in 1870.[7] In December of that year, during the coldest period of the Siege, Hachette advertised the upcoming publication of Guizot's *Histoire de France racontée à mes petits enfants*, whose title indicates the grandfatherly role Romantic historians played in the twilight of the Second Empire. They were born from the French Revolution, envisioning history through highly lyrical narratives based on archival research, a drastic departure from the tracing of dynastic lineages and so many "life-at-the-court" tableaux so prized by historians of the pre-revolutionary *ancien régime*. Romantic histories, inspired by the revolutionary conception of nationhood, inaugurated a form of historiography that placed the people, rather than a monarch, as guarantor of the French state. What were Siege diaries other than a narrative of *le peuple* written by *le peuple*?

However, there were new forces influencing the French conception of history, notably the more scientifically-minded German schools of thought. Despite the French defeat in 1871, this German influence continued well into the Third Republic, eventually leading to the so-called positivist[8] historiographical tradition and to the professionalization of French historians.[9] Intellectual historians now situate this

6   Michelet, *Le Peuple*, 5th ed. (Paris: Calmann Lévy, 1877), p. 10.
7   My understanding of Romantic historiography and the shift to positivist methodologies championed in the universities of the Third Republic is influenced by Charles-Olivier Carbonell's *Histoire et historiens: une mutation idéologique des historiens français* (Privat, 1976); Antoine Compagnon's *La Troisième République des lettres* (Seuil, 1983); Isabel Noronha-DiVanna's *Writing History in the Third Republic* (Cambridge Scholars Publishing, 2010); Lionel Gossman's *Between History and Literature* (Harvard UP, 1990); William Keylor's *Academy and Community: The Foundation of the French Historical Profession* (Harvard UP, 1975); and Maurice Samuels's *The Spectacular Past: Popular History and the Novel in Nineteenth-Century France* (Cornell UP, 2004).
8   There is considerable debate over whether to call the historians of the late nineteenth century "positivist." While they certainly did borrow from other positivist scientific traditions, they never claimed to be positivist themselves. Isabel Noronha-DiVanna opts for the appellation *école méthodique*, which is certainly less anachronistic than "positivist." However, since this chapter is primarily interested in the *tools* of these historians—which are expressly positivist—rather than the theoretical differences between each historian in this movement, I will use both terms interchangeably.
9   See Keylor's *Academy and Community* and Carbonell's *Histoire et historiens*.

tradition—sometimes called the *école méthodique*—squarely during the Third Republic; that is, as a sort of segue from the Romantic historians of the earlier nineteenth century to the more meta-narrative professionals of the twentieth most clearly represented by the Annales School.

Such attempts to categorize Third Republic historiography often overlook the essentially heterogeneous nature of history writing in the decades following the Franco-Prussian War. Isabel Noronha-DiVanna argues that no attempts have been made to define what, exactly, brings these historians together into a coherent school, other than that they are "Protestant, republican historians in institutions of higher education in Paris."[10] Noronha-DiVanna's approach, on the other hand, isolates a number of historians (Fustel de Coulanges, Gabriel Monod, Charles-Victor Langlois, Ernest Lavisse, and Charles Seignobos) in order to highlight, not their institutional affiliations or their contributions to the professionalization of historians, but instead the specific characteristics of their conception of history. In doing so, she undermines the traditional narrative of Third Republic historical consciousness as trickling downward from elite intellectual institutions, in favor of a more organic reading of each writer's engagement with current historiographical trends.

Perhaps due to their amateurism, Siege diarists were not explicit about how they reshaped Romantic historiography in ways that anticipated positivist views of French history. Much like Romantic writers, they wrote from personal observation, meaning that they participated in the making of history at the same time as they wrote their own histories. However, they were less concerned than their Romantic forebears with the past as a problem to be overcome. The French Revolution no longer loomed ominously in their memory, freeing them from the Romantic imperative to make sense of that moment of rupture with the past. Instead, they grappled with the complicated legacy of that Revolution as expressed through the myriad insurrections and political reversals of the nineteenth century, one of which they were living through. In writing history, Siege diarists turned their view from the past to the present.

The heightened historical consciousness of people who lived through the Siege is present not only in the sheer volume of diaries written but

---

10   Noronha-DiVanna, *Writing History in the Third Republic*, p. xvii.

also as direct pronouncements within those texts. The diarist Eugène Loudun framed his work in no uncertain terms, writing that he was contributing "to the composition of this canvas, always being retouched but never finished, of which each century sketches a fragment and is called history."[11] Diarists wrote individually, but together they painted a picture of the Siege in ways that a single-author book could not. This broad narrative conception of history owed much to Romantic historiographical traditions that located legitimacy in the personal and the collective. However, the historical ego, the organizing and structuring voice that Michelet used to lend legitimacy to his writing, was absent.

When Siege diarists explained their reasons for writing, they relied on superlative language to express the unprecedented nature of their historical moment. The balloonist Gaston Tissandier, at the start of writing his own history, noted that future historians would have two subjects of amazement when faced with the Siege, the political and the social:

> The historians who recount the drama of the Siege of Paris will take it upon themselves to judge the crimes of the Empire, its never-before-seen negligence, its senseless ignorance; they will say that the capital of the world, just before falling under the enemy's sights, had not a single cannon on its ramparts, not a soldier in its forts. But what they will not forget to confirm is that the inhabitants of Paris, living through the most nefarious hours of their history, found renewed energy in the tragedies that had just struck France, without pity, without reprieve; their energy seemed to grow in direct proportion to the dangers they faced.[12]

Even if Tissandier's role as a balloonist during the Siege seems to imply that he would be telling his story from a bird's-eye view, his account has more to do with the goings-on in the streets of Paris. Historians, he implies, will place political judgments before human experience; in his own diary, he eschews the political, focusing instead on the renewed energy of Parisians faced with growing dangers. The very act of describing historians' work sets Tissandier apart from their ilk.

11   Loudun (Balleyguier), *Journal d'un Parisien* (Paris: Lachaud, 1872), p. 5. I will comment on this citation in more detail below.
12   Tissandier, *En ballon! Pendant le siège de Paris. Souvenirs d'un aéronaute* (Paris: Dentu, 1871), p. 1.

Another diarist—this one anonymous—placed the distinction between the professional and the personal at the heart of his chronicle:

> This is why, dear reader, instead of writing a book I have only made a simple diary, in other words a sequence of events that occurred during the Siege of Paris. This is also why my diary does not carry my name, for obscurity, I believe, is a dearer friend than myself. Is this not real freedom?

Lest we mistake his anonymity for bashfulness, he goes on to suggest that anonymity is the only way to allow readers to relive the experience he recounts, with the implication that authored histories fall short of representing the collective tragedy:

> Those who were present and acted in this great drama will find here the history, so to speak, of each hour. For those who were absent, it will be easy for them to understand our anguish. What I want most to say here is that my diary was made with the most scrupulous exactitude and that what you'll read here was written from day to day, which is to me the only merit of my work.[13]

The authors of Siege diaries did not claim to have any special information to share other than the observations they gleaned as Parisians. Their authority did not come from an insider status as political figures, professional historians, public intellectuals, or even journalists, since what they saw and what they knew could have been seen or known by anyone who lived through the event. In this way, anonymity brings with it a promise of direct interaction with source material: a "scrupulous exactitude" not the result of heuristic analysis of archival sources but transcribed as it happened.

However, basing one's authenticity on one's subjectivity presents a paradox since many of these diaries were published anonymously or pseudonymously. Even if the stories are intensely personal, there is little information that could be used to identify the writer. The events in these books have been directly observed by a real individual whose anonymity frustrates any attempts at authorial attribution. It is difficult to apply Philippe Lejeune's theory of the "autobiographical pact" to

---

13   *Journal du siège par un bourgeois* (Paris: Dentu, 1872), pp. vii–viii.

these texts, since Lejeune states that any authenticity or authority must flow from the author's "intention to honor their *signature*."[14] The only piece of identifying information in one such diary is the epithetical title, "by a bourgeois of Paris." While this diary certainly does present the observations of a bourgeois—his class is palpable in his adherence to moderate republicanism, a distrust of the *communards*, and far-from-modest dining habits under siege—this can hardly be considered a signature in any meaningful or responsible way. Resolving this paradox requires reading Lejeune in light of the historiographical theories developed in the very prefaces of these diaries. Echoing Loudun's definition of history as "this canvas always being retouched," another writer, Francisque Sarcey, imagines that the history of the Siege will be written incrementally rather than authoritatively:

> Little by little, day by day, each person giving the information they possess and offering their testimony; and later, there will be some writer, a lover of truth, who will verify all these stories, one against the other, will organize them, and with them will compose this veritable history that we cannot and do not want to do today.[15]

Each writer is only responsible—and only capable—of writing about their own personal experience. By limiting their scope to some compositional aspect of a larger "veritable history," diarists need only honor their signature insofar as they restrict themselves to representing the masses of ordinary Parisians who lived through the event.[16] Therefore, these diaries are autobiographical in their commitment to relating the development of an individual, but historical in their desire to represent a larger body of humanity.

The anonymous *Journal du siège par un bourgeois de Paris* also identifies the dual nature of the intended readerships of all Siege diaries.[17] These were written both for people who had lived in Paris and *les absents*,

---

14   Lejeune, *Le Pacte autobiographique* (Seuil, 1975), p. 26; emphasis in original.
15   Sarcey, *Le Siège de Paris: impressions et souvenirs* (Paris: Lachaud, 1871), p. 4.
16   I use the term "ordinary" to distinguish between professional historians/politicians and those writing outside of institutional and professional structures. In the case of the "bourgeois de Paris," the author obviously only intends to speak for himself and his fellow bourgeois.
17   For more on the intended, and slippery, readership of diaries, see Chapter 5.

those who had no other way of experiencing the Siege than through these written accounts. This dual readership is mirrored in the intended readership of Romantic and positivist historians: the former wrote almost lyrical narratives of the past for the average literate reader, the latter wrote using scientific documentation that made the events understandable for the well-educated. Chaumorot, with one foot in Romantic historiography, wrote via the outpouring of her heart. Other diarists, one foot in positivist historiography, made efforts to document events and transcribe rumors that would not have appeared in the newspapers and therefore may have escaped notice. For readers who were not in Paris, these diaries offered a glimpse into the lived experience of fellow citizens during a historic period. If these stories had not been written, the history of the Siege of Paris may not have been integrated into the collective memory of France; reading daily accounts of the event functioned as a way to experience it for oneself.

Documentary Narratives: The Positivist Turn

There was a man who worked in the telegraph office of the *mairie* (or municipal building) of the seventh *arrondissement* when the Prussians cut the telegraph lines leading into the city. These lines were vital not only for communication with the outside world but also for his job. So much for modern convenience. Our man in the *mairie* had formidable technical skills that no longer seemed relevant. Luckily, there were plenty of other municipal activities he oversaw during the investment, one of which was collecting census data to organize the distribution of food to improvised city-run markets. He often went to the central market of les Halles to take stock of the state of comestibles and made copious notes in his diary:

> I've just come from les Halles: there are a good number of vendors, but little merchandise and in what a state! The few vegetables that one can find there are ripped up from the gardens between the forts and the ramparts of the city: half-rotten or half-dried out vegetables, and everything is selling despite the prices. Because in a few days there will be no more green vegetables. Here are a few prices: a fist-sized cabbage 60 to 75 centimes, leafy greens 90 c., the leeks cost one *sous* per foot and

for a little packet of 8 or 9 carrots or turnips you need a franc or more, and so forth. And it's all selling.[18]

The author certainly intended these prices to shock the reader, but his goals were primarily documentary rather than impressionistic. He was concerned with making information available to future readers of his diary and to those who were absent, always on the lookout for "a fact that will not be reported."[19] For example, when he launched into a story about the shelling of the city, he stopped himself halfway through, noting that "these are daily things that the newspapers are talking about."[20] He was selective about his anecdotes, his sources, and his figures, in order to complement other sources—like newspapers—rather than supplant them.

The Romantic inclination favored personal narrative based on authorship and the convincing angle of telling a story about a people as a whole. However, the man in the *mairie* departed drastically from the Romantic school through his inclusion of statistics and his awareness of available sources. As we have seen, many diarists wrote for later generations, adding their voice to the continuous and laborious work of history writing, and so they wrote with the concerns of historians in mind. The professional historians Charles-Victor Langlois and Charles Seignobos outlined these concerns in their 1898 text, *Introduction aux études historiques*, often considered to be a field guide to positivist historiography:

> History is made with documents. Documents are the traces left by the thoughts and deeds of men of the past. Among the thoughts and deeds of men, there are very few that leave visible traces, and these traces, when they occur, are rarely lasting: one accident can erase them [...] Without documents, the history of large periods of the past of humanity is forever unknowable. For nothing can stand in for documents: no documents, no history.[21]

The importance of documentary research expressed in Seignobos and Langlois's conception of historiographical heuristics also finds voice in

18   BHVP, Ms 1073, fol. 4v.
19   BHVP, Ms 1073, fol. 15v.
20   BHVP, Ms 1073, fol. 24v.
21   Langlois and Seignobos, *Introduction aux études historiques* (1898) (Éditions Kimé, 1992), p. 13.

Siege diarists' mission to present the panoply of thoughts, actions, and events of the Siege. Their diaries emerged from the historical need for evidence to support claims, even if they were writing while the event itself was unfolding. Writing for the future, they conceived of their present as a soon-to-be past needing documentation.

Where our man in the *mairie* used facts and figures to understand his historical moment, others like Jules Claretie relied on textual evidence. Claretie, like Chaumorot, was a product of his time. Journalist, author, historian, playwright, literary and theater critic, he achieved fame in the aftermath of the *année terrible* mostly due to his writings during and about the Siege. In the 1880s and 1890s, he was president of the Société des gens de lettres, director of the Comédie-Française, and a member of the Académie française. Immediately after the war, he wrote a series of historical texts that firmly anchored his early fame around the events of 1870–1871: *La Débâcle* (1871), *Le Champ de bataille de Sedan* (1871), *La France envahie* (1871), *La Guerre nationale* (1871), and his massive *Histoire de la révolution de 1870–1871* (5 vols., 1872). He also wrote and later published a Siege diary that attested to his personal involvement in the events that he, as a historian, took as a major subject. He wrote in the preface of the 1898 edition of his diary that "This is not a book, it's the deposition of a witness. I didn't see everything, but what I did see I saw well. I have not said everything, but what I say is true."[22] This Rousseauesque autobiographical pact, frank about its dishonesty, clear yet unspecific about its gaps, nonetheless situates Claretie in the tradition of diarists who participated in the stories they told.

Claretie participated in even more fundamental ways than other amateur historians, as his name constantly appeared in newspaper bylines. The articles he penned in *Le Rappel* and elsewhere mostly fell under the categories of theatre criticism and *chronique parisienne* (Parisian chronicle). This was a particularly apt rubric for articles that would eventually find their way into his published diary. The manuscript for this diary[23] offers a glimpse into Claretie's affinity for documentation, especially when it concerned other texts he had written. The diary is essentially composed of a series of press clippings, with his own interstitial commentary tying them together. However,

22   Claretie, *Paris assiégé: tableaux et souvenirs* (Paris: Lemerre: 1871), p. iii.
23   BHVP, Fonds Jules Claretie, section XII, vol. 20, *Journal du siège de Paris.*

the published edition makes no citational distinction between his published articles and his manuscript diary. For example, on the entry dated September 23, 1870 in his handwritten diary, we read: "Hastily, I wrote the following lines": followed by a newspaper clipping.[24] A reader of the published edition would have no idea *where* he wrote this line as nothing separates it textually from the rest of the diary, but indeed, these lines were written in a newspaper and transcribed into his diary. This lapsus is fortunate, as it points to the complete integration of documentary sources in his historiographical methodology: the diary essentially reads as an anthology of Claretie's journalism during the Siege. The manuscript also shows his affinity for lists; for example, he dedicates two pages to reproducing a list of new newspapers that have appeared during the Siege, a list which was originally published in *Le Journal des débats*. His commentary on this transcription reveals his reasons for including such a document in his diary, even if it was eventually cut from the published edition:[25]

> One newspaper is publishing a list of all the newspapers that have appeared since [the proclamation of] the Republic. This is a curious document and already feels historic, since the year 1870, only dead for three days, seems so far away … someone might be interested in reading [this document] here.[26]

The Seignobos and Langlois of the twenty-first century certainly will be interested in this document. Claretie implicitly argued for the importance of historical evidence in his diary, especially considering that many of these newspapers, like *La Défense nationale*, *Le Salut public*, and *Le Peuple souverain* only published one issue before folding. As Seignobos and Langlois feared, many historical events leave traces that are "rarely lasting." Claretie was preparing for positivist historians before they had even founded their school.

Siege diarists may have wished to present documents for future historians, but their diaries themselves were (and are) historical documents. When Édouard Thierry, director of the Comédie-Française, published his history of that same institution in 1887, *La Comédie-Française pendant*

---

24   BHVP, Fonds Jules Claretie, section XII, vol. 20, September 23, 1870.
25   For more information on the differences between Claretie's manuscript and the published diary, see Chapter 8.
26   BHVP, Fonds Claretie, section XII, vol. 20, p. 246.

les deux sièges (1870–1871), the preface insisted ambiguously that this is less a diary, more a historical document itself:

> This volume made itself, and without any plan. The general administrator of the Théâtre-Français, the same since the end of the year 1859 to his retirement in 1871, had his desk diary open next to him. In his desk diary, as is common in most businesses, during the last ten months of his administration, each day is supported by a few sentences. Each day shows what happened, what was in store for the next day. The days and the sentences piled up, the pages were filled, the diary or rather the diaries, since there were two, went off as time passed, just as yesterday's newspaper and last year's calendar are left behind.[27]

The claim that Thierry had little to do with the publication of these desk diaries clearly seems to situate this text as one of historical, rather than narrative interest. However, the description of these diaries uses much of the same language one could use to describe Siege diaries: written daily, without knowledge of their natural end point, and (in 1887 as today) representing a chronicle of an event that has become but was not yet historically relevant. The preface states that Thierry "became convinced that the interest of such a diary as this was precisely that it was not the work of an author, and that it leaves the last word to the facts themselves just as they had the first word." The language is ambivalent: is this a "diary," the daily writing of an individual with authorial perspective, or "the facts themselves" devoid of subjectivity? Thierry's diaries offer more than facts and figures, even if one can rely on them for historical research.[28] His "I" is very present during his feud with Hugo, when he worries about paying his actors, and when he frets over the future of the Theater, as outlined in Part I. Reading Thierry's book as a historical document destined for heuristic analysis, as Seignobos and Langlois suggest we should, would be to miss the narrative elements that tell a more dynamic and

---

27   Thierry, *La Comédie-Française pendant les deux sièges (1870–1871)* (Paris: Tresse et Stock, 1887), p. v.
28   In Chapters 1 and 2, for example, I base much of my analysis of the practical information about operating the Theater on Thierry's fastidious accounting, supported by other documents. These chapters also explain his feud with Hugo in greater detail.

certainly not objective story of the people in and around the Theater.[29]
However, if we ignore the data-centric aspects of his diary we risk
missing how the field of historiography was changing at the moment
of publication. Thierry's agendas, like the diaries of Chaumorot and
Claretie, must be read as attempts to reconcile numbers and narrative,
artifact and artifice. Or at least as attempts to avoid responsibility for
ideological rhetoric under the guise of objectivity.

As literature, Siege diaries relied on many of the same narrato-
logical and historiographic structural elements as the medieval
chronicle. This form of history writing, which has roots in Roman
histories like the *Annals* of Tacitus, were composed in chronological
order, often as the events themselves transpired. Gabrielle Spiegel
has argued that the thirteenth-century transition from verse to prose
chronicles carried with it the double imperative of reaching a larger
audience and uncoupling historical truth claims from matters of
style.[30] Similarly, Siege diarists wrote histories intended for a large
audience, and eschewed stylistic constraints in favor of the language
of witnessing, or at least they believed this was their duty; Caroline
Chaumorot apologized for her lack of elegance in her opening letter,
even if her truth claims arose precisely from her inelegant style.
Other comparisons might include, as Sophie Marnette has claimed
for the chronicles of Joinville, Villehardouin, and Robert de Clari,
the reliance on what she terms "external focalization of witnessing,"[31]
which allowed for the narrators of medieval and Siege chronicles
to imply both a personal witnessing of an event and the notion of
collective witnessing. While none of the diarists during the Siege
explicitly indicated his or her inheritance of the medieval chronicle,
the comparison of these genres points to new ways of writing history
that emerged during the Siege: the chronicle, once a respectable form
of historiography, was seen by many historians in 1870 as simply a

29   If we include texts like diaries into the corpus of history writing, the
relevance of Hayden White becomes much more obvious, whose book *Metahistory:
The Historical Imagination in Nineteenth-Century Europe* (Johns Hopkins UP, 1973)
asserts the idea that one can apply literary techniques of analysis to supposedly
neutral historiography.
30   Spiegel, *Romancing the Past: The Rise of Vernacular Prose Historiography in
Thirteenth-Century France* (University of California Press, 1993).
31   Marnette, *Narrateur et points de vue dans la littérature française médiévale. Une
approche linguistique* (Peter Lang, 1998).

primary source that required an authoritative and structuring voice in order to be incorporated into history writing.

These diaries, half-medieval and half-modern, are contradictions. Their authors present them simultaneously as histories of the Siege that perform the function of historical evidence *for studying* the Siege. As "histories," they are Romantic narrative accounts of a seminal moment in French history. As "history," they are documents intended for later analysis by other historians wishing to tell the whole story of the past event. This is due to the Siege's position as a turning point between two conceptions of history. In this light, these diarists' insistence on the present—"the present circumstances"—highlights the feeling that they existed and wrote at a seminal moment. However, more surprising than these diaries' double nature was their authors' complete indifference to reconciling documentation and narrative, a holdover from the calculated Romantic histories for which "the source of their truth or legitimacy does not come from outside but is constituted in the process of writing and making history (in both senses of that term)."[32] Their very ambivalence is refreshing when compared to the meta-historical musings of the Romantics and the cold manifestos of the *école méthodique*.

The diarists of 1870–1871 also showed less concern with what sorts of topics historians—even amateur ones—can write about. The positivist turn brought with it a disdain for writing histories of the present;[33] note that Seignobos and Langlois cited documentary evidence as necessary only in reconstructing a past so distant that its visible effects have already faded. Another historian, Gabriel Monod, specifically denied the possibility of histories of the present in his inaugural essay for the *Revue historique* in 1876, using the example of medieval chroniclers:

> Without a doubt the Middle Ages had among their chroniclers some remarkable writers such as Joinville, Villani, or Froissart, but they were not, strictly speaking, historians. Their subject was

---

32 Linda Orr, *Headless Histories: Nineteenth-Century Historiography of the Revolution* (Cornell UP, 1990), p. x.

33 A disdain now less pervasive in some historiographic cultures. See the establishment of the Institut d'histoire du temps présent, and books like Henry Rousso's *La Dernière catastrophe: l'histoire, le présent, le contemporain* (Gallimard, 2012).

the present not the past. They wanted to preserve for posterity the memory of the events that they saw and in which they participated rather than to retrace for their contemporaries a faithful image of older times. Their literary merit is found in life, in movement, in the passion that animates their stories, not in the art with which the work is composed, in the equal balance of its parts, in the impartiality of its judgments.[34]

Monod's distinction lay precisely in the subject matter of medieval chroniclers. They wrote about the present rather than the past, making them active participants in the history they were relating; they were too close to their subject to be objective. Siege diaries fell under this same category. Monod could easily have been writing about Chaumorot's text, which wants to "preserve for posterity the memory of the events that they saw" and functions like the "outpouring of a heart" as Chaumorot describes her letters.[35] Real historians, he says, write about the past in serious works organized by more scientific means than chronology.

Parisians were so conscious of the passage of time that newspapers as well as diarists began counting the days that had passed since the first day of the blockade. This way of ordering time, which could be called "siege time," differed from the standard calendar year. For one, siege time was measured linearly rather than cyclically. Unlike the seasons, which come, go, and return, the days behind the walls aligned together in a tireless march forward. Whereas one could count down to a certain date in a calendar year—the anticipation of Christmas or the new year, for example—siege time had no way of distinguishing one future date from another. The hundredth day of the Siege had no more significance than the thirtieth, the eighty-sixth, or any other day. Parisians experienced time without memory. They had no dates to refer to other than day one, the day siege time began. Chaumorot's diary begins, after her cover letter, with the day of the year and the inscription "86th day of blockade." Whereas our man in the *mairie* began his diary with the first day of blockade, Chaumorot, still conscious of the linear passing of siege time, began on an arbitrary

34   Monod, "Introduction. Du progrès des études historiques en France depuis le XVIe siècle," *Revue historique*, vol. 1 (1876), pp. 5–6.
35   Chaumorot, BHVP, Ms 1074, fol. 91.

date. This entry begins: "I can't continue like this, I have to speak with you."[36] This day, December 11, may have had special meaning for her, but the "eighty-sixth day of siege" carried no special significance, as it was without a past or a future: there has never been nor will there ever again be an eighty-sixth day of the Siege of Paris. Each day of the investment was unique because it will never happen again, and yet each day seemed meaningless. The juxtaposition of this arbitrary date and the sudden "outpouring" of Chaumorot's heart only serve to heighten the absurdity of siege time as a calendar not tailored to human experience. Hauréau lamented that there is "nothing more monotone than a diary under siege"[37] amid his descriptions of bombings, frost, news of battles, and of his own promotion to director of the Imprimerie nationale. Things certainly *happened* during the Siege, but the feeling of monotony remained.

The disturbing continuity of siege time was one symptom of living through a historical event as it unfolded. We can now look back to the Siege and count the days backwards, towards its end, but this is the privilege of historians. For the besieged, time was an arrow that began at a fixed point in the past and gestured vaguely beyond the present. This conception of time is very different than that of the Romantic or positivist historians but is very close to that of the medieval chroniclers so maligned by Monod.

Amateur Politics

The amateur historians who penned Siege diaries pushed against prevailing practices and attitudes that privileged one type of history over another: political over personal, military over meditative. Despite the fact that the field of history has become more willing to embrace multiple historical conceptions of historiography in the past several decades with the advent of women's studies, queer studies, and cultural history, texts like those of the authors present in this chapter still do not impact the way we imagine the history of history.

Who could write history in the nineteenth century, and what could

36   BHVP, Ms 1074, fol. 93.
37   BHVP, Ms 1113, fol. 45. Of course I disagree with his assessment of his writings.

they write about? In addressing this question, Bonnie Smith remarks that amateurism has long been associated with female historians who wrote about cultural, social, and domestic concerns, and maintains that this division still exists today:

> Female authors, with their ardent readership, disappear from historiography; far from informing history, they seem to clot it. Social and cultural history, especially when addressing women's concerns and issues of everyday life, come to have little value. No matter how much cachet social history may have had from time to time, politics and the men who write about it are the "meat and potatoes" of great history.[38]

Smith's book tells the story of a hidden set of authors who, on closer inspection, had not always been hidden. While she often relies on the well-known author Germaine de Staël, she shows that many other women historians of the nineteenth century were beloved by their readers and amassed a considerable number of them, too. Smith shows that, as the field became more professional (roughly corresponding to the move from Romanticism to the *école méthodique*), women became more marginalized since history was being done in male spaces like universities while women were associated with a domestic perspective. Amateurism had to define itself in contrast to professionalism, and so as the two gendered spheres separated, two distinct forms of history developed.

The historiography of the Siege and the Commune observed a similar dichotomy. Many of the famous histories of the year 1870–1871 share some commonalities with the type of professional historiography described by Smith. Maxime du Camp, perhaps now most famous for his friendship with Gustave Flaubert, wrote a multivolume history of the *année terrible*, entitled *Les Convulsions de Paris* (1878–1880), which was organized along two guiding principles: that the events of 1870–1871 were predominantly military and legislative, and that the Commune was the detestable result of disorganization under siege. Du Camp's narrative, which in part earned him a seat at the Académie française, has all the characteristics of a professional, state-centric history. He denounces besieged Parisians for allowing the

---

38 Smith, *The Gender of History*, pp. 70–71.

Commune to happen ("Paris lacked authority")[39] and the Commune for bringing shame to France. He reinforced bourgeois indignation over the reasons behind the Commune, and in doing so, defined it as a criminal aberration without any right to inscribe itself in the long history of French revolutions.[40] Du Camp was clearly writing from the perspective of the victor, one of the *amis de l'ordre* who opposed the Commune and had to find a way to use the Siege to explain it. His accounting of the Siege had to be political rather than personal, since the Commune was, in his telling, a direct response: lost battles, missed signals, resigned ministers, and storming of the *hôtel de ville*.

Du Camp employed language strikingly similar to the *école méthodique*, even if he was writing about an event that had recently ended. His concern for Langlois and Seignobos's *traces visibles* (visible traces) emerges in a passage on his search for documentary evidence:

> The large deposit of unpublished documents that could tell the history of the Commune is not yet open: in vain did I knock on its doors, which I believe will remain closed for a long time [...] The registries of military justice and criminal justice are closed: when the time comes to open them, we will find an anecdotal and moral history of the Commune that we cannot write today.[41]

Du Camp opposes his work to "anecdotal" history that might be written once the archives relative to daily life are released, but he stops short of defining his own history. The preface to the work guides the reader, especially his chosen epigraph, a quote from Pascal: "Violence follows a narrow path, whereas truth endures forever."[42] In his search for Pascal's "truth" he worked with the documents that *did* exist,

39   Du Camp, *Les Convulsions de Paris*, Vol. I (Paris: Hachette, 1881), p. 3.
40   Du Camp also inaugurated a long tradition of reading the Siege in light of the Commune, a perspective that tends to obscure the lived experience of the Siege which this book argues against.
41   Du Camp, *Les Convulsions de Paris*, p. iv.
42   Du Camp abbreviated the quotation, which he gives in the original French as "la violence n'a qu'un cours borné, au lieu que la vérité subsiste éternellement." Here is the original French, taken from Pascal's *Lettres provinciales*: "Qu'on ne prétende pas de là néanmoins que les choses soient égales: car il y a cette extrême différence, que la violence n'a qu'un cours borné par l'ordre de Dieu, qui en conduit les effets à la gloire de la vérité qu'elle attaque: au lieu que la vérité subsiste éternellement, et triomphe enfin de ses ennemis, parce qu'elle est éternelle et puissante comme Dieu même."

including other monographs—perhaps even some published diaries, considering their ubiquity in 1871–1872—to construct his history. The task was not simple. Du Camp felt that he needed to look beyond the emotive element of first-person accounts as they were not scientific, unbiased, or fair, as we are to assume his history will be. He writes that the *année terrible* was an event "that those who had the misfortune of witnessing [...] will never forget and that history will hardly understand."[43] His dichotomy between witnessing and understanding mirrors the split between chronicles and scientific history developed by the *école méthodique*: participating in an event precludes one from writing about it. While the Siege diarists may remember what happened, they were incapable of understanding it.

Du Camp, like Monod, Seignobos, and Langlois, considered historians like the Siege diarists to be too close to history to write it. The positivist claims of objectivity were based on the assumption that documents and testimony cannot lie, but they cannot tell the whole truth either. Du Camp was able to co-opt the history of the Siege into the history of the Commune precisely because he had written his account with hindsight. Furthermore, his insistence on the political over the personal gave his history the veneer of objectivity. Smith observes similar claims throughout the century and even today:

> [I]n an ironic twist, political history came to serve as a sign of neutrality, whereas other subfields (for example, cultural and economic history in the late nineteenth century, and today's labor, ethnic, and gender history) were interpreted as being "political" and thus biased.[44]

Smith uses "ironic" here to point out that political history has always been biased since it privileges male historians who have been trained by male-dominated institutions. While I certainly do not disagree with Smith's claims, I have tried in this chapter to point to other types of amateurism, also coded as feminine, but that were defined not by the training of their authors but by the types of truth claims those authors made. Not once did the diarists I present here worry about their methodology or make broad statements about the truth of history, unless it was to relinquish to others the task of writing a history "held

43   Du Camp, *Les Convulsions de Paris*, p. 2.
44   Smith, *The Gender of History*, p. 131.

together in a pure and elegant style" as Chaumorot defined it. Diarists wrote personal histories because they had lived through it, not because they lacked archival evidence like Du Camp.

Another "irony" of the positivists' claims to truth is that the political history written by professional historians like Du Camp tended towards a kind of nationalist presentism. By yoking the history of the Siege to the history of the Commune, bourgeois revisionism saw criminal revolution everywhere during the four months of the Prussian investment. Trying to find a reason for the events of the Commune, historians like Du Camp focused on the Siege government's failure to maintain order rather than on the Commune's failure to produce a lasting revolution. On the other hand, Siege diarists had no historical reason to explain the existing government since it was still subject to change: they had no idea what was going to happen to their Republic once the war was over. This lack of interest in causality created dynamic accounts of the Siege that vacillated from optimism to pessimism within the same page. Our man in the *mairie*, for example, had changed his mind on a number of issues by the time he finished writing, most notably about the movement for the Commune. On October 31, he wrote with the complacency of a man of his station about the overtaking of the *hôtel de ville* by revolutionaries calling for the dissolution of the government. When the National Guard managed to remove them, his judgment foreshadowed Du Camp's conservatism: "Thanks to the vigor of the men of the government of national defense, everything is restored to its original order."[45] However, for our man in the *mairie* as for many other diarists, political thinking had evolved by the end of the Siege and especially in the wake of the humiliating armistice signed by the *gouvernement de la défense nationale*. Even the most conservative of Parisians felt betrayed by the deal, especially those who had lost a loved one or had been destitute during the Siege. Their resistance to the enemy seemed to have been futile.

---

45   BHVP Ms 1073, fol. 46r. The word *ordre* came to be very charged by the end of the Commune. Thiers had once been a part of the *parti de l'ordre* under the Second Republic, a party composed of monarchists wishing for a return to "order"—that is, an escape from revolutionary insurrection. The *amis de l'ordre* (which I mention earlier in this chapter) were the group of Parisians who opposed the Commune in 1871. Even in the context of October 1870, it should be read as an indication of conservative, status quo politics.

By the end of January, our man in the *mairie* would have taken offense to the nickname I have been using to identify him, as he no longer supported the government he worked so hard to uphold even during the darkest times of the Siege. When insurrection began to foment in the popular neighborhood of Belleville, where food storage and hygiene standards were the lowest during the privations of the Siege, he sympathized: "But the revolutionaries of Belleville were right to want the Commune: the government is a traitor twice over. In accepting the revolution, we might have at least avoided this disaster."[46] Coming from the same pen that just months earlier had urged his fellow citizens to uphold the Siege government, this reversal points to the most striking of lessons these diaries could teach their readers: if history is a science of facts, the present is a laboratory where facts are partial, contradictory, or unreliable. For all of these Siege diarists, writing history meant negotiating truth rather than imposing it.

★   ★   ★

The type of history imagined by people like Chaumorot, Claretie, and our man in the *mairie* was also a product of the rising literacy rates of the nineteenth century, and specifically of the sophistication of the publishing industry that encouraged such writing. The emergence of these diaries owed as much to changing conceptions of historiography as it did to the publishing industry, which many diarists correctly anticipated would warmly receive personal accounts of the Siege in 1871 and beyond. These diaries reveal the unsteady détente between two schools of historians, but they also point to institutions of literary production. Many diaries were published simply because the public wanted to read them and their editors saw a profit to be made. There was an industry around publications about the Siege that was interested in less lofty goals than providing archival resources for future historians.

The majority of texts written and published during the Siege were more overtly rhetorical and patriotic than Siege diaries. Diaries expressed the loftier goals of Siege literature than, say, the militant revolutionary pamphlets discussed below in Chapter 7. Writing for *les*

---

46   BHVP, Ms 1073, fols. 153v–154r.

absents, Siege diarists rhetorically employed the human and experiential side of living in an unstable regime while foreign troops besieged the capital. However, rhetoric is still rhetoric: just as our man in the *mairie* saw his diary as a documentary snapshot of a period in time, he also saw it as an opportunity to expose his political beliefs, making history (by voting in the referendum, for example) at the same time he was writing it. Writing the present, these diarists also knew that they were living it, inscribing their contributions to besieged Paris into "the composition of this canvas, always being retouched but never finished, of which each century sketches a fragment and which is called history," as the diarist Loudun mused. Siege diarists turned an old adage on its head: instead of history being written by the victors, they became the victors by writing their own history. Since they were the only ones to witness the events of the Siege, they had a total monopoly on how it would be remembered.

Part IV

In Print

Chapter 7

De-Modernizing Publishing

Many Parisians wrote, read, and published as a form of patriotism, as resistance to the enemy, or simply to pass the time. But many others wanted to ensure the viability of the business of literature. The Société des gens de lettres, an author advocacy organization headquartered in the French capital, even applauded some consequences of the Siege, namely the complete freedom of the press announced by the government. When the members of the Société met on September 12, 1870, they wished that the "minutes show the satisfaction with which the Committee welcomes the decree rendered by the government relative to the freedom of the press and of the bookseller, a freedom that the Société has always demanded."[1] To read their monthly bulletin, which continued to be published during the Siege, is to watch an organization deal with the hardship of war without ever calling it a tragedy. Satisfied with their newfound freedom, the Central Committee of the Société decided to meet every day from 2 to 3 p.m.

They were eager to keep things moving smoothly. To celebrate the government shining its graces upon the industry the Société pledged to protect, its members offered an honorary position to Jules Favre, the vice president of the newly proclaimed Republic. This was as much to honor the politician as it was to keep the gears of their institution turning; many members of their executive committee had fled before the Prussians began the blockade, so they would have been eager for restaffing. In another sign of maintaining the status quo, the October edition of their bulletin ended with announcements of new publications:

---

1 *Chronique de la Société des gens de lettres*, October 1870.

a realist novel by Hector Malot, George Sand's sentimental *Malgrétout*, an historical novel by Ponson du Terrail. Nothing indicated that France was at war.

France was not just at war, but also on the edge of a political revolution, with many publications, politicians, and public intellectuals openly calling the new government a sham. The leaders of the Société, unable to remain apolitical, felt the need to explain the institution's lack of political engagement. In the November 1870 bulletin, members anonymously announced their neutrality in affirming that theirs was an organization "in which are grouped all opinions under the neutral flag of literary confraternity and free thought." Claiming institutional independence above the vagaries of politics, the Société did not want to prejudice itself. So-called neutrality prevailed to the point where the Société's bulletin often made no mention of the events that surrounded and engulfed it. But remaining apolitical, especially as a literary advocacy group, was a luxury only powerful institutions could afford.

The Société des gens de lettres acted like an institution, protecting the modern publishing industry that it had helped to create and that had created it. Despite its members' claims to the contrary, the Société had its own politics independent of the politics of the authors it aimed to support. It was concerned with the future of the French state but only insofar as that future state benefitted the well-being of the institution, so dependent on the status quo: the continual publishing of books, the functioning of the presses, the financial stability that only political stability could offer. The Société had been founded in 1838 to protect authors at a moment when publishing in France was very profitable and, increasingly throughout the nineteenth century, when authors had less influence over the production and dissemination of their works. Complex legal and social networks of editors, printers, authors, guilds, and syndicates had made publishing a more modern, collective, and structured endeavor. Publishing was an industry.

However, some institutions and individuals wanted to rock the boat, disrupting the modern literary industry and national politics in the process. This chapter details how fissures in the economic and regulatory structure of the publishing industry allowed for new, topical publications to emerge during the Siege. The next chapter dives into these publications not as products of historical systems but as literary texts. The new freedom of the press and of booksellers expressed itself as an explosion of these new non-periodical works and new printers in the city, finally able to publish without fear of censorship or without the burden of costly start-up permits from the government. Small printing presses began churning out new books and pamphlets written by the besieged, for the besieged; turning away from established authors like George Sand whom the Société protected, these new printers instead published engaged texts like political manifestos, first-hand accounts of fighting on the ramparts of the city, and patriotic poetry written by soldiers. Books appeared constantly, emerging as if "from the street" itself, as one historian wrote in 1874.[2] The bestseller of the Siege, Victor Hugo's anti-Napoleonic poetry collection *Les Chatîments*, sold more than twenty thousand copies—so many that his official printer, Claye, ran out of coal to run his presses. Smaller, upstart printers were happy to print more copies without the approval of the government, the Société, or Hugo. The Société actively tried to suppress these illicit copies, what they saw as literary misdemeanors, threatening to bring legal complaints against underground printers and newspapers that failed to cite the names of authors whose texts they published.[3] Outside of the walls, there was a war between France and Prussia; inside, there was another between traditional literary industries and the cottage industries born of the freedoms of the Siege.

The bureaucracy and administration of modern publishing, the very economic structures that made publishing so profitable, provided the greatest obstacle to the publication of books during the Siege. Readers demanded books about their present situation as quickly as possible. Modern publishing could not keep up. To satisfy this demand, smaller printers began producing books in basements, courtyards, and homes, sidestepping the complicated publishing practices inherent to the modern industry. To remain relevant during the Siege, the publishing industry had to de-modernize.

As the traditional publishing industry was slow to change and unwilling to abandon the economic and material machinery of publishing, new presses, publishers, and authors jumped at the opportunity to create a grassroots and nimble cottage industry of works that, written and published quickly, spoke to the present moment. Despite the competing interests of these two groups of publishers—the

2   Firmin Maillard, *Les Publications de la rue pendant le siège et la Commune: satires, canards, complaintes, chansons, placards et pamphlets* (Paris: Aubry, 1874).
3   *Chronique de la Société des gens de lettres*, October 1870.

established and the improvisational—everyone associated with the business of books believed that literature was the foundation of a new republic. The slow bureaucratic entrenchment of established institutions and the emergence of a small-scale basement industry were two responses to the unavoidable conclusion that, during the Siege, producing literature was a political act motivated by profit.

The Rules of Modern Publishing

The November edition of the bulletin of the Société des gens de lettres reproduced some decrees of the provisional government. First, the government decreed the professions of printer and of bookseller to be *free*, or not subject to governmental or regulatory approval. This was an extraordinarily broad and radical deregulation of an industry that had been the center of considerable debate with ferocious lobbying on either side. The government's opening up of these professions amounted to a win for those with liberal tendencies who considered regulation tantamount to political censorship. According to these decrees, anyone wishing to become a printer or a bookseller simply had to declare themselves as such to the Ministry of the Interior. Anytime a book was printed, it had to bear the name of the printer and it had to be registered at the *dépôt légal*, a register which indicated the author, *éditeur*, printer, page count, and print run of every book published in France and whose use the provisional government of the Siege carried over from the Second Empire.[4] But even these two modest regulations would not have had much effect: it would have been difficult to enforce such policies during a siege, even if all entries in the *dépôt légal* included the name of a printer.

This register lists roughly eight hundred and sixty non-periodical publications between September 1870 and January 1871. Nearly one hundred and sixty of these were specifically about the Siege, the new Republic, or the war, or took these circumstances as their explicit or implicit context for publication. These included shorter texts like tracts, slim nonfiction histories, poetry, political tirades, and textual speeches. Some of these were republications of much older texts (like

---

4   The Introduction explains the process of official record keeping of all books published in France.

the *Déclarations des droits de l'homme*) while others were necessarily written during recent events (like the narrative account *Un mois dans les lignes Prussiennes*). Other publications took a more practical perspective on the Siege, offering advice on cooking under blockade (*La Cuisinière assiégée* or *La Cuisine pendant le siège*), relating official reports (*Report of the Universal Israelite Alliance*, in English), or institutional proceedings (*Thèses présentées à la faculté de Science de Paris*). However, the *dépôt légal* shows that even if Parisians and their publishers understood that the Siege was a momentous occasion, the vast majority of published books seemed uninterested in the importance of the moment. Publishers' timetables knew neither famine nor regime change.

The publishing industry was caught between institutional inertia and the impetus of current events. Throughout the nineteenth century, the publishing industry had grown immensely, and in order to achieve this fantastic growth had become somewhat inflexible, meaning that the majority of books published during the Siege were published *despite* rather than because of current events, but represented the fruit of likely months or years of collaboration between *éditeurs*, authors, printers, and booksellers. The nineteenth century saw the term *éditeur* take on its "modern understanding," as a distinct professional figure emerged,[5] acting as a sort of literary entrepreneur: the *éditeur* was the gateway to the world of publishing, acting as a talent scout for authors, a financial backer for publication costs, a contract negotiator between printers and authors. In assuming the risks associated with publications, *éditeurs* also stood to gain enormous profits. To do so, they relied on their intimate knowledge of presses, of contract and press laws, and of the tastes of the expanding reading public. However, these bodies of knowledge meant little during the Siege. Given the impossibility of assuring prompt publication of books, the financial uncertainty of the country, and the reading public's abrupt interest in all things Siege-related, the modern *éditeur* no longer had much of a role to play in the economics

5   Odile and Henri-Jean Martin, "Le Monde des éditeurs," in *Histoire de l'édition française*, Vol. 3, edited by Roger Chartier and Henri-Jean Martin (Fayard, 1990), p. 176. The entirety of the third tome of this series, entitled "Le Temps des éditeurs," points to the seminal role that *éditeurs* acquired over the century in the increasing accessibility of published literature. I follow Christine Haynes's practice of maintaining the French word *éditeur*, which could be translated as "publisher." See Haynes's *Lost Illusions: The Politics of Publishing in Nineteenth-Century France* (Harvard UP, 2010).

of publishing.[6] There were other competing interests at stake. On the one hand, the Société des gens de lettres had been establishing itself as a vital author advocacy group, protecting intellectual property rights and contractual agreements and assuring the proper, long-term functioning of the literary industry. Other groups, like the Cercle de la librairie, "organized by and for publishers,"[7] lobbied the government on behalf of business interests. In fact, throughout the nineteenth century many of these potentially adversarial groups found common ground to resist an even more ominous enemy: the government. Authors and *éditeurs* formed a sort of "solidarity" due to the fact that any infringement on the regulatory and legal framework established by the government led to punishment of both parties.[8] The publishing world was so enmeshed in bureaucratic and legal frameworks and so preoccupied with competing factions that it responded slowly and poorly to external forces like the Siege.

The Siege upended the delicate balance of the publishing world. The Revolution of 1789 had thrown open the doors to what had previously been a tightly regulated profession, leading to a century-long divide between "two camps: one nostalgic for the Old Regime and the other committed to revolutionary liberalism."[9] The Siege effectively reversed the positions of these groups, as those who had previously lobbied for less regulation of the literary market now grew anxious to return to a legal system that ensured contractual relationships between *éditeurs*, authors, and printers. The margins of the publishing world, the illegal and unregulated side of literature, had taken advantage of the chaos of regime change. As the Siege wore on, many of the more timely publications revealed themselves to be work the work of direct, unmediated collaboration between author and printer, thus eliding

6   For the legal and social place of the *éditeur* and printer in the nineteenth-century publishing, see Haynes's *Lost Illusions* and the work of Robert Darnton, especially Robert Darnton and Daniel Roche, editors, *Revolution in Print: The Press in France 1775–1800* (University of California Press, 1989), and Jean-Yves Mollier's *L'Argent et les lettres. Histoire du capitalisme d'édition* (Fayard, 1988).

7   Haynes, *Lost Illusions*, p. 120. Haynes's devotes a chapter to this publishers' advocacy group.

8   Christophe Charle, "Le Champ de la production littéraire," in *Histoire de l'édition française*, Vol. III: *le temps des éditeurs*, edited by Roger Chartier and Henri-Jean Martin (Fayard, 1990), p. 132.

9   Haynes, *Lost Illusions*, p. 49.

the burdensome requirements that came with publishing through a more established and respectable *éditeur*, now rendered unnecessary by the near complete deregulation of the industry. As an example of this pseudo-black market approach: many of the books published during the Siege were produced at the expense of the author rather than that of a speculative *éditeur*.

Backyard Printers

During the Siege, most printers had complete autonomy in what they could publish, due in part to the softening of publishing regulations, but mostly because the provisional government was too busy to enforce the few regulations that were left. On the other hand, Paris had a surprising lack of printing presses given its highly literate market, meaning it was no longer fear of censorship or regulation that limited publishing; it was the dearth of available printing resources. This meant that the most productive areas of publication were in the formerly sleepy parts of the industry: those tiny printers and the authors who had relationships with them. This led to a grassroots reorientation of the market, away from large-scale printers and towards small, politically active ones. Gisèle Sapiro has reached similar conclusions about literature produced in the period around World War II and the Occupation: writers' politics meant less for overall output than did the ideologies of institutions, whose "more or less marked propensity to respond to external demand must be understood within their histories and their means of survival."[10] Books did not appear *ex nihilo*, but rather as a function of changing sociological and economic forces.

Parisian printers and printing presses were suddenly much more important than before the blockade. As Frédéric Barbier has written,[11] Paris was just too small to accommodate large printing workshops, which by the mid-nineteenth century had come to rely on cumbersome but efficient steam-powered presses. As a result, Paris only housed roughly 7 percent of France's total printers in 1879. When the Prussians

---

10   Sapiro, *La Guerre des écrivains* (Fayard, 1999), p. 255.
11   Barbier, "Les Imprimeurs," in *Histoire de l'édition française*, Vol. III: *le temps des éditeurs*, edited by Roger Chartier and Henri-Jean Martin (Fayard, 1990), pp 69–89.

cut off the capital, they deprived *éditeurs* of their regional distribution networks as well as the very means of production: the presses. The *éditeur* Pierre-Jules Hetzel managed to print a small number of Hugo's *Napoléon le petit* at his company workshop on 18 rue Jacob,[12] but the majority of copies came from the Jules Claye presses, an impressive facility at 5–7 rue Saint-Benoît that had also been printing *Les Châtiments*, along with many other publications. Claye had become one of the largest Parisian printers during the Second Empire[13] and could handle the demand for Parisian books during the Siege. The lack of printing options must have frustrated more than just *éditeurs*: the *dépôt légal* becomes a long list of repetitive printers: Berthélémy, Claye, Chaix, Dubuisson, Paul Dupont, and Seringe dominate the register as the largest operating at the time in Paris. While many of these employed steam-powered presses within Paris, the blockade presented other difficulties. Coal, their primary power source, was a limited commodity. As Hetzel noted in December 1870, "Lacking coal to power the steam presses, the shuttering of presses is imminent."[14] Despite his fears, the lack of coal did not greatly affect these printers. Overall numbers of publications actually increased in December 1870 and January 1871.

Besides the large printers, many of those that were active during the Siege were very small and specialized in niche material, many of them having arisen in the more lax, later years of the Second Empire when publishing political pamphlets became less dangerous.[15] For example, by 1868 the longstanding printer Gaittet had become the haunt of many radical republicans who later participated in the Commune. One such figure, Maxime Vuillaume, described the printing workshop and its owner, which in 1870 was a woman known as "Mother Gaittet":

12   There were other *imprimeurs-éditeurs* that managed to operate their Parisian workshops during the Siege, the most prolific being perhaps Damase Jouaust.

13   Mollier describes (*L'Argent et les lettres*, pp. 151–168) how Hetzel and the former Claye printing workshop had almost exclusive rights to Hugo's work in the 1880s.

14   As reported by Hugo on December 19 in his diary published as *Choses vues* (Gallimard, 2002).

15   Philip Nord has shown, in *The Republican Moment* (Harvard UP, 1995), that growing republicanism in the late Second Empire did much to solidify the later legitimacy of the Third Republic.

I can still see [...] the cobblestone courtyard covered with all sorts of equipment, hand carts, outdated furniture and tools. In a corner, a little boutique stuffed with printed papers, behind which a cobbler pounded on shoes. Through a gray door, there was the printing press, where the owner quickly arrived, a tall, graying woman eternally wearing a bluish fustian dress, et perpetually followed by a large jaundiced greyhound, its snout thinning in old age.[16]

From this dark print shop emerged a number of publications during the Siege, notably pamphlets like *Faut-il pendre les propriétaires?* and the newspaper *Le Père Duchêne*, modeled after the ribald Cordelier and first appearing in 1790 during the Revolution.[17] During the Siege, political presses like that of Mother Gaittet profited from the restricted number of Parisian printers and the almost nonexistent regulation of printing presses[18] insofar as they suddenly produced a sizeable portion of Parisian print market.

Some printers, emboldened by their newfound freedoms, extended their political influence during the Siege. Formerly a printer, then director of the Papeteries d'Essonnes, then a wholesale paper merchant in Paris,[19] Amédée Gratiot was elected the inaugural president of the Comité central des fabricants de papier in August 1864,[20] but during the Siege he was best known as the author of four pamphlets, eventually entitled *Les Petits livres du siège*,[21] that ranged from imagined dialogues

16   Vuillaume, *Mes cahiers rouges pendant la Commune* (Paris: Ollendorf, 1909), p. 100.
17   Vuillaume eventually took over the publication of this newspaper during the Commune.
18   The French have long tightly regulated printing presses, requiring them to attach their name to everything they produce—still a near universal requirement today. Fees levied in punishment for flaunting these laws have been high in France: In 1850, Auguste Garnier was fined 2,000 francs for forgetting to attach his name to a *brochure* (Martin and Martin, "Le monde des éditeurs," p. 169). However, the Siege government gave complete freedom to presses and *libraires*, meaning that they would escape such strict scrutiny. Some took advantage: the *dépôt légal* lists fifteen publications with no indication of who printed them.
19   Nécrologie, *Le Moniteur de la papeterie française*, June 1, 1881.
20   *Le Moniteur de la papeterie française*, October 15, 1864.
21   First published in *Le Figaro*, then published by the Librairie nouvelle as separate brochures in 1870, their titles being: "Peau neuve," "La nuit du

on the ramparts, "fantasies"[22] that fictionalize supposedly true events, and a letter to Queen Victoria chastising her for not coming to France's aid. The newspaper *La Liberté* remarks that the small-format books do not present themselves as escapist literature: "It is a time of war and not of reading, but it is fair to make an exception for the two pamphlets, completely topical, published by M. Amédée Gratiot."[23] In *Peau neuve*, Gratiot engages in a type of bland political rhetoric that espoused republicanism but stopped short of revolutionary sentiment. A dialogue between two unidentified characters, one a civilian, one a soldier, their exchange is prefaced with a simple situational note: "Along the ramparts, September 21, 1870." The dialogue is Socratic, one character asking questions of the other in order to interrogate his logic. The two topics these characters explore are the enemy outside the gates and the internal political divisions that threaten the nation. The natural conclusion to their debate, like most other republican-leaning literature during the Siege, is that only a republican government is capable of uniting warring parties and defeating the Prussians. More of a simple declaration of solidarity than an endorsement of the current composition of the government, this form of republicanism argued that the best form of government is one that defends against the Prussians. What results is a poetry for the ramparts.

Pamphlets like *Peau neuve* failed to see beyond the blockade, a representational limitation that mirrored their political conservatism. Any expression of the future of the French nation fell into ambiguity. After a long digression on the historical moments of French republicanism and how they differ one from another, one character asks the other how France is to discover the one, true Republic whose iterations have ended in despotism and defeat. Can the new government simply suppress their monarchist, Bonapartist, legitimist, and bourgeois adversaries in order to build that ideal state?

> "So then, we must discard, in one fell swoop, the current generation that is defiant against the Republic?"
> "No."
> "Then what do we do?"

6 novembre," "Le Châtiment d'Angleterre," and then after the Commune, "La Carte à payer."
22   "La Nuit du 6 Novembre," *Le Figaro*, November 14, 1870.
23   *La Liberté*, December 13, 1870.

"Shed our skin [*faire peau neuve*]."[24]

Gratiot was suggesting the impossible. How could France simply shake off a century of political traditions, of bitter disagreement, and of foundational revolutions, republican and otherwise? The argument behind this claim seems to imply that the only way France can move forward is to renounce its own history and "faire peau neuve"—start over again completely, just as an insect sheds its skin in order to grow. Whether or not Gratiot's central premise is practical, however, does not affect the way in which he formulated it, and the means by which he hoped to arrive at his goal: no matter which type of government France needed, only a certain type of engaged literature could argue for it during the Siege. His argument meant less than did the conditions behind the pamphlet's production, its humble origins a guarantee of its status as grassroots literature.

Gratiot was cautious in his political pamphlets.[25] Other small printers ran afoul of the authorities. Since around 1864, Gustave Georges Balitout had operated a small-scale press on rue Baillif. Before the Siege, this printer produced around forty small publications per year of around forty pages apiece. During the Siege, Balitout printed items such as a six-page pamphlet containing a patriotic poem by Pitre Merlaud;[26] a revolutionary newspaper called *La Défense nationale*, a daily publication edited by the future encyclopedist Jules Trousset that only produced one issue; and Maurice Joly's "Speech on the Commune of Paris." Balitout's most famous publication, however, is most likely the first version of *Les Chants de Maldoror*, the poetic novel of the Count of Lautréamont that appeared anonymously in 1868 and later inspired the surrealists. In April and June of 1870, Lautréamont published two books of poetry, *Poésies I* and *II* with Balitout, before the poet's death on November 24, 1870. Balitout's most infamous publication, however, was a short pamphlet by Félix Pyat entitled "Les Soldats"

---

24   Amédée Gratiot, *Peau neuve* (Paris: Librairie nouvelle, 1870), pp. 17–18.
25   Gratiot was later accused of supplying paper to the *communard* leader Raoul Rigault, a charge he adamantly rejected, claiming that "at that time I was resolved not to give any paper to any publication," as reported in *Le Pays* of August 19, 1871. It is unclear but likely that he had stockpiles of paper during the Siege.
26   Also known as the judge Pierre Mathurin Merlaud, who gave his name to a street in Angers.

that encouraged all of France's armed forces to lay down their arms. Two thousand copies of the pamphlet were distributed among soldiers in Paris before Pyat and Balitout were caught and sentenced to short prison sentences, four months and fifteen days, respectively.[27]

The liberal turn of the Second Empire had allowed for a slight growth in specialized Parisian printing. The law of May 11, 1868 is most often cited as the point at which the Second Empire relinquished repressive control of political content in newspapers, giving rise to pamphlet-makers like Gaittet and emboldening those like Balitout. However, this law also allowed newspapers to establish their own printing presses for their exclusive use. Unbeknownst to those dailies that took advantage of this, having one's own Parisian press amounted to a necessary fact of survival during the Siege. These presses essentially stuck to their purview of publishing their own papers, only branching out in rare cases: *Le Soir* published a translation of Benjamin Disraeli's *Lothair* on November 23, *Le Figaro* published Octave Féré's *Le Dernier criminel* in a single volume on October 15, and *Le Siècle* published the *La Double vue* by Elie Berthet on October 18. None of these publications were topical to the Siege or the war. Newspapers owned the rights to the works they were publishing as standalone books, since all of these titles had already appeared in serial form in their pages.

Other Parisian presses were attached to municipal or governmental entities. Édouard Vert, for example, was the official printer of the third *arrondissement*'s City Hall, but during the Siege he published more than municipal edicts, delving into paid publicity with the *Echo des concerts parisiens* and into patriotic publications like the *Almanach chantant de la garde nationale*, a collection of "unpublished patriotic songs by the citizens A. Philibert and Hip. Chatelin, dedicated to the noble defenders of Paris."[28] On the other hand the former Imprimerie impériale, quickly rebaptized the Imprimerie *nationale*, was a large operation, counting

---

27　Fernand Drujon, *Catalogue des ouvrages, écrits, et dessins poursuivis, supprimés ou condamnés depuis le 21 octobre 1814 jusqu'au 31 juillet 1877* (Paris: Rouveyre, 1879), p. 363.

28　Philibert and Chatelin, *Almanach chantant de la garde nationale* (Imprimerie Vert, 1871), cited in Maillard, *Publications de la rue pendant le siège et la Commune*, p. 5.

some nine hundred employees and mostly producing posters for the *gouvernement de la défense nationale.*[29]

Despite its ownership of municipal presses, the government had little impact on publishing during the Siege. Christine Haynes notes that, given its republican and liberalist leanings, the new government's "move to free the book trade from the licensing requirement is not surprising," and that those who spearheaded the policy claimed to be motived by "a concern for national defense."[30] While the abolishment of the licensing requirement had a significant impact in the later years of the Third Republic, it made virtually no impact on publishing during the Siege since there was simply not enough time to obtain the printing machinery or the physical space required to operate as a printer or bookdealer and take advantage of the newly open market. The only effect this law could have had for national defense was to rid the government of the prospect of paying a civil servant to administrate the issuing of these licenses.

With the *éditeur* relegated to the margins of the industry, the publication practices of the Siege resembled those of the late eighteenth and early nineteenth centuries, but now without government regulation. Authors contacted presses directly or went through the intermediary of the *libraire* or bookseller who then arranged for printing. When an ex-*zouave*[31] of the 1st Regiment wrote a diatribe against Napoléon III, he took just such a route to see his pamphlet published: *Le Lâche de Sedan* was published by the bookseller Lefranc, 10 rue des Poissonniers, and printed by the Association typographique of Berthélémy and Company, one of the larger Parisian printers alongside Claye and Dupont. When the polemical pamphleteer known as "Le citoyen Vindex" (Citizen Vindex) began publishing his salacious accounts of the Bonaparte family,[32] he was aided by the Librairie Martinon at 14 rue Jean-Jacques-Rousseau, near the Palais

---

29   Gwladys Longeard has written a very thorough history of the Imprimerie nationale during the Siege and the Commune: "L'Imprimerie nationale pendant la Commune de 1871," *Revue d'histoire moderne et contemporaine*, vol. 1, no. 52, 2005, pp. 147–174. The director of the new national presses was Barthélémy Hauréau, whose letters I study in Chapters 5 and 6.

30   Haynes, *Lost Illusions*, p. 227.

31   The *zouaves* were members of certain light infantry regiments serving in North Africa, known for their orientalist uniforms.

32   I will discuss Vindex's texts in Chapter 8.

Royal, the early nineteenth-century hub for bookshops and *cabinets de lecture*.[33] Once the Siege had stripped the *éditeur* of his power, authors reverted back to the practices of the early century, publishing directly with small-scale *libraires-éditeurs* or with printers.

If *éditeurs* such as Hetzel, Hachette, and Charpentier did little to affect publishing, the Société des gens de lettres still wielded power, given its role in influencing public policy and *éditeurs* large and small. However, this power came more from its cultural visibility and less from its ability to adapt their lobbying practices to the crisis. As an author advocacy group, the Société argued that *éditeurs* had to honor current contracts with authors before they looked for new opportunities, contributing in large part to the publication of works during the Siege that included such seemingly incongruous titles as *Synthèses de pharmacie et de chimie* or *Les Géants de la mer*, a history of whaling. The Société pressured *éditeurs* to ensure a regular market for authors even at a moment when it made more financial sense to capitalize on the growing interest in publications about the Siege.

The Société des gens de lettres participated in the business of publishing during the Siege in much more visible ways than did printers and booksellers. The Société's institutional means of survival was that of an advocacy group for authors, and as such it promoted policies that kept authors' livelihoods the most regular. This often put its members on the offensive against printers who wished to publish new texts to capitalize on the sudden demand for Siege literature. On the other hand, the Société also had some of its own cash flow problems: in November 1870, it essentially stepped away from the publishing industry when it ceased paying out advances for original works or printers' fees for authors. Previously, this type of financing had put the institution in the market position of an *éditeur*, making financial decisions about investing in certain authors and books in the hopes of recuperating costs. But its departure from the business of publishing did not mean it was leaving authors out in the cold. The bulletin stated that the money the Société saved would be put to good

33   For more on the Palais Royal's importance for early nineteenth-century reading practices, see Claude Pichois, "Les Cabinets de lecture à Paris, durant la première moitié du XIXe siècle," in *Annales*, vol. 14, no. 3, 1959, pp. 521–534. Balzac lampooned the bookseller's outsized role in determining literary success in his novel *Illusions perdues*.

use, as advances to established authors in financial need: "all of our resources [must] be reserved to respond to requests for urgent help,"[34] the bulletin declared, participating in the general push towards charity that prevailed in the capital.[35] Not only was the Société bailing out authors who had a hard time placing articles or publishing already written books, the organization also chastised newspapers for printing "passages of news articles or letters from the theater of war without mentioning the name of their authors," and threatened legal action for those who continued to ignore their responsibility. Every month, its bi-monthly periodical announced a list of "new publications," which never included the types of circumstance-specific literature that abounded during the Siege, promoting titles like *Souvenirs d'un hirondelle, Eucharis,* and *Le Secret de Gilbert.* Its main mission was to ensure the payment of current contractual relationships between *éditeurs* and authors at the expense of new titles that may have been more profitable.

The most consistent genres of publications that sidestepped *éditeurs* were political pamphlets and poetry written by soldiers (or at least presented as having been written by soldiers) and by ordinary Parisians. Poetry generally appeared in individual published poems rather than in collections in order to get texts out into the public as fast as possible, leading to very slim pamphlets of two to fifteen pages in general. Many of these poems, unsurprisingly, read as pastiches of Hugo's *Les Châtiments,* an obvious bid to capitalize on its success. This is why we see titles reminiscent of Hugo's prophetic and denunciating style, like *Le Lâche de Sedan,*[36] *La Délivrance,*[37] *Rêves et vérités,*[38] produced by small-scale Parisian printers. Other poets intended to raise morale within the city, publishing poems with titles like "L'Avenir,"[39] "L'Heure suprême,"[40] as

---

34 *La Chronique de la Société des gens de lettres,* November 1870, p. 1.
35 Theaters, for example, converted their spaces into makeshift hospitals, and when they finally began performing again, donated much of their proceeds to the founding of cannons. See Chapter 1 for more.
36 Édouard Daner, *Le Lâche de Sedan: à Louis-Napoléon Bonaparte* (Paris: Lefranc, October 31, 1870).
37 J.-B. Davanne, *La Délivrance* (Paris: J. Rigal, November 21, 1870).
38 Alfred Cauvet, *Rêves et vérités* (Paris: Lacroix, December 29, 1870).
39 August Roussel, *L'Avenir: poésie* (Paris: Claye, September 26, 1870).
40 Dreux, *L'Heure suprême. Actualité, scène dramatique, au théâtre des Menus-Plaisirs, le 24 novembre 1870* (Paris: Chez l'auteur, December 27, 1870).

a sort of call to arms. Others were more prescient, looking to Alsace and its Franco-German culture as a symbolic space to represent this war between neighbors. However, all of these poems shared a common appeal to Parisian resistance, to French glory, and, most importantly, to shared lived experience. Poems appeared in cheap volumes, were recited on stage, and were often reprinted in newspapers. They wielded the populist power to flow within institutional networks. Poems such as Émile Bergerat's "Les Cuirassiers de Reichshoffen"[41] did not merely exist on the printed page; they had a long afterlife as the subject of other poems, as spectacular panoramas, set to music and sung in clubs, contributing in general to the legend of Parisian suffering and heroism. This poetry was not necessarily valued for the quality of its composition or its style, but instead for its potential to be reproduced, reprinted, and reused elsewhere. In other words, these poems were meant to be ephemeral.

Many soldiers who found themselves with little to do during their long, uneventful stations on the ramparts began to write amateur poetry. The first example of this dates from November 2: "Le Chant de réveil" written by Jules Bailly, "sous-lieutenant à la 5ᵉ compagnie du 60ᵉ bataillion." Bailly made no pretense to professionalism. The poem is prefaced with the indication "air à faire" (musical accompaniment to be written)—meaning he had not yet found suitable music to accompany his verses, or, more likely, that he merely intended others to set it to music. The poem itself is less than thrilling:

> Peoples, wake up! It's a new era!
> The age of tyrants is going to end:
> Liberty rises up and her voice calls you
> Her finger points to the future!
> Look! The east changes color
> To a purple and brilliant clarity.
> Alert! On your feet! It's the dawn
> Of the great day of Liberty![42]

The reader should have the vague impression that "the tyrants" in question are Napoléon III, Bismarck, and King Wilhelm of Prussia, but mostly through Hugolian intertext. The poet felt that the invocation of

---

41   Bergerat, *Les Cuirassiers de Reichshoffen* (Paris: Lemerre, November 8, 1870).
42   Bailly, *Le Chant de réveil* (Paris: Parent, 1870).

some sort of tyranny trumped the identifications of those tyrants. The "day of Liberty" could either be the proclamation of the Republic or the day Paris might defeat the Prussians—most likely the latter, given the poet's occupation. The more specific the poem was, the less likely it would become a hit. The poet's vague references made it easy for others to impose their own beliefs onto his words. Bailly wanted his text to become a sort of anthem to raise morale: the best way to accomplish this was to avoid specificity, but also to indicate that his verses could be sung while soldiers idled at their posts on the ramparts.

Poems often became songs during the Siege and vice versa, continuing a generic commonplace during the revolutionary nineteenth century. The "Marseillaise" was the gold standard to which all other patriotic chants aspired. This patriotic hymn often spontaneously broke out during other performances at the Comédie-Française and elsewhere when spectacles included other patriotic anthems like many of these Siege poems. As an example, the newspaper *L'Ami de la France*, written for the scores of foreigners living in Paris, published a poem set to the tune of "La Marseillaise":

> Nous, étrangers par la naissance,
> Mais les enfants par notre cœur,
> Nous accourons à ta défense
> Brave France! en voyant ton malheur
> Prêts à donner tous notre vie
> Pour repousser l'envahisseur:
> Nous combattrons avec ardeur
> Sous ton drapeau, France chérie!

> [We, foreigners by birth,
> But children in our hearts,
> We run to your defense
> Brave France! Upon seeing your misfortune
> Ready to give our lives
> To push out the invader:
> We will fight fervently
> Under your flag, dear France!][43]

---

43 Jules D'Herpent, "Chant des amis de la France," *L'Ami de la France*, November 19, 1870. I have included the original French to show the cadence of the "Marseillaise."

A poet's surest way to expose as many people as possible to his or her verse was to set it to a popular tune such as the "Marseillaise." As a result of this generic slippage from poetry to song, the publication history of most Siege verse must be understood in the context of their performance on stage, in clubs, and among soldiers. Even those poems that were not set to music were recited on stage. François Coppée's soldier poem *Lettre d'un mobile breton*[44] was performed twice before its publication, meaning that by the time it appeared in print, many readers had already heard it. Eager to participate in the immediate literature of the Siege, theaters were complicit in what the Société des gens de lettres saw as the erosion of authors' rights.

Public Relations

The Société may have intervened often in public debates, such as the co-organization of the reading of *Les Châtiments* at the Paris Opéra[45] with the goal of raising money to forge a cannon, but this public engagement only served to underscore the importance of economic stability for authors in urgent circumstances. The organization's interest in founding cannons, performing Hugo, and lobbying the government for more freedoms for printers, authors, and *éditeurs* certainly did contribute to republican-coded causes, such as resistance to the enemy and open public debate. However, the spontaneous generation of republican revolutionary gusto was not the result of the Société's politics, but instead a symptom of its institutional entrenchment. Its members participated in the war effort as a way to further the interests of their institution, lauding the liberalization of their industry while simultaneously resisting the orientation towards anonymous and small-scale publishing that tended to favor more revolutionary practices.

The Société was not the only association that navigated the Siege according to institutional logic. As an advocacy group for the publishing industry, the Cercle de la librairie continued to produce its *Bibliographie de la France* throughout the Siege, cataloguing the books that had been submitted to the Ministry of the Interior's *dépôt légal*. This bibliography usually carried with it a *chronique*, offering reports on governmental

44   Coppée, *Lettre d'un mobile breton* (Paris: Lemerre, November 25, 1870).
45   An event I describe in Chapter 2.

sessions and decrees relative to the industry. By December 10, 1870, the Siege had rendered this type of journalism too burdensome. In its "Nécrologie" ("Obituaries") section—which had come to dominate the *chronique* for the first few weeks of military investment of the city—the Cercle shows how the conditions of the Siege had had little effect on their institutional mission of "solidifying the moral community of the book trade" through such obituaries:[46]

> In the middle of the painful events that for the past four months our country has suffered without destroying its faith, literature and the bookselling trade have felt the blow of public tragedies. Our bibliographic review has suspended its weekly publicity for a few weeks, and various branches of literature, science, and law have suffered tangible losses and would pass into oblivion if the *Journal de la librairie*, always loyal to the memory of the deceased, did not pay its regular respects in recalling the principal works they have authored.[47]

Equal insistence is given to those whom the trade has lost and the Cercle's mission of paying its respects to the deceased. There is even a certain pride in the aside that the corporation has "always" done so, signaling that the "painful events" of the Siege cannot extinguish the institution's commitment to its values. This type of engagement with the war effort did double duty as civic service and institutional publicity. The Société des gens de lettres began fundraising efforts that flowed from its institutional mission, such as charity readings of poetry. The Cercle de la librairie set up a book drive for wounded soldiers, which certainly did represent a civic intervention, but might also have resulted in more books being bought and published. According to the activities and rhetoric of such literary associations, human tragedies called for institutional responses.

Book drives were common, most usually at the instigation of *éditeurs* or advocates within the industry. The Cercle had its own subscription, which—to be fair—was primarily addressed to *éditeurs* and authors to donate books for wounded soldiers and civilians. The Cercle claimed that its members "want to do this quickly, convinced that each of us

---

46   Haynes, *Lost Illusions*, p. 136.
47   E.B., "Nécrologie" ("Chronique"), *Bibliographie de la France: ou Journal général de l'imprimerie et de la librairie*, December 10, 1870, p. 166.

would like to contribute to giving some distraction to our soldiers during their long stays in our hospitals."[48] Before the blockade shut down transit in and out of the city, the Cercle even collected books to be sent to Berlin for the benefit of French prisoners of war, a proposal suggested by the German jurist and professor Baron Franz von Holtzendorff, who intended for such prisoners to have "a good bit of French reading, both consoling and instructive," suggesting that it would be a "pleasure for these prisoners to stay in intellectual contact with their country."[49] Parisian newspapers seconded the Cercle's efforts by reprinting the request for books both used and new. By December 10, three thousand five hundred books had arrived at the central collection depository located at the presses of Napoléon Chaix and Company, 20 rue Bergère, but it remains unclear how the besieged Cercle intended to get these books to Berlin. General charity for the wounded of Paris fared much better, collecting 24,805 books for distribution within the city.[50]

Other successful charities strengthened ties between authors, printers, and *éditeurs*. In July 1870, Lieutenant Colonel Ferdinand Staaff published the last tome of a long series of pedagogical instruction manuals in French literature entitled *La Littérature française*.[51] Like many pedagogical textbooks of the time, it consisted of a series of curated excerpts from famous poets and novelists, with introductions and analysis from diverse literary critics and journalists; these textbooks looked more like what we would now call literary anthologies. Staaff himself was a rather obscure figure in French letters despite his role as an officer of *instruction publique* and of the *légion d'honneur*. He born in 1823 in Stockholm and spent most of his life in his native Sweden, but in 1862, he was named military attaché in Paris, where he developed an affinity for French literature.[52] His foreignness may have also spoken to French citizens who thought of the war as a fight

48   "Chronique," *Bibliographie de la France*, August 27, 1870, p. 151.
49   Von Holtzendorff, letter published in *Bibliographie de France*, August 27, 1870, p. 150.
50   Figures from the *Bibliographie de la France*. The fate of these books is unknown. We know that the *ambulances* in the Comédie-Française and the Théâtre de l'Odéon received some books, but they may not have been from the Cercle's collection.
51   Staaff, *La Littérature française: depuis la formation de la langue jusqu'à nos jours*, Vol. 3 (Paris: Librairie académique Didier et Cie., 1870).
52   Leche, Meijer, Nyström, Warburg, Westrin, editors. *Nordisk Familjebok:*

between brothers—Germany and France—who shared a commitment to literature and intellectual culture more than any two countries in Europe. Reading an anthology of French literature written by a foreigner may have served as a reminder to French readers that while their country could be invaded, their culture still influenced a vast part of the world.

During the Siege, Staaff and his *éditeurs* at the Librairie académique Didier and Company reprinted *La Littérature française* with the express purpose of distributing them to the convalescent. As reported in the newspaper *Le Réveil*, another example of *éditeurs* receiving free publicity through civic engagement, "300 copies" of the 600-page book were offered gratis to wounded Parisians. "Another generous idea" was behind the book being offered at half price to any Parisian— sick or well—who bought the book directly from the author at his home. The article, written by the revolutionary Charles Delescluze, ends with a strange appeal: "May each of us, according to our abilities, also try to satisfy a need that, unfortunately, in the middle of so many others, becomes more and more urgent every day!"[53] It is not clear from the context if Delescluze means that each Parisian should buy a copy (unlikely), but he does indicate that Staaff and his *éditeurs'* patriotic gesture correspond to their "abilities" ("facultés"), meaning that he thinks every individual can contribute something, according to their talents, to the country. Every individual, but also every institution.

Book drives of this magnitude were only possible due to the physical infrastructure of presses, *éditeurs*, and booksellers in the city. While the Siege did not vastly redefine these spaces, some literary advocates argued for more intentional spaces for the public consumption of literature in the city. In late November 1870, Jules Claretie wrote an open letter to Jules Ferry, then the mayor of Paris, imploring him to reopen the municipal libraries, provisionally closed at the outset of the Siege. He went further, sketching out a plan for new libraries to be opened in each *arrondissement* that would serve the national interest and edify the new republican citizenry:

A library is a reading and conference space. This is precisely the

---

Konversationslexikon och realencyklopedi (Stockholm: Nordisk familjeboks tryckeri, 1917), pp. 861–862.

53   Delescluze, "Livres pour les blessés," *Le Réveil*, November 22, 1870.

right moment to do so if one was only thinking of right now, and if one only took the examples of the founders and the first defenders of the Republic in France.

Through his invocation of libraries as spaces of congregation and of erudition, Claretie implicitly argued that these spaces could become alternatives to political clubs, especially if they were modeled after the wishes of the earliest republicans in France. He explained that their predecessors assigned themselves the role of "educators" and "civilizers" of the French people. For the republicans of 1870, he claimed that libraries could be the sites of this important civilizing mission as well as places where the study of the history and literature of France could explain that very mission. For those fighting for the future of the country, "the history of the Revolution would show them how we win, and Corneille how we die," Claretie suggested.[54] Claretie's proposal directly addressed the reasons why literature could save the country and how such spaces should be built into the geography of the city. Literature, wrote Claretie, can inspire ordinary citizens during extraordinary times by representing to them fictional or nonfictional moments of strife in French culture. Corneille's *Horace* had as much to teach republican readers as, say, Michelet's *Histoire de la Révolution française.*[55]

His proposal aligned directly with the new ways that Parisians thought of literature as a way to teach the historical and political events of French history, but also with the pseudo-utopian ideas of *éditeurs*, authors, and printers about literature's ability to save the soul and the borders of France. On the one hand, these libraries could take the place of political clubs (as a "conference space"), making it easier for the current and future governments to monitor and maintain healthy spaces for political discussion. This meant that Claretie's libraries would have a practical purpose during moments such as the Siege. Second, they would continue to act as educational spaces ("reading

54 Claretie, Letter to Ferry, *Le Journal officiel*, November 26, 1870.
55 Claretie's evocation of Corneille is relevant. The seventeenth-century playwright was often read during the Siege, especially *Horace*, which dramatizes how an international war can rip apart families. Franz Beauvallet wrote a play, *Le Forgeron de Châteaudun*, which is an explicit rewrite of *Horace* involving a Franco-German romance suddenly torn apart by the war. This play is discussed in Chapter 2.

space") during moments of peace, as a way of reminding patrons of the revolution of September 4, 1870 and of its inscription into a longer history of revolutions, back to the founders of the original French Republic and their civilizing mission. Claretie, like all promoters of literature during the Siege, imagined that literature could serve political purposes, either conservative or revolutionary. Claretie's proposal sought to inscribe literature's civic mission into the geography of the city, looking towards a political future that would seek to teach the types of republican liberalism that allowed the publishing industry to become so profitable and so productive. But these plans could not come to realization. The top-down education of republican citizens would have to wait. In the meantime, smaller printers took over Paris. The types of radical rhetoric and sensational history they published probably would not have been appropriate for municipal libraries dedicated to the lofty values of French letters.

Chapter 8

To Make the Past Public

The upstart and sporadic nature of publishing during the Siege favored radical politics, and in particular revolutionary republicanism. To break with the past, to turn public opinion against the politics of the Second Empire that had just fallen, Parisian printers and *éditeurs* turned to the etymological definition of publication: to make matters public. Many Parisians felt that they had been betrayed by Napoléon III, betrayed by their military leaders, and perhaps even betrayed by their own revolutionary traditions that had inspired the former Emperor's coup d'état of 1851. The national sentiment of 1870, born of distrust, created an atmosphere in which Parisians longed for the transparency that many believed had been lacking under Napoléon III. The Siege saw the publication of hundreds of books that wished to expose secrets, shed light on lies, and emanate truth. However, this light only shone in one direction: towards the past. Accusatory publications exposed the crimes, both real and imagined, of the Second Empire, leaving future affairs murky.

The accusatory publications of the Siege espoused a denunciatory rhetoric that played into French revolutionary traditions. This explains the popularity of Victor Hugo's *Les Châtiments*, among which the poem "Lux" perhaps best encapsulates the collective frenzy for publications that expose what was hidden:

> Banished! Banished! Banished! Such is destiny.
> What is flowing in the morning will be
> Taken back on the ebb.
> Bad days will flee without us knowing their number,

And joyous peoples, peering over shadows
Will say: this is no more!

Happy times will shine, not only for France,
But for all. Within this deliverance,
Deadly only to the past,
All humanity will sing, covered in flowers,
As a master who returns to the deserted home,
From which he had been chased.[1]

Hugo evokes the cyclical passage of time—the ebb and flow of revolutions—in order to create a dichotomy between light and dark which plays a major thematic role in this poem and in his collection as a whole, bookended with the poems "Nox" (night) and with this, "Lux" (light). Bending over the shadows of the past, Siege publications were shining the light of the Republic over its secrets for the world to see, just as Hugo predicted they would: "O, Universal Republic, / You are yet but a spark, / Tomorrow, you will be the sun!"[2]

Hugo's metaphor of revolution as a light shining upon the country inspired many other writers. Just as Parisians began writing diaries to document their experience of this seminal moment in French history, many of the literary professionals in Hugo's wake believed that they were not only publishing for their own fame, but also to spread the gospel of the new Republic, to root out tyranny and to abolish oppression through the dissemination of published texts. Hugo imagined that the Republic would spread like the light of dawn; in reality, it spread through vast and irregular networks of *éditeurs*, printers, libraries, and bookshops. Ironically, the clerk of the *dépôt légal* was yet another actor in this revolution, an unwitting agent of light, storing and cataloging these new publications for inclusion in France's *patrimoine nationale*.[3]

The rest of France may not have been interested in the suffering of Parisians in defense of a republic with which they were unfamiliar. The names of these new politicians, Trochu, Favre, Ferry, Picard, Simon, meant little to them, perhaps even less than the major events that cemented the republican regime's leadership within the capital: the occupation of the Tuileries on September 4, 1870, the storming of the

---

1   Hugo, *Les Châtiments* (Paris: Hetzel, 1880), p. 443.
2   Hugo, *Les Châtiments*, p. 433.
3   A clerk presented in the Introduction.

hôtel de ville on October 31, the subsequent referendum of the urban population in favor of the incumbent government, the closing and reopening of theaters, the multiplication of new political periodicals, or even the unprecedented deregulation of the publishing industry. Parisians had to convince their provincial compatriots that the events of the Siege mattered to everyone, and that the history of Paris was synonymous with the history of France. To do so, they published books, which unlike newspapers offered longevity and material durability,[4] giving readers—even today's readers—the possibility of reliving the events that led to France's political situation after the Siege. Parisians saw books and their repositories, like national and municipal libraries, as sites of republican propaganda and as pillars of the new French nation. The books that were published during the Siege intended, in Eugen Weber's terms, to turn peasants into Frenchmen.

This included publishing the Second Empire's archives, as well. Jules Claretie began this work in the early September 1870, sifting through materials in the Salon Louis XIV of the Tuileries Palace, a former dining room transformed into dumping ground for the fallen Empire's official documents. Claretie was not a member of the new *gouvernement provisoire de la défense nationale*, hastily assembled on September 5 after the fall of Napoléon III, nor did he aspire to join their ranks. Instead, the writer, journalist, and theater critic had been charged with what he called "a historian's job,"[5] the lonely task of sifting through all the papers found at the Tuileries palace, which just a week earlier had been the private residence and public office of the Bonaparte family. Claretie worked on this project of publishing the Second Empire's most secret documents for nearly a month, but when *Les Papiers trouvés aux Tuileries* (*Papers Found in the Tuileries Palace*) were published, his name was curiously absent. In his published diary of 1871, *Paris assiégé*, he carefully removed any indication of his role at the Tuileries Palace,[6] as if he had never participated in the publication of these scandalous texts

---

4   Bound books did not suffer from the same paper shortages as newspapers did. As a result, such books published during the Siege were printed on the same high-quality paper as before the investment. The exception to this were many political pamphlets, which—because they were often made by small printers—appeared on more fibrous and less durable paper, often in striking colors like red, green, or blue.

5   Claretie, BHVP, Fonds Jules Claretie, section XII, vol. 20, p. 6.

6   This assertion is based on a cross-analysis of Claretie's published diary, *Paris*

that became one of the bestsellers of the Siege of Paris. What happened? Why did Claretie back away from his "historian's job" of publishing the secrets of the Second Empire?

When Parisians heard of Napoléon III's capture by the Prussians, they stormed the Tuileries palace, the hallowed halls of French kings, queens, and emperors since 1564.[7] By all accounts, these revolutionary revelers arrived mere hours after Napoléon's wife, Eugénie de Montijo, had escaped through a back door, possibly disguised as a man and with the help of her English hairdresser. While Parisians took turns sitting in the freshly abdicated throne, the new republican government quickly set aside any and all documents found in the Tuileries, including the correspondence of the former emperor, Empress Eugénie's personal library, and internal memos of the imperial censorship bureau. The government organized a commission, headed by the director of the newly reinstituted *Journal officiel*, André Lavertujon, whose purpose was to select excerpts destined for publication in major newspapers and for a future book edited by Garnier frères in 1871. At the time, Claretie was little known outside the world of journalism but, due to his constant presence during the Siege and the books he later published about the event, he eventually was named a member of the prestigious French Academy and director of the Comédie-Française. However, in September 1870 this project was one of his most high-profile. Lavertujon was doing him a favor.

To explain Claretie's disappearance from this publication, we need to look at the context in which the *Papers Found at the Tuileries* appeared, notably the return of the eighteenth-century genre of the *libelle*, or short, salacious pamphlet. He quit the commission around the same time that Parisians had their first contemporary experience of this genre, which appeared as a series of bound pamphlets exposing the so-called criminality and amorality of the Bonaparte dynasty. The eighteenth-century incarnation of the *libelle* had been less discriminate

assiégé: tableaux et souvenirs (Paris: Lemerre, 1871), and the manuscript available at the BHVP, cited above.

7   Catherine de Medici ordered the construction of the Tuileries palace in 1564, right in front of the Louvre. There it stood until 1871, when it was nearly destroyed during the Commune and never rebuilt. The ruins remained as a sort of romantic monument and political reminder until 1883, when the City removed the last traces of the former seat of French royalty.

in its target of attack, however. Robert Darnton shows the origins of the genre in the decades before the Revolution of 1789, when such lascivious tales took aim at the women of the court. Darnton pays particular attention to the *Anecdotes sur Mme la Comtesse du Barry*, published in 1775, which he calls "a classic of the genre," but concedes that "as the genre is now extinct, the book has been forgotten."[8] However, the *libelle* returned in a very similar form during the Second Empire and reached its peak during the Siege. Darnton proposes a definition of the eighteenth-century *libelle*, but it applies to certain books published in 1870:

> It reads like an off-color Cinderella tale or sexual success story, because du Barry sleeps her way from a brothel to the throne. But the sex only added spice to the main appeal of the plot, which gave uninformed readers a chance to know the inside story of life in Versailles […] As a "historian," the narrator promises a double treat: an accurate account of life at the top and a story that will read like a novel.[9]

In other words, these stories perform the impending Revolution through the cultural work of representation. In robbing the court of its mystery and in painting the élite as a band of misfits, the *libelle* leaves the reader with the impression that no divine will could have placed these people in such a powerful position. This anticipated the Revolution insofar as it symbolically exposed the ruling class as perpetuating a centuries-long hoax.

What sort of political work was the *libelle* of 1870 doing? The people already knew that Napoléon III was not infallible, since he had just been captured. While many believed that he had made dupes of a bellicose French population, many of those same people believed that they had to save France's honor by fighting to the end the war that Napoléon III started. The near century that separated eighteenth-century *libelles* from those of the Siege had brought with it many different regimes, all of which had proved unable to create a lasting dynasty. In a way, regime change had become as central to France as the ruling parties themselves. To put it bluntly, the *libelles* were not revolutionary in 1870.

---

8   Darnton, *The Forbidden Bestsellers of Pre-Revolutionary France* (Fontana Press, 1997), p. 137.
9   Darnton, *Forbidden Bestsellers*, p. 137.

Siege-time *libelles* probed the limits of the new Republic, investigating the ideological and political contours of the revolution of September 4, if it can even claim to be a revolution. Printers and presses had obtained unprecedented liberties in 1868 and in 1870: how serious and how unlimited were these liberties? Bordering on the obscene, the *libelle* pushed the limits of its public and seemed to dare the government to suppress its publication. Under the guise of writing history, the authors of these pamphlets profited from republican fervor and the collective anger at Napoléon III for having started the war. They were explicitly republican, seeming to care as little for fact-checking as for good taste. As Paris's publishing industry was reconfigured into older networks of unmediated collaboration between printers and authors, the *libelle* demonstrates that the types of books produced by this collaboration were also partly modeled on the clandestine publishing mentalities of the *ancien régime*. The *libelles* of the Siege acted like Darnton's so-called forbidden bestsellers, but they were neither forbidden nor as bestselling as other more moderate books, like Hugo's *Les Châtiments*.

Around fifteen *libelles* appeared in the winter of 1870–1871. They capitalized on the reading public's desire for the publication, the making public, of formerly taboo topics. Hugo's *Les Châtiments* contributed to the success of this new model of publishing, as did *Papers Found in the Tuileries*. However, the *libelle* was the radical, obscene cousin of other texts that fought for transparency. The *libelles* were highly rhetorical, viscerally denunciatory, and deeply conspiratorial, announcing their stance in titles like *Note secrète sur la mission occulte du Second Empire* (*Secret Note on the Occult Mission of the Second Empire*), *Histoire des amours, scandales, et libertinages des Bonaparte* (*History of the Loves, Scandals, and Libertinage of the Bonapartes*), and *Les Deux cours et les nuits de Saint-Cloud* (*The Two Courts and Nights at Saint-Cloud*). The printer Berthélémy published the latter on October 24. An eighty-eight-page volume, *Les Deux cours* was written by the journalist Hippolyte Magen, who had been in exile throughout the Second Empire and who refused Napoléon III's amnesty, much like Victor Hugo. Magen wrote the book while in exile, first publishing it through the London-based publisher Jeffs in 1852—another parallel to Hugo, who published *Les Châtiments* the same year in Brussels. Magen's book, subtitled *Customs, Debauchery, and Crimes of the Bonaparte Family*, attacked both Napoléon I and III, but saved particular rancor for the female members of the family, as in this description of the mother of Napoléon I:

> Madame Laetitia Ramolini Bonaparte was a very comely Swiss woman; just recently married to a clerk from Ajaccio, she began an affair with M. de Marbeuf in Corsica; this lover took care of her financially; as soon as he had left his island, Madame Bonaparte opened a brothel there.
>
> In 1793, she came to France with her two sons Napoléon and Lucien; her niece Arena, whom Napoléon assassinated later, breastfed them for many months.
>
> She again took up the title of pimp, and opened a *house* in Marseille; there, she prostituted her two daughters Pauline and Elise; Caroline, aged thirteen, acted as the messenger of love for her sisters.[10]

Magen's particular brand of fictitious history spoke to a population that wished to see the Second Empire and its élite dragged through the mud, and, given the explicit nature of many of these descriptions, needed a little bit of pornography to spice up these already exaggerated stories. For Magen and others who published similar stories about the Bonaparte family, the only way France could move on from its past was to deny the legitimacy of its former rulers. Thus, Napoléon I became the son of a whore, and Napoléon III things much worse.

Magen was not the only author to attack the imperial family. His book was republished in Paris in October 1870, along with the original publication of what became a long series of slim volumes denouncing the crimes and debauchery of the defunct ruler's loved ones. Their author, the most prolific writer in this genre, signed his works under the pseudonym "Citizen Vindex" but was also known later to publish using his given name, Guenot-Winger. During the Second Empire, Guenot-Winger was the vicar of Ménilmontant, but lost his faith in the final years of the regime, according to his 1871 book *Les Révélations d'un curé démissionné* (*Revelations of a Former Vicar*).[11] Before he published this enumeration of the crimes of the

---

10 Magen, *Les Deux cours et les nuits de Saint Cloud* (Paris: Berthélémy, 1870), p. 4.

11 Little is known about Guenot-Winger, not even his first name. I cannot confirm his identity as a former vicar, but his contemporaries, even the most

clergy, he had published at least nine different tracts during the Siege itself—ranging from eight to eighty pages each—about the rulers of France and Prussia. Their titles are not particularly inventive, but I reproduce here a few examples:

> *Le Clan des Bonaparte: le sieur Bonaparte, sa vie et ses crimes*
>   (*The Bonaparte Clan: Sir Bonaparte, His Life and His Crimes*)
> *La Femme Bonaparte, ses amants, ses orgies*
>   (*The Lady Bonaparte, Her Lovers, Her Orgies*)
> *Monsieur Guillaume, roi de Prusse, sa vie et sa condamnation à
>   mort*
>   (*Monsieur Guillaume, King of Prussia, His Life and His Death
>   Sentence*)
> *Tribunal du genre humain*
>   (*The Human Race on Trial*)

Guenot-Winger attracted more attention that Magen, whose contribution to this bibliography of scandalous histories was limited to his *Les Deux cours et les nuits de Saint-Cloud*, and much more than J.-G. Prat, whose sole contribution, *Les Exploits du deux décembre* (*The Exploits of December Second*) (1870), condemned the Bonaparte family without alluding to their sex lives.

While these erotico-historical tales began to flood Parisian bookstores, Claretie was still at work in the archives of the Second Empire. He had some affection for a certain member of the Bonaparte family: Eugénie de Montijo, the wife of Napoléon III who had escaped the Tuileries in company of her hairdresser on September 4, bound for London where she waited out the war. As Claretie catalogued the books in Eugénie's personal library, his admiration for her and her family grew:

> Visited the apartments of the Empress in the Tuileries [...] Books: Victor Hugo, Proudhon [...] The works of Victor Hugo among the books of the Empress were all signed "Eugénie." She had great admiration for him. "Her father was," Hugo told me, "aide

critical, did not question his bona fides. See Firmin Maillard, *Les Publications de la rue pendant le siège et la Commune: satires, canards, complaintes, chansons, placards et pamphlets* (Paris: Aubry, 1874): "En somme, ces *révélations*, faites avec toute l'ardeur et toute la vivacité d'un défroqué, sont assez amusantes et je les lisais avec plaisir, que le ciel me pardonne!" (p. 157).

de camp for my father [...] Mme de Montijo did not forget this, and brought me many times to the Place Royale around 1844, 1845, and 1846 to hear her daughter sing my poetry with other young Spanish girls."[12]

Like Eugénie's mother, and like most of Paris in 1870, Claretie idolized Hugo. His words quoted in Claretie's diary most likely came from the mouth of the poet himself, whom Claretie visited nearly every day during his time archiving the Tuileries papers. He realized, going through her affairs and through his discussions with Hugo, that Eugénie was more complicated than just the wife of a tyrant, and that her story was more bound up in respectable literary circles than Magen and Guenot-Winger had described.

Eugénie was more than just the wife of a tyrant for others, too: she was reprehensible on her own merit. On October 24—the same day Magen republished his *Les Deux cours et les nuits de Saint-Cloud*—Guenot-Winger alias "Citizen Vindex" released another so-called secret history of the Bonaparte clan, entitled *La Femme Bonaparte*, this time with more contemporary characters. His description of Eugénie is at odds with Claretie's impression of her after inspecting her library:

> As for her morals, no intellectual culture whatsoever, no brightness of wit, complete absence of gravity in her ideas. Unfamiliar with the arts, with literature, she demonstrated masculine tastes very early on. Good at riding, she could have kept up with the stable keepers. In terms of novels, the beautiful damsel liked the action as much as the story. Disguised as an Empress, then Majesty, she basked in the freely given praise of her innumerable troop of courtesans.[13]

Neither Claretie nor Hugo would have recognized in this description the Eugénie they had come to know. Vindex's criticism of her, however, stayed within the same categories as Claretie's praise. She either read widely or not at all. She had a young woman's education of music and poetry, or she read novels for the action and preferred horseback riding. Clearly, Vindex was attempting to set the record

---

12   Claretie, *Paris assiégé*, p. 20.
13   Guenot-Winger (alias Vindex), *La Femme Bonaparte* (Paris: Jacquiet, 1870), p. 2.

straight on public opinion of the former empress, using her own reputation against her.

Although he never wrote this explicitly, Claretie resigned his post on the commission charged with publishing the Tuileries papers because of the popularity of these libelous tracts. Claretie believed himself to be better equipped than Citizen Vindex to tell the true story of life in the imperial court, given his daily examination of the most private papers of the Bonaparte family. However, he came to very different conclusions than Vindex and others. Claretie's overall impression is one of governmental mismanagement and of pettiness, but not of crime. Magen's entire project revolves around uncovering crime and debauchery, offering a look "behind the scenes, where the charlatans are unmasked."[14] The *Papiers trouvés aux Tuileries* appeared around the same time as these tracts, meaning that the public would have associated them, given their similar mission of giving transparency, to the recent government. Claretie may not have wanted his name attached to yet another denunciation of the imperial family.[15]

The authors of these tracts were not necessarily interested in getting at the truth of the history of the Second Empire, so what were they doing? Their popularity certainly was tied to the publication of the *Papiers trouvés aux Tuileries*, which appeared in installments on the front pages of nearly every major newspaper in late September and early October 1870. However, just as Claretie did, the public began to turn against the types of publications that exposed the supposed crimes of the fallen regime. On November 15, 1870, when the fourth installment of libelous tracts appeared, targeting Mathilde-Laetitia-Wilhelmine Bonaparte, its author, Citizen Vindex, spent half of his publication defending himself against critiques levied by journalists. So, the question becomes double: why were these tracts initially so popular, and why did that popularity wane?

The answer is that they were socially useful despite their lurid exaggerations. Darnton insists that *Anecdotes sur Mme la Comtesse du Barry*, the eighteenth-century precursor to the *libelle* of the Siege,

14 Magen, *Les Deux cours*, p. 66.
15 Even if Claretie edited out of his published diary any indications that he served on the committee, he does mention that he read some of the papers at the Tuileries palace, commenting on some discoveries of political corruption: "How disgusting. So much cowardice uncovered" (*Paris assiégé*, p. 5).

should be read as a history of the end of the monarchy, and that it can—despite the sexual details—shed light on the actual workings of the court. The author of the *Anecdotes*, Mairobert, may have used real documentation to craft his story: "By sifting through this material and piecing together 'anecdotes,' he has constructed a general history of the last years of Louis XV's reign," Darton claims.[16] However, anyone who read Magen and Vindex alongside the *Papiers trouvés aux Tuilieries* in 1870 would have known that the latter relied upon real documentary evidence while the former dealt in gossip and exaggeration; this much is clear from the critiques levied against them. But they both had the veneer of truth, or the rhetorical stance of telling truth to power, even if that power had just been deposed.

When the *libelle* returned, it was for different reasons than its late eighteenth-century incarnation. The secret histories of 1870 attempted neither to oust any ruler from his throne nor tell an unknown but true story. Instead the Siege *libelles* inscribed France's current tragedy into a longer history of governmental decadence reaching back to the *ancien régime*. By the very fact of their reappearance, these books signaled the end of another era, urging their readers to consider their present in relation to other revolutionary moments.[17] Through intertextual references, these histories suggested that there was no difference between Louis XV and Napoléon III; tyrants had led France into disaster since the beginning of the French state. Magen and Vindex wanted to punish and humiliate a tyrannical figure who had brought so much punishment and humiliation on the people. But what sorts of solutions did they offer? Do these Siege *libelles* present any alternatives to the endless cycle of revolution and repression that they clearly wish to recall?

While there was nothing particularly republican in Mairobert's *Anecdotes sur Mme la Comtesse du Barry*, Vindex often alluded to alternative forms of government couched in republican terms. The pseudonym under which he published, "Le citoyen Vindex," is the

---

16   Darnton, *Forbidden Bestsellers*, p. 149.

17   The *libelles* were not the only genre to reappear during the Siege. The return of the newspaper *Le Père Duchêne*, the republication of countless history books about the Revolution, and the constant newspaper articles about previous revolutions attest to Parisians' understanding of the new Republic as yet another reincarnation of that ur-Republic of the eighteenth century.

most forward of these allusions, *citoyen* and *citoyenne* having been employed since the Revolution of 1789 to refer to fellow Frenchmen or -women sympathetic to the republican cause. Guenot-Winger appends to this honorific the name "Vindex," which could refer to the Roman senator Gaius Julius Vindex, a Gallic revolutionary who led a violent rebellion against the emperor Nero around 67 AD. That the Roman senator inspired his name is all the more likely considering that the Catholic author and journalist Louis Veuillot published a dialogue in 1848 entitled *L'Esclave Vindex*. Written in the aftermath of the 1848 Revolution, Veuillot's text endeavored to show that the conservative party (read: "monarchist") needed to understand "the urgency of calling the Church to help society."[18] Guenot-Winger, having given up his place in the Church in order to denounce its excesses, would have relished the opportunity to rewrite the story of the Roman senator marching against tyranny. In taking the name Vindex, Guenot-Winger was able to incorporate two foundational myths of the French Republican tradition: the legend of Gallic resistance to the crimes of the Roman Empire and the increasing secularization of republicanism after 1848.[19]

Aside from his choice of pseudonym, Guenot-Winger offered other evidence of his fervent republicanism in his citations. At the beginning of his first tract, *Le Sieur Louis Bonaparte, sa vie et ses crimes*, he established his credibility by placing two unattributed quotations from Hugo's *Les Châtiments*: "City sown of infamy and glory ..." from the poem "Toulon," and "No, scoundrel; the ossuary of kings is forbidden to you" from "La Caravane." During the Siege, authors evoked Hugo's name and works primarily to ride his popularity, but also to include their works in a republican corpus of texts.[20] Guenot-Winger's choice of quotations reveals the same intentions for his *libelles*. His second quotation establishes generic boundaries, telling the reader that what follows will be a summary of crimes committed against the French,

18   Veuillot, preface to *L'Esclave Vindex* (Paris: Gaume frères et Duprey, 1862), p. 1.

19   Vindex and those republicans who believed in a secular state were disappointed to see how monarchists like Thiers slipped into the highest ranks of the Third Republic. Their presence created a form of conservative republicanism described by Sanford Elwitt in his *The Making of the Third Republic* (Louisiana State UP, 1975).

20   For more on Hugo's popularity, see Chapter 2.

which precludes the perpetrator's entrance into French historical reverence. The first citation is more complex: the evocation of a city risen out of both glory and infamy seems to designate Paris[21] as a city whose revolutionary past cannot be forgotten, neither the bloody nor the peaceful moments.

This quotation of Hugo should give us pause. Why would Guenot-Winger have wished to put both the good and the bad moments of the revolutionary century on equal footing? On the contrary, it seems like his *libelles* are intended to remove the Bonaparte family from the annals of French history. His preface to the first installment offers more insight into this seeming contradiction:

> Many volumes would be needed to detail the shameful intrigues of the tyrant who for eighteen years crushed us under his boot [...] The people must know in all his hideousness the dreary showman who was showered so long with the titles of *Sire, Majesty,* and *Emperor.* This mountebank needs to be completely unmasked. We will drag him naked to the pillory.[22]

Without citing republicanism explicitly, Guenot-Winger nonetheless deploys the rhetoric of publication as "making public": the unmasking of fraud, the imperative of truth, and the publicizing of that which was private. Even though Claretie's job of publishing the Tuileries papers was less sensational, the same motivation was at work. As much as Hugo's poetry avoided the female members of the Bonaparte family, Guenot-Winger's citations of the poet make sense in the context of the *libelle* insofar as both *Les Châtiments* and *Le Sire Bonaparte* attempt to lead criminals to justice through the act of publication.

The expressions of urgency and necessity in the above passage of *Le Sire Bonaparte* ("Many volumes would be needed ... the people need to know ... the mountebank needs to be completely unmasked ...") explain why Guenot-Winger and others wished to linger on the darker moments of French history in order to move forward. The *libelle* appeals to its readership not only to take pleasure in the making public of supposed crimes but also to act on this information. There

---

21 Hugo's poem actually was describing Toulon, but since Guenot-Winger did not make that clear, readers would have reasonably imagined the citation to be concern Paris.

22 Guenot-Winger, *Le Sire Bonaparte* (Paris: Librairie Martinon, 1870), p. 2.

was a sense of the imperative in these books, urging citizen-readers to learn from the mistakes of their leaders. The "ebb" and "flow" of revolution, as Hugo phrased it in "Lux," are the same *infamy* and *glory* that he contrasted in another poem, "Toulon," also quoted in Guenot-Winger's *libelle*. Revolutions can be good or bad—for Hugo, 1830 and 1852, respectively—but looking back on them and making judgments about their merit can educate the public as to what a successful, legitimate revolution looks like. It can also serve as a lesson to revolutionaries who take over the government as a way of ensuring democratic processes. Philip Nord has commented on this potential end to the revolutionary cycle:

> The prospects of a democratic transition brighten, the argument goes, when elites, old and new, have learned from violent past experience to avoid confrontation. Bloody memories of former repressions can have a sobering effect on incumbent authorities. When faced with a new democratic challenge, the landlords, generals, and bureaucrats in power may hesitate to embark on yet another round of violence.[23]

In this passage, Nord is specifically comparing twentieth-century South American revolutions to the origins of the Third Republic, but his argument about the memory of violence certainly holds for the Siege. The proclamation of the Republic of September 4, 1870 was made without a single drop of blood spilled in Paris. On the other hand, there were no throngs of people clamoring for a republic, no struggle to oust a dictator, no cathartic moment of release. The government and the people it served may not necessarily have felt any real need to maintain this sort of republic for lack of anything better once the Siege was over and France was at peace. Nord says as much when he claims "the Republic survived [the elections of winter 1871–1872], governed by men who felt only a minimal attachment to its institutions or principles."[24] Siege publications functioned as a way of instilling republican values within these men and the people they governed, even if the history of the Third Republic shows us that these publications may not have been read attentively.

23 Nord, *The Republican Moment* (Harvard UP, 1995), p. 6.
24 Nord, *Republican Moment*, p. 3.

According to the authors of Siege publications, it wasn't just the newly named members of the *gouvernement provisoire* that needed to learn this lesson, but also the French people at large. By November 1870, Guenot-Winger's radical critique of anything and anyone associated with the Bonaparte family had not garnered him many allies. Claretie was not the only one to disassociate himself from the methods of *libellistes* even if he may have sympathized with their goals at first. Journalists were particularly quick to denounce Guenot-Winger's tactics, to whom he responded:

> Looking deeply into [the lives of the Bonapartes], [we] will be even better able to judge the miserable people whom religion dared call, from on high, the elect of God; whom judicial authorities, crooked and corrupt, gave complete respect; whom degraded authors did not hesitate to glorify.[25]

The last line is particularly important, since the critics of the *libelles* were predominantly other authors. Arthur Picard, an editor at the newspaper *L'Electeur libre*, had accused Vindex "of feeding garbage to the public,"[26] to which the latter responded by accusing Picard of harboring Bonapartist sympathies. This, his last tract published on November 15, was by far the shortest of the series, and he devoted a considerable part of it to arguing that authors had a solemn duty to defend truth amid the temptations of political favors. In typical fashion, he relied on attacking the female members of the Bonaparte family in order to illustrate this point. Mathilde, the target of this pamphlet, had made some friends within literary circles, much as Hortense de Beauharnais and Eugénie de Montijo had, the latter of whom he had earlier accused of having "no intellectual culture whatsoever," in contrast to the testimonial of Hugo and Claretie:

> [Mathilde] figured out how to gain some independence without sacrificing (a life of *freedom without limits*) the homages of the literary, artistic, or other renowned creative disseminators, from whose strictness women rarely escape with impunity.
>
>   This grand idea of flattering the vain coterie of artists and poets in order to receive a certificate of good life and morals, we

25   Guenot-Winger, *La Fille Mathilde* (Paris: Librairie Martinon, 1870), p. 2.
26   Cited in Guenot-Winger, *La Fille Mathilde*, p. 3.

suspect that Mathilde borrowed it from another celebrity in her family. She had watched her aunt, Hortense de Beauharnais, and had learned from the adulterous mother of Sir Louis Bonaparte in her use of a suite of ingenious practices.[27]

Guenot-Winger accused artists, authors, and other "disseminators" ("distributeurs") of having colluded with Mathilde in a sort of lascivious pact, whereby they exchanged good press for sexual favors. This, he claimed, was the trademark of all Bonaparte women and symptomatic of the conditions of writing under the rule of Bonaparte men. It is interesting that he used the word "disseminator" to designate the intellectual elite, as it reveals his own definition of culture: authors, artists, and journalists distributed ideas among the population, actively creating public opinion. As public intellectuals, they became accomplices to the crimes of the ruling class when they used that influence for their own fame. In contrast to what he saw as self-serving intellectuals, Vindex suggested that he was fighting for truth in a world of deceit and manipulation. Two could play at dissemination.

Authors were fully aware of their role as public intellectuals. When the city organized a free and open-to-the-public reading of *Les Châtiments* at the Paris Opéra, the goal was to perform the fall of Napoléon III in a bid to legitimize new republican leadership. Guenot-Winger also wrote to impress upon his readership the crimes of their fallen tyrant, and to lead him "naked to the pillory"—a symbolic pillory since, despite their exaggerated rhetoric, these *libelles* never advocated violence in response to violence. The genre was born in pre-revolutionary fervor, but Vindex takes care not to resurrect the guillotine with it.

As a genre, the *libelle* had a short shelf life in the bookstores of Paris, but its resurgence speaks to a new conception of literature and to a new meaning of publication in the months Paris was isolated from the rest of France. News about Napoléon III's capture at Sedan was spotty, coming to Paris in the form of anecdotes and short dispatches from the outside world. When information was lacking, republicans like Vindex turned to literature in order to represent the event itself. In publishing a creative, perhaps false story of the imperial family, he was urging his readers to understand the events they were living through within

27 Guenot-Winger, *La Fille Mathilde*, p. 7.

a fatalistic conception of French history. Thus, Napoléon III's capture was not merely a military disaster that could be corrected when France was again at peace; the end of Napoléon represented the end of tyranny, and the opening of a new, enlightened period in French history.

Hugo's poetry and the *libelles* participated in historical revolutionary politics. This backward-looking ideology attempted to interpret history in a revolutionary way rather than enact revolution in the present. Accusatory publications never made lists of demands or even pointed out ongoing wrongdoings; they appealed to the past to form their rhetorical stance. Beyond simply speaking about the then-toppled Second Empire, both *Les Châtiments* and the *libelles* were texts with formal ties to the past. *Les Châtiments* was already a historical document by 1870, having been written when the poet first entered exile in 1852. During the Siege, it told its readers things they already knew, predicted an event that had already happened. The *libelles* were a throwback to the original Revolution, a fiery punishment fit for monarchs, not emperors. In a sense, both texts re-enacted older revolutions. They were not performative publications intended to stoke the fires of revolution in a city racked by convulsion. No, they were much more conservative, confirming things their readers already knew, spouting a form of truth that confirmed rather than challenged readers' beliefs. These sorts of comforting lies perhaps represent the only form of escapist literature that was published during the Siege: a way for Parisians to believe that their suffering was out of their control, that their past determined their future. The revolutionary century was coming to an end in a sort of anti-revolution. No wonder, then, that many of the newly cast republican readers of *Les Châtiments* failed, just months after extolling Hugo's calls for political rebirth, to recognize the *communards'* claims as legitimate inheritors of French revolutionary politics.

Coda
The Siege and State Violence

In his 1889 novel about the events of 1870–1871, Georges Darien describes how quickly—and how visibly—the Republic was declared. The narrator of *Bas les cœurs!*, a young boy who experiences the Franco-Prussian War and the Commune from his home in Versailles, forms his political beliefs from this experience. The proclamation of the Republic signals the end of the only regime he has ever known, as was the case for anyone under the age of eighteen. Despite his unfamiliarity with the phenomenon, the narrator finds that a revolution can be seen primarily as a visual event, manifest in the spectacles and gestures of everyday life:

> We are in a republic, which is clear to see: they removed the eagle from the flag on city hall and replaced it with a spearhead. They erased the word *imperial* from the pediments of buildings and everyone's calling the Emperor "Badinguet."
>
> "It's a beautiful spectacle," repeats my father ten times per day, "this peaceful revolution."
>
> "Indeed," approves Monsieur Beaudrain. "We could have feared so much violence, disorder …"[1]

Beaudrain's relief, of course, turns out to be premature. Disorder and violence reigned when, in the months following the Siege, the Commune of Paris questioned the legitimacy of the new and unelected republican government. In response, the French army brutally stamped out this revolution in May of 1871, bringing a bloody end to the *année terrible*.

---

1   Darien, *Bas les cœurs! 1870–1871* (Paris: Savine, 1889), p. 114.

But much like the narrator's father, Parisians seemed generally relieved by the September 4 proclamation of the Republic. They, too, found it manifest. The new Republic shined in particular on the media and publishing industries, giving editors, publishers, and journalists rare liberties in the types of discourses that could enter the public sphere. The explosion of new periodicals can attest to this. The literary equivalent of giving Napoléon III his demeaning nickname "Badinguet" came at the Paris Opéra in November 1870, during the free and open-to-the-public reading of Victor Hugo's *Les Châtiments*. Inspired by the revolutionary nature of their daily life, literate Parisians took up their pens to write a type of grassroots history in their diaries, intertwining personal political awakenings with national events, suggesting that pens had replaced pitchforks. The director of the Comédie-Française removed the "imperial" insignia from the architecture of the august theater, replacing it with republican iconography kept in storage as if regime change was a part of business. In Darien's *Bas les cœurs!*, the narrator's political mentor, Merlin, speaks of revolution in just such economic terms, dismissing the Republic as "a new sign on an old boutique."[2] Despite all the celebration, there was little to indicate that the Third Republic would be any different than the Second Empire. Despite all the fanfare, one could wonder if there had been a revolution at all.

The cultural proliferation of republicanism did not come at the government's request. Instead, the adoption of revolutionary rhetoric happened as a result of economic forces within the cultural industries of the Siege. With the exception of the *Châtiments* reading at the Paris Opéra, there were few instances of blatant cultural propaganda at the behest of the state authorities. The Provisional Government of National Defense was, after all, concerned with other issues. As Parisians found out, the state did not need to use propaganda; it appeared without state intervention. The scale, power, and influence of Parisian cultural institutions, suddenly faced with a market free of regulation during the Siege, tended towards a type of conservatism that enforced the political status quo. This was true even though that status quo was barely established at the fall of the Second Empire and most certainly subject to reversals and upheavals in the future. The Government of

2   Darien, *Bas les cœurs!*, p. 116.

National Defense could hardly have been considered stable, and yet republican rhetoric emerged instinctively from a city that had, after all, been through a century of revolutionary moments.

In the 1870s and 1880s, literary representations of the event revealed the hollowness of the regime change and the inauthenticity of republicanism during the Siege. For Henry Céard, the Siege taught no lessons, or at least its lessons went unheeded. In his short story "La Saignée," published in the *Soirées de Médan* in 1880, it is France's willingness to interpret the Siege of Paris as heroic resistance rather than, Céard suggests, a catastrophic miscalculation that informs the tragedy of 1870–1871. The short story centers on Huberte de Pahauën, a universally beloved Parisienne, as comfortable in aristocratic salons as drinking with soldiers, who embroils herself in an affair with the fictional General-in-Chief of the defense of Paris. After a scandal when de Pahauën embarrasses the general in front of his military council, he exiles her to Prussian-occupied Versailles. Languishing outside the capital, she eventually strikes a deal with a Prussian officer for a pass to re-enter the city in exchange for sexual favors. She arrives and lifts Paris's spirits again, only for the Siege to end in devastating defeat.

As she passes through the no man's land between French and Prussian forces, her return seems to signal that Paris will always be Paris, on the hunt for pleasure in even the most incongruous circumstances. Even the Prussians cannot help but stop and soak in the spectacle that would have brought down the house at a cabaret:

> Mme de Pahauën cuts an apotheotic figure, standing upright in her boat, as she crosses the bloody Seine. She smiles at the rowers hunched over their oars. Officers on the German bank wave amicable goodbyes; officers on the French bank call to her with intimate familiarity, and amid the immense devastation of the ruined banks, she passes, confirming in the middle of slaughter the invincible power of her flesh, the insolent triumph of her sex.[3]

Through its association with feminine sexuality and national decadence,[4] Céard implies that this short ceasefire, during which men

---

3 Céard, "La Saignée," in *Les Soirées de Médan* (Paris: Charpentier, 1880), p. 216.
4 For more on feminine bodies in 1870–1871, see Colin Foss, "Sarah

of all flags lay down their weapons to ogle, explains the senselessness of the war. The linking of the "bloody" Seine and the triumphant floating "flesh" on the boat creates a continuity between sexual lust and warfare, a masculine cycle in which feminine flesh is made complicit in the massacre. It is not just that men perpetuate this cycle, but that women encourage it. De Pahauën hardly leaves the center of the short story and Céard gives her the agency and the power to stop the senseless violence, given her influence over men in high-ranking military positions. Instead, she thinks only of herself. As embodiment of the carnal pleasures of the Second Empire, Huberte de Pahauën emerges on the battlefield as a Helen of Troy for a self-obsessed city.

The final image of the short story, a rare page where Huberte de Pahauën is completely absent, is of soldiers, dead and dying, their bodies littering the outskirts of the city in the aftermath of the Parisians' last attempt to break the blockade. De Pahauën's return had raised morale, leading to another disaster caused by a particularly Parisian hubris, or so Céard would have us think. Nothing had changed between the fall of the Second Empire and the end of the war, no lessons had been learned, and no figure emerges victorious— except of course de Pahauën, whose treasonous familiarity with the enemy only increased her fame. Nothing indicated that the culture responsible for the Franco-Prussian War would be any different under a republic.

Without mentioning the Commune, Céard wanted to blame the self-centeredness of Parisians, and *Parisiennes* in particular, for the senselessness of 1870–1871. While "La Saignée" clearly finds guilt among the rich, the politicians, the strategists, and the women of Paris, it does so in order to question whether France could ever truly change as long as national rhetoric continued to mistake folly for heroism. The France of "La Saignée" is averse to revolution, unable to progress even in the face of bloodshed. Céard was clearly writing with hindsight for a public that, he believed, still had not seen how the Siege and the Commune represented two tragedies born of the same sin.

From a historical perspective, it would almost be cruel to expect that besieged Parisians, those gawking at de Pahauën from the shores of the Seine and reveling in the heroism of their resistance, be aware that

Bernhardt's Bodies: Feminine Fame during Wartime in Her Memoirs and Henry Céard's *La Saignée*," *Dix-Neuf*, 23:2, 2019, pp. 136–150.

France was about to lose the war. Can we blame Parisians for finding hope in the return of a Parisian icon? Can we blame de Pahauën for perhaps self-interestedly wishing to be there, to be present, to heed the call of "il faut être là!" ["you must be here!"] emblazoned on newspapers and peppered in Parisian discussions in late August and early September 1870? And if the Siege is meant to stand in for the Commune, it is neither fair to women such as de Pahauën nor to the working-class *communards* to place blame for the massacre of Parisians on the excessive and persistent culture of the Second Empire. Given the relatively peaceful nature of the regime change on September 4, it was almost unthinkable in 1870 that the French army could massacre tens of thousands of Parisians during and after the Bloody Week of the Commune.

Parisians' optimism—or naivete—was not a purely psychosocial consequence of the conditions of the Siege. High-level machinations, like those of Céard's fictional commander of the Parisian defense, trickled down into culture, leading to an atmosphere in which Parisians believed that there was a certain heroism in remaining Parisian despite the circumstances. Parisian stubbornness emerged from and contributed to the stubbornness of institutions imbued with cultural authority. For as much as institutions such as the Comédie-Française, moderate but long-established newspapers, and some publishers of political pamphlets cynically adopted the language and the symbols of revolution, the people who engaged within these politico-economic systems—the authors, readers, and spectators—became aware that social and political manipulation works insidiously within a liberalized regime. Culture did not need to be impressed into the war effort, to be actively surveilled or regulated, or subject to censorship to produce texts and spectacle that promoted militaristic patriotism or that co-opted revolution for the bourgeoisie. Céard saw Parisians as complicit in the government's machinations. Other authors believed that they had been duped.

There were some signs of the horrors that would rain down on the Commune. The literature of the Franco-Prussian War attests to a growing realization that the state's primary purpose was to legitimize violence in service of the nation. Perhaps as a result of their inability to predict or even influence their fates during 1870–1871, the French "began to believe that they—not just the government—were responsible for preparing the nation for future armed conflict," as Rachel Chrastil shows for the period before the First World War.[5] Stéphane Audoin-Rouzeau also points to the similarities between the Franco-Prussian War and the First World War, the military, strategic, and economic aspects of 1870 having set the path "upon which France would march a half-century later."[6] During the Siege, Parisians learned that their nation and fellow citizens were capable of throwing them into threatening and dangerous situations without their consent and outside of their control. They became aware of the mechanisms of diplomacy and of war mongering that had direct and sometimes fatal influence over their lives. They learned that newspapers, in their zeal for sensationalism, spread rumors that spies lurked in Paris, leading to surveillance among the besieged. Much like the Prussians outside Paris, the French government itself was capable of setting in motion a series of events that posed an existential threat to its people. The violence of the state cut both ways, within and without its borders. The culture of the Siege might best anticipate not the First but the Second World War. Given the institutional mechanisms of war put in place or inspired by the Franco-Prussian War, Isabel Hull has argued that "Genocide can also happen as the by-product of institutional routines and organizational dynamics as they operate during wartime and generate 'final solutions' to all sorts of problems."[7]

The representations of the Franco-Prussian War that appeared in the decades following the event might appear less dependent on the economic conditions of their production, but they nonetheless insist on the hidden structures behind state violence and propaganda. Mary Donaldson-Evans writes that another short story from the *Soirées de Médan*, Guy de Maupassant's "Boule de suif," seduced readers into believing that "France's wounds, still far from healed, had been self-inflicted."[8] She is not alone in reading Maupassant's representation of the Franco-Prussian War and the Siege as imbued with a "strongly polemical element,"[9] that can be read as an oblique reference to the

---

5   Chrastil, *Organizing for War: France 1870–1914* (Louisiana State UP, 2010), p. 2.

6   Audoin-Rouzeau, *1870. La France dans la guerre* (Armand Colin, 1989), p. 16.

7   Hull, *Absolute Destruction: Military Culture and the Practices of War in Imperial Germany* (Cornell UP, 2005), p. 2.

8   Donaldson-Evans, "Doctoring History: Maupassant's 'Un coup d'état,'" *Nineteenth-Century French Studies*, vol. 16, nos. 3–4, 1988, p. 351.

9   Donaldson-Evans, "Doctoring History," p. 352.

Commune. Writers such as Maupassant and the gang behind the 1880 short story collection *Les Soirées de Médan* wrote about the war and the Siege as a way not just of writing about the Commune, but in general about how violence seems to arise *ex nihilo*, no longer the result of high-level diplomatic decisions but as a collaborative effort among actors entangled within economic, institutional, and social structures. Both Céard and Maupassant show victims as complicit in the violence they suffer, but Maupassant absolves them of guilt.

Maupassant's 1883 short story, "Deux Amis" ("Two Friends") dramatizes the absurdity of modern state violence that seems to come from nowhere and yet exists everywhere. The story concerns two Parisians—a watchmaker and a haberdasher—who often run into each other when they go to fish in the suburbs of Paris. Their friendship is comfortable and easy, as they only see each other when they fish, and only exchange a few banal words about the weather. The blockade interrupts their *parties de dimanche*, as the Prussians forbid any travel out of the city. However, one wintery Sunday, the watchmaker runs into the haberdasher on an exterior boulevard in the city. Pleasantries are exchanged, and after ducking into a cabaret for a couple of absinthes, they decide to brave the enemy and return to their fishing hole.

The sky is clear, a rare occurrence during an otherwise cloudy and snowy winter. The weather, the fishing, the company, or a combination of the three quickly make the friends forget the Siege. The fishing that day is good, and the conversation even better. Their newfound loquacity brings them to the most ordinary topic—politics—but they are less patriotic than the types of discourse this book presents. "The Republic would never have declared war," says one. The other replies in more sinister terms: "With kings we had war outside. With the Republic we have war within."[10] The anticipatory evocation of the Commune, almost magically, brings a dark cloud over the friends' outing. A group of Prussians sneak up on them, rifles aimed. The two have never laid eyes on a Prussian before, but "They had felt them there for months, around Paris, ruining France, pillaging, massacring, bringing famine, invisible and all-powerful."[11] For besieged Parisians, the Prussians posed a threat more theoretical than physical. Even when

10 Maupassant, "Deux Amis," in *Mademoiselle Fifi: nouveaux contes* (Paris: Ollendorf, 1898), p. 266.
11 Maupassant, "Deux Amis," p. 262.

Prussian shells hit the city, death came quickly and without warning, as quickly as the Prussian officer appears before the two friends.

The officer accuses them of being spies and threatens to have them shot. However, if they are willing to give up the code word that would grant the Prussians access to the city, the Parisians will be spared. The two friends, terrified, remain silent. Refusing to give up their city, they say goodbye to each other before they are shot by a firing squad, "the twelve shots coming together as one."[12] After throwing their bodies into the Seine, the Prussians sit down to enjoy the fish that the two Parisians had caught during their day of reprieve from the anguish of the Siege.

Maupassant's story is remarkable not just for his representation of life under siege, or more specifically about life on the outskirts of siege. It also is an early example of absurdist literature, perhaps best read as a precursor to Albert Camus's 1947 novel *La Peste*, in which two characters, quarantined in Oran, break through their own blockade to take a moment to swim in the ocean, another moment of blissful homosociability. Camus's novel has been read as an allegory of many different historical situations, most notably of life under the German occupation of France during World War Two. Both Camus and Maupassant explained the logic of oppression, how violence most often comes without a face, and how administrative forces designed to protect citizens can often lead to tragedy dismissed as inevitable.

The Siege foreshadowed the Commune and the two world wars by introducing the idea that violence is "invisible and all-powerful." However, as we see during the Siege, there were ways of combatting the threat of being caught between two bellicose nations or in the firing line of one's own nation. Maupassant's characters express regret that, with any form of government, war was inevitable. They may not have been capable of imagining a form of regime beyond bellicose monarchy and divisive republic, but at least they, unlike Huberte de Pahauën and her general-in-chief, are aware of the structure of political systems. Despite feeling cheated by both republic and king, Maupassant's Parisians refuse to give up the code word, in an acknowledgment that even in unjust systems, personal decisions have political consequences. Their refusal is tantamount to a revolutionary act in

12   Maupassant, "Deux Amis," p. 271.

which sacrifice is made out of loyalty to fellow citizens rather than loyalty to the state. The poignancy of their refusal lies in the fact that the code word is likely to have been almost useless to the Prussians. This story takes place in January 1870, when Paris was "starving and gasping."[13] The Siege would have been over soon whether or not they gave up the code word.

Reading literature represented neither a complete disengagement from political practice nor a noble and heroic resistance. A student of Céard would interpret the cultural boom of Paris as another example of Parisian navel-gazing; a good reader of Maupassant would see the same enthusiasm as loyalty to one's principles. However, both retrospectives capture the ambiguity of assigning any ideological meaning to a phenomenon resulting from a complex market of ideas, political persuasions, and economic constraints. When Parisians wrote diaries, they were trying to stave off the boredom of blockade just as much as they were making sense of the events around them as they happened. The generic limitations of diaries—the inability to see the end of history, to fabricate a coherent narrative of everyday life— allowed for writers to come to terms with not knowing the ends of their own stories. Professional histories proved unwilling and unable to see the events of the Siege from the human perspective. When petty publishers pushed back against the rigid institutional mechanisms of the massive and bureaucratic publishing industry, producing poetry written by soldiers and anonymous political pamphlets, they were also pushing back against the obscure framework that tended to promote already established voices in the literary marketplace. Theaters like the Comédie-Française found themselves in the predicament of having to promote popular political messages without becoming propaganda tools of the government. When the city organized a free and open-to-the-public reading of Hugo's republican poetry, it indicated to Parisians that literature should be democratic, serving the people rather than the state. The failure of that performance to attract the democratic readership it intended showed Parisians that the government, and the cultural institutions that prop up the government, might have cynical reasons to stage such political performances. The production and consumption of cultural products took place within a negotiation

---

13 Maupassant, "Deux Amis," p. 257.

of differing political ideologies and confrontational political interpretations. Every book, diary, performance, and newspaper improbably emerged from the tense but necessary relationship between individuals and institutions. This book has attempted to show how writers, readers, and publishers encode cultural and political information into the shape, size, price, and availability—in other words the social existence—of literature.

"Deux Amis" seems to take a fatalist approach to this materialist methodology, according to which culture is produced, manipulated, weaponized but never enjoyed. The fruits of the fishermen's labor, after all, are destined to satisfy Prussian hunger. In her analysis of Maupassant's literary pessimism, Mariane Bury has called the execution of the two Parisians "cruelly farcical" since their deaths are "useless."[14] By extension, the Siege of Paris might appear farcical as it, too, proved useless. On the other hand, an absurdist reading of the Siege might encourage a more positive interpretation in which perseverance against obviously insurmountable obstacles can form the basis of rebellion or revolution. Maupassant's characters do not give up the code word but it is not clear why. The text leaves open the possibility that they remain silent due to some allegiance to their country, but Maupassant does not seem interested in state secrets. "Deux Amis" is a touching story because they share a moment of reprieve in the midst of continual struggle. They are able, albeit fleetingly, to escape from oppression. Giving up the password would have represented a betrayal not of the state, but of their shared moment. While much of the literature produced during the Siege specifically addressed politics, arguing for specific reforms of government or proposing new readings of French history, when seen as a whole, this literature resembles the idle talk of the two Parisians on the banks of the Seine: a moment of peace that they had fashioned within the invisible and unknowable forces that structured their lives and led to their deaths. Before the friends knew that the Prussians had them in their sights, they breathed a Sisyphean sigh of relief: "The gentle sun poured its warmth between their shoulders. They heard nothing. They thought of nothing. They were unaware of the rest of the world. They were fishing."[15]

---

14   Bury, "Maupassant pessimiste?" *Romantisme*, vol. 61, 1988, p. 81.
15   Maupassant, "Deux Amis," pp. 264–265.

Bibliography

Primary Sources

Archives

Archives nationales (AN), F18(III) 128, Dépôt légal ouvrages non-périodiques
    AN F18(IV) 158-161, Dépôt légal ouvrages périodiques
    AN F18(V) 157-164, Dépôt légal ouvrages périodiques publés par livraisons
    AN F18 9, circulaires 1870–1871
    AN 55AJ 1-99, Théâtre de l'Odéon
    AN AJ13 445-529, Théâtre national de l'Opéra

Bibliothèque historique de la ville de Paris (BHVP), *Lettres de Caroline Chaumorot*,
    Ms 1073
    BHVP *Journal d'un Parisien*, Ms 1074
    BHVP Paul du Boys et fils, Ms 1075
    BHVP Rapports de Police, Ms 1083
    BHVP Correspondance générale, Ms 1113
    BHVP Fonds Jules Claretie

Periodicals and Newspapers (Partial List)

L'Ami de la France
Bibliographie de France: Journal générale de l'imprimerie et de la librairie
Chronique de la Société des gens de lettres
Le Cloche
Le Combat
Le Conseiller des dames
Le Constitutionnel
Correspondance Havas
Le Cri du people
L'Écho des étrangers
L'Électeur libre
Le Figaro

Le Gaulois
Le Journal-ballon
Le Journal-poste
Le Journal des débats littéraires et politiques
Le Journal officiel
La Lanterne
Lettre-Journal de Paris: Gazette des absents
La Lutte à outrance
Le Moblot
Le Moniteur de la papeterie française
Le Moniteur des arts
Le Moniteur des citoyennes
Le National (edited by Ildefonse Rousset)
La Patrie en danger
Le Père Duchêne
Le Petit Journal
Le Petit Moniteur
La Presse
Le Réveil
La Revue des deux mondes
Le Siècle
Le Temps
Le Trac
L'Univers
La Vie parisienne

Published Diaries (Partial List)

Adam, Juliette. *Mes illusions et nos souffrances pendant le siège de Paris*. Paris: Lemerre, 1906.

———. *Le Siège de Paris: journal d'une Parisienne*. Paris: Lévy, 1873.

Bernhardt, Sarah. *Ma double vie*. Paris: Charpentier et Fasquelle, 1907.

Boissonnas, Mme B. *Une Famille pendant la guerre de 1870–1871*. Paris: Lemerre, 1871.

Claretie, Jules. *Paris assiégé. Tableaux et souvenirs*. Paris: Lemerre, 1871.

Dabot, Henri. *Griffonnages quotidiens d'un bourgeois du Quartier latin*. Péronne: Imprimerie E. Quentin, 1895.

Fonvielle, Wilfrid. *Le Siège de Paris vu à vol d'oiseau*. Paris: Hetzel, 1894.

Gaboriau, Émile. *Journal d'un Garde national mobilisé pendant the siège de Paris*. *Petit Journal*, January 5–April 6, 1871.

Gautier, Théophile. *Tableaux du siège*. Paris: Charpentier, 1871.

Goncourt, Edmond de. *Journal des Goncourt. Mémoires de la vie littéraire*, Vol. 4. Paris: Charpentier et Fasquelle, 1892.

Hugo, Victor. *Choses vues*. Paris: Gallimard, 2002.

Journal du siège de Paris par un bourgeois. Paris: Dentu, 1872.

Laucassade, Auguste. *Le Siège de Paris*. Paris: Lemerre, 1871.

Loudun, Eugène (Balleyguier). *Journal d'un Parisien. La révolution de septembre et la Commune.* Paris: Lachaud, 1872.

Manet, Édouard. *Lettres du siège de Paris.* Paris: Alidades, 2002.

Michel, Adolphe. *Le Siège de Paris: journal d'un Parisien.* Paris: Arléa, 2012.

Paradis, Jacques-Henry. *Journal du siège.* Paris: Dentu, 1872.

Pascal, Edmond. *Journal d'un petit Parisien pendant le siège de Paris (1870–1871).* Paris: Picard et Kaan, 1893.

Sarcey, Francisque. *Le Siège de Paris: impressions et souvenirs.* Paris: Lachaud, 1871.

Schuler, Pierre. *Journal d'un Suisse pendant le siège de Paris.* Neuchâtel: Bienne, 1871.

Sheppard, Nathan. *Shut up in Paris.* London: Bently, 1871.

Thierry, Édouard. *La Comédie française pendant les deux sièges (1870–1871). Journal de l'administration générale.* Paris: Tresse et Stock, 1887.

Tissandier, Gaston. *En Ballon! Pendant le siège de Paris. Souvenirs d'un aéronaute.* Paris: Dentu, 1871.

Wey, Francis. *Chronique du siège de Paris (1870–1871).* Paris: Hachette, 1871.

Non-Periodical Works Published during the Siege (Partial List)

Bacon, Francis. *Œuvres complètes.* Paris: Casse, Sept. 21, 1870.

Bailly, Jules. *Le Chant de réveil.* Paris: Parent, Nov. 2, 1870.

Beauchesne, A. de. *La Vie de Mme Elisabeth, sœur de Louis XVI.* Paris: Plon, Dec. 23, 1870.

Belly, Félix. *Les Amazones de la Seine et la police.* Paris: Chez l'auteur, Oct. 26, 1870.

Bergerat, Émile. *Les Cuirassiers de Reichshoffen.* Paris: Lemerre, Nov. 8, 1870.

———. *Le Maître d'école. Poésie dite au Théâtre-Français par M. Coquelinau le 27 novembre 1870.* Paris: Lemerre, Dec. 5, 1870.

Berthet, Elie. *La Double vue.* Paris: Bureaux du Siècle, Oct. 18, 1870.

Bornier, Henri de. *Châteaudun; Une Petite bourgeoise; Les Assiégés.* Paris: Lachaud, Nov. 30, 1870.

Boutron, Jacques-Marie. *Le Cri du cœur.* Paris: Gaittet, Oct. 4, 1870.

C., M.J. de. *Le Breton au siège de Paris. Ballade lue le 6 novembre 1870 à la réunion de la société bretonne d'assistance aux blesses et aux maladies.* Paris: Dupont, Dec. 15, 1870.

Caussade, Auguste. *Cri de guerre. Vae victoribus.* Paris: Lemerre, Jan. 7, 1871.

Cauvet, Alfred. *Rêves et vérités.* Paris: Lacroix, Dec. 29, 1870.

Chéreau, Achille. *Guillotin et la Guillotine.* Paris: Aux bureaux de l'Union médicale, Nov. 12, 1870.

Claretie, Jules. *La Débâcle: 4 septembre 1870.* Paris: Librairie centrale, Dec. 28, 1870.

Coppée, François. *Lettre d'un mobile breton.* Paris: Lemerre, Nov. 25, 1870.

Corneille. *Horace: annoté par Nicholas-Auguste Dubois.* Paris: Delalain, Oct. 13, 1870.

Couitat. *Un honnête homme: comédie en cinq actes et en vers*, 2nd ed. Editor unknown, Sept. 28, 1870.

La Cuisinière assiégée, ou l'art de vivre en temps de siège, par une femme de ménage. Paris: Laporte, Jan. 16, 1871.

Damé, Frédéric. *L'Invasion, 1792–1870.* Paris: Lemerre, Jan. 7, 1871.

Daner, Édouard. *Le Lâche de Sedan: à Louis-Napoléon Bonaparte.* Paris: Lefranc, Oct. 31, 1870.

Davanne, J.-B. *La Délivrance.* Paris: J. Rigal, Nov. 21, 1870.

Déclaration des droits de l'homme et du citoyen. Paris: Moquet, Oct. 20, 1870.

Deline, N. *La Mitrailleuse française, chant national de 1870.* Paris: de Morris, Dec. 6, 1870.

Despierres. *Strasbourg, poésie en vers.* Paris: Chaix, Oct. 29, 1870.

Destaminil. *La Cuisine pendant le siège: recettes pour accommoder la viande de cheval et d'âne.* Paris: Librairie des villes et des campagnes, Nov. 25, 1870.

Les Deux blessés. Conférence sur l'Evangile. Paris: de Dubuisson, Nov. 17, 1870.

Disraeli, Benjamin. *Lothair.* Paris: Aux bureaux du Soir, Nov. 23, 1870.

Dreux. *L'Heure suprême. Actualité, scène dramatique, au théâtre des Menus-Plaisirs, le 24 novembre 1870.* Paris: Chez l'auteur, Dec. 27, 1870.

Dreyfus, Abraham. *Le Bombardement de Gomorrhe: strophes dites par M. Saint Germain.* Paris: Lachaud, Jan. 15, 1870.

Dunant, Jules-Henry. *Un souvenir de Solférino.* Paris: Hachette, Nov. 16, 1870.

Duverne, Félix. *Le Ballon d'Etat: satire héroïque.* Paris: les marchands de journaux, Dec. 6, 1870.

Erckmann-Chatrian. *Histoire d'un paysan. Le Citoyen Bonaparte.* Paris: Hetzel, 1870.

Fayol. *Le Voyageur aérien.* Paris: de Dubuisson, Nov. 5, 1870.

Féré, Octave. *Le Dernier criminel.* Paris: Bureaux de l'administration du Figaro, Oct. 15, 1870.

Fleuriot, Zénaide. *Siège de Paris. Entre absents. Aux mères françaises.* Paris: Lecoffre, Jan. 25, 1871.

Frank, Félix. *La Horde allemande.* Paris: Lemerre, Nov. 25, 1870.

Gaboriau, Émile. *Journal d'un Garde national mobilisé.* Paris: *Petit Journal,* serialized Jan. 5–Apr. 6, 1871.

———. *Un Mariage d'aventure.* Paris: *Petit Journal,* serialized Sept. 7–28, 1870.

———. *Promettre et tenir.* Paris: *Petit Journal,* serialized Sept.–Oct. 1870.

———. *La Route de Berlin.* Paris: *Petit Journal,* serialized Sept.–Dec. 1870.

Gautier, Eugène. *Publication patriotique: le siège de Vienne.* Paris: de Chaix, Oct. 18, 1870.

Geruzez, Nicholas-Eugène. *Études littéraires sur les ouvrages français.* Paris: Delalain, Oct. 13, 1870.

Gonzales, Emmanuel. *Les Sabotiers de la forêt noire.* Paris: Plon, Dec. 14, 1870.

Gouraud, Julie. *Marianne Aubry.* Second Edition. Paris: editor unknown, Dec. 5, 1870.

La Grande chierie des diables. En vers. Paris: lith. Manoury, Nov. 26, 1870.

Gratiot, Amédée. *Le Châtiment de l'Angleterre.* Paris: Librairie nouvelle, Dec. 27, 1870.

———. *La Nuit du 6 novembre.* Paris: Librairie nouvelle, Nov. 17, 1870.

———. *Peau neuve.* Paris: Librairie nouvelle, Oct. 3, 1870.

Guenot-Winger. *La Femme Bonaparte.* Paris: Jacquiet, Oct. 24, 1870.

———. *La Fille Mathilde.* Paris: Jacquiet, Nov. 15, 1870.

———. *Histoire des amours, scandales, et libertinages des Bonaparte.* Paris: Jacquiet, Oct. 28, 1870.

Guenot-Winger. *Le Sire Bonaparte.* Paris: Librairie Martinon, 1870. Day unknown.

———. *Tribunal du genre humain.* Paris: Jacquiet, Jan. 3, 1871.

Hugo, Victor. *Les Châtiments.* Paris: Hetzel, Sept. 14, 1870.

———. *Napoléon le petit.* Paris: Hetzel, Nov. 25, 1870.

Joly, Maurice. *Discours sur la Commune de Paris.* Paris: Balitout, Oct. 28, 1870.

La Landelle, Gabriel de. *Les Géants de la mer.* Paris: Cadot, Dec. 14, 1870.

Lavergne, Alphonse de. *Nouvelles et romans choisis.* Paris: Bureaux du Siècle, Oct. 26, 1870.

Leconte de Lisle. *Le Sacre de Paris: strophes dites par Mlle Agar.* Paris: Lemerre, Jan. 10, 1871.

Legouvé, Ernest. "De l'alimentation morale pendant le siège." *Conférences parisiennes* (Paris: Hetzel, 1872).

———. *Les Deux misères: poésie lue par l'auteur à l'ambulance du Palais-Royal et dédiée aux dames infirmières.* Paris: Hetzel, Nov. 10, 1870.

Lescot, Bernard-Eugène. *Synthèses de pharmacie et de chimie: présentées le jeudi 17 novembre 1870 pour obtenir le titre de pharmacien.* Paris: École supérieure de pharmacie, Nov. 22, 1870.

Magen, Hippolyte. *Les Deux cours et les nuits de Saint-Cloud.* Paris: Berthélémy, Oct. 24, 1870.

Manuel, Eugène. *Bonjour, bon an! Compliment au public, récité à la Comédie-Française le 17 janvier 1871.* Paris: Michel Lévy, Feb. 3, 1871.

———. *Les Pigeons de la république.* Paris: Lévy frères, 1871.

Marchand, Alfred. *Le Siège de Strasbourg: la bibliothèque, la cathédrale.* Paris: J. Cherbuliez, Dec. 28, 1870.

Marc-Henri. *Les Sept interventions.* Paris: de Dupont, Nov. 8, 1870.

Un mois dans les lignes prussiennes: par un chirurgien. Paris: Dentu, Nov. 25, 1870.

Moreau, Eugène. *Les Parricides: pièce de vers.* Paris: Imp. de Cordier, Jan 15, 1871.

Nadar, Félix. *Les Ballons en 1870: ce qu'on aurait pu faire, ce qu'on a fait.* Paris: Chatelain, 1870. Day unknown.

Parelon, Paul. *Les Volontaires de 1870.* Paris: Voitelain, Dec. 15, 1870.

Puyparlier, Faulte. *Régime des aliénés en France.* Paris: Masquin, Oct. 19, 1870.

Pyat, Félix. *Les Soldats.* Paris: Balitout, 1870, Dec. 1870.

Rancurel, J. *La Déchéance.* Paris: N. Goupy, Sept. 6, 1870.

Ratouis, André. *Les Deux journées.* Paris: Imprimerie nouvelle, Oct. 22, 1870.

Report of the Universal Israelite Alliance. Paris: Marechal, Oct. 8, 1870.

Retour du voyage des pays des neutres: chant populaire. Paris: Imp. J., Dec. 10, 1870.

Riche-Gardon, Luc-Pierre. *Note secrète sur la mission occulte du Second Empire et sur ses moyens machiavéliques de réalisation par le concours de la Prusse.* Paris: Publication de la "Bonne Nouvelle du XIXe siècle," Nov. 26, 1870.

Roussel, Auguste. *L'Avenir: poésie.* Paris: Claye, Sept. 26, 1870.

———. *Les Quatre animaux.* Paris: Rochette, Nov. 2, 1870.

Simonin, Louis. "Le Canon Krupp et le bombardement de Paris, par un officier de secteur." *Revue des deux mondes,* 2e période, vol. 91 (1871), pp. 467–468.

Souetre, Olivier. *La Parisienne de 1870: au citoyen Félix Pyat.* Paris: J. Rigal, Nov. 19, 1870.

Staaff, Ferdinand. *La littérature française: depuis la formation de la langue jusqu'à nos jours: Tome III.* Paris: Librairie académique de Didier et Cie, Nov. 2, 1870.

Stupuy, Hippolyte. *Ceux qui marchent; poésie dite par M. Maubant le 21 décembre 1870.* Paris: Imp. De Cordier, Jan. 21, 1871.

Theuriet, André. *Les Paysans de l'Argonne.* Paris: Lemerre, Jan. 7, 1871.

Thierry, Édouard. *La Comédie-Française pendant les deux sièges (1870–1871).* Paris: Tresse et Stock, 1887. Day unknown.

Vitet, Louis. *Lettres sur le siège de Paris.* Paris: Sauton, 1870–1871. Day unknown.

Secondary Sources

Adamowicz-Hariasz, Maria. "From Opinion to Information: The *Roman-Feuilleton* and the Transformation of the Nineteenth-Century French Press." *Making the News: Modernity and the Mass Press in Nineteenth-Century France,* edited by Dean de la Motte and Jeannene M. Przyblyski. UMASS Press, 1999.

Agulhon, Maurice. *1848 ou l'apprentissage de la République.* Seuil, 1973.

Alexis, Paul. *Émile Zola: notes d'un ami.* Paris: Charpentier, 1882.

Altman, Janet. *Epistolarity.* Ohio State UP, 1992.

Anne-Claude Ambroise-Rendu. "Le Fait divers." *La Civilisation du journal,* edited by Kalifa et al. Nouveau Monde Éditions, 2011.

Arendt, Hannah. *Between Past and Future.* Viking Press, 1961.

Audoin-Rouzeau, Stéphane. *1870. La France dans la guerre.* Armand Colin, 1989.

Balaev, Michelle, editor. *Contemporary Approaches in Literary Trauma Theory.* Palgrave Macmillan, 2014.

Beauvallet, Frantz. *Le Forgeron de Châteaudun.* Paris: Tresse, 1871.

Bergerat, Émile. *Souvenirs d'un enfant de Paris,* Vol. I. Paris: Charpentier, 1911.

Berleux, Jean. *La Caricature politique en France pendant la guerre, le siège de Paris, et la Commune.* Paris: Labitte, 1890.

Birch, Edmund. *Fictions of the Press in Nineteenth-Century France.* Palgrave Macmillan, 2018.

Birnbaum, Pierre. *Les Fous de la République: histoire politique des juifs d'État, de Gambetta à Vichy.* Fayard, 1992.

Bloy, Léon. *Sueur de sang.* Paris: Georges Grès, 1914.

Bonnassies, Jules. *Le Théâtre et le peuple, esquisse d'une organisation théâtrale.* Paris: Armand le Chevalier, 1872.

Bourachot, André and Henri Ortholan. *Les Deux sièges de Paris.* Bernard Giovanangeli, 2016.

Brosman, Catharine Savage. "The Functions of War Literature." *South Central Review*, vol. 9, no. 1, Spring 1992, pp. 85–98.

Brubaker, Rogers. *Citoyenneté et nationalité en France et en Allemagne*. Belin, 1997.

Bury, Mariane. "Maupassant pessimiste?" *Romantisme*, vol. 61, 1988, pp. 75–83.

Camus, Albert. *La Peste*. Gallimard, 1947.

Carbonell, Charles-Olivier. *Histoire et historiens: une mutation idéologique des historiens français*. Privat, 1976.

Carel, Alfred. *Histoire anecdotique des contemporains*. Paris: Chevalier-Marescq, 1885.

Caruth, Cathy. *Unclaimed Experience: Trauma, Narrative, and History*. JHU Press, 1996.

Cazanave, Claire. "Le dialogue au XVIIe siècle: un genre français moderne?" *Dix-septième siècle*, no. 3, 2005, pp. 427–441.

Céard, Henry. "La Saignée." *Les Soirées de Médan*. Paris: Charpentier, 1880.

Certeau, Michel de. *L'Invention du quotidien*, Vol. 1: *arts de faire*. Gallimard, 1990.

Chanet, Jean-François. *L'École républicaine et les petites patries*. Aubier-Histoires, 1996.

Charle, Christophe. "Le champ de la production littéraire," *Histoire de l'édition française*, Vol. III: *le temps des éditeurs*, edited by Roger Chartier and Henri-Jean Martin. Fayard, 1990.

Chrastil, Rachel. *Organizing for War: France 1870–1914*. Louisiana State UP, 2010.

——. *The Siege of Strasbourg*. Harvard UP, 2014.

Cixous, Hélène. "Le Rire de la Méduse," translated in *New French Feminisms: An Anthology*, edited by Marks and Courtivron. University of Massachusetts Press, 1980.

Claretie, Jules. *Le Mariage d'Agnès*. Paris: Fasquelle, 1907.

Clayson, Hollis. *Paris in Despair: Art and Everyday Life under Siege (1870–1871)*. University of Chicago Press, 2002.

Cohen, Deborah. "Une institution musicale entre repli et implication politique: le quotidien de l'Opéra de Paris pendant la guerre de 1870 et sous la Commune." *Le Mouvement social*, vol. 208, 2004, pp. 7–28.

Compagnon, Antoine. *La Troisième République des lettres*. Seuil, 1983.

Curtius, Ernst Robert. *European Literature and the Latin Middle Ages*. Princeton UP, 2013.

Darien, Georges. *Bas les cœurs! 1870–1871* Paris: Savine, 1889.

Darnton, Robert. *The Forbidden Bestsellers of Pre-Revolutionary France*. Fontana Press, 1997.

Darnton, Robert and Daniel Roche, editors. *The Revolution in Print: The Press in France 1775–1800*. University of California Press, 1989.

Daudet, Léon. *Contes du lundi*. Paris: Lemerre, 1880.

Debord, Guy. *Society of the Spectacle*. Black and Red, 1983.

Debuchy, Victor. *La Vie à Paris pendant le siège*. L'Harmattan, 1999.

Deluermoz, Quentin. "Le Crépuscule des Révolutions: 1848–1871." *Histoire de la France contemporaine*, Vol. 3. Seuil, 2012.

———. "Les étrangers sous la Commune: la fin du rêve nationalitaire du XIXe siècle?" *Migrance*, first semester, 2010, pp. 23–34.

Les Deux sièges de Paris, album pittoresque. Paris: Bureaux du journal *L'Eclipse*, 1871.

Dewald, Jonathan. *Lost Worlds: The Emergence of French Social History*. Penn State UP, 2006.

Donaldson-Evans, Mary. "Doctoring History: Maupassant's 'Un coup d'état." *Nineteenth-Century French Studies*, vol. 16, nos. 3–4, 1988, pp. 351–360.

Drujon, Fernand. *Catalogue des ouvrages, écrits, et dessins poursuivis, supprimés ou condamnés depuis le 21 octobre 1814 jusqu'au 31 juillet 1877*. Paris: Rouveyre, 1879.

Du Camp, Maxime. *Les Convulsions de Paris*. Paris: Hachette, 1878.

Elwitt, Sanford. *The Making of the Third Republic: Class and Politics in France 1868–1884*. Louisiana State UP, 1975.

Erckmann-Chatrian. *Correspondance inédite (1870–1887)*. Presses universitaires de Blaise-Pascal, 2000.

Faivre-Zellner, Catherine. *Firmin Gémier*. Actes Sud, 2009.

Febvre, Frédéric. *Journal d'un comédien*, Vol. I: 1850–1870. Paris: Ollendorf, 1896.

Felman, Shoshanna and Dori Laub. *Testimony: Crises of Witnessing in Literature*. Routledge, 1992.

Ferguson, Sam. *Diaries Real and Fictional in Twentieth-Century French Writing*. Oxford UP, 2018.

Foss, Colin. "Engaged Theater during the Siege of Paris 1870–1871: Corneille Rewritten." *French Forum*, vol. 43, no. 3 (2018), pp. 375–389.

———. "Sarah Bernhardt's Bodies: Feminine Fame during Wartime in Her Memoirs and Henry Céard's *La Saignée*." *Dix-Neuf*, vol. 23, no. 2, 2019, pp. 136–150.

Fournier, Eric. *La Commune n'est pas morte: les usages politiques du passé, de 1871 à nos jours*. Libertalia, 2013.

Fuchs, Maximilien. *Théodore de Banville (1823–1891)*. Slatkine, 1972.

Furet, François. *La Gauche et la Révolution au milieu du XIXème siècle*. Hachette, 1986.

Galtier, Brigitte. *L'Ecrit des jours: lire les journaux personnels*. Honoré Champion, 1997.

Gautier, Théophile. *Tableaux de siège: Paris 1870–1871*. Paris: Charpentier, 1871.

Geffroy, Gustave. *L'Apprentie*. Paris: Fasquelle, 1904.

Gerson, Stéphane. *The Pride of Place: Local Memories and Political Culture in Modern France*. Cornell UP, 2003.

Gossman, Lionel. *Between History and Literature*. Harvard UP, 1990.

Guiral, Pierre. "La Presse de 1848 à 1871." *Histoire générale de la presse française*, Vol. 2, edited by Claude Bellanger, Jacques Godechot, Pierre Guiral, and Fernand Terrou. Presses universitaires de France, 1969.

Hanna, Martha. "A Republic of Letters: The Epistolary Tradition in France during World War I." *The American Historical Review*, vol. 108, no. 5, 2003, pp. 1338–1361.

Harvey, David. *Paris: Capital of Modernity.* Routledge, 2003.

Haynes, Christine. *Lost Illusions: The Politics of Publishing in Nineteenth-Century France.* Harvard UP, 2010.

Henryot, Arnold. *Paris pendant le siège.* Paris: Armand le Chevalier, 1871.

Howard, Michael. *The Franco-Prussian War: The German Invasion of France.* Macmillan, 1961.

Huff, Cynthia. "'That Profoundly Feminine, and Feminist, Genre': The Diary as Feminist Practice." *Women's Studies Quarterly*, vol. 17, nos. 3–4 (fall–winter 1989), pp. 6–14.

Hugo, Victor. *L'Année terrible.* Paris: Michel Lévy, 1872.

———. *Les Misérables.* Paris: Testard, 1890.

Hull, Isabel. *Absolute Destruction: Military Culture and the Practices of War in Imperial Germany.* Cornell UP, 2005.

Hyde, Ralph. *Panoramania: The Art and Entertainment of "All-Embracing" View.* Trefoil Publications, 1988.

Jones, Colin. *Paris: Biography of a City.* Penguin, 2012.

Jordan, David. *Transforming Paris.* Simon & Schuster, 1995.

Kalifa, Dominique. *Les Bas-fonds: histoire d'un imaginaire.* Seuil, 2013.

———. "Faits divers en guerre (1870–1914)." *Romantisme*, vol. 97 (1997), pp. 89–102.

Kalifa, Dominique et al., editors. *La Civilisation du journal.* Nouveau Monde Éditions, 2011.

Kamuf, Peggy. *The Division of Literature, or the University in Deconstruction.* University of Chicago Press, 1997.

Kaplan, Alice and Kristen Ross. "Introduction." *Yale French Studies*, no. 73, 1987, pp. 1–4.

Keylor, William. *Academy and Community: The Foundation of the French Historical Profession.* Harvard UP, 1975.

Kracauer, Siegfried. *Jacques Offenbach and the Paris of His Time*, translated by Gwenda David and Eric Mosbacher. MIT Press, 2002.

Krackovitch, Odile. *Hugo censuré: la liberté au théâtre au XIXe siècle.* Calmann-Lévy, 1985.

Labarthe, Gustave. *Le Théâtre pendant les jours du siège et pendant la Commune.* Paris: Fischbacher, 1910.

Langlois, Charles and Charles-Victor Seignobos, editors. *Introduction aux études historiques.* 1898. Éditions Kimé, 1992.

Lecaillon, Jean-François. *Le Souvenir de 1870, histoire d'une mémoire.* Bernard Giovanangeli, 2011.

Leche, Wilhelm, Berhnard Meijer, et al., editors. *Nordisk Familjebok: Konversationslexikon och realencyklopedi.* Stockholm: Nordisk familjeboks tryckeri, 1917.

Legouvé, Ernest. *Conférences parisiennes.* Paris: Hetzel, 1872.

Le Jean, Sébastien. "La Comédie-Française et ses administrateurs (1849–1871)." *Les Spectacles sous le Second Empire*, edited by Jean-Claude Yon. Armand Colin, 2010, pp. 97–108.

Lejeune, Philippe. *Le Pacte autobiographique*. Seuil, 1975.

Lidsky, Paul. *Les Écrivains contre la Commune*. La Découverte, 2010.

Liston, Mairi. "'Le Spectacle de la rue': Edmond de Goncourt and the Siege of Paris." *Nineteenth-Century French Studies*, vol. 32, 2003–2004, pp. 58–68.

Loliée, Frédéric. *La Comédie-Française. Histoire de la Maison de Molière*. Paris: Lucien Laveur, 1907.

Longeard, Gwladys. "L'imprimerie nationale pendant la Commune de 1871." *Revue d'histoire moderne et contemporaine*, vol. 1, no. 52, 2005, pp. 147–174.

Lyon-Caen, Judith. *La Lecture et la vie: les usages du roman au temps de Balzac*. Tallandier, 2006.

Lyons, Martyn. *Readers and Society in Nineteenth-Century France: Workers, Women, Peasants*. Palgrave, 2001.

———. *Reading Culture and Writing Practices in Nineteenth-Century France*. University of Toronto Press, 2008.

Maillard, Firmin. *Histoire des journaux publiés pendant le siège de Paris et sous la Commune*. Paris: Dentu, 1871.

———. *Les Publications de la rue pendant le siège et la Commune: satires, canards, complaintes, chansons, placards et pamphlets*. Paris: Aubry, 1874.

Malot, Hector. *Souvenirs d'un blessé*. Paris: Michel Lévy, 1872.

Mannarelli, Giuliana. "Un projet de normalisation et d'intégration du peuple: les *Romans nationaux et populaires* d'Erckmann-Chatrian." *Romantisme*, vol. 16, 1986, pp. 83–96.

Marnette, Sophie. *Narrateur et points de vue dans la littérature française médiévale. Une approche linguistique*. Peter Lang, 1998.

Martial, A.P. *Les Femmes de Paris pendant le siège*. Paris: Cadart, 1871.

Martin, Henri-Jean, Roger Chartier, and Jean-Pierre Vivet, editors. *Histoire de l'édition française*, Vol. 3: *Le temps des éditeurs*. 1985. Fayard, 1990.

Martin, Marc. *Médias et journalistes de la république*. Odile Jacob, 1997.

Martin, Michèle. "Conflictual Imaginaries: Victorian Illustrated Periodicals and the Franco-Prussian War (1870–1871)." *Victorian Periodicals Review*, vol. 36, no. 1, 2003, pp. 41–58.

Martin, Michèle and Christopher Bodnar. "The Illustrated Press under Siege: Technological Imagination in the Paris Siege, 1870–1871." *Urban History*, vol. 36, no. 1, 2009, pp. 67–85.

Marx, Karl. *The Eighteenth Brumaire of Louis Bonaparte*, translated by Daniel de Leon. New York: International Publishing Co., 1898.

Maslan, Susan. *Revolutionary Acts: Theater, Democracy, and the French Revolution*. Johns Hopkins UP, 2005.

Maupassant, Guy de. *Boule de suif et autres histoires de guerre*. Flammarion, 2009.

———. *Mademoiselle Fifi: nouveaux contes*. Paris: Ollendorf, 1898.

Mayeur, Jean-Marie. *Les Débuts de la Troisième République*. Seuil, 1973.

McCready, Susan. *Staging France between the World Wars: Performance, Politics, and the Transformation of the French Canon*. Lexington Books, 2016.

Merriman, John. *The Margins of City Life*. Oxford UP, 1991.

———. *Massacre: The Life and Death of the Paris Commune.* Basic Books, 2014.

Michelet, Jules. *Histoire de France.* Paris: Lacroix et Cie, 1880.

———. *Le Peuple.* Paris: Calmann Lévy, 1877.

Mitchell, Gaston. *Journal des deux mondes pendant le siège de Paris.* Paris: Lacroix, 1871.

Molinari, Gustave de. *Les Clubs rouges pendant le siège de Paris.* Paris: Garnier, 1871.

Mollier, Jean-Yves. *L'Argent et les lettres. Histoire du capitalisme d'édition.* Fayard, 1988.

———. *Histoire de la librairie Larousse.* Fayard, 2012.

Monod, Gabriel. "Introduction. Du progrès des études historiques en France depuis le XVIe siècle." *Revue historique,* vol. 1, 1876, pp. 27–28.

Monzie, Eugène de. *La Journée de Reichshoffen.* Paris: Palmé, 1876.

Mordey, Delphine. "'Dans le palais du son on fait de la farine': Performing at the Opera during the Siege of Paris." *Music and Letters,* vol. 93, 2012, pp. 1–28.

Murphy, Steven. *Rimbaud et la Commune, 1871–1872.* Classiques Garnier, 2009.

Nass, Lucien. *Le Siège de Paris et la Commune.* Paris: Plon, 1914.

Noiriel, Gabriel. *Le Creuset français.* Seuil, 1988.

Nord, Philip. *The Republican Moment: Struggles for Democracy in Nineteenth-Century France.* Harvard UP, 1995.

Nordmann, Jean-Thomas. *Taine et la critique scientifique.* Presses universitaires de France, 1992.

Noronha-DiVanna, Isabel. *Writing History in the Third Republic.* Cambridge Scholars Publishing, 2010.

Orr, Linda. *Headless Histories: Nineteenth-Century French Historiography of the Revolution.* Cornell UP, 1990.

Parrain, Josette. "Censure, théâtre, et la Commune." *Le Mouvement social,* vol. 79, April–June 1972, pp. 327–342.

Pichois, Claude. "Les Cabinets de lecture à Paris, durant la première moitié du XIXe siècle." *Annales,* vol. 14, no. 3, 1959, pp. 521–534.

Prendergast, Christopher. *Paris and the Nineteenth Century.* Blackwell, 1992.

Quinet, Edgar. *Le Siège de Paris et la défense nationale.* Paris: Lacroix, 1871.

Raoul, Valerie. "Women and Diaries: Gender and Genre." *Mosaic: An Interdisciplinary Critical Journal,* vol. 22, no. 3, summer 1989, pp. 57–65.

Rich, Adrienne. *On Lies, Secrets, and Silence: Selected Prose, 1966–1978.* W.W. Norton, 1979.

Roseau, Katherine. "A Diary Without the 'I': Embodiment and Self-Construction in Felix Hartlaub's Extrospective World War Paris Writings." *Textual Practice,* published online Oct. 26, 2018. doi: 10.1080/0950236X.2018.1533574.

Ross, Kristen. *Communal Luxury: The Political Imaginary of the Paris Commune.* Verso, 2015.

———. *The Emergence of Social Space: Rimbaud and the Paris Commune.* University of Minneapolis Press, 1988.

Rougerie, Jacques. *Paris insurgé.* Gallimard, 2006.

———. *Paris libre: 1871.* Seuil, 1971.

——. *Le Procès des Communards*. Juillard, 1964.

Roussier-Puig, Marianna. "Michelet, Hetzel, et les véroniques du peuple." *Romantisme*, vol. 23, 1993, pp. 6–20.

Rousso, Henry. *La Dernière catastrophe: l'histoire, le présent, le contemporain*. Gallimard, 2012.

Samuels, Maurice. *Inventing the Israelite: Jewish Fiction in Nineteenth-Century France*. Stanford UP, 2010.

——. *The Spectacular Past*. Cornell UP, 2004.

Sapiro, Gisèle. *La Guerre des écrivains, 1940–1953*. Fayard, 1999.

Sauget, Stéphanie. "Enterrer les morts pendant le double siège de Paris (1870–1871)." *Revue Historique*, vol. 317, no. 3, July 2015, pp. 557–585.

Scarry, Elaine. *Resisting Representation*. Oxford UP, 1994.

Schivelbusch, Wolfgang. *The Culture of Defeat: On National Trauma, Mourning, and Recovery*. Translated by Jefferson Chase. Metropolitan Books, 1991.

Schwartz, Vanessa. *Spectacular Realities: Early Mass Culture in Fin-de-Siècle Paris*. University of California Press, 1999.

Smith, Bonnie. *The Gender of History*. Harvard UP, 2000.

Spang, Rebecca. "'And They Ate the Zoo': Relating Gastronomic Exoticism in the Siege of Paris." *MLN*, no. 107, 1992, pp. 752–773.

Spiegel, Gabrielle. *Romancing the Past: The Rise of Vernacular Prose Historiography in Thirteenth-Century France*. University of California Press, 1993.

Steinlitz, Rebecca. *Time, Space, and Gender in the Nineteenth-Century British Diary*. Palgrave Macmillan, 2011.

Taine, Hippolyte. *Histoire de la littérature anglaise*. Paris: Hachette, 1866.

Tal, Kali. *Worlds of Hurt: Reading the Literatures of Trauma*. Cambridge UP, 1996.

Terdiman, Richard. *Present Past: Modernity and the Memory Crisis*. Cornell UP, 1993.

Thérenty, Marie-Ève. *La Littérature au quotidien. Poétiques journalistiques au XIXe siècle*. Seuil, 2007.

Thiesse, Anne-Marie. *Écrire la France: le mouvement littéraire régionaliste de la Belle-Époque à la Libération*. Presses universitaires de France, 1991.

Tillier, Bertrand. *La Commune de Paris, Révolution sans images?* Champ Vallon, 2004.

Tombs, Robert. *The Paris Commune, 1871*. Longman, 1999.

——. *The War against Paris, 1871*. Cambridge UP, 1981.

Trailles, Henri de. *Les Femmes de France pendant les deux sièges de Paris*. Paris: Polo, 1872.

Vaillant, Alain. *L'Histoire littéraire*. Armand Colin, 2010.

Vaillant, Alain and Marie-Ève Thérenty. *L'An 1 de l'ère médiatique: étude littéraire et historique du journal La Presse, d'Émile Girardin*. Nouveau Monde Éditions, 2001.

Varley, Karine. *Under the Shadow of Defeat: The War of 1870–1871 in French Memory*. Palgrave Macmillan, 2005.

Verne, Jules. *Les Forceurs de blocus*. Paris: Hetzel, 1871.

Veuillot, Louis. *L'Esclave Vindex*. Paris: Gaume fr. et Duprey, 1862.

———. *Paris pendant les deux sièges*. Paris: Vivès, 1876.

Vuillaume, Maxime. *Mes cahiers rouges pendant la Commune*. Paris: Ollendorf, 1909.

Wagneur, Jean-Didier. "Les Chiffonniers de la petite presse. Hottes et crochets médiatiques." *Revue d'histoire littéraire de la France*, vol. 118, no. 3, 2018, pp. 547–558.

Wallbank, Adrian. *Dialogue, Didacticism, and the Genres of Dispute*. Routledge, 2016.

Wardhaugh, Jessica. *Popular Theatre and Political Utopia in France, 1870–1940*. Palgrave, 2017

Wawro, Geoffrey. *The Franco-Prussian War*. Cambridge UP, 2003.

Weber, Eugen. *Peasants into Frenchmen*. Stanford UP, 1976.

Weil, Patrick. *Qu'est-ce qu'un français? Histoire de la nationalité française depuis la Révolution*. Grasset, 2002.

White, Hayden. *Metahistory: The Historical Imagination in Nineteenth-Century Europe*. Johns Hopkins UP, 1973.

White, Nicholas. "The Fog of War: Impressionism and Zola Revisited." *Lucidity: Essays in Honour of Alison Finch*, edited by Ian James and Emma Wilson. Legenda, 2016.

———. "Zola and the Physical Geography of War." *Dix-Neuf*, vol. 21, nos. 2–3, 2017, pp. 155–166.

Winter, Jay. *Sites of Memory, Sites of Mourning: The Great War in European Cultural History*. Cambridge UP, 1995.

Yon, Jean-Claude, editor. *Les Spectacles sous le Second Empire*. Armand Colin, 2010.

Zola, Émile. *La Débâcle*. Paris: Charpentier, 1892.

Zola, Émile et al. *Les Soirées de Médan*. Paris: Charpentier, 1880.

Index

absence 7, 15, 37, 39, 54, 137, 145, 146–147
Achard, Amédée 98–101, 105–106
Adam, Juliette 129–130, 141
alcohol 91, 209
Alsace 86, 113, 180
ambulance (field hospital) 39
    in theaters 36–37, 39, 44, 45–47, 48, 184n50
anonymity 3, 6, 12, 30, 32, 72, 94, 95, 97, 101, 103, 127–128, 141, 145–146, 166, 175, 182, 215
art, visual
    caricature 71–72
    illustrated newspapers 79, 84
    painting 129–130, 131
    panorama 112–115
    sculpture 45–47
artillery *see* bombardment

balloon (aircraft) 79, 124, 125
Banville, Théodore de 3, 34–35, 63–64
Barbey d'Aurévilly 93
Beauvallet, Frantz 107–111
Beauvallet, Léon 11–12
Belleville (neighborhood) 61, 160
Bergerat, Emile 101–113, 180
Bernhardt, Sarah 26, 48–49
Blanqui, Auguste 15, 54n6, 80–83, 88n46

see also newspapers, *La Patrie en danger*
Boisgobey, Fortuné de 84–85, 92
bombardment 2, 6, 12, 17, 36, 41, 43–44, 94, 99, 121, 127, 136–137, 141, 148, 155, 214
boredom 11–12, 17, 27, 29–30, 32, 34, 37, 90, 121–122, 215
see also death
boulevards 4, 12, 25–27, 30–33, 36–37, 60–62, 131, 213
bread 12, 30n11, 71
Brindeau, Edouard 43
Britain 79, 129
    people of 93, 100, 192

cannon
    defensive 144
    founding of 30, 59–60, 66, 182
    see also bombardment
Céard, Henry 209–211, 213, 215
censorship 4, 8, 14–15, 21, 38, 58, 76, 81, 90, 167, 168, 171, 192, 211
Cercle de la librairie 170, 182–184
charity 30, 36, 46, 56, 179, 183, 184–185
Les Châtiments 2, 3, 4, 20, 38, 51–53, 55–67, 167, 172, 179, 182, 189–190, 194, 200–201, 204, 205, 208

chronicle (genre)
    historiography 21, 151–155, 158
    in newspapers 74, 75, 149
citizenship
    civic responsibility of 119–120,
        133–134
    commemorative culture and 98, 147
    education and 16, 185–186,
        201–202
    history writing and 139–140, 147,
        160, 177, 184–185
    patriotism and 93–95, 104, 176,
        214–215
    spectacle and 27–28, 61, 63, 67,
        108, 112–113
    state violence and 9, 212, 214
Claretie, Jules 25–27, 28–29, 110–111,
        126–127, 149–150, 185–187,
        191–192, 196–198, 201, 203
Claye, Jules 4, 167, 172, 177
Cochinat, Victor 55–56, 61
Comédie-Française 9, 12, 18, 20,
        25–26, 27, 28–29, 36–50, 56–59,
        67, 101–102, 106–107, 110, 126,
        149, 150–151, 181, 184, 192, 208,
        211, 215
commemoration *see* monuments
Commune of Paris 7–11, 15, 35n25,
        51n1, 61–62, 101n10, 102n11, 119,
        133n33, 136, 156–160, 172–173,
        175, 177n29, 192n7, 207, 210–214
Coquelin, Constant 102, 106
Coquelin, Gustave 46
Corneille, Pierre 62, 64, 108, 110, 186
costume
    military 43, 72
    theatrical 37, 43–44
Cresson, Ernest 51–52, 56, 60
crime
    of Commune 8
    in fiction 85
    of Napoléon III 55, 65–66,
        144, 189–190, 194–196, 198,
        200–201, 204
    in Paris 91–92

Crimean War 101n10
curfew 27, 30, 32
    closing of theaters and 25–27, 29,
        35, 43, 57, 191

Dante (Alighieri) 55–56
Darien, Georges 207–208
death
    boredom and 11–12
    of Jules de Goncourt 32n18
    memory and 183, 214, 216
    soldiers and 91–92, 98–99, 101,
        103, 109, 112
Delimal, Odilon 54
Delpit, Albert 34
dépôt légal 1–2, 22, 72, 168–169, 172,
        173n18, 182, 190
diaries
    autobiography and 120, 145–146,
        149
    gender and 120–121, 129–130,
        133, 156
    as history writing 139–141, 146,
        152–154, 157–158
    see also letters
domesticity 6, 14, 39, 41, 63, 72–73,
        102, 121, 129–130, 130–133, 140,
        156, 185, 190
Du Camp, Maxime 156–159
duty 26, 29, 34–35, 43, 72, 76,
        93–94, 125, 126, 133, 136, 152,
        203, 211

economics
    of newspapers 15, 73, 75–79, 82
    of publishing industry 19, 160,
        165–167, 169–171, 173,
        178–179, 187, 194
    of theaters 26, 59–60, 151, 208
editor (*éditeur*)
    of newspapers 73, 74–75, 87, 94,
        203
    in publishing 6, 19, 168–171, 172,
        177–178
education *see* citizenship

epistolarity 122–123
espionage 93
Eugénie, Empress 49, 55, 192, 196–197, 203
exile 20, 50, 51, 53, 55–56, 81, 194, 209
L'Expiation (poem in *Les Châtiments*) 64–65

fait divers 73–75, 90–94
famine 2–3, 12–13, 27, 41, 66, 121, 136, 141, 147–148, 160, 169, 213, 215
fatherhood 34–35, 103–104, 142, 196–197, 207
    see also motherhood
Favart, Marie 26, 44
Favre, Jules 166, 190
Febvre, Frédéric 43
Ferry, Jules 185–186
feuilleton
    current events and 73, 74–75, 84–85, 92
    experience of time and 75, 85, 87, 92–93
    poetics of 16, 73–74, 87–89, 92–93
    profitability 75

Gaboriau, Emile 84–89, 92, 95, 106
Gautier, Estelle 102
Gautier, Théophile 31, 33–34, 43–44, 102, 106–107
gender
    historiography and 140–141, 156, 158
    patriotism and 48, 103, 132–133, 193, 204, 209–210
    wartime conventions and 34–35, 120–121, 129–130
generational change 98, 142, 174–175, 207
    among revolutionaries 36, 66
geography 14, 31, 33, 39, 51–52, 61, 125, 131, 160, 187–188

Goncourt, Edmond de 6, 31–32, 41, 72n4, 73
Got, Edmond 57
Government of National Defense
    actions 79, 80, 177, 208
    composition of 191, 203
    critique of 80, 136, 159
    mandate of 54n6, 134, 208–209
Grimm, Thomas 87–88
Guenot-Winger 195–197, 200–204

Hachette 142, 178
Hauréau, Barthélémy 74n14, 94n61, 123–126, 134, 155, 177n29
    see also Imprimerie nationale
Haussmannization 60–61
Hernani 59
heroism 3, 48, 53, 55, 62, 98–102, 108, 120, 180, 209–211, 215
Hetzel, Pierre-Jules 172, 178
historiography
    positivist (école méthodique) 128, 139, 142–143, 147–150, 153–154, 158–159
    Romanticism 21, 139, 141–144, 147, 148, 153, 156
home *see* domesticity
hôtel de ville 49, 88
    storming of 10, 15, 54n6, 64n23, 133, 157, 159
Hugo, Victor 2, 4, 7, 20, 34, 37, 38, 43, 50, 51–67, 99–100, 103, 106–107, 151, 167, 172, 179–180, 189–190, 194, 196–197, 200–205, 208, 215

Imprimerie nationale 176–177
    see also Hauréau, Barthélémy

journalism *see* editor; reportage
judgment
    aesthetic 5, 106, 107–108
    civic 18, 66–67
    historical 126, 136, 144, 153–154, 202–203

July Monarchy 58, 141

Kératry, Emile de 28

Labarthe, Gustave 107
labor 45, 47, 78–80, 130, 148, 151,
    166, 170–172, 178–179, 191, 216
    class and 9, 35n25, 61–62
    geography of 61, 63–64
    unemployment 36–37, 41, 71, 147
Langlois, Charles-Victor 143,
    148–149, 150, 151–152, 153,
    157–158
Lautréamont 175
Lavertujon, André 192
Legouvé, Ernest 16, 38–41, 57–58
Lemerre, Alphonse 107
letters
    dialogic function of 120–122, 126
    as diary 119–120, 125–126
    as mail 119–120, 123–124
    see also diary
libelle 22, 85n42, 192–205
library 55, 185–187, 191, 192,
    196–197
lighting
    of homes 12, 128
    of streets 30, 32, 73
    of theaters 33
Loliée, Frédéric 43
London 71, 79, 194, 196
Lorraine 86
    see also Alsace
Louis XIV 60

Mac-Mahon, Patrice de 21, 100–101,
    102, 103–105, 109, 111–112
Magen, Hippolyte 194–199
mail *see* letters
La Marseillaise 37, 43, 62, 66, 181
Maubant, Henri-Polydore 43
Maupassant, Guy de 212–216
Mendès, Catulle 34
Michelet, Jules 4, 141–142, 144, 186
Monod, Gabriel 153–154

monuments 61, 98, 192n7
    see also myth
morale 21, 26–27, 38, 73, 100, 111,
    179–180
motherhood 65, 131, 195, 197, 204
    see also fatherhood
music 38, 42, 180–182, 197
    see also song
myth
    of populism 60, 62
    of Third Republic 21, 111–112,
        115, 200
    of triumph in defeat 53, 97–101,
        105–108

Napoléon I 64–66, 99, 105–106,
    112–113, 194–195
Napoléon III 1, 3, 4, 7, 14–15, 16, 22,
    25–26, 35–36, 46, 49, 51–54, 55,
    64–65, 80–81, 99, 104–106, 113,
    135, 177, 180–181, 189, 191–192,
    193–196, 199, 204–205, 208
"Napoléon le petit" (poem) 53, 172
National Guard 34, 38, 43, 45, 79,
    85, 91, 133n33, 159, 176
Nefftzer, Auguste 73, 94
news
    and poetry 29–30, 100–104
    and theater 29–30, 107–108,
        110–111
    dissemination of 136, 148, 150,
        155, 179
    poetics of 14, 16–17, 73–75, 84,
        113–114, 204
    truth claims of 79, 88–89, 93–94,
        115, 204, 212
    see also reportage
newspaper hawkers 71, 73, 103
newspapers
    Le Combat 35, 41, 45–46, 77, 83,
        93
    Le Constitutionnel 63, 77, 83
    L'Électeur libre 62, 78, 83, 203
    Le Figaro 64, 85, 90, 173n21,
        174n22, 176

Le Journal officiel 31, 33–34, 43–44, 106, 186n54, 192

Le Moniteur de la papeterie française 71, 72–73, 76–78

Le National 34, 63–64, 81–83, 90, 91–92, 93n56

La Patrie en danger 15, 35, 77, 80–82, 83, 88n46

Le Père Duchêne 173, 199n17

Le Petit Journal 28, 63, 85, 87–89

Le Petit moniteur 28n5, 55, 77, 84–85, 91–92, 93

La Presse 75n18, 77, 111, 114n33

Le Rappel 63, 149

Le Réveil 35, 83, 185

Le Siècle 77, 176

Le Soir 100, 103, 109, 111, 176

Le Temps 73, 85, 90, 94, 111, 130

L'Univers 15, 47, 77, 82–83

obituaries 183
    see also death

Opéra de Paris 20, 37, 42, 51–52, 60–64, 66, 182, 204, 208

pamphlets 3–4, 13, 14, 160, 167, 172–176, 177–178, 179–180, 191n4, 192–198, 203–204, 211, 215
    see also libelle

paper 71–74, 76–83, 191n4

Passy (neighborhood) 131

Picard, Arthur 203

Picard, Ernest 78, 83, 190

poetry 4, 17, 18, 34, 56–66, 101–107, 111, 167, 168, 175, 179–182, 183, 197, 201, 205, 215
    see also Les Châtiments

Ponsard, François 26, 46

populism 7, 18, 36, 58, 60, 62–64, 66–67, 104, 142, 180

poverty 9, 12–13, 41, 60–61, 131, 136

pricing
    books 185, 216
    comestibles 147–148

newspapers 77–80, 82–83
paper 21, 77–80
theater 46, 61, 79

printer *see* editor

propaganda
    of daily life 84
    monarchist 53
    republican 7, 20, 36–37, 191, 208, 215
    war 7, 36–37, 88, 212

Prussians 1, 2, 7–8, 12–13, 16, 27, 32, 35, 41, 45, 64, 77, 78, 85, 86–87, 93, 94, 98–99, 105, 108, 114, 119, 128, 147, 171–172, 174, 181, 192, 209, 212, 213–216

publisher *see* editor

Pyat, Félix 83, 133n33, 175–176

ramparts 4, 5, 27, 32–35, 40, 85, 91, 144, 147, 167, 174–175, 180–181

readership
    and competitive markets 21, 73, 76, 78–80, 82–83, 167
    education of 45–46, 160, 185–186, 193, 199, 201–202, 212
    of personal writing 14, 120, 122–127, 132, 137, 141, 145–148, 156
    as political actors 54–55, 56, 83–84, 86–95, 98, 109–110, 114–115, 185–186, 193, 199, 201–202, 204–205, 211–212
    within and without Paris 6, 15–16, 79

religion 36, 45–50, 77–78, 81, 200, 203

reportage 16, 35–36, 75, 84, 89, 93, 99, 110, 112, 115, 128
    see also news

republicanism 7, 15, 16, 20, 27–28, 30, 35–36, 39, 41–42, 45–50, 53–55, 60–61, 62n22, 64–67, 76, 80–82, 86, 88n46, 89, 106, 112–113, 129n26, 134, 143, 146, 168, 172, 174–175, 177, 182,

185–187, 190–191, 194, 199–202,
204, 208–210
Revolution
    of 1789 10, 36, 45, 47, 52, 53, 65,
        66, 67, 81, 86, 88, 170, 193,
        199–200
    of 1848 35n25, 36, 49, 52, 65, 80,
        88, 89–90, 130, 200
    of 1871 *see* Commune of Paris
Rochefort, Henri 15, 53
Romanticism (aesthetic) 59, 192n7
    see also historiography
Rome (antiquity) 60, 152, 200
Rousset, Ildefonse 81–83

Sand, George 4, 166, 167
Sarcey, Francisque 29, 85, 146
Sedan 7, 28, 53, 65, 86, 88–89, 95,
    119, 149, 177, 179, 204
Seignobos, Charles 143, 148–149,
    150, 151–152, 153, 157–158
silence 12, 48, 119, 128, 214, 216
Simon, Jules 58, 60, 63, 66, 190
Société des gens de lettres 22, 51,
    54, 57, 58, 60, 149, 165–168, 170,
    178–179, 182–183
Les Soirées de Médan 209, 212–213
song 10n20, 18, 176, 180–182
    see also music
spectators *see* readership
"Stella" (poem in *Les Châtiments*)
    56–57

Théâtre de l'Odéon 12, 48–49, 66,
    184n50
Théâtre de la Porte Saint-Martin 20,
    37n27, 44, 59–60
Thierry, Edouard 9n14, 18, 27, 36,
    40n30, 41–47, 49–50, 56–59, 62,
    67, 126n18, 150–152
Thiers, Adolphe 15, 159n45, 200n19
Tissandier, Gaston 144
trauma 8–9, 11–13, 132
Trochu, Louis-Jules 53, 133n33, 190

Versailles 8, 193, 207, 209
Vert, Edouard 176
Veuillot, Louis *see* newspapers,
    Le Univers
victimhood 8, 13, 39, 121, 213
Vindex *see* Guenot-Winger
violence 9–10, 11–12, 47, 90–92, 121,
    157–158, 202, 204, 207, 209–210,
    211–216
Voltaire 45–47, 49, 57
voting 54n6, 133–134

Waterloo (battle) 98–100, 105, 107,
    111–113
witnessing 2, 8, 17, 22, 84, 89, 97,
    114–115, 126, 136, 149, 152, 158,
    161
    see also reportage
wood (fuel) 6, 12

Zola, Emile 6, 8, 140